*Sylvia.S*

## Praise for Bar[

'A compelling new series' *Sunday Telegraph*

'A melting-pot mix of mystery' *Sunday Express*

'An intricate story around the lives of ordinary people and the devastation that is caused when people are not what they seem . . . A good read, very enjoyable' *Eurocrime*

'A skilled and experienced writer' *Shotsmag*

'A wide-reaching commentary on the social and cultural problems facing normal people scratching out a life in the metropolis' *Raven Crime Reads*

'Found the Arnold and Hakim duo deliciously addictive . . . Definitely recommended for those who like PI thrillers with a bit of a difference and who like complex believable storylines' *The Crime Warp*

## Also by Barbara Nadel

### Hakim and Arnold Mysteries
*A Private Business*
*An Act of Kindness*

### The Inspector Ikmen series
*Belshazzar's Daughter*
*A Chemical Prison*
*Arabesk*
*Deep Waters*
*Harem*
*Petrified*
*Deadly Web*
*Dance With Death*
*A Passion for Killing*
*Pretty Dead Things*
*River of the Dead*
*Dead of Night*
*Death by Design*
*A Noble Killing*
*Deadline*
*Body Count*
*Land of the Blind*

### The Hancock series
*Last Rights*
*After the Mourning*
*Ashes to Ashes*
*Sure and Certain Death*

# BARBARA NADEL

## POISONED GROUND

### A Hakim and Arnold Mystery

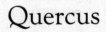

Quercus

First published in Great Britain in 2014 by Quercus Publishing Ltd
This paperback edition first published in 2015 by Quercus Publishing Ltd

Quercus Publishing Ltd
Carmelite House
50 Victoria Embankment
London EC4Y 0DZ

An Hachette UK company

Copyright © 2014 Barbara Nadel

The moral right of Barbara Nadel to be
identified as the author of this work has been
asserted in accordance with the Copyright,
Designs and Patents Act, 1988.

All rights reserved. No part of this publication
may be reproduced or transmitted in any form
or by any means, electronic or mechanical,
including photocopy, recording, or any
information storage and retrieval system,
without permission in writing from the publisher.

A CIP catalogue record for this book is available
from the British Library

PB ISBN 978 1 84866 422 7
EBOOK ISBN 978 1 84866 421 0

This book is a work of fiction. Names, characters,
businesses, organizations, places and events are
either the product of the author's imagination
or used fictitiously. Any resemblance to
actual persons, living or dead, events or
locales is entirely coincidental.

10 9 8 7 6 5 4 3 2 1

Typeset by Jouve (UK), Milton Keynes

Printed and bound in Great Britain by Clays Ltd, St Ives plc

To anyone who has ever been depressed,
delusional, heard voices,
suffered from anxiety, self harmed,
gone high as a kite or felt suicidal. For once,
this is a book dedicated to you.

She had fifteen minutes and one opportunity.

What nationality the girl who'd opened the window had been was anybody's guess. Staff could be from anywhere, as long as they were cheap. Indistinct voices from the end of the corridor made her heart pick up its beat.

'Can you open a window for me, please?' she'd said. 'It's hot.'

The girl, a pale, thin character in a cleaner's tabard had said, 'The what?'

'The window,' she'd said. 'Open it?'

'No.'

The girl had shaken her head. Health and safety.

'Look, I'm not asking you to open my bedroom window,' she'd said. That was no good anyway. That had bars. 'The one in the corridor. Up there.'

The girl had looked up at the window. Its lower sill was two metres off the floor.

'How I do that?' the girl had asked. 'It locked.'

She was new. They always were.

'You open it with a hook on the end of a pole,' she'd said. 'They keep it in the cleaning cupboard. Do you have a key to the cleaning cupboard?'

Her voice had only wavered very slightly. She'd been proud of
that.

'I don't know.' But the girl had looked in the pocket of her
nylon tabard where she'd found a small nest of keys.

'It could be one of those. Try them.' The girl had looked at her
as if to say 'don't tell me what to do', but she'd gone to the cupboard anyway and she'd tried each key until she'd found the
right one. The girl had quickly found the pole with the hook and
opened the window.

'Better?' she'd said when she'd finished.

'Better, thank you, yes.'

The girl had gone on her way to the ward where they stored
the old women who smelt of jaundice. The staff liked it over
there with them. If you were old and mad, then that was
natural.

She carried the chair from beside her bed and put it underneath the corridor window. For a moment she looked at it from
the open door of her room. Then she went and stood by her bed.
She'd need a decent run-up if she were to get some momentum
going.

Treating it like a game. For her it was the only way. Games
were exciting and then, when they were over, you went inside
the house to your mum and you had your tea. She'd seen kids do
that on TV a thousand times.

She hadn't run for months and at first she wondered whether
she could still do so. But when her right foot hit the chair, she
vaulted effortlessly up onto the window ledge. It was exhilarat-
ing and for just a moment she wondered whether there was
some hope, even though she knew that there wasn't. If she
hadn't looked down at that moment, she would have gone right
then. But she did look down.

The drop was enormous, it had to be at least six metres. Bile entered her throat and then, when she heard a door open somewhere behind her in the corridor, she lost control of her bladder.

Someone shouted, 'For God's sake!'

This wasn't how it was supposed to have been. She moved one wet leg out into the nothingness beyond the window. The siren began to scream. Her father's face smiled in her mind and she began to cry.

'Come down, love! Come on!'

It was Michelle. She liked Michelle. It wasn't her fault.

The siren drilled into her head and she felt as if her brain would explode. She closed her eyes. If she looked down at the drop again, or at Michelle, she would be lost. Against every impulse in her body she pulled her second leg out over the ledge to join the first and just hung there. She lay along the window-sill, both her legs out in space, urine dripping down her feet into the void. Would she also soil herself as she fell? She'd never envisaged this. She might have guessed.

She heard Michelle mount the chair even though she didn't see her. Eyes still closed, she allowed her bottom to follow her legs outside and then, at the end, motivated by fear of capture more than by sacrifice, she just let go.

# 1

To be fair to Lee, he'd told her he didn't often eat a proper lunch. His thing was usually a sandwich, or a bag of cakes at his desk. But even so . . .

'Babe, you know if you keep on pushing that fish around it'll sit up and lump you one,' she said.

Lee Arnold looked at her with his big, brown eyes and Susan felt herself come over all maternal. There were times when he looked just like that sad-eyed cat in the Shrek movies. So what if he didn't want his dinner?

She put a hand on his and said, 'Sorry, darlin', don't mean to nag.'

He shook his head. 'You're not.'

He'd suggested they go to Lake Vembanad, a small Indian restaurant tucked away at the top of High Street North, East Ham. Specializing in food from the south Indian state of Kerala, Lee had taken Susan's love of unusual curries seriously. They were sharing something called *meen pollichathu*, a fish curry, with *kappa*, a tapioca dish.

'This is gorgeous,' Susan said as she helped herself to more food. 'Don't know how you can resist it.'

He shrugged. He'd shut his office to come and take her out for lunch and, even though Susan had only been with Lee for a month, she knew already that this was some concession. Although she was desperate to celebrate their first full month together, Susan hadn't been able to persuade her bosses at the Southend Casino to let her have the night off. It had been Lee who had suggested lunch. That assistant of his, Mumtaz, could look after the office while they were eating – and maybe, later, something more. But then bloody Mumtaz had been called out on some job . . .

Susan looked up from her plate but Lee had his profile to her, staring out of the window. She'd met him when he and a load of his old copper mates had come for a night out by the seaside. Lee had been tagging along behind some rough old female bobby who had got visibly narked when he'd hooked up with Susan. At first, Susan had thought he was a copper himself. He'd only told her he was ex-job, now a private detective, once he'd jumped into her bed. But she hadn't cared. He'd been on holiday, and so three more days of great sex had followed and now Susan was hooked. She pulled her dress down a little further than she should at the front, just to get a bit more tit on show for him.

'I don't have to be at work 'til eight tonight,' she said. She had to drive back to Southend, which was thirty odd miles, but that was nothing.

Lee turned back towards her and smiled at the adjustment to her clothing. Then he sighed. 'But I can't leave the office for more than an hour . . .'

'What about Mumtaz? When will she be back?' Susan asked. Bloody woman! Why was what she was doing so important?

'I dunno,' Lee said. Leaning on the table, over his uneaten food, he took out a packet of cigarettes, which he turned over in his hands.

'Why not?'

'Because it's delicate, what we do. Often we have to talk to people when they're at their most vulnerable. Know what I mean?'

'So how vulnerable are these people Mumtaz is talking to, then?'

'Can't tell you,' he said. But Susan reckoned that he could, if he'd wanted to.

'We have to operate according to strict rules regarding confidentiality,' Lee said. 'And that includes our partners and children.' He smiled and Susan suddenly felt as if everything was all right again. 'It's not personal, darlin'.'

'I know. And yet it does sort of bleed over into your personal life . . .'

'Take me on and you take on what I do, I'm afraid,' Lee said and then Susan didn't feel all right any more.

She frowned and began to push her fish around on her plate. She looked up at Lee, and saw that he had turned his head away to look into the street again. She'd never known him as distracted as he was now. It was almost as if closing his office down for an hour had somehow brought him to a halt.


Mumtaz knew that haunted look. Even though the woman was smiling, the expression hung around her eyes. Once you had it, it was impossible to shift. When she passed her a tiny cup of coffee, Mumtaz wondered if the woman could see the same thing in her own eyes.

'Thank you.'

The woman nodded her head. Then she went and sat on a cushion in a dark corner of the room. She said, 'I imagine, since I told you my name on the telephone, that you know I am a person of interest to the police.'

'Yes.' Mumtaz, unlike her hostess, sat on a chair. It was hard and she shuffled about, trying to make herself comfortable in vain.

'My husband has been in prison for eight months for something he did not do.'

Nobody had ever really done anything wrong. Lee had taught her that. 'Nobody in Stir is ever guilty,' he'd told her. 'It's bullshit, but that's how we all think about our own. We have to, to stay sane.'

'My husband was framed,' the woman said. Both Mumtaz and Lee had known who Salwa el Shamy was as soon as she had given her name over the phone. Originally an Egyptian national, Salwa el Shamy was married to Hatem el Shamy, another Egyptian, in whose work locker police had found a homemade bomb. Hatem had used the 'framed' defence, but no one had believed him. A known hard-line Islamist, Hatem had left Egypt with Salwa during the President Mubarak years, when people like him were routinely tortured and sometimes 'disappeared' by the regime. Logic would dictate that once Mubarak was ousted, Hatem and Salwa would have returned to Cairo, but they hadn't. Salwa said it was because their children were happily settled at schools in Newham.

'How was your husband framed?' Mumtaz asked. 'And by whom?'

Salwa shrugged. She was a large woman, with meaty shoulders that were only barely contained by the sleeves of her kaftan. 'I don't know how. But the pig who did it was el Masri.'

'El Masri?' Mumtaz sipped Turkish coffee, which burnt her lips. She put it down beside her on the coffee table, leaving it to cool. Salwa drank hers down in one gulp. It was clearly something one had to be born to.

'He is a psychiatrist,' Salwa said. 'A blood-soaked follower of the criminal Mubarak.'

So it was personal, too. Lee had warned her about this. Hatem el Shamy had been a psychiatric nurse at Ilford Hospital, across the border in the London Borough of Redbridge. It had been well known that he'd had political issues with a fellow Egyptian who had been one of his superiors at the institution.

'Your husband named a psychiatrist at the time of his arrest,' Mumtaz began. 'He was exonerated.'

'He framed my husband,' Salwa said. Having finished her coffee she put a sweet into her mouth.

'And why was that?' Mumtaz asked. 'Was it because of their political differences?'

Salwa looked down at the floor. 'Not just that. It was because of a shameful thing.'

'Which was?'

Mumtaz was aware that she was coming across as abrupt. It was difficult for her not to. She remembered the el Shamy case well. When police had found the homemade bomb in Hatem el Shamy's locker at Ilford Hospital, they'd worked out it contained enough explosive to destroy the two wards in its immediate vicinity. Had it detonated, fifty people could have lost their lives. That was a difficult statistic to forget.

'El Masri was taking sexual advantage of his patients,' Salwa said. She looked up into Mumtaz's eyes. 'And Hatem knew.'

Mumtaz felt a shiver. She'd not heard this story before. 'Did he tell anyone?'

'Yes,' she said. 'He told the hospital.'

'And what did they do about it?' Mumtaz asked.

'Nothing. They didn't listen. Why would they? My husband was just a nurse and el Masri was a doctor. Which one do you think, Mrs Hakim, is the more valuable?'

Mumtaz's parents had always been great believers in the

National Health Service. Free to all, it had saved her mother's life when she'd suffered an ectopic pregnancy. Compared to what her father always described as the 'nothing health service' back in Bangladesh, it was marvellous. But in recent years a succession of scandals regarding hospital funding, death rates and sexual abuse had brought certain institutions and some clinicians into disrepute. Salwa's story was not without precedent.

Mumtaz picked up her coffee again and sipped. This time it was cooler. 'Tell me about it.'

'To begin with my husband admired el Masri,' Salwa said. 'Not for his politics, but for the way he was with his patients. He listened to them. But then Hatem also noticed how he was sometimes different with vulnerable young women. Too familiar. He touched them, usually when they were sedated. And such patients were often sedated. In fact, that was what Hatem originally complained to the hospital management about.'

'Over-medication?'

'Yes. But they did nothing. They said that issues of medication were for doctors to decide.'

'What did your husband do then?'

'He began to stay late a lot, to protect the patients. Then one night he told me he saw el Masri violating a female who was entirely unconscious,' she said. 'The next day he went straight to Mr Cotton, the chief consultant psychiatrist and el Masri's immediate superior.' Her eyes became wet. 'Mr Cotton said to Hatem that he must have been mistaken and told him to take some time off. Then, after Hatem had gone back to work, a woman under el Masri's care took her own life.'

'Had el Masri been abusing her?'

'I don't know for sure,' she said. 'Hatem never said he had seen that patient being assaulted by him. But that doesn't mean that he didn't touch her. She was only a young girl. She had her whole life before her.'

'But she was mentally ill,' Mumtaz said.

'And that is exactly el Masri's defence! And the hospital's!' Salwa said. 'All the girls were mad and my husband hated el Masri because he was a supporter of President Mubarak.'

'The girls were ill and it is well known that your husband . . .'

'You know how it was in Mubarak's Egypt?' Salwa's face had gone red and her English crumbled. 'They have dogs to train to rape Muslim women. The prisons, full of brothers torn to . . . to . . . into pieces. They . . . Mubarak was . . . I . . .'

'Mrs el Shamy, I don't know how it was for you in Egypt. My knowledge of your country comes from newspapers and the internet,' Mumtaz said. 'But I do know something about psychology and about hospitals and so I am aware that the mentally ill are not always believed.'

'The Muslim women here in Manor Park say you have a degree in psychology. I chose you for that, and because of your faith.'

'Yes.' Mumtaz was, as far as she knew, the only female Muslim private detective in Newham, if not the whole of London. And in a borough where a lot of Muslim women lived, that gave her both a certain reputation and some responsibilities. The reputation meant that she never turned a woman away, whatever her religion, while her main responsibility was to be honest with her clients. Many of the women's partners and husbands were not worth the anxiety, work and love that these women lavished on them.

'The hospital, they know about el Masri,' Salwa said. 'But they say nothing and they don't want to do anything. The police know only that el Masri and my husband came from different political directions.'

'Your husband didn't tell them that el Masri abused his patients?'

'No.'

'Why not? If he had cited the sexual abuse the police would have had to contact the hospital management.'

Salwa shrugged. 'I can't say. He still won't. I've tried to persuade him.'

Mumtaz didn't like this. Why would anyone withhold information from the police, whatever its nature, if that information might get one released?

'Hatem is innocent,' Salwa said. 'When he went back to work after Mr Cotton gave him time off, el Masri tried to make him abuse women too. He said, "Be quiet now, Hatem, and you can have pretty girls also." He thinks Hatem is one of those bad Muslims. But he isn't. Hatem refused and one week later the police arrive and find a bomb in his locker. Hatem wouldn't know how to make a bomb. The police ask him how he made it and he couldn't tell them. He was framed by el Masri. That is for certain.'

But then why, Mumtaz wondered, had el Masri gone to all the trouble of building a bomb to frame Hatem if the hospital either chose to believe or were convinced by the consultant's story anyway? Putting an explosive device in Hatem's locker seemed like using a hammer to crack a nut. She felt there had to be something else that connected the men. 'Did Hatem know el Masri back in Egypt?' she asked.

'No.'

'You're sure?'

'El Masri comes from Heliopolis, it is like the Kensington of Cairo. Hatem was born in Boulaq. That is like those places you hear about in south London where young people get shot – worse than that even. How could they meet? No, Hatem and el Masri met first at Ilford Hospital.'

'How did Hatem know that Dr el Masri was a supporter of President Mubarak?'

'Because they are two Egyptians at the same place of work,' Salwa said. 'They had a conversation about our country. And my husband has a beard, el Masri didn't like that. I am sure that you have seen pictures of Hatem on the television.'

She had. Hatem el Shamy's bearded face, his skull cap – the classic radical Muslim look for a lot of people – was well known.

'The only way to prove that Hatem is innocent is to prove el Masri's guilt,' Salwa said. 'To me this means that someone has to find him committing lewd acts on his patients. That person must also be prepared to tell the police.'

'Hatem's colleagues . . .'

'No good,' she said. 'They are frightened for their jobs. They will be called liars and make-believers, just as Hatem was. Hospital has a service called advocacy, made up of volunteers, that is supposed to report patient complaints, but that too is threatened if it makes trouble.'

'So what is the point of it?' Mumtaz asked.

Salwa shrugged. 'I don't know. Hatem didn't know. But advocacy could be a way in. It can be useful to us.'

'What do you mean?' Mumtaz said.

'A person needs to get into the hospital to watch el Masri and find the truth,' Salwa said. 'It must be someone who knows how to watch and also someone who knows about mental illness, too. Hatem always told me that advocacy group all the time need people. Few want to work with the mad. A person of education, like you, would be valuable to them.'

'Oh, I see.' Mumtaz paused. 'You want to employ me to be your eyes and ears . . .'

'Exactly. To collect evidence to give to the police.'

'Does your husband know you want to do this?' Mumtaz asked.

'No. It's not good he know.'

'Because people will think he's put pressure on you to get him out?'

'Exactly. I never went to Ilford Hospital or met any of the people he worked with. So it is only Hatem's word that I have. But he is an honest man and a good Muslim, Mrs Hakim, and I believe him.'

Mumtaz took a deep breath. 'You know, Mrs el Shamy, even if we can prove that Dr el Masri is abusing his patients, that doesn't also necessarily prove your husband's innocence. All that will demonstrate is that the doctor is an unreliable witness.'

'Which means that they will search his house, where they will find explosives.'

'Not necessarily.'

'What else do I have?' Salwa said. 'Eh? What? Sit here with my four children and wait to be deported? Leave my husband to lie in jail for the rest of his life? Mrs Hakim, I will pay you to go into that hospital, join that advocacy group and find out what el Masri is doing. I can think of nothing else. Please, help me.'


Lee Arnold shook his head. 'I think it's well dodgy,' he said.

Mumtaz, two steps above him on the iron staircase outside the back entrance to the office, said, 'Lee, every bone in my body rebelled against the idea of listening to that man's wife. But what if Hatem el Shamy was right about Dr el Masri? Hatem's guilt or innocence aside, patients in that hospital could be being abused right now.'

'I take your point but . . .' Lee puffed on his cigarette. It tasted odd after all the chilli and garlic in that fish curry. He smoked it anyway. 'I can't think why el Shamy didn't tell the police about the psychiatrist. However religious he is, it's not his "shame", is it? It's el Masri's.'

'Maybe he didn't because the police wouldn't have believed him.'

'Or maybe he made it up.'

'Just for his wife's ears? Why?'

'I don't know, I'm just putting it out there.'

'I can't stand by and let mentally ill women be abused,' Mumtaz said.

He looked up at her. 'Mrs el Shamy certainly knew which of your buttons to press, didn't she?'

'She knew I had a degree in psychology.'

He said nothing. Since Mumtaz had come to work for the Arnold Agency, he was all too well aware of how her reputation had preceded her, especially amongst the local female Asian community.

'Mrs el Shamy will pay me to work for the Ilford Hospital Advocacy,' Mumtaz said. 'Depending on how many hours they give me – should I be recruited – and how much work I have to do on the case, that's good money.'

She'd appealed to him on behalf of several possible clients before through the prism of money and it had always worked. Although not as skint as she was, he wasn't far off, especially now he had a girlfriend.

He said, 'If you want to go undercover, it'll be difficult.'

'Why?'

'Because as if working for Salwa el Shamy wasn't contentious enough, if you find any substance in her story you have to be squeaky clean yourself, and going in as a private detective is not squeaky clean. Just like the police, we can be accused of entrapment. But then going in as Mumtaz Hakim, PI won't work either, because the advocacy service won't take you. And if Salwa el Shamy is right, and el Masri likes attractive young women then . . .'

'But, Lee, I'm not a patient, I'm not vulnerable.'

He stared into her eyes and for a moment Mumtaz became silent. Such a job was fraught with hazard, both physical and ethical, and she knew it.

She said, 'Let me contact the hospital advocacy service. Let me go for an interview. It's mental health, they always need people.'

Lee looked down at his cigarette. 'No.'

The outright negative took her by surprise.

'Hatem el Shamy is a suspected terrorist – we can't touch it. The police . . .'

'The police don't know his story about el Masri. They just think Hatem and the doctor are political opponents,' Mumtaz said. 'The hospital authorities didn't take him seriously—'

'Maybe because it's not true.'

'But what if it is?' she said. 'What if, irrespective of el Shamy's status as a suspected terrorist, this doctor is abusing his patients? And there's something else too, Lee.'

'Which is?'

'If el Masri had the support of his employers, then why go to the trouble of planting a bomb?'

'*If* he did that.'

'If he did that, yes,' she said.

'This is really a job for the coppers . . .'

'But they're not going to do it, are they? They don't know,' she said. 'Hatem won't tell them and so Salwa is using us to get to the truth by a different route.'

'Does Hatem el Shamy know what his wife is doing?'

'She says not. What are you thinking?' When he didn't answer, she sat down next to him on the metal steps. 'Lee, I don't know what's really going on in that hospital. But if Dr el Masri did go to the trouble of building a bomb to frame Hatem el Shamy—'

'A known Islamist back in Egypt.'

'Yes. But if he went to all that trouble then I can't accept that he was "just" covering up his own sexual behaviour. That, to me, speaks of something more, something that would have killed people. If el Masri framed Hatem, he was prepared to kill to do it. And if that is so, that makes him a very dangerous person.'

Lee Arnold put out his cigarette and then lit up another. Mumtaz didn't like it when he chain-smoked but she knew that he usually did it when he was in some sort of turmoil.

She said, 'I had a CRB check done when I worked for that mental health charity just before I got married . . .'

'They're not called the Criminal Records Bureau any more.'

'Whatever they're called, then. It's still valid. Although it is in my maiden name, Huq.'

'Mumtaz, be quiet,' Lee said. 'I'm thinking.'

'Sorry.'

'Ssshh.'

They sat in silence for a good five minutes. She knew that both of their cars needed servicing within the next two months and that business had been slow. She also knew how his mind worked.

Eventually she said, 'A girl died, Lee. I looked it up online. Last year. She was called Sara Ibrahim and she threw herself out of a second-floor window. She was under el Masri's care and she was very, very beautiful.'

They stared into each other's eyes until, eventually, Lee blinked.

'You know,' he said, 'you sometimes remind me of my Auntie Jean.'

Mumtaz cocked her head to one side. 'Why?'

'She was what they used to call a "Women's Libber" back in the 1970s.'

'A feminist.'

'She worked in one of the first battered women's refuges in the country,' he said. 'She'd do anything for women in trouble.'

'That's not a fault, Lee,' she said.

'I didn't say that it was.'

'So what are we going to do?' she asked.

He stood up and then helped Mumtaz to her feet. For a moment their bodies almost touched. She moved away slightly and looked down.

'You volunteer for the Ilford Hospital Advocacy as Mumtaz Huq,' he said. 'And let's see what happens.'

'So we can take Salwa el Shamy's money? '

'Reluctantly.' He shrugged. 'You have to know that I can't believe her story. Her old man could've killed loads of people with his bomb and I find that difficult. Know what I mean?'

'I do, but surely we have to keep an open mind?'

'Yeah.' Lee ground his cigarette end out with his boot. 'But just don't go into this thinking you're gonna suddenly find out Hatem el Shamy is innocent.'

'I'm not. I told his wife that even if Dr el Masri is guilty of sexually abusing his patients, that doesn't prove that her husband didn't make that bomb.'

'Good.'

'So now I contact Ilford Hospital Advocacy,' Mumtaz said.

'No.' He put his cigarettes and lighter in his jacket pocket and walked up to the office door.

She frowned.

'Go through that volunteer centre up Forest Gate,' he said. 'It'll take a bit longer but it'll make you look more kosher. If you go straight to the hospital and this doctor is abusing his patients while being protected by his colleagues, you rocking up out of the blue might make them all a bit windy. Know what I mean?'

Mumtaz, following, said, 'Yes.'

'The devil's always in the detail.' He shook his head. He wasn't happy.

She changed the subject. 'How did your lunch work out?' she asked. 'Was it nice?'

'Yeah, it was good,' Lee said.

'I'm glad. I'm just so sorry I couldn't have been here to keep the office open,' Mumtaz said. 'Did you have enough time to enjoy your meal?'

'Yes,' he said. 'Plenty.'

The girl walked into the house with the 'Sold' sign outside without so much as a glance at him. But Naz just smiled. The arrogant little tart would get hers one day, what did he care? And now that her late father's house was sold, her rather tasty stepmother would be giving him a nice wedge of cash in the not-too-distant future. He looked down the street, trying to ignore the old white man staring at him from across the road. The silly old shit sometimes 'kept an eye out' for the Hakim women. How did he honestly think he could protect himself, much less anyone else?

Then there she was, the stepmother, Mumtaz Hakim, in that terrible old Nissan Micra she drove, pulling up on the concrete slab that her late husband, Ahmet, had once used for his Merc. Unlike her kid, she'd seen Naz. When she got out of the car she walked over to him and pulled him away from her property. Her forcefulness excited him.

'What do you want?' she said in a low voice.

'Just checking on my investment,' he said. 'Making sure you haven't changed your mind.'

'And why would I do that?' She pulled the front of her headscarf a little further down her forehead. Naz knew that in his presence she always felt the need to try to hide. With good cause. 'I've exchanged contracts with Mr and Mrs Singh,' she said. 'We're just waiting for a mutually convenient day for completion. You'll get your money.'

'And you'll get a lovely new home in . . .? '

'Never mind where I'm going,' she said. 'Our business together will be at an end.'

'Oh, will it?' he said.

'Yes.'

The old white man across the street stopped gardening and called over, 'Everything all right, Mrs Hakim?'

'Mind your own fucking business. Cunt!'

She was amazingly strong when she wanted to be. When she pushed him, Naz nearly lost his footing.

'Oh, Ron, I'm so sorry for that!' she said to the old white man. 'My nephew. Mannerless! What can you do with these young people?'

'Oh, well . . .' The old git clearly didn't know what to say. He probably fancied her and so he'd almost certainly let it go.

But then she pushed him forward. 'Apologize immediately, Naz,' she said. He didn't and just looked down at his feet. 'Now!'

He mumbled something, simply to stop the whole thing. It wasn't 'sorry' but it seemed to satisfy the old bastard because he went inside his house.

When he'd gone, she said, 'Don't abuse my neighbours. Don't abuse anyone around me.'

He leant against her next-door neighbour's wall. 'Or what?' he said.

'Or one day someone will really lose it with you,' she said. 'Like the people who've just bought my house.'

'Sikhs.'

'Mrs Kaur is a lawyer and her husband is a very good amateur boxer,' she said. 'Don't mess with them.'

'I won't,' he said. 'Why would I?'

'Just don't even think about it,' she warned him. Then she started to walk towards her house.

The Woodgrange Estate in Forest Gate was a lovely place to live. The houses were substantial Victorian villas set in large gardens on tree-lined streets that were almost always quiet. If one could afford such a place, it was a good area to bring up kids. But it wasn't cheap, even though the Sikhs Mumtaz Hakim had sold to had got a bargain. But then she'd been in a hurry to sell.

Just before she opened the front door and let herself in, Naz heard Mumtaz Hakim say, 'Soon we'll all be free of my husband's debts and, consequently, you, thank God.'

She closed the door behind her.

Naz, smiling, knew that her relief was way premature.

# 2

Salwa didn't tell any of her children about her meeting with Mumtaz Hakim except her eldest girl, Rashida. She was fifteen and so she could understand. But Rashida didn't like it.

'My father won't get off,' she said. 'The world will end first.'

'Don't say that!'

'It's true. And if Baba knew you were doing this he'd go mad,' the girl said. Sitting at the kitchen table, doing her homework while her mother washed up, Rashida went back to her books.

'You're not to tell him!'

'I won't.'

'But if this detective can catch el Masri hurting his patients . . .'

'Baba told you that the doctor had sex with them,' Rashida said. 'I heard him.'

'I didn't want to say . . .'

'We live in London, Omy, everybody talks about sex.'

Salwa put the dishes away and sat down opposite her daughter. 'We have to do everything that we can to help your father,' she said. 'Ever since we came here, he has been under suspicion.'

But Rashida said nothing. Unknown to her mother she was trying as hard as she could to concentrate on her History coursework. It helped.

'Even now the long arm of Mubarak and his supporters stretches over land and sea and we are never safe,' Salwa continued. 'Look at your father! Mubarak had already fallen when he was arrested.'

The coursework, Medicine Through Time, had become particularly gruesome. Leeches were involved. But that was far preferable to what her mother was saying – and where her mother's words were going.

'It's because of monsters like Mubarak that people in Europe think that Muslims are fanatics,' Salwa said.

In some hospitals leeches were being used again, apparently. There was a chemical in their saliva that acted as an anticoagulant.

'So many martyrs! And now at last we have a government that wants to institute Sharia law and all the Egyptians can do is complain . . .'

Rashida bit her tongue. Whenever the modern Egypt of the Muslim Brotherhood was discussed it was always held up as a paragon of virtue. But if it was so good, why hadn't her family gone home?

'Omy, I have to finish my homework . . .'

'Yes. Yes.'

Salwa got up from the table and went over to the cooker. She lifted the lid on a large pot of *kushari*. Lentils, pasta, rice and chickpeas in a tomato and garlic sauce, it was a family favourite, as well as being cheap. Salwa had to watch her money now that Hatem was in prison and she was living on benefits. Thanks be to Allah that her parents were paying for this private detective, even if it did come at a price. She watched Rashida get on with her homework and then, suddenly infuriated by the girl's apparent calmness, she said, 'I don't know how you can just work like that with your father in so much trouble.'

Rashida looked up, adjusted the scarf that covered her head and said, 'What good would it do for him if I stopped studying and just gave up?'

Salwa frowned. 'We had paparazzi out in the front garden . . .'

'That was months ago,' Rashida said. 'The world has moved on, Omy. Nobody is interested in us any more.'

'But when he goes to court . . .'

'When he goes to court it will be bad again.'

'And what if they find him guilty?'

She looked to her daughter for some reassurance, but didn't find any. The girl just sat with a straight face, occasionally looking at the books on the table. Infuriated, Salwa said, 'You think more of those books than you do of your father! Selfish, that's what you are, Rashida.'

But Rashida didn't answer.

'You care more about your future than you do about your family,' Salwa said. 'Well, let me tell you, Miss, we have plans for you so don't get too comfortable with your school books.'

Rashida's already pale skin turned white. She knew what this meant but it was the first time she'd heard anything about it. 'You mean marriage?'

'Of course. What else?' The woman stared into the girl's eyes and the girl stared back.

Then Rashida said, 'I won't consent to it.'

'You won't have a choice,' Salwa told her. Then she went back to the cooker and stirred the *kushari*.

'Omy, I don't want to get married –'

'You wish to be an old maid? You want people to pity you?'

'I want to have a job,' Rashida said. 'I'd like to be a psychiatric nurse like Baba.'

'Working with mad people? Don't be ridiculous.'

'Why is it ridiculous?' Rashida said. Her homework was well and truly interrupted now and so she left the table and went over to the cooker to stand by her mother.

'Because it isn't nice for girls to be around mad men who expose themselves.'

'They don't all—'

'It's not going to happen,' Salwa said. She held up a hand. 'No. Your cousin Anwar is very suitable. He has a good job and will provide for you.'

'Anwar?' Rashida shook her head. 'You mean football hooligan Anwar?'

'He's not a football hooligan. Don't be silly.'

But Rashida shook her head. 'He's an Al Ahly ultra-fan,' she said. 'Ask anyone. Ask Auntie Rabbah! She's his mother and she doesn't like it.'

'Anwar is a good boy. He prays five times a day, he always observes Ramadan . . .'

'He tries to gouge people's eyes out at football matches!'

Salwa felt her face go hot. 'Well, you're marrying him and that is that!'

'No, I'm not!'

'Yes, you are.'

'I'm not!'

'The family have decided . . .'

'Yes, but I haven't, have I?'

Salwa pointed a *kushari*-scented spoon at her daughter. 'It's done,' she said and then she turned back to the cooking. For almost a minute there was silence.

Then Rashida said, 'Omy, don't press me to marry that pig.'

'It's—'

'Because if you do, I don't know how I will be able to keep quiet about Baba.'

For a second it seemed as if Salwa hadn't heard her, but then, without looking up from her cooking, she said, 'What do you mean "keep quiet"? About what?'

'You know what, Omy.'

When Salwa did look at her daughter it wasn't with love.

Shocked if not surprised by her mother's expression, Rashida said, 'Don't make me marry that bastard from Cairo and then you'll never have to worry about it, will you?'


Newham could be a bit of a village. Mumtaz's father often told her that even in the mega-city of Dhaka, back in his old home of Bangladesh, gossip spread like wildfire.

'You couldn't so much as walk across the street sometimes without some nosy parker telling your father some nonsense about how you'd looked at someone else's sister,' he would say. 'Silly buggers without enough to do.'

And although Mumtaz didn't think that there were many 'silly buggers without enough to do' in Newham, she was aware that when she went to somewhere like the Volunteer Network Centre there was always a chance that someone would recognize her as 'that Mrs Hakim the private detective'. So, to minimize contact, she completed the registration pack online. The centre didn't just handle volunteer vacancies from the borough but also from places outside Newham, too. She knew for a fact that they worked with Ilford Hospital Psychiatric Unit because she'd found a reference to the Volunteer Network on the hospital's own website. But she'd already decided to go into her interview as a relative innocent. She wanted to volunteer, she had a degree in psychology that she wanted to use and which made her suitable for a position in mental health services.

Just over a week after she'd completed her volunteer registration, Mumtaz got a call from a woman called Amina. She invited her in for a chat about her 'options'.

Mumtaz was slightly nervous when she walked into the centre, which was on the Romford Road. It was a little bit too near her house for comfort. But she didn't see anyone she knew and Amina, a small, uncovered Muslim girl in her twenties, took her through into a side room almost immediately.

'I see you've got a degree,' Amina said as she offered Mumtaz a chair.

'Yes.'

'What are you doing now?'

Mumtaz smiled. 'These days I'm a full-time mother,' she said. 'My husband died and so I feel it is important to be at home for my daughter as much as I can.'

'Sure. Sure.'

Whether Amina was one of those girls who believed that all covered sisters were oppressed, Mumtaz didn't know, but she had a feeling it was possible. Whenever Amina looked at Mumtaz's headscarf she tended to stare, and not in a good way.

'So do you have any idea about what you'd like to do?' Amina asked.

'Not really,' Mumtaz said. 'Something useful . . . My daughter will be leaving to go to university in just over a year and I would like to get some work experience now so that I can look for a job when she goes.'

Amina narrowed her eyes and Mumtaz wondered whether the girl had recognized her. Or her family name. But then Huq was common.

'Cool. With volunteering, doing something that you like is very important,' Amina said. 'But if you want to get back in the workplace then it has to be in line with your skill-set to some extent, too.' She looked at Mumtaz's application on her computer screen. 'You can drive?'

'Yes. I have my own car.'

'That's always good. But I don't suppose you want to drive for a living, do you?'

'I don't really know. I'm just looking at options.'

'Sure.' She looked back at the screen. 'I guess ideally you'd like to use your degree?'

'Well, yes, I would actually. That would be ideal, but—'

'Psychology, isn't it?'

'Yes.'

'Cool.'

It was difficult trying to be casual when all Mumtaz wanted to do was get inside Ilford Hospital and find out what was going on. But Lee had been adamant about patience. He'd said, 'Look, all these volunteering types know each other. Come over too eager about mental health at the volunteer centre and they'll tell the hospital you're some sort of nutter. Believe me, they exist.'

'Ever thought about bereavement counselling?' Amina asked. 'I'm thinking psychology, yeah. The organization I'm looking at will train you.'

'Mmm.'

Amina looked up. 'Not you?'

'Yes, but . . .' Mumtaz shook her head. 'A bit close to home.'

'Oh, your husband . . .'

'Yes.'

'Right.' She looked back at her screen and clicked her mouse a few times. 'You know there is a car service attached to Newham General if you do want to drive . . .'

Mumtaz leant forward. 'Which is?'

'It's for elderly or disabled people who find public transport difficult. You take them backwards and forwards to their outpatients appointments and they pay your petrol costs. It's driving, but you do get to meet people.'

'Mmm.' She didn't want to say 'no', but it wasn't close enough to the advocacy programme. She said, 'The trouble is, to be honest, that I do have to drive my daughter about quite a lot.'

'So you don't want to do more of that than you have to? Cool.' Amina looked back at her screen again.

To her credit, Amina tried just about every type of volunteering remotely related to mental health before she got to advocacy. To *her* credit, Mumtaz didn't jump for joy when she did finally get there.

'So, mental health advocacy at Ilford Mental Health Unit. Used to be called Ilford Hospital Psychiatric Unit?' Amina said. 'That's representing patients, speaking on behalf of them to medical and administrative staff.'

'In what way?' Mumtaz asked.

Amina looked back at her screen. 'Like, when they have a complaint about something,' she said. 'Often they don't feel confident enough to speak up for themselves. So they have an advocate. But anyway this project, Ilford Advocacy, train.' She looked up, expectantly.

'Mmm.'

'I mean, I know it's like *real* mental health, which is why I left it till last,' Amina said. 'It's cool if you say, like, no, because it's not the best environment. I mean, like, it's a unit now and not an actual hospital but it's still . . .'

'Mmm.' Mumtaz played at considering her options and then she said, 'Yet if I don't like it I don't have to . . . ?'

'Oh, you can leave any time you like,' Amina said. 'Volunteering is so up to you.'

With difficulty Mumtaz left it for a moment and then said, 'OK, I'll try the advocacy.'

Amina smiled. 'Cool!'


Doing the advocacy surgeries on the regular wards was bad enough, but on the forensic unit it could be pointless. If something had kicked off in the last twenty-four hours, or if one of the patients had tried to kill themselves, then all anyone – patients and staff alike – would do was sit. The patients because they were drugged up to help them deal with whatever had gone on, the staff because they were knackered.

Shirley sat down at her desk and switched her computer on. She was down to just two reliable volunteers and doing it all almost on her own was as much fun as toothache. But she couldn't let her service users down. It wasn't their fault if most people who chose to volunteer to help them were either ill themselves, suddenly decided they couldn't stand the mentally unwell or wanted to bring Jesus, by force if necessary, into their lives.

Booted up, the computer let Shirley into her email. Her heart sank. There were the usual 'To all staff' bulletins from the hospital management. These told her what term was correct to use when talking about patients this week, how well the Trust was doing financially and included numerous invitations to team-building events with staff on acute wards one and two, the forensic unit or the chronic ward. Every one of them redefined the word 'tedious' and so Shirley deleted them all. However one email did catch her eye: 'Possible New Volunteer'. When she opened it, Shirley felt a vague glimmer of hope.

# 3

Lee had his head in the gas cooker when the doorbell rang. It was only seven o'clock in the fucking morning and he was up to his rubber-gloved elbows in oven cleaner. He swore out loud, took the gloves off, threw them in the kitchen bin and walked to the front door. In the living room, Chronus, his mynah bird, shouted, 'West Ham till we die!'

Lee ignored him. He'd indoctrinated the poor thing with West Ham United songs and chants, which he yelled out whenever anything happened in the flat. Lee only had himself to blame. He opened the door and saw a fifty-something woman in a cheap but stylish purple skirt-suit smoking in his porch.

'Hi, Vi,' he said. 'It's seven o'clock. What's the emergency?'

'No emergency,' Detective Inspector Violet Collins said as she pushed her way past him into his hall. 'What you up to?'

'Cleaning the oven,' he said.

'Don't you have a woman to do it for you?' She walked into the living room and blew a kiss at the mynah bird, who squawked in response. She took a packet of cigarettes out of her pocket and looked at Lee. 'Fag?'

He shrugged. She threw a cigarette at him, he caught it and they both sat down.

'I'd've thought that your bird would've done that cooker for you,' Vi said.

'What? Chronus? He don't have opposable thumbs.'

'Not the fucking parrot,' Vi said. 'Your woman. You know, what's-er-name from Sarfend . . .'

Lee lit his cigarette and said, 'Don't be jealous, Vi, it doesn't suit you.'

'Don't flatter yourself.' But she looked away from him when she spoke.

The night he'd met Susan at the casino he'd been with Vi, her DS, Tony Bracci, and a bunch of other colleagues from his old nick in Forest Gate. Coppers on a night out with booze and gambling included wasn't a pretty sight by anyone's standards, but one croupier, Susan, hadn't minded. Well, she hadn't minded Lee. If he recalled that night correctly, she'd not exactly taken a shine to Vi Collins. But then Vi had been arse'oled and she had said some less than complimentary things to Susan once she'd realized she had her cap tipped at Lee. He might have expected something like that. Although Lee had occasionally slept with Vi over the years since his divorce, it wasn't a serious relationship, not on his part. Vi, on the other hand, in spite of her liking for the young lads she had sex with on her holidays, had wanted more from Lee Arnold for a long time.

'So, to what do I owe the pleasure?' Lee asked. Vi's eyes were wet with what could be tears. That wasn't her at all.

'Gotta have a bit of time off,' she said. 'Thought I'd better let you know.'

The wet eyes, as well as the fact she'd come to see him, told Lee it was serious. When Vi went on a sex trip to Morocco she just buggered off.

Lee smoked. 'So what's the deal?'

'I go into the London in two weeks' time,' Vi said.

'The London?'

'Hospital,' she said. 'You know, Whitechapel . . .'

'I know where it is, but . . .'

Vi put a hand up to her neck. 'It's gotta go,' she said.

'What, your—'

'Gordon's time has come,' she said.

'Oh, fuck.' He leant forward in his chair, both wanting and not wanting to take her hand. Vi had a goitre, or enlarged thyroid gland, which she called 'Gordon', round her throat which had been there for years. And although in her case the goitre wasn't an indication of a malfunctioning thyroid, Lee knew that it sometimes bothered her by interfering with her breathing. But it had been doing that for years. What, suddenly, had changed?

Vi laughed. 'Oh, Christ,' she said, 'you look as if you've seen a ghost.'

'What?'

'Gone all pale and interesting, love.'

'Yeah, but Gordon . . .'

'Gordon's been a pain in the arse for years, as you know,' Vi said. 'And when I went to see the endocrinologist a couple of months ago he said that Gordon had got bigger and needed to go.'

'So you're going to have it removed?'

'Yeah.' And then she gave him one of those tight little smiles she only ever dished out when she was absolutely terrified.

'I see.'

The only thing Lee Arnold had ever known to frighten Vi Collins was her own body. Police medicals were a nightmare for her and any visit to a hospital meant that she had to take beta-blockers in large doses. He'd never known her to have an operation.

'The boys'll look after the cat,' she said. Vi had two sons who worshipped the ground she walked on and so Lee had no doubt that they'd do a lot more than just feed her moggie. 'Should be back at work a fortnight after the op.'

'A fortnight?' Lee said. 'Don't they have to cut your throat when they take out your thyroid gland?'

'Course they do, doughnut!' she said. 'But once it starts to heal, provided I don't get MRSA, or that thing where your skin goes black and . . .' She lurched forward and howled. 'Fucking hell, I'm frightened!'

Although he'd known her for decades, Lee didn't know whether to give Vi a hug or not. Sometimes she hated that 'sentimental stuff' and sometimes she took it as some sort of sexual invitation. In the end he just spoke. 'You'll be fine,' he said. 'It's a good hospital.'

She looked up, her eyes red. 'That don't make no difference these days! What if I get something like that flesh-rotting thing? I can't expect my boys to look after me if the hospital chucks me out with my legs rotting off!'

'They won't.' He walked over to her, squatted down by her chair and this time put an arm around her shoulder.

'When my brother Tommy went into the old Poplar Hospital to have his appendix out, my mum said he'd never come out again except feet first and she was right.'

Part of Vi's problem with hospitals stemmed from her mother. A deeply superstitious Irish gypsy, Vi's mum had helped to form her children's opinions via reference to folk beliefs and the more lurid manifestations of Catholicism. Her Jewish father had been mainly absent during Vi's childhood.

'Vi,' Lee said, 'your mum's long dead and so are the nineteen sixties.'

'East End was still wrecked by the war back in the old days.'

'Yeah and you knew people who'd had polio and TB – even I remember a few,' Lee said. Ten years Vi's junior, Lee could nevertheless remember most of the things she talked about when she referred to the 'old days'. They had lasted for a very long time in the East End of London, especially in Newham, where in places the 'old days' still persisted. He kissed her on the cheek. 'I'll come and visit you. You'll be fine.'

But Vi shook her head. 'Don't you read the papers, Arnold?' she said. 'People are terrified of hospitals these days. Full of dirt and psycho doctors and nurses who don't give a shit. Most people'd rather die at home on the floor than go into one of them places. It's going back to how it was before the National Health Service – if you ain't got money they don't give a fuck about you.'

It had to be one of the last working bins in the country. That was what psychiatric hospitals or asylums had been called, 'bins' – somewhere you chucked away the rubbish. However, since the arrival of modern psychiatric drugs in the 1950s, the bins had gradually closed as patients were moved out into their local communities with varying degrees of success – and more than a few dramatic failures. However, Ilford Hospital Psychiatric Unit, or Mental Health Unit, as its management preferred it to be called, seemed to be an exception.

Mumtaz looked around at dirty cream walls, scarred doors – one of which was an incongruous shade of lime green – and the lino-covered floor flecked with strands of tobacco and the odd sweet wrapper. In spite of the litter, the lino itself shone and, underneath the smell of urine that pervaded even the corridor she had been sent to wait in, there was a faint odour of disinfectant. Ilford was that rare thing, a working bin that housed up to a hundred patients at any one time. The bored receptionist who had sent Mumtaz to this benighted corner of the building had told her it was closing 'soon', but she had no idea when.

By the look of it, Ilford Hospital had been built in the late 1800s. During her time at university, Mumtaz had once visited a semi-derelict asylum in Kent. It reminded her of that. All long corridors, vast windows high off the floor and a grand central clock tower. Late Victorian philanthropic splendour.

'Miss Huq?'

A woman with long iron-grey hair pushed the lime-green door open and smiled at her.

Mumtaz walked towards her. 'Mrs Mayfield?'

'Shirley.' She was probably about sixty, a little overweight and clearly had a liking for cheesecloth. 'Come in.'

The advocacy office was vast. Mumtaz had imagined it would be an afterthought, a tiny sliver tacked onto the side of a ward. Shirley sat down behind an old wooden desk in front of a huge bay window and asked Mumtaz if she'd like tea or coffee. Soon both the women were talking.

'We don't often get people as qualified as you coming to us to be advocates,' Shirley said. She had the yellow-stained fingers of the avid cigarette smoker, Mumtaz noticed.

'As I explained to the girl at the Volunteer Centre, my daughter is due to leave home to go to university in just over a year and I'd like to get some work experience.'

'Goodness me, you were a young mother!' Shirley said.

But Mumtaz just smiled. Then she said, 'I wrote my dissertation about the demise of the asylum system.'

'What do you think about Care in the Community?'

'I think it needs more resources to make it work properly,' Mumtaz said.

Shirley smiled. 'We get a lot of criticism here in this old place,' she said. 'People look on the secure psychiatric wards as symbols of repression. Not that they ever want our service users living on their doorsteps when they do get out of here.'

'NIMBYism,' Mumtaz said.

'Not In My Back Yard. Yes.'

'And yet, now the process has started . . .'

'Oh, there's no going back,' Shirley said. 'Although quite how the community would deal with some of our chronics if any of them were ever to be discharged, I don't know. But that's not on the cards, as yet.' She shook her head and then smiled again and said, 'Well, anyway, for the moment there are three main wards here at Ilford. One is an old cubicle-style dormitory, which is for our long-term chronic service users, while the other two are made up of small single and twin units designed for short-stay acute clients. There's also a very small forensic unit for mentally disordered offenders, which is used mainly for clients awaiting transfer from big institutions like Broadmoor and Ashworth back to a more community-based type of accommodation.'

'And the Advocacy services all these wards?'

'That's what we're contracted to do, yes. We have one formal advocacy surgery per ward per week where service users can come to us with their complaints, worries et cetera, plus we go out to patients when requested, tour the wards on a regular basis, help out in Admissions and also at mental health tribunals. I've two trained volunteer advocates at the moment, but of course they're only part, time. As the coordinator, I'm the only full-time paid worker. It's varied and demanding, often frustrating, and we're not always popular with the hospital staff.'

'Because you represent the views of the patients?'

'We call them service users or clients. Yes. We're chronically short-staffed too,' Shirley said. 'Getting volunteers like yourself to come up here and talk to very often completely disconnected people about things that cannot possibly be real is not easy.'

'Are the complaints the service users make always just artefacts of their illnesses?' Mumtaz said.

'No, of course not. We always take what a client is saying as gospel, but . . .' She sighed. 'But sometimes patients can take against members of staff for no real reason. This can be very distressing and possibly career-destroying for staff and so one has to be careful how one proceeds.'

'I see.' Mumtaz wanted to say, 'But surely, as an advocacy service, we're here for the patients and the patients alone,' but she felt that although Shirley might agree with that notion, she would not welcome the opportunity to say so.

'We have to tread carefully,' Shirley said. 'However, if there is anything you don't understand or are unsure about, I'm always here for you.'

Mumtaz asked if there was any formal training on offer. Shirley told her this would consist of shadowing her and the other advocates. 'And of course you'll be instructed about how to fill out paperwork.'

Ah, yes, the infamous institutional paperwork, the Kafkaesque nightmare that many said was in the process of strangling the UK's public health service.

'So, let me get this right,' Mumtaz said. 'We always believe what a pati – a service user tells us, on principle.'

'In essence,' Shirley said. 'But particularly where complaints against staff go, I'd have to say you should always run it by me first. I know this client base. Their preferences, sometimes their obsessions and delusions.' She laughed. 'But if they complain about the food then go straight ahead!'

'Is it bad?' Mumtaz asked.

'Well, if you do decide to come and volunteer for us you'll find out.'

They talked for another half an hour. Shirley photocopied Mumtaz's CRB certificate as well as her birth certificate and then she asked her whether she thought that advocacy was going to be for her.

'I'd like to give it a try,' Mumtaz said.

Shirley smiled. 'I'm pleased,' she said. 'I think you'll enjoy working with our small team.'

'I'm sure that I will.'

'And the hospital staff are very nice too, very caring,' Shirley said.

'And the patients – sorry, the service users?'

'Oh, well, they are why we're all here, aren't they?' Shirley said. 'Nobody wants to be in hospital these days, do they? Bless them.'

But then her face fell and Mumtaz felt a small cold ripple snake down her spine.

Shirley brightened again. 'Can you start tomorrow?' she said.


Derek Salmon was not the sort of solicitor who wrapped things up in nice language.

'The fucking shit's done a runner,' he said as he pushed a photograph of a good-looking blond man in his thirties across his desk towards Lee Arnold.

'And you want him . . .'

'He owes money to a client of mine.'

'A lot?'

'Proceeds from a house sale,' the solicitor said. 'Client's his ex-wife.'

Lee looked up. 'Wasn't the property included in the divorce settlement?'

'Yes and no.' He shook his head. 'Phil Rivers, the misper, is a bit of a bad boy, but one of those with a good body and a "heart of gold". You know the type.'

Lee rolled his eyes. Yes, he knew that type. In his experience those Jack-the-Lad blokes either ended up being kept by gullible women or they went to prison for something petty where they were repeatedly sodomised by hard nuts.

'My client, the wife, who is a lady of no small fortune, let Phil stay in the house after they got divorced on condition that if he wanted to move or she needed to sell the place it could be sold and they'd split the profits.'

'What happened?'

'Phil scammed her,' Derek said. 'Put the house up for sale privately, online. It's in a nice part of Wanstead and so it went quickly.'

Lee narrowed his eyes. 'Right.' Even if Phil Rivers had advertised his house online, how had he managed to actually sell it without his wife's permission?

'You're thinking how did he do the conveyancing, transfer the funds? Well, that was done through a bogus firm of solicitors called Myerson & Jackson. On their very kosher-looking paperwork they claim to have an office in Harlow. In fact they don't and have never existed.'

'But the vendor's solicitors transferred their funds into Myerson & Jackson's account.'

'Correct.'

Lee shook his head. 'I've heard about this but not come across it myself.'

'Oh, it's a growing problem,' Derek said. 'In this case Phil Rivers and/or whoever Myerson & Jackson really are got away with a cool one point two million quid.'

'Fuck me.' Lee looked around Derek Salmon's brand-new chrome and glass office on Stratford Broadway and wondered what it had cost. 'Derek, this is a criminal matter. Surely the buyers have contacted the police?'

'Oh yes, but they've drawn a blank. The money was transferred, taken out of the bogus solicitor's account, account was closed and Myerson & Jackson ceased to exist. It's probably offshore now. Although whether that account is in the name of Phil Rivers is a moot point. The description given by Myerson & Jackson's bank of the person who opened that account doesn't bear any resemblance to Phil.'

'He wasn't working alone.'

'Probably not.'

'What about the wife?' Lee said. 'Surely she wants her money?'

'Ah, there we have a complication,' Derek Salmon said.

'Why?'

The solicitor, who was tall, thin and aristocratic-looking, nevertheless retained his Canning Town accent. 'Still loves him, soppy mare.' He shook his head. 'She wants Phil found, not so much because she wants her money back, but because she's worried about him. She don't want the police involved.'

Lee said. 'This geezer's broken the law and as for the bogus law firm . . . What about the buyers? They must still be pushing the coppers?'

'Well, they were . . .'

'What do you mean?'

Derek sighed. 'They withdrew their statement against Phil Rivers and Myerson & Jackson when Mrs Rivers, the wife, paid them off in full.'

Lee was speechless. Not only was this Mrs Rivers very rich she was also, he felt, very stupid, too.

'So the coppers aren't looking for him,' Derek said. 'But Mrs Rivers is, which is where you come in. Of course, if you do find him, Phil's story may well be that Myerson & Jackson cheated him, too.'

'That's bollocks!'

'Probably.'

'Definitely.'

'We have to proceed with caution.' Derek leant back in his large leather chair and smiled. 'Sandra Rivers, Phil's wife, is a very good client of mine.'

He made a lot of money out of her.

'So, much as I might want to put a stop to scams like this one, on this occasion, I can't assume that Phil Rivers is involved,' the solicitor said. 'Phil may or may not be Myerson & Jackson. Hopefully we'll discover that when you find him. And for the moment, that is all I want you to do, Lee. Find him and tell me where he is, don't attempt to engage with him yourself.'

'Understood.'

Lee had worked on and off for Derek Salmon for a number of years and so he knew that he understood East London and its people. But he was also a lawyer, which made him, by definition, dodgy to an ex-copper like Lee. If he found this Phil Rivers, one way or another, he'd find out if his Myerson & Jackson stunt was a one-off. With money in the millions on offer, he suspected that it could become habit-forming.

'So you'll take it?'

'Yes,' Lee said.

The solicitor took a plastic wallet out of his briefcase and flung it across the table towards Lee.

'That'll answer most of your questions about Phil Rivers,' he said. 'Some homework for you.'

Lee opened the wallet. 'He local?'

'North Woolwich,' Derek said. 'But his parents moved out to Southend ten years ago. Oh, and if you're thinking that maybe he might have gone abroad, Phil doesn't fly. Got a phobia about it.'

'He can presumably get on a boat.'

'Yeah, imagine he can. But Sandra reckons that if he can find a way to stay in the UK he will. She used to take him all over the world when they were married, but he hated "abroad" according to her.' He shrugged. 'How anyone can dislike St Tropez in the summer is beyond me.'

'St Tropez?'

'Sandra has a house there,' Derek said. 'And before you ask, Lee, she made her money from an online shopping site she has since sold on. Not bad for a girl from Shoreditch back in the days when it was a shithole.'

'She's older than Phil?'

'When she met him he was working as a bit of extra muscle for a mate of Sandra's dad. Remember Brian Barber?'

'Oh, God.'

Brian Barber had been an old-time old lag who had run his antiquated crime firm, based around clocking cars, out of a shabby lock-up in Canning Town. Brian, who had been old when Lee remembered him, had been dead for a good fifteen years. Broken by illness and the enhanced security in modern cars,

he'd died a virtual pauper. If Sandra Rivers' dad had been Brian
Barber's contemporary, then how old was she?

'Sandra's almost sixty,' Derek said. The two men exchanged a
look and then he continued, 'So, all clear for now?'

'I'll get on to it,' Lee said.

'I'll leave it with you.'

When he left Derek's office and went to pick his car up, Lee
looked at his watch. It was five o'clock and he imagined that
Mumtaz would be out of her meeting up at Ilford Hospital and
that Vi would have left the station to go home. He imagined Vi's
anxiety as she packed a small bag to go into hospital the following morning and wondered whether he should phone her. Later.

By the time Mumtaz got home she was drained. Being in the
institutional atmosphere of the hospital for so long – Shirley
had given her what had turned out to be a thorough guided
tour – had tired and depressed her. How she was going to cope
emotionally being there twice a week, she didn't know. She
started first thing the next morning!

Mumtaz had always believed that the mentally ill were the
least regarded souls and what she'd seen up at Ilford had not
changed her mind. It was particularly true on the chronic ward.
As if the shabby clothes weren't bad enough, the patients' lack
of curiosity had made her want to cry. That wasn't good
medicine.

But when she walked into her living room she saw something
that made her feel better. She'd been dreading packing up the
china. Yet here was her stepdaughter, Shazia, doing just that.

'It's Wednesday,' the girl said by way of explanation. Wednes-
days were short days at her sixth form college and students

could either go home to do some private study or take part in one of its enrichment programmes.

'Shazia!'

From the look of it, most of the china had already been packed. Mumtaz hugged the girl. When she'd first married Shazia's father, Ahmet Hakim, the girl had been resentful of Mumtaz. But when Ahmet had started to sexually abuse Mumtaz, Shazia, abused by him herself for years, realized that she had an ally. And after Ahmet's death they had become even closer.

'Thank you so much, darling. I was dreading the china.'

Shazia wrapped a delicate teapot in newspaper and put it into a crate. 'Well, I think that's it,' she said. 'Would you like a cup of tea, Amma?'

Mumtaz sat down on the nearest comfy chair. 'You're an angel.'

Shazia laughed. 'You don't know what I want in return yet,' she said.

Mumtaz shook her head. 'Whatever it is, you can have it. And yes, I would like some tea, please.'

'OK.' Shazia began to walk towards the kitchen. But then she stopped. 'Oh, some man called today.'

Mumtaz turned to look at her. 'What man?'

'Quite old, Asian. I didn't know him. He asked me to tell him where we were moving to.'

Suddenly Mumtaz's welcome home turned sour. A 'quite old' Asian man could, possibly, be Zahid Sheikh, Naz's father and head of the clan that had beggared her husband through his weakness for gambling – and who had killed him. After his death, Ahmet's debt to the Sheikhs had become Mumtaz's and she'd had to sell the house to pay it. Shazia knew nothing of this. Mumtaz, controlling her voice, said, 'And did you tell him?'

'No!' Shazia said. 'Of course not. I didn't know him. Why would I?' Then she went into the kitchen to make the tea.

Mumtaz breathed more easily again. She was under no illusion – the Sheikhs weren't going to leave her alone any time soon. Naz had made it clear that he wanted Shazia while she was still young and Mumtaz knew she'd have to pay, one way or another, to keep her daughter safe. But she didn't want to make anything easy for the Sheikhs. No doubt they'd find out where she'd moved to soon enough.

Mumtaz remembered that she hadn't called Lee to tell him about her interview at the hospital. She took her mobile out of her handbag and brought up his number. When he answered she said, 'I start tomorrow.'

# 4

A man who was tall, broad and whose face was smoke-dried to the colour of dust, was crying. 'They' had been flying over in planes and dropping his father's cremated ashes on the hospital. Why weren't the staff doing anything about it?

Shirley, who had been trying to make eye contact with this service user to no avail, said, 'Terry, I know it's hard to accept, but no one can stop planes flying.'

'They can stop them dropping ashes! But they keep on doing it! Year in, year out!' He looked as if someone had poured ashes over his head; grey hair and face, agonized grey eyes.

Shirley let him cry. Sitting in silence beside her, Mumtaz wondered what Shirley was going to say next. The man was in the grip of a delusion that was clearly real to him. She knew what she would say to him, with her text-book knowledge, but what would Shirley do?

'This issue of your father's ashes is very distressing to you, Terry,' Shirley said. 'And I also know that it is really happening – for you.'

He looked up.

'But it isn't happening that way for me or for the other staff here,' she said. 'I don't know why that is but . . .'

'I'm not mad.' His voice, if not his face, was wounded. All hysteria had gone.

'Nobody's saying that you are,' Shirley reassured him. 'But sometimes, Terry, we all have to accept that the way we see the world is not necessarily the way other people see it.'

'The pills they give you here don't help either,' Terry said. 'I don't take them. Make you mad, they do! Look at all these barmy patients in here! Couldn't see a plane if their lives depended on it. Staff are the same. Druggies, all of them!'

Terry started crying again and eventually Shirley called over a nurse, who wordlessly led him back to his room.

'Chronic patients like Terry can seem almost normal when they're not on their particular hobby horses,' Shirley said as they walked out of the locked ward and into the open air. 'With Terry it's his father's cremation. He's fixated on it.'

'Does anyone know why?' Mumtaz asked.

'Not that I know of. But he's far too sick to leave so he'll never have to deal with normal life.'

Knowing what she did about mental health and its reputation as the 'Cinderella service' within the NHS, Mumtaz wondered if anyone had ever asked Terry to explain what his fears meant to him. The nurses on the chronic ward had looked almost as torpid and badly dressed as the patients, the TV had been on at full volume, cranking out chat show nonsense, and every chair she'd come across had been stained beyond redemption. How could anyone work effectively in such an environment? How could the patients ever get well? But then she remembered that they weren't expected to.

'You'll notice,' Shirley said, 'that I didn't collude in Terry's delusion.'

'No.' Mumtaz hadn't imagined she would. Whatever iniqui-
ties remained within mental health services, the propagation of
patient delusions was not one of them. Acknowledging a different perspective while retaining one's own point of view had
been a standard therapeutic response for many years.

'You give the service user respect as an individual with a
unique position while at the same time not playing a game of
pretending to believe them just to make them happy and give
yourself a quiet life,' Shirley continued.

'What about Terry's idea that the medication the patients are
given isn't working?' Mumtaz asked.

'Well, it's nonsense.' Shirley smiled. 'And he does take his
meds, in spite of what he says. He has to, he's sectioned.' Then
she said, 'Do you smoke?'

'No.'

'Well, I need a fag. You'll find that most of the service users
and most of the staff smoke. But these days we have to do it outside. We've got a smokers' corner behind the old laundry block,'
Shirley said. 'If you want to join me, you're welcome. You'll get
to meet just about anyone who is anyone in this place if you do.'

'OK.'

They walked the length of the chronic wing until they came
to a low red-brick building. Where there had once been windows, now there were wooden boards and a large chimney at
one end, which looked as if it was in danger of collapse. Shirley
led Mumtaz round the back of the building.

'All the laundry used to be done on-site,' she said. 'But when it
was decided that the hospital would close, it was contracted out
to some private company. That chimney is over where the old
laundry copper used to be.'

'When is the hospital supposed to be closing?' Mumtaz asked.

'This time?' Shirley shook her head. 'Officially 2014, but in reality God knows. This place has been "closing down" since the 1980s to my knowledge. Hiya, Kylie.'

They were suddenly in amongst a large group of people.

'Hi, Shirley.' Kylie was a young girl, probably no more than eighteen or twenty, and she wore one of those nylon tabards Mumtaz recognized as the uniform of the hospital's cleaners. She smiled at Mumtaz. 'All right?'

'This is my new advocate, Mumtaz.' Shirley lit a cigarette.

'Hiya.'

'Hi,' Mumtaz said.

Mainly nurses, care assistants and cleaners, the smokers consisted of one large, apparently cheerful group, plus two smaller collections of people. One of these was made up of patients. Clustered around a blocked-off doorway, most of them sat on cracked paving stones and scrub grass sharing roll-ups. Occasionally one or other of them would glance up at the larger group and then look away quickly.

Shirley said, 'They wait around for dog-ends. When we go, they'll pounce on this patch.'

Mumtaz remembered when she'd worked with mental health service users briefly before her marriage and how keen they'd always been to have a branded cigarette. One of the group, a young man in a pair of baggy tracksuit bottoms, stood up and began to pace.

'And we've got some doctors,' Shirley said. The other group, more distant from the main group than the service users, was well dressed and exclusively male. 'Psychiatrists smoke like troopers.'

There were four of them. All dressed in suits, the one that stood out for Mumtaz was a tall, blond man of about fifty. He was so thin that she wondered whether he was unwell. To his right were two smaller men of about the same age, one slim, the other overweight. Both looked Asian. The fourth man was younger than the others and was white with dark hair.

'The tall skinny chap is Mr Cotton, the chief psychiatric consult,' Shirley said.

'He looks to me as if he's got cancer or something,' Kylie said.

'He did have it about eighteen months ago,' Shirley said. 'One of his legs. But he's all right now, just thin.'

'That why he walks a bit funny?'

'The cancer? Probably.'

'That young good-looking one is Dr Golding,' Shirley told Mumtaz.

Kylie smiled. 'Everyone fancies him.'

'He won't stay long,' Shirley said.

'Why not?'

'He just won't.'

Maybe she was influenced by Shirley's words, but to Mumtaz the young doctor didn't look comfortable. While the other three men chatted easily, he was a little on the periphery and she thought he looked as if he didn't want to get any closer.

'Who are the other two?' Mumtaz asked.

'The slim one's Dr D'Lima and the fat one's Dr el Masri.'

Mumtaz saw Dr D'Lima laugh and then look at the tall, white consultant and nod his head in agreement. Dr el Masri had a good head of hair and a moustache and his face was smooth, but his teeth stuck out. Other than that he seemed ordinary.


Lee looked at his watch. Eleven-thirty. He wondered whether Vi had had her operation. She hated hospitals and so they could be having problems calming her down. Either her blood pressure or her pulse went loopy whenever she got near a hospital, he couldn't remember which.

He looked down at the plastic file on his desk, located a telephone number, and dialled it. He waited for a few moments until he heard a woman say, 'Hello? Yeah?'

'Mrs Rivers?' he asked.

'Yeah?'

'Hello, Mrs Rivers, my name's Lee Arnold, I'm the private investigator your solicitor Mr Salmon has engaged to locate the whereabouts of your husband, Philip.'

'Oh, yeah,' she said. 'Del's mate. He said you'd be in touch.'

Lee wasn't sure he liked being described as 'Del's mate' but he let it go.

'It would be helpful if we could have a chat about Philip as soon as possible,' he said. 'As I'm sure you can appreciate, if I'm going to look for him I need to know as much about him as I can.'

'Course.'

'Convenient to you . . .'

'Oh, I'm not doing nothing,' she said. She sounded young even though he knew that she wasn't. He had an image in his head of a petite blonde in high heels and hot pants.

'I can come to you or we can meet at my office,' Lee said. 'I'm in Green Street, Upton Park.'

She laughed. 'Green Street? Gawd blimey, I remember Green Street! Don't think I've been down there for twenty years. Me and me dad used to go buying old toot for a laugh in junk shops on Green Street when I was a kid. Got me buyer's eye in down there.'

'Not many junk shops these days,' Lee said.

'I know. Been Asian restaurants and shops for donkeys' years,' she said. 'Not the same.'

Lee waited for her to elaborate on what wasn't 'the same' but fortunately she didn't. Instead she said, 'Why don't you come here?'

'If that'll be better for you.'

'Well, at least you'll be able to park,' she said.

He looked back down at the file. 'West Heath Road, Hampstead?'

'That's the one,' she said. 'There's gates but if you just press the buzzer on the wall when you get here, I'll let you in. Do you wanna come over now, Mr Arnold?'

He thought about how long it was going to take him to get all the way across north London. And he wanted a bit more time with Phil Rivers' file before he met his missus. He said, 'How's two?'

'Fine,' she said. 'See you then.'

'Thank you, Mrs Rivers.'

'Anything to know where Phil's gone,' she said and then rang off.

Lee leant back in his chair and picked up the file. Phil Rivers was the product of one of those old council tower blocks that had been built in North Woolwich back in the 1960s. Phil's father, Ken, had been a docker and had lost his job just a few years after his son's birth when the Royal Docks had closed in 1981. He'd been in his forties then and hadn't worked since. It had been Phil's mum, Bette, who had kept the family going by increasing her hours at the Tate & Lyle sugar factory at Silvertown. In terms of male role models, Phil's first had been a jobless man who had probably been infuriated by what he had almost certainly seen as his emasculation. Lee had had uncles like that himself. Ex-dockers embittered by unemployment and loss of status. Uncle Charlie had thrown himself under a tube train.

According to Derek Salmon, Ken Rivers knew what his son had done and that he was missing. Phil's mother was in the early stages of dementia and so she didn't. Lee had considered going to visit the old couple but had then changed his mind. Parents could be too close to their children to be honest and so he'd decided to simply observe them. Ken and Bette Rivers had moved to Southend, not too far from Susan. A couple of days by the Thames Estuary, combined with some time with his girlfriend, would be very nice. Mumtaz was perfectly capable of taking care of the office on her own for a few days. Although he knew that she had a lot on her plate, what with her house move and the el Shamy assignment. Maybe he'd pop back occasionally, depending upon what he found in Southend.

He looked at his watch again. There was no way of knowing whether Vi was having surgery or not unless she phoned him. He was suddenly lonely. Mumtaz was doing her 'voluntary work' at Ilford Hospital and he wished she was around. Lee went out onto the metal steps outside the office and smoked a cigarette. He looked at people moving about, loading and unloading fruit and vegetables to and from lorries, men chatting and laughing in languages he couldn't understand, kids making noise for the hell of it. He knew he should be mugging up on Phil Rivers' biog so that he was ready for his meeting with the ex-wife. But Lee also needed to absorb what he knew about Rivers so far. With the exception of the few years when he'd worked for the old car thief Brian Barber, Phil Rivers had spent most of his life being funded by women. First his mum, then his wife. Until he'd met Sandra he'd never even left home and yet it had been Phil who had divorced her. Why? Unless he'd planned to sell the house and bugger off for some time, it seemed to Lee as if Phil was blowing his life up. Phil's wife had kept him. Derek Salmon had been of the opinion that Sandra was besotted with her husband and let him do whatever he liked. So if he'd wanted to cheat on her he could probably have got away with it. On the face of it, the divorce didn't make sense.

There were four photographers outside the front of the house, one from each of the tabloids. Salwa was just grateful that the children had gone to school before they'd arrived. She'd phoned Rashida to tell her to pick the younger ones up after school. Her daughter had said, 'Only if you say I don't have to marry Cousin Anwar.' Salwa had not agreed to that, but she knew that Rashida would collect her siblings anyway.

Some Yemeni preacher had tried to get a visa for the UK and had been denied because of his open support for al Qaeda. This story had led to other cases, both old and new, about so-called Muslim 'hate preachers' in the national press. And although Salwa's husband Hatem had never preached a word either for or against al Qaeda since he'd come to Britain, his continued incarceration in Belmarsh Prison, and especially its cost, had become newsworthy again. Salwa heard one of the men outside shout, 'How much do you get a week while your husband's in prison, Mrs el Shamy?' and 'Now the Muslim Brotherhood are in government in Egypt, why can't you go home?'

Salwa hid in her kitchen. Newspapers like the *Daily Mail* and the *Sun* had already decided that Hatem was guilty of planning to blow up his hospital and nothing she could say would change what they wrote. But when Mumtaz Hakim got evidence against Ragab el Masri for sexual misconduct, the whole case would unravel. She was confident. Salwa put a boiled sweet into her mouth and told herself that again. But her teeth ground nervously against the pear drop and eventually she crunched down too hard and broke a molar. Salwa cried.

Susan would have loved Sandra Rivers' house. Old and beautifully restored on the outside, it was completely new, shiny and minimalist inside. The lounge, in common with Susan's much smaller version, contained a TV, sofas and a coffee table. There was not a book or a newspaper in sight. That was the bit that Lee didn't like. The antiseptic cleanliness was delightful, the rest of it gave him the heebie-jeebies. But he'd been spooked even before he'd got inside.

Sandra Rivers had opened her electronic gates remotely and had met Lee in person at the front door. She hadn't been the petite blonde in high heels and hot pants he had imagined. At first he'd wondered whether the stout middle-aged woman in a yellow sack dress was in fact the 'help'. But she shook his hand. 'Sandra Rivers,' she said. 'Pleased to meet you.'

Coffee was offered, which he accepted, and cake, which he declined. When she returned from making the drinks she was smiling.

'You were with Phil for almost fifteen years, Mrs Rivers,' Lee said.

'Sandra.' She put his coffee down on the table in front of him. 'Call me Sandra. Yes, I'd just sold me old ladies fashion shop on Brick Lane and I'd been online with budget vintage fakes dot com for about six months.'

He could smell sugar on her breath. She'd sneaked something to eat when she'd made the coffee. 'How was the site doing?'

'Oh, brilliant,' she said. 'It took off right from the get-go.'

Lee had looked up Sandra Rivers online. When she'd eventually sold her budget vintage clothes website back in 2010 it had netted her twenty million pounds. But then what was not to like about a company that sold fake vintage clothes made in China for pocket money prices? Women who liked that sort of thing could look funky and different without spending a fortune.

'Derek Salmon told me you met Phil through one of your dad's friends.'

Sandra smiled, her big cheeks rising to make her eyes look small. 'Ah, yes, dear old Brian,' she said. 'Del told me you used to be a copper in Newham so you must've known Brian Barber.'

'A bit.'

'Oh, he and my dad were best mates from, like, years ago, back in the thirties, you know,' she said. 'My dad's family was originally from Italy, see, and so they had a hard time of it when the war started. The Barbers, Brian's family, were friends and neighbours of theirs in Shoreditch and didn't care about the Italian business. After the war, when Brian's lot moved to Canning Town, they stayed in touch.' She smiled again. 'My dad was a cobbler by trade but when he was young he was a bit of a tearaway and I've no doubt he went out on the rob with Brian back then. But not later on, and especially not when Brian started to get hard men in to protect his business.'

'Like your husband.'

She shook her head. She had a lot of beautiful thick brown hair. 'Phil wasn't really a tough guy,' she said. 'He just did a lot of bodybuilding and looked as if he could handle himself. Brian took him on as a favour to Phil's Uncle Bob who'd been inside with Brian back in the eighties.'

'And was it love at first sight?'

'I thought so.' Her smile disappeared immediately. The lack of it made her look her age and Lee noticed that her hands began to fidget. 'I know what you're thinking about the age difference, Mr Arnold.'

'Lee.'

'Lee.' She smiled again briefly then she said, 'But Phil was in love with me. I was married and divorced before Phil and so I know when a man is or isn't in love. Phil was.'

'And so why did he ask you for a divorce at the beginning of last year?'

She thought, shook her head and then she said, 'I can't tell you and that's the truth. We were happy in the house in Wanstead. Phil was doing lots of gym work, which was what he liked to do. Driving about – he had a Jag. He loved to bomb down the A127 to Southend to see his mum and dad.'

'You didn't go with him?'

'No.'

'What did you do once you'd sold your business, Sandra?'

Her hands began to work nervously again. 'Not a lot,' she said. She shook her head. 'Oh, what am I doing? I can't keep things from you if you're going to find Phil for me, can I? The truth is that when I gave up the business I had a breakdown. When you've worked all your life and suddenly there's nothing to do, however much money you have just doesn't make up for that.'

'How did this breakdown . . .'

'Look, I've never been exactly thin in me life, but I'm now a size twenty-four, know what I mean? Eating and crying and eating . . . I couldn't sleep half the time and whenever Phil was out I had panic attacks. Eventually I got help.'

'Treatment.'

'I didn't go to hospital,' she said. 'But, you know, pills and therapy and that. Luckily I could pay for the best. Slowly I started to feel better. When Phil said he wanted a divorce the worst of it was over.'

'He supported you through it.'

'Yeah. Then he said he wanted to be on his own.'

'Derek Salmon told me your divorce was based on irreconcilable differences.'

'That was what Phil wanted, not me,' she said. 'I asked him if there was anybody else and he said no. I had no evidence to make me believe there was another woman . . . we had a normal sex life right up until he asked for the divorce.'

Lee finally got round to his coffee, which was fresh and very good. 'Why did you let Phil stay in the Wanstead house after your divorce?' he asked.

She shrugged. 'He wanted to,' she said. 'And I'd already bought this. As soon as Phil said we were over I looked for another place. I couldn't've stayed in the Wanstead house after that, not with all those memories in there.'

'So you moved out?'

'Yes. I went to my place in St Tropez for a couple of weeks first then I came back and found this. I expect Del's told you that the arrangement that we came to, all legal, was that Phil could live in the house rent-free for as long as he wanted. But if he moved out, it had to be sold and we would split the profits between us. I never thought for a second he'd scam me. If he scammed me . . .' She looked for a moment as if she might cry. Then she said, 'Imagine what a fool I felt when I realized that he'd advertised our house online! Me, an Internet retailer! Talk about being slapped in the face.'

And it had been a huge slap.

'Has he used his credit or debit cards since he disappeared?' Lee asked.

Tracking the use of credit or debit cards would have been the first thing that the police would have done.

'No,' she said.

So either he had transferred the money into another account or someone was looking after him. But if he had transferred the money, how had he done it and where had it gone?

Lee said, 'Do you know if Phil had any debts? Did he gamble?'

'No and no. He had an allowance for his car and general expenses, and he never went over it or asked for any more.'

'What about friends and relatives? Any of those in trouble as far as you know?'

'No. His old man liked the odd little flutter on the gee-gees but what bloke his age don't? Phil never said it was a problem.' She sighed. Then she riffled in the pockets of her sack dress and took out a chocolate bar. 'God help me. I'm sorry, I have to eat something now.'

Lee smiled. 'It's OK.'

'Put me right back, all this,' she said. 'Back on meds too.' She shook her head. 'No, Phil's mum and dad live in Southend in a flat by the sea and are very happy and settled, in spite of Bette's dementia. Or they were until Phil went missing.'

'You've spoken to them?'

'To Ken, yeah. I never saw either of them that much, but we always got on.'

'What about any new people in Phil's circle?' Lee asked. 'Did he come into contact with anyone you thought might be a bit dodgy or maybe had a bad influence on him?'

'No,' she said. 'Phil just went to his gym, which I had built for him in the garden, he went out in his car sometimes and that was really all he did. When we was first together he used to go down the pub sometimes with Brian's son, Barry, but then that all stopped years ago. Phil told me that all Barry ever wanted to do was pull birds and he wasn't interested in that and so he knocked it on the head. I never once got any sort of feeling or heard any rumours that Phil was playing around with other women.'

'Which pub did Phil and Barry go to?'

'The George on Wanstead High Street,' she said. 'But that was years ago. Since me and Phil got together we did most things together, especially after I got ill. Poor Phil saw almost no one during that time because he had to be with me. I think I saw more people than he did, coming in to help me get well. Phil was just left to his own devices. Maybe that was why he wanted a divorce? Maybe he couldn't bear the thought of going through all that with me again? What do you think, Lee?'


The patients (she could call them that in the privacy of her own head) and some of the staff said that the long corridor that connected the chronic block to the building containing the two acute wards was haunted. Some patient who had committed suicide back in the 1900s, supposedly. Shirley knew that a lot more had taken that route out of Ilford Hospital since then. Luckily she hadn't been at work the day that young Sara Ibrahim had thrown herself out of the window. People who had seen it were still having trouble with it. Now that was haunting.

'Mrs Mayfield.'

'Mr Cotton.'

He'd appeared through a door ahead of her. There were several in the corridor but they were usually locked.

'I saw a young woman I didn't recognize with you this morning. Do you have a new volunteer?'

'Yes. Miss Huq,' she said.

'Promising?'

'I think so.'

They walked, he as usual with some difficulty.

Shirley was on her way to the car park via the acute wards. Inducting a new volunteer was always tiring and she wanted to get home and put her feet up.

'There was a minor incident on the forensic ward this afternoon,' the chief psychiatric consultant said. 'Don't know if it's come to your notice.'

'No. I didn't hear the alarm go off.'

Even a minor incident on the forensic ward would necessitate the sounding of the old Second World War siren alarm.

'As I say, it was a very minor incident,' he said. 'However, it may come to your attention. A male patient may ask you to institute an investigation into the conduct of a member of my staff.'

It was all right for him to use 'patient' because he was a doctor. It was also quite permissible for him to refer to 'his' staff. But he was also sending her a message and they both knew it.

'Thanks for the heads-up,' she said.

He smiled. 'I'm sure you'll do whatever is appropriate, Mrs Mayfield. I have confidence in you.'

He strode off purposefully. Bad leg or no bad leg, Mr Cotton could put on a turn of speed when he wanted to. He could also leave a nasty metaphorical smell in his wake. Because Shirley knew that she would do whatever was 'appropriate' should that forensic patient contact her and she didn't like herself for it.

# 5

Feeling excited and pissed off at the same time was exhausting, especially after a long evening shift followed by not much sleep. Susan staggered out of bed and walked unsteadily into her kitchen. She was useless before her first cup of tea. As she waited for the kettle to boil and flung a teabag into a mug, she wondered whether Lee would pop in on his way to the job he had on. Even though she was working every evening that week, he was going to stay over for a few days anyway. If she let him.

When he'd first called and told her that he was coming to Southend, Susan had been excited. She'd accepted that he had to work for much of that time and she'd been happy when he'd asked her if he could stay. But then he'd gone on about that old copper woman he used to work with when he was in the police. She'd had some sort of operation on her throat and when he'd been to see her in hospital she hadn't been able to speak. It had spooked him and he'd clearly been worried. And while Susan accepted that it was normal to worry about a sick friend, to go on about it to someone who didn't give a stuff had been a bit tiresome. And weird. But then, the first time she'd met Lee it had been obvious that Vi Collins had been jealous. The old girl had a thing for him and Susan wondered why he encouraged it by hanging out with her. Lee said it was because it was always useful for private investigators to have contacts in the police. But Susan wondered whether he also enjoyed the attention.

She made her tea and took it back to bed with her. Once she felt human, she'd get up. She hoped that her mood would lighten. She didn't want to be pissed off with Lee when he arrived. He was the best bloke she'd been out with for years and she didn't want to frighten him off by appearing too clingy. Men like him didn't walk into the casino every day. Most of them were either loud-mouthed car dealers who fancied themselves as Mafia dons or pathetic gambling addicts, too old and nervous to go on the internet to feed their habit. Then there was the odd high roller. At the moment there were two, a young black guy from south London and an old man who always dressed up in a full evening suit when he played the tables. The younger man spent heavily and won heavily, while the old guy was all about big stakes and even bigger losses. Whatever happened he was, strangely, always cheerful.

Lee had been such a breath of fresh air in the darkened, velvet atmosphere of the casino. He hadn't gambled what he couldn't afford – only one of those coppers had. He'd very clearly just been out for a laugh and that simplicity, as well as his dark good looks, had attracted Susan. She'd been out with Tony Soprano wannabes in the past and she was done with them. All the flash cars that turned out to belong to rich customers, as well as the mortgaged-to-the-hilt houses and unpaid credit card bills, were as tiresome as the men themselves. As far as she could tell, Lee was honest. He had a scruffy old car, a small flat in Forest Gate and a business that he openly admitted was struggling. He still supported a teenage daughter who lived with his ex-wife and he smoked more than Susan would have liked – she'd have to work on him about that. But he didn't drink at all, which was

refreshing. Most middle-aged blokes did drink and, as a conse-
quence, talked a lot of shit. But Lee didn't talk shit and if she
were honest the only time anything he'd said had really upset
her had happened when he'd phoned to tell her about Vi Collins.
He'd been, to Susan's way of thinking, far too involved and she
hadn't liked it.

Susan finished her tea and tried not to be annoyed.


'Have you met el Masri?'

Mumtaz had had to run up the stairs and open up the office
as quickly as she could to take the call.

'I've seen him, Salwa.'

Some blurry photographs of Salwa el Shamy, albeit from a distance, had been in a couple of the tabloids that morning. The
decision by the Home Office to bar a radical Yemeni Islamic
cleric from the UK had reignited the debate, particularly in
right-wing circles, about a range of issues around immigration.
This included the status of people like Salwa el Shamy.

'You haven't met him yet?'

She sounded agitated, but then she would be. The photographs Mumtaz had seen showed Salwa trying to hide as much
of herself as she could behind her front door as she let her children into the house. The headline accompanying the pictures
had screamed some odious invective she had immediately put
from her mind. Salwa quite naturally wanted to hear some good
news.

'No,' Mumtaz said. 'But I'm volunteering twice a week and so
I will meet him. The Advocacy has regular meetings with the
hospital staff and that includes the doctors. Don't worry, it's in
hand.'

She heard Salwa sigh. 'You see my family are in the newspapers today?'

'Yes. I'm sorry you had to go through that.'

'They are like vultures. There's no respect here for Muslims. I don't know if I can do this any more! I can't be in this country!'

She was becoming hysterical.

Mumtaz said, 'Salwa, whatever is happening, you must support Hatem. That's what you've decided to do, isn't it? Stay until Hatem's trial?'

'And for children.'

'Yes, for them too. They're all at school.'

'Yes, but . . .'

'Salwa, what you have to understand is that newspapers like that don't have respect for anyone. They don't actually care whether you're a Muslim, a Christian or a Hindu. If they can make a story out of something they will. And in this case it was the banning of Sheikh al-Kabir.'

'I don't know this Yemeni holy man!'

'I know that, but his story reignited the debate—'

'They say all Muslims are terrorists! This is not true!'

'Of course it isn't, but because this Sheikh has said some things about how it is all right to kill non-believers and because Hatem is in prison on suspicion of terrorist offences, some of the newspapers have connected them. Wrongly. But it will stop soon, Salwa, trust me. Tomorrow the papers will find another story and you will be forgotten. It won't be the same as it was when Hatem was arrested.'

For a moment Salwa was quiet and then she said, 'You know this free speech they talk about here? It doesn't happen for Muslims.'

'It can seem that way sometimes,' Mumtaz said. 'But, Salwa,

you do have to be strong for Hatem and your children. I am doing my best for you but getting the evidence you want may take some time. I have to become part of the hospital so that el Masri becomes used to me and, hopefully, ignores me. I have to ask questions without seeming to ask questions. Do you see what I mean?'

'You must not make suspicious.'

'That's right.' She saw her mobile phone begin to flash and looked at the screen. It was Naz Sheikh. She switched it off. 'Salwa, I will tell you as soon as I have any news.'

'You will tell to me first?'

'Of course.' Mumtaz crossed her fingers behind her back. There was no way she would pass on material as sensitive as this direct to the client without telling Lee first.

Salwa sighed. Calmer now, she said, 'OK.'

'OK,' Mumtaz said. 'Now, Salwa, you go and start your day. Are there any photographers outside your house this morning?'

'No.'

'Good. Then just go about your business,' Mumtaz said.

'I will. *Ma'is salama.*'

Although Mumtaz knew that meant 'goodbye' in Arabic she responded in English, just as she did with her English-speaking Bangladeshi clients. That she was a Muslim of Asian heritage was helpful sometimes in her work but it was also incidental. If she was to be free from accusations of bias she had to keep a professional distance.

After she put the phone down, Mumtaz looked at her mobile again and switched it back on. Naz Sheikh hadn't left a message. He'd only called to wind her up and she could do without that. At the weekend she'd have to load the car up with stuff from the garage to take down to the tip in Barking. It was a dirty job that she wasn't looking forward to; the last thing she needed was Naz or any other member of his family hassling her for her new address. That, or some exhortation for her to be a 'better' Muslim woman. As if she were some sort of whore. And coming from a sexual predator like him! But then the Sheikhs and their ilk had double standards, not unlike Salwa el Shamy. Her reference to the Yemeni preacher who urged the faithful to kill unbelievers as a 'holy man' had not been lost on Mumtaz.


Ken and Bette Rivers' flat occupied the lower half of an Edwardian house on a street just off the eastern side of the seafront, known as Southend's Golden Mile. It sounded grand but although it had been tidied up in recent years, Lee could easily see it hadn't changed that much. For a start there were still all the slot machine places with their promises of easy money and cheap teddy bears. Pubs he remembered his dad getting plastered in – ruining everyone's day – didn't seem to have changed at all. The Foresters, the Cornucopia and, of course, the Hope Hotel which, back when he'd been a copper, some Essex plod had told him used to rent out rooms by the hour. Then there was the smell. A combination of frying onions, sugar and chips.

Sandra's casino was at the other end of the seafront, on the western side of the famous 'longest pier in the world'. A much tidier and more sedate area, the western seafront had once been famous for its ornamental gardens on slopes known as 'the cliffs'. But in recent years the land had become unstable and vast areas of the gardens had been cordoned off as too dangerous for the public. But it was still preferable to the Golden Mile.

Lee Arnold lit a cigarette and then stared down a kid who had been on the verge of asking him for one. The kid changed his mind. Lee walked past the Rivers' flat, put his cigarette out and then wandered into a small cafe at the end of the road. On one side its windows looked out to sea, while on the other they faced the house Lee was watching. He sat down at the fixed plastic table that gave him the best view of the street and, when the waitress came to ask him for his order, he said, 'Cup of tea and a plate of chips, please.'

Susan hadn't given him so much as a glass of water when he'd turned up at her flat half an hour earlier. She'd been in a bad mood about something and so he'd just dropped his bag in the bedroom, she'd given him her spare key and he'd left. He'd asked her if she really did want him to stay and she'd said that she did, but Lee wondered. Had she gone off him? Met someone else?

Lee looked at some of his fellow diners. Seaside towns always had a selection of easily recognisable types. By the front door was the regulation alcoholic, age indecipherable, talking to a man so thin he had to be a junkie. An old woman in a battered Persian lamb hat lifted a transparent cup of frothy coffee to her crinkled lips with purple and brown veined hands, while a young couple with a baby in a buggy made roll-ups in preparation for leaving. A middle-aged woman, who could only be a prostitute, pulled her V-necked t-shirt up a little to hide her cleavage. Off-duty, she was enjoying a bacon sandwich before, no doubt, returning to her bedsit somewhere behind the Golden Mile where the local ladies of the night had always lived. Unemployment was high in seaside towns: poor people flocked in with the vain hope their lives would be better by the sea where rents were cheap. It had been like that for decades, but since the recession, this trend had got worse.

Lee saw the junkie turn to look at him and wondered how long it would be before he tried to tap him up for some cash.

Would there be some story about how he'd left his wallet somewhere and couldn't pay for his tea? Or would he just come over and beg?

Outside, a young woman came out of the Rivers' house with a baby in a car seat. She had purple hair and wore hot pants over thick black tights. She put the car seat in a battered Mini and drove off as if the police were pursuing her. The Rivers owned their flat. Bette Rivers had bought their old council flat in North Woolwich back in the 1990s under the Right to Buy scheme. Selling it had enabled the couple to buy the Southend place, which they owned outright. Lee ran his gaze up and down the street outside again and still couldn't find much to recommend it. But then, if Ken and Bette Rivers liked it then that was all that mattered.

The waitress put a mug of tea and a plate of chips down in front of him without a word. She was middle-aged and had a disappointed air; Lee knew how she felt. Because he had to pay his bills he'd let Mumtaz take that dodgy el Shamy job. As if the idea of working for such a contentious client wasn't enough – if the press got to know they'd have a field day – he wasn't exactly happy about her going into what could be a dangerous environment either. The mad (who were connected in Lee's mind with the addicted, in the shape of his alcoholic father and brother) could kick off over nothing. Mumtaz might just walk on to one of those wards and get a punch in the face. He'd told her, but she'd laughed. She'd thought he was being overcautious and ignorant. Maybe he was, but even Mumtaz hadn't been able to laugh about the predatory doctor.

'Mate, you got a fag I could buy off you?'

It was the junkie, as Lee had predicted.

'I'll give you thirty pee for one,' he pleaded.

Lee took a cigarette out of his packet and gave it to him. 'No, that's all right,' he said.

The man smiled. 'Oh, thanks. Can I have one for me mate?'

Lee frowned. But he gave him another cigarette and said, 'That's your lot.'

The man shuffled away. Lee put a chip in his mouth and took a swig of tea, which was so dark it made his teeth wince. He filled the cup with as much sugar as he could tolerate and carried on watching the street. If he remembered correctly, there was an old seaside rock factory somewhere on one of the streets off the seafront, but he couldn't remember where. A white van came and parked in front of the Rivers' house while the driver delivered a parcel to another house across the road and then left in a cloud of exhaust fumes. When the smoke had cleared there was an old man outside the house, coughing and smoking a fag. He was a bit of a state – limp trousers pulled up to his chest, a vest on underneath an old sports jacket – but there was definitely a resemblance to the picture of Ken Rivers that had been in Phil Rivers' file.

Lee watched him. He didn't do much. Ken Rivers used his front gate to hang on to and when he did move it was clear that his legs were stiff. Several people came and went down the pavement in front of the old man but he didn't speak or even look at any of them. Ken Rivers didn't want to talk to anyone. Decades of unemployment could do that to a person. But Lee thought that there was also something hard behind his eyes, something inbuilt. Lee could see Phil in his father but what he couldn't spot, along with the younger man's good looks, was the innocence that shone through from all the photographs he'd seen of Phil. Whatever people said, and in spite of what he had done, Lee couldn't accept that Phil Rivers was mean. Unlike his father.

Shirley waited for her clued-up new advocate to answer her mobile, but she didn't. Shirley hung up without leaving a message. It hadn't been important. She'd wanted to talk to someone she could communicate with easily. It wasn't that Mandy and Roy, her other two advocates, were useless but they were both ex-service-users and there were times when Shirley felt that that was a barrier. Roy, in particular, took quite heavy meds and could be difficult to get through to.

But even if Shirley had been able to speak to Mumtaz, she didn't know what she would have said. She would probably have just chatted, talked platitudes and then said how much she was looking forward to seeing her again the following week. She wouldn't have been able to share. How could she?

The service user Mr Cotton had spoken to her about had called her first thing in the morning. He'd been segregated and was being 'specialled' – accompanied by a nurse at all times. So the interview she'd had with him had been strained. Dylan was young, street-drug dependent, angry and a self-harmer. He was what Shirley had come to recognize as a 'typical' forensic service user. He came from a family in the nearby London Borough of Tower Hamlets notorious for its criminality and Dylan himself was on the unit because he'd killed someone. By turns delusional, furious and sad beyond consolation, Dylan had been involved in what Mr Cotton had called a 'minor' incident on the unit. However, the first thing that Shirley noticed when she walked in the room was that Dylan had lost a front tooth.

'Timothy knocked my tooth out,' Dylan said.

'Timothy Pool? The ward manager?'

'Yeah, man.'

Shirley felt her heart sink. Timothy Pool had managed the forensic unit for as long as anyone could remember. A small, efficient nurse originally from Mauritius, nobody who knew Dylan would have been surprised that he'd got into a spat with Timothy. One of Dylan's family's hobbies was racism and Timothy was black.

As if he'd heard her thoughts, Dylan said, 'I never called him nothing racist.'

The nurse observing cleared his throat.

'So what happened?' Shirley asked.

'I wanted to go outside for a tab and Timothy said I couldn't.'

Since the indoor smoking ban had come into force, there had been trouble over fags on all the wards. Back in the old days, cigarettes had been used to reward good behaviour – in fact on one of the acute wards they still were – but Timothy had always been a virulent anti-smoker and so on the unit that practice had ceased a long time ago. Patients were still allowed to go outside to smoke their 'tabs', dependent upon treatment compliance and good behaviour, but their friends or relatives outside the hospital had to supply the smoking materials.

'Why not?' Shirley asked.

'Because he can,' Dylan said.

'That's no reason. What do you mean, Dylan?'

He looked up. His eyes were bloodshot and half closed and his clothes smelt of stale tobacco.

'He wanted a ruck with me, man,' he said. 'He knew I'd kick off if he didn't let me smoke.'

'Why would he want that to happen?' Shirley asked the question, but part of her knew the answer anyway.

'Because he thinks he's like some sort of fucking god,' Dylan said. Then he looked up at the nurse and added, 'You all stick your tongues up his arse.'

The nurse said nothing. But Shirley knew Dylan was right.

Timothy Pool, nurse, ward manager and devout Christian, was also a massive egotist. And because he'd been in charge of the unit for over a decade it had become his personal fiefdom. Ruling his staff with a mixture of guile, fear and favouritism, Timothy was not the excellent manager Mr Cotton thought he was. But he did everything the chief consultant said. In fact, Timothy was all over anyone who could put 'Dr' in front of their name.

'What happened?' Shirley asked.

Dylan licked his lips, which still had some dried blood on them. 'I asked to go into the yard for a smoke and Timothy said no. I asked him why I couldn't when I'd taken all me meds and not kicked off and he said it was because I was cutting up.'

'Were you?'

'No!'

She looked at his arms. They were covered with scars, but none of them looked new.

'I showed him me wrists and I offered to take all me clothes off so he could check, but he didn't want me to do that,' Dylan said. 'He said, "You know you've done wrong, Dylan," and then he turned his back on me. Cunt.'

The nurse said, 'Easy.'

'Oh fuck off,' Dylan mumbled. He said to Shirley, 'He knows that people ignoring me sets me off and so he done it deliberate.'

'What did you do then, Dylan?'

'I never hit him. He says I did, but I never. I just tapped him on the shoulder to get his attention, like. Then he's screaming and next thing I know he's punching me in the mouth while him,' he pointed at the nurse, 'and that lesbo Tricia, look on.'

Shirley knew that Timothy Pool and the nurses would tell an entirely different story. When she saw Timothy to hear his account, he barely looked up at Shirley. It wasn't just because she personally disliked him that Shirley didn't believe what Timothy said but because she'd been in this situation too many times before. The management of the forensic unit was rotten to the core. The acute and chronic wards weren't much better. But Mr Cotton, his doctors and the hospital management were happy and that was all that mattered. Except that it wasn't. Shirley felt guilty every day she went to work and when she'd heard that Sara Ibrahim had killed herself she'd almost lost her mind. But she'd taken Mr Cotton's shilling anyway.

As she was leaving the ward she saw Dylan again, who mumbled, 'I know you won't do nothing, but I had to ask, you know?'

And Shirley Mayfield had wanted to die.

# 6

Everything hurt. Throat, shoulders, arms, head, chest. Vi held up a piece of paper with the words: 'It fucking hurts.' Her companion, an overweight middle-aged man said, 'Well, it will do, you've had your throat cut.'

The man, Tony Bracci, had been Vi Collins's detective Sergeant for just over five years and he knew her well. Blond and blue-eyed, Tony's vast family was originally Italian, although he looked more like a Viking than a Latin.

'Know when you'll be back?' Tony asked. He wanted to offer his guv a cigarette because he knew she'd be gagging for one but then he also knew that it wasn't allowed. If she coughed she could burst her Frankenstein-like staples, which didn't bear thinking about.

Vi wrote down, 'Two weeks.'

'Oh, well, that's not too bad.'

She gave him a look that said it was worse than he could ever think possible and then, bored with writing things down, she hissed, 'What's going on?'

'Don't worry about all that. Just get better.'

But he was on her turf, in her house, where even more than at the station she was mistress of all she surveyed. Vi didn't have to speak to get Tony to talk.

'Non-fatal stabbing on High Street North, perp was at the scene and gave himself up. He was the victim's brother. Shit over an inheritance.' He shrugged. 'Peeping toms in East Ham Leisure Centre. That was yesterday afternoon.'

'Peeping toms?' Vi whispered. 'More'n one?'

'Three,' Tony said. 'Young lads who need to get laid. Nearly frightened the bejesus out of a pair of young ladies in swimwear. Oh, and that mini-mart on Katherine Road got done over again.'

Vi rolled her eyes. Some businesses, for reasons she'd never been able to fathom, seemed to have a sort of catnip effect on villains.

'A typical two days in the life of a busy London borough,' Tony said. 'Oh and I went down North Woolwich yesterday evening to take a look at the old Gallions Hotel.'

Vi frowned.

'You know, the old pub where . . .'

'I know Gallions,' she said hoarsely. 'What about it?'

'Well, there's been rumours about it being either sold or rented out for ages. Who knows what the new people'll do with it? I took some photographs, of the outside, like, while I still can.'

A little-known fact about Tony Bracci was that in the months since the Olympics he had become an active tweeter on Twitter. And although he didn't have a lot to say to his followers, he did like to post up pictures of what he thought were significant local landmarks. Vi Collins thought that he probably wasn't getting laid. But she looked at his photographs anyway. They showed a large Edwardian building surrounded by modern blocks of flats.

'My mum's brothers used to go up Gallions when it was called the Captain's Brothel,' Vi said. 'And yeah, they went for the reasons the name implies.'

Vi's uncles, like her mum, had been travellers who had made their living as itinerant builders and part-time farriers in and around East London. The first time Vi's Jewish dad had met her mum, she'd been selling 'lucky' heather sprigs outside pubs.

'I expect it'll be turned into flats in the end,' Tony said. 'Everything seems to be, these days. Unless they make it a Tesco Metro.'

Vi shook her head. She hated the trend for turning once-thriving pubs into small, urban supermarkets. It robbed the world of boozers and also threatened corner shops and mini-marts.

'Oh, and I'm bird-sitting for Lee Arnold's mynah,' he said.

'Chronus? Where's Arnold?'

'Don't know. Didn't ask. Off the manor somewhere. He should be back by the weekend. He didn't mention it to you?'

'No.'

There was a bit of an awkward silence. Tony knew only too well what his boss thought about Lee Arnold and he knew that she wouldn't be happy that he'd kept her out of the loop. He was probably only trying to spare her worrying about him. But Vi Collins wouldn't see it that way.

Tony changed the subject. 'So, apart from the pain, how are you, guv?'

'Bored shitless.'

Tony looked around what was a very comfortable living room well stocked with books and DVDs.

'Well, you've enough to keep you busy here,' he said.

'Yeah, but I want to be out there, don't I?' Vi said. 'Fuck knows what you and the rest of the wooden tops'll get up to while I'm laying on me sofa looking at *Judge Judy*. How's Venus?'

Paul Venus, superintendent at Forest Gate nick was Vi's and Tony's boss. A middle-aged, middle-class man with an eye for a younger woman, he didn't impress either of them or any of their colleagues. To his credit he was a good negotiator with villains who'd lost the plot, but he was next to useless when it came to supporting his officers against bureaucratic bullshit from the Metropolitan Police high command and central government. Also, he didn't like upsetting gangsters and that disturbed Vi in particular. Venus was either too frightened to be useful or he was in with them.

Tony said, 'Still a tosser.'

'Consistent.' She imagined that Venus was enjoying the break from her skinny, middle-aged smoke-dried face. She was everything he disliked in a woman.

They sat in silence then. They'd had a chat and Tony had put the flowers he'd brought her in a vase and arranged them artlessly. With no work to talk about there was nothing left to say.


This time, when Naz called, Mumtaz answered her phone.

'What do you want? I'm at work,' she said.

'Ah, but your white boyfriend isn't with you, is he?' Naz said.

Had he been watching the office or was he just guessing because she'd answered him promptly and not in a whisper?

'What do you want? I haven't got a moving date yet. When I do, I'll let you have it.'

'Oh, you mean when you're going to move to Sebert Road? Just by the cemetery?' he said.

Mumtaz felt her mouth dry up. She'd been so careful not to tell anyone – except her immediate family, Shazia and Lee. She'd found the ground-floor flat through one of her brothers and so it wasn't even as if a letting agent had been involved. How had he found out?

'I don't know why you tried to hide where you're going,' he said.

Mumtaz coughed to lubricate her throat. 'I didn't. I just didn't feel the need to tell you. How did you find out?'

'Oh, we can find out anything.'

She remembered that a man who could have been Naz's father had called at the house and asked Shazia where they were going. But she'd said she hadn't told him anything. Maybe Shazia had told some of her college friends and word had got out that way?

'I don't know why it's of interest to you,' Mumtaz said. 'I told you I'd pay you in full and I will.'

'Will you?'

'Look, it's more important to me to get you off my back than it is to have money,' she said. 'I will pay you and we'll be done.'

Her chest tightened. She didn't believe her own words.

'Oh, I don't think so,' Naz said. 'You'll still owe our admin fee, which is twenty-five per cent of the purchase price of your house. Then there is my charge.'

She began to notice her own heartbeat at the same time her hands started to shake. But Mumtaz knew she had to keep control. She'd expected something but this was worse than anything she'd imagined. She had to find out what these charges were. 'What do you mean "admin fee"? For what? And what is your charge? I don't understand.'

'It's quite simple,' he said. 'We take an admin fee from people who owe us money to cover the paperwork we've had to do to recover the debt.'

'What have you had to do? Nothing!' She was losing control and she couldn't afford to. But the office had just shifted on its axis and she'd started to feel hot, then sick. She grabbed hold of the side of the desk for support.

'We have to instruct our bank, our solicitors, we have people we have to pay with the money we've been waiting on from you, Mrs Hakim,' he said.

'Twenty-five per cent . . .'

'Oh, that's very fair.'

That was another hundred thousand pounds. It meant she'd be paying the Sheikhs forever. She couldn't speak.

'And as for my own charge, well, that's more to do with keeping something quiet for you.'

Although Mumtaz knew what he was going to say she still felt her ears try to close themselves against it.

'If your stepdaughter got to know the real circumstances surrounding her father's death . . .'

'Stop!'

Mumtaz's husband, Ahmet, had been murdered by Naz Sheikh. Mumtaz and Ahmet had been walking across Wanstead Flats, the open space between Forest Gate and Wanstead, when a young man had appeared. At the time Mumtaz hadn't known who he was and had only taken in that he was handsome. Even when he'd stabbed her husband, and Ahmet lay dying, she'd still not been able to take her eyes off him. She'd been so grateful.

Later she'd discovered that his name was Naz Sheikh and that he belonged to a family of gangsters. Ahmet had owed them money. As well as physically and sexually abusing both Shazia and herself, Mumtaz's husband had suffered from other vices. Principal amongst these was gambling, losing money to people far more powerful than himself. Ahmet had always been a show-off. All the money she'd been paying to the Sheikhs since his death had been to cover his debts.

'You remember that evening when Ahmet died, don't you, Mumtaz?' Naz said. She could hear how much he was enjoying this.

'Yes.'

When the police had asked her to describe her husband's attacker, she'd only given them a generic description. Young, dark-haired, wearing trainers. It could have been almost any young man in the borough. And yet she could have told them about every item of clothing he wore, his silver trainers, the tiny blemishes on his fine, smooth cheeks. He'd been like the hero in an old story her mother had told her when she was a child, the brave and handsome Silver Prince who had saved Bengal from all sorts of mythical beasts and bloodthirsty despots. She'd been so naive. With a first-class honours degree in psychology, she'd fallen prey to the oldest myth in the book – the saviour prince.

'You didn't know who I was then.'

'No.'

And when she had found out, she'd been too terrified to go to the police. Not because she was afraid they might find out about her collusion in the escape of her husband's killer, but because Naz had made threats that involved Shazia. And because it always worked, he hadn't stopped since.

'So, we have an agreement in principle?' Naz said. 'You pay me and my family what you owe and Shazia need never know what you did. Or rather what you didn't do. And she'll be safe, you have my word.'

He'd drooled over Shazia. Watching her as she left the house to go to college. Mumtaz had seen him sitting in his car or casually walking on the opposite side of the road. Because he knew that Shazia had been raped by her own father, Naz looked on her as little more than a prostitute.

Mumtaz closed her eyes. 'We have an agreement,' she said.

'Then I'll get a document drawn up for the administration fee,' he said. 'My charge we'll keep between ourselves. An agreement between friends.'

It seemed he didn't always want to share everything with his father and his brother.

Only just managing to stop herself crying, Mumtaz said, 'Why are you doing this? Why us? What did Ahmet ever do to your family that was so bad?'

There was a moment of silence. Then he said, 'You know, Mrs Hakim, your husband was always full of excuses. Whenever the time came for him to pay us, there was always a reason why he couldn't. The stress of it made my dad quite ill and I find that hard to forgive.'

'Yes, but that was Ahmet . . .'

'And you are his wife,' Naz said. 'Mumtaz, I'm doing this because I can. If I wanted to work and be like an ordinary person I'd've bought myself a little mini-mart somewhere or studied hard and become a solicitor. But Allah has chosen another path for me . . .'

'Allah? Allah! Allah has nothing to do with what you are!'

'Or you, I think, a whore who works on her own with a Christian man,' he said. And then his voice dropped to a hiss. 'Don't disrespect me or the Holy Name of Allah, Mrs Hakim. You saw what I did to your husband.'

He cut the connection and for a moment Mumtaz just sat and looked blankly at the phone. Although she'd never told Lee about the Sheikhs, she was aware that he knew she was in trouble. He'd suspected she owed money to people like the Sheikhs and he'd warned her that unless she went to the police she'd never be free. But how could she do that?

If Naz was found guilty of Ahmet's murder, she'd have to admit to her own part in it. Shazia would know everything and, although she had hated her father, how would she respond to Mumtaz if she knew she had murdered him? Would she hate her? And even if Naz went to prison, that would still leave his father and his brother on the loose and what would they do to her then?

Not that Naz was likely to be found guilty of Ahmet's murder.

A more likely scenario was that Naz would be exonerated. He'd have had all sorts of false alibis in place before he set out to murder Ahmet. She'd be accused of making a false allegation, which would raise more questions about her than about the Sheikhs. If she accused her dead husband of sexual abuse she could ruin Shazia's reputation, in some people's eyes, at least. And even a free and easy, western-dressing girl like Shazia valued her reputation, even if she said that she didn't. More importantly, contact with the police would enrage the Sheikhs. What they'd do to punish her, Mumtaz didn't dare think. Even running away wasn't an option for her. If she and Shazia just disappeared, how would they live? Who would console her parents when they went mad with worry? What would it do to Shazia's education? And how could she ever leave Lee Arnold on his own with the office, the bills and a queue of enraged clients?

Oh, why had he had to go to Southend this week?

Ken Rivers did a lot of what Lee's mother Rose called 'faffing about'. The previous day he'd spent most of his time in a seafront pub nursing two pints of bitter and looking at a copy of the *Racing Post*. But he hadn't gone to put a bet on. Unless he did it online which, at his age, seemed unlikely. He'd spoken to the barman about television and the weather and later he'd had a chat with another elderly man about his ailments. He had arthritis, angina and also what he called 'prostrate trouble', which probably meant he had a leaky bladder. He hadn't mentioned his missing only child at all and he had seemed neither unduly disturbed or upset. When he'd left the pub he'd bought a pint of milk and a packet of fags in a local shop and then gone home. Lee had watched the flat until it got dark and then he'd gone back to Susan's.

She'd still been off with him when he'd arrived a second time and had gone away to the casino, leaving Lee to fend for himself, food-wise. He'd bought a bag of chips from a local takeaway and waited for her to come home. When she'd got in she'd been all loved-up again and they'd had sex. But Lee was no more enlightened about what had been wrong with her to begin with. Not for the first time, he wondered why he tried to work out what made women tick.

Southend high street was mostly pedestrianized. This made it easier to walk about but also seemed to make Lee notice the squashed patties of old chewing gum on the pavement. They made him long for a wallpaper scraper. Ken Rivers went into Greggs the bakers and came out carrying a small paper bag. Although Lee knew that Bette Rivers had dementia and probably couldn't leave the flat he was shocked at Ken's behaviour. Since he'd been observing him, Ken had been out in the day most of the time. Who was looking after Bette?

He followed the old man up the High Street in the direction of the Victoria Shopping Centre. All along the street were the sorts of businesses he associated with Southend, like bookies and pawnbrokers, but also some that he didn't, like posh coffee places and even a university. He'd heard that the town was coming up but he hadn't quite believed it; even when he'd spent those few days with Susan back in early September he didn't remember noticing it. Although he didn't see what he would have regarded as many well-heeled people about, there were a lot of young students as well as a selection of the sorts more usually seen around the seafront. Ken Rivers made for a branch of NatWest and Lee followed him in. In spite of all the self-service options on offer to pay in or take out money, Ken walked up to one of the two cashiers' desks and took either a cheque or paying-in book out of his pocket. Lee went to a cash machine and took out thirty pounds. He also got a personal account statement that almost put him off what he was doing.

But then he heard Ken Rivers speak. 'I'll have it in fifties, please, love,' he said.

And while Lee didn't catch what the cashier said back to Ken, he did watch as she counted out notes in front of him. She did it for some time. When Ken Rivers left the bank, Lee reckoned that he'd folded at least a thousand pounds into his battered old wallet. Once he was outside the bank, the old man ate the jumbo sausage roll he'd bought from Greggs and then threw the paper bag on the ground. Lee Arnold itched to pick it up.

Salwa watched her daughter walk towards a group of lock-up garages under the railway bridge on Balmoral Road in the mistaken belief that she hadn't seen her. But Rashida had. She took a key out of her pocket and then turned to look at her mother.

'What you doing, Omy?' she asked.

Salwa answered her in Arabic. The girl spoke to her in English when she wanted to annoy her with her superior language skills. 'What are *you* doing, Rashida?'

'Don't you know?' Rashida still held keys in her hands. 'If you didn't know, why did you follow me?'

'I didn't . . .'

'You followed me from school, Omy,' she said. 'What've you been doing, watching me?'

It was lunchtime and usually Rashida had her food at school.

Her mother pulled the bottom of her jilbab up across her mouth like a naughty schoolgirl. Then, suddenly angry, she pulled it away and said, 'Why aren't you having school dinners?'

Rashida shook her head. 'You're unbelievable! Omy, tell me why you're here! Go on, tell me, we both know!'

Salwa took a deep breath. Then she took another. She said, 'It was what you said after the private detective came. About . . . not keeping quiet. I saw you come here yesterday, by chance, and . . . I know this place, Rashida. We both know.'

Salwa had come upon Rashida as she went a convoluted way home from the shops on Upton Lane. That time she hadn't seen her. Rashida had stood outside the lock-up, looking anxiously from left to right and then back again.

'Well, if you admit you know, then tell me I don't have to marry Cousin Anwar and I'll never come here again.'

'You can't come here again.' Salwa looked over her shoulder. 'We shouldn't be here now.'

'Then why were you here yesterday "by chance"?'

Salwa looked away. 'I come to check, sometimes.'

'Check for what? You don't have a key. I do.'

'I didn't know where it was. Where did you find it?'

'It doesn't matter. I got it,' Rashida said.

'You mustn't go inside!' Salwa looked over her shoulder again. 'We have to leave, there are people about.'

'I've never been inside,' Rashida said.

'Then what—'

'It doesn't matter why I'm here. That isn't your business, Omy.'

'You are my daughter.'

'Who you want to marry off to a football hooligan, yes!' Rashida said. 'Omy, if you promise not to give me to Cousin Anwar then I will never come here again. I promise.'

'A man is coming!' Salwa grabbed hold of her daughter's arm and pulled her away from the lock-up garages and towards the Romford Road. 'Come! Come!'

The girl was reluctant to move but she did. There was a man walking in their direction.

'Rashida!'

She walked beside her mother. 'So?'

'So what?' Salwa said. 'What do you mean?'

'Cousin Anwar . . .'

Salwa flung her arms up in exasperation. 'I cannot do anything about Cousin Anwar,' she said. 'The family have decided. There is nothing I can do.'

'Then I'll come back to the lock-up,' Rashida said.

'No. You will give me that key and you will never come here again.'

Rashida stopped. 'My baba gave it to me. He trusted me. I won't give it to you.'

For a moment, Salwa was too shocked to speak. Then she said, 'You will.'

'Make me.'

Salwa walked towards her. 'Rashida, I will lock you in the house if necessary. But don't make me. You should go to school. I want you to.'

'What for?' She began to cry. 'What will Cousin Anwar do with an educated woman? Omy, men like that want a slave. He will beat me and make me stay in the house all the time. He's not a man like my baba. He doesn't have morals or beliefs or . . .'

'Anwar is a good Muslim and you will do your duty,' Salwa said.

'I won't!'

Salwa grabbed the girl by the back of the neck and pulled her along the road. 'You will. You will come home with me now and there will be no more of this nonsense.'

But Rashida was hysterical. 'I won't!'

Salwa pulled her along the road, aware that people were looking at them. 'You're making a spectacle of yourself,' Salwa hissed.

'I don't care! I don't!'

Salwa slapped her face. Then there was silence.

## 7

Ken Rivers' not so hard-drinking stint on the first day of Lee's observation seemed as if it had been an anomaly. A more usual morning consisted of a painfully slow walk up the High Street, into Greggs for either a meat pie or a jumbo sausage roll and then on to NatWest to withdraw a large sum of money. On the way back to his flat he'd eat whatever he'd bought and then he'd stay indoors for an hour or so. For the rest of the day, if the sun was out he'd sit by the sea and chain-smoke. If it rained he'd go into one of the seafront cafes and nurse cups of tea in the same way he'd nursed pints in the pub. All the waiters and waitresses knew him. In spite of being a small spender it was all 'Hello, Ken' and 'How you doing, mate? How's your legs?' But no one ever asked him about his wife. Was it because they were too frightened to ask, given Bette's condition? Or did Ken just live his life outside the flat as if she didn't exist? He spent precious little time in the flat, apart from after dark, and once again Lee wondered who, if anyone, looked after the old woman. He'd phoned Sandra Rivers, but she didn't know. She'd only spoken to Ken in recent years.

It wasn't warm even though it was sunny, so Lee was glad that he could sit in one of the small Edwardian cabins that shielded those contemplating the Estuary and, in the case of Ken Rivers, two cabins along from him, smoking roll-ups. If the old man did know where his son was, he certainly wasn't visiting him, and Ken hadn't seen anyone who could have been Phil. Lee wondered whether it was Phil who was looking after Bette back at the flat; perhaps that was why Ken was able to roam about so freely. But he'd recced the flat twice when Ken had been out and had seen and heard nothing. He hadn't even been able to make out an old woman inside, much less a youngish man. The place had been like a Chapel of Rest – dark, silent and a little bit frightening. There was a part of Lee that wanted to call the police to find out if Bette was all right. But the coppers wouldn't come out unless they had some sort of proof the old girl was in danger. And maybe she was in a care home, anyway? Maybe that was what all the money had been for? Those places cost a fortune.

His phone rang.

'Hello?'

'Lee, it's Mumtaz.'

'How's things?'

She hesitated just a little and then said, 'Fine. Lee, Mrs Mayfield at the Advocacy in Ilford has just called me to ask if I can come in today. She's been let down by both of her other advocates and she has a Care Programme Approach meeting for one of her clients today at the same time as the advocacy surgery on the acute wards. CPA meetings are important so she can't just skip it. I said I'd see what I had on today and get back to her. If I do it, it will mean that the office will have to be closed this afternoon. Is that all right or not?'

'Do you think that doing this surgery will help?' Lee asked. 'What I mean is, in terms of your job?'

'I don't know,' Mumtaz said. 'I still haven't met Dr el Masri and I don't know whether he'll be at the hospital this afternoon.

But one just never knows. The girl who killed herself, Sara Ibrahim, the one Salwa el Shamy reckoned was abused by el Masri, had been on one of the acute wards and so there is a chance that some of the patients may remember her.'

'Mmm.' Lee thought for a moment and then he said, 'All right.' It was only one afternoon and it was a Friday when they could often be quiet. And the answerphone message included his mobile number. 'Just be careful what you ask people. You're new, remember.'

'I know.'

'This is almost certainly going to be a long game.'

'Yes.'

He went back to observing Ken Rivers, who'd got into conversation with an elderly woman with a shopping trolley. He heard the old man say, 'My missus used to have a thing like that to do the shopping.'

'Oh, they're very handy,' the woman replied. 'Especially if your arms have gone.'

'Absolutely,' Ken said. And then, in a change of subject that frankly left Lee Arnold staggered, he said, 'Here, you live local or you just down here on a beano?'

The woman blushed.

'Not often I get to see a pretty face round these parts,' Ken said, his eyes twinkling.

'Oh, well, I'm sort of local, Thorpe Bay . . .'

'Very nice. Very tasteful part of town, that is.'

'Oh, well, yes . . .'

The old dog was trying to pick her up!

Lee's phone rang again.

'Mr Arnold?'

He didn't recognize the voice, which was male and gruff.

'Yes?'

'It's Barry Barber,' the man said. 'You left a message for me to call you. Something about Phil Rivers . . .'

'Ah, yes, Mr Barber.' He was Phil Rivers' old boss's son. 'Thanks for getting back to me. I'm a private detective. Mr Rivers is missing and I'm trying to find him.'

'Phil's missing?'

'Yes, I'm afraid so. I wondered if you'd seen him recently. I understand from his wife that you and Phil used to drink together.'

'Years ago, yeah. But I've not seen Phil for ages. I wouldn't have a clue where he might have gone. Don't Sandra know?'

'No,' Lee said. 'But she's very worried even though she's no longer with him.'

'They split up?'

'Yeah.' Lee didn't want to go into the details so he just said, 'Irreconcilable differences.'

'Oh. I see.' And then he went quiet for a moment.

'Mr Barber?'

Another silence and then Barry Barber said, 'I think that maybe we should meet somewhere so we can talk.'

'Well, I'm outside London at the moment,' Lee said. 'Can't you tell me—'

'Not now, no,' he interrupted. 'Look, I do Saturday nights behind the bar at a pub in Dagenham, the Cross Keys. I don't know if you know it? It's an old-fashioned place.'

'Yeah.' Back in his dim and distant past Lee could remember going out to what looked like an old coaching inn in Dagenham with his ex.

'Well, if you meet me outside there this Saturday night, eleven-thirty, I'll just be finished with me shift.'

Ken Rivers and the old woman were laughing at something. Lee had promised Susan that he'd spend some time with her on Saturday but he'd have to go back to London that night. Tony Bracci couldn't carry on going in to bird-sit Chronus forever, even if his home life was dead miserable.

'Yeah, that's fine,' Lee said.

'I'll be outside in the car park.'

'OK.'

The call finished and Lee heard Ken Rivers say to the old woman, 'I'd ask you to go for a drink, love, but I'm a bit skint at the moment.'

She said, 'Oh, don't worry about that, I'll buy you one.'

'Well, that's very nice of you, I must say, Mavis.'

Lee Arnold thought, *Ken Rivers, you old liar!*


She felt like an idiot. Sitting at a table in the day room with a rough handwritten sign saying 'Advocacy' in front of her and not being approached by anyone. Admittedly, at least four of the service users were asleep, while a large group was outside smoking. Those that remained and were conscious seemed to be mesmerized by Jeremy Kyle on the TV. Mumtaz wondered whether it was always like this, or whether her headscarf was putting the mainly white British service users off. Maybe she'd been wrong to wear it for this job? But whenever she could have her head covered in public, she preferred to do so.

It had been Ahmet who had insisted that she cover when they got married. Given what kind of 'Muslim' he had been – a drinker, sexual abuser, gambler – that had been a joke. But then Mumtaz had discovered that she preferred it. Covered, men didn't look at her, or rather Muslim men didn't. Other men, and occasionally women too, sometimes grimaced as she passed. The bombing of the World Trade Centre in America in 2001 and then the London bombings of 2005, both perpetrated by Muslim extremists, had delivered a massive blow to the reputation of all Muslims, which saddened her. But in spite of the drawbacks, she still felt better when her head was covered.

An elderly woman woke up and said, 'Henry?' She looked around the room with an expression of complete confusion on her face and then began to cry. Mumtaz didn't know what to do. The purpose of the advocacy service was to try to resolve service users' issues on matters such as sectioning, accommodation, staff conduct and access to activities. Shirley had told her that comforting patients in any way that went beyond a verbal 'there, there' was strictly prohibited. But the old lady was sobbing her heart out. Who was Henry? Her husband? Her son?

'Henry! Henry!'

Mumtaz leant forward in her chair. What could she say that would help? In her experience only the comfort of some sort of contact with another person . . .

'Oh dear, Hilda.' A woman Mumtaz recognized as a nurse came and sat down next to the old lady. Briefly she smiled at Mumtaz. 'I'm sorry, darling, Henry isn't here any more,' she said.

The old woman carried on crying. The nurse picked up the TV remote control and turned the volume down. Eventually the old woman managed to say, 'So, where is he then? Henry?'

'He's gone, Hilda,' the nurse said.

'Where? To Jesus?'

'No, he went to Norfolk, didn't he?'

'Norfolk? Why'd he go there? Why isn't he here? What's he doing in Norfolk?' With every question she became more agitated.

The nurse said, 'Look, why don't you and me have a little stroll outside? It's a nice day. Not too cold and you've got a thick cardie on.'

But the old woman just looked at her as if she was talking gibberish. Then she pointed at Mumtaz. 'Who's that?'

'That's the lady from the Advocacy,' the nurse said. 'She's here to find out if you've got any problems.'

'Well, I have. I want my Henry, that's my problem. Do you know where Henry is, love? Do you?'

'No, I'm—'

'Not those sorts of problems, Hilda,' the nurse said. 'Now come on, let's go outside for a bit. You know you like it outside and you can have a smoke.'

'A smoke? Oh.' The old woman smiled and then stood up. 'Yes, I'd like that.'

'Well, let's do that then, shall we?' The nurse guided Hilda out of the day room with a small smile back at Mumtaz as she went.

*Jeremy Kyle*, on faintly in the background now, rolled back into the silence and Mumtaz was left feeling useless. She could have at least gone and sat with the old lady when she started crying.

'Ah, so you're the new Advocacy volunteer then?'

The voice was foreign and male and when she looked up to see where it was coming from she found herself staring into Dr Ragab el Masri's eyes.

'Oh.' To come upon him out of the blue was a shock.

He sat down opposite her. Overweight and buck-toothed, he nevertheless had a pleasant smile and wore a pair of almost invisible glasses that looked as if they had cost a fortune.

'I am Dr el Masri, consultant psychiatrist,' he said. But he didn't offer to shake her hand. As a Muslim himself he would know that physical contact wasn't always appropriate with a woman who covered her head. Usually Mumtaz didn't mind a handshake but on this occasion she was grateful he had observed that convention. If he was guilty of what Hatem el Shamy claimed, she didn't want to shake his hand. 'And you are?' he asked.

'Ah, Mumtaz Huq,' she said.

'Mumtaz,' he smiled. 'And what qualifies you to work with our patients, Mumtaz? Have you worked in a psychiatric setting before?'

'Um.' She hadn't expected an ad hoc job interview. But he was still smiling and so she assumed it was a friendly question.

'Well?'

His teeth were very heavily stained.

'I have a degree in psychology,' Mumtaz said. 'And I've worked in a community setting with people with mental health problems on a volunteer basis before.'

'Oh. Where?'

'Here in London,' she said. She didn't want to get specific. And she didn't need to, he wasn't her boss.

'Good,' he said. 'You know, I get on very well with Mrs Mayfield – Shirley. It's good to see that she now has someone like you to help her.'

Mumtaz didn't know how to respond to that. What did he mean? One of the service users, a sleeping middle-aged male, began to snore. The doctor looked over at him and the smile on his face faded.

'I mean, these ex-patient advocates are all very well,' he said. 'But they have no clarity of judgement. They always favour their own kind over others.'

By 'others' he meant the staff.

'I think you'll find, Dr el Masri, that advocates are impartial,' Mumtaz said.

His smile came back again. 'And I think you will find, Miss Huq, that that is simply the theory,' he said.

'I can't comment on colleagues I've not even met,' she said. 'But I think you're wrong.'

'If only I were.' He stood up. 'But good to see you, and I hope that we can work together as well as Mrs Mayfield and myself do. If you need to discuss anything with me, my office is on the second floor. My door is always open to you. If I'm out, please feel free to leave a message with my secretary.'

'Thank you,' Mumtaz said. 'I will.'

He bowed slightly. 'I will leave you to your labours.' And then he walked away. Leaving behind him a suspicion about Shirley Mayfield that Mumtaz had felt right from the start. Shirley had been very quick to point out that complaints against hospital staff were to be treated with extreme caution. She'd said she was happy to receive complaints about food and other 'housekeep-ing' issues. But what did she do with the complaints that she wasn't happy about? And had she received such complaints from her advocates on behalf of some of Dr el Masri's female patients? If so, what had happened?


Without Vi, Tony and the other 'erberts from Forest Gate, the casino was dull. Lee had gone along because Susan had wanted him to and because she'd been able to get him in for nothing. But they couldn't spend time together. She was working on what was apparently called an American roulette wheel. This was per-manently surrounded by squawking women with orange skin and bad jewellery and men in dinner jackets clearly going for a 'brick shithouse' vibe. It was like looking at an East End gang-ster's wedding from the nineteen sixties – all big hair, false eyelashes and knuckle-dusters. It also left Lee hanging about on his own with nothing much to do.

Lee had given up booze at the same time he'd given up his painkiller addiction. His divorce, plus memories from his service as a soldier in Iraq in the early 1990s had made him an unhappy man and a very bad cop. It had been Vi Collins who had sorted him out. She'd just appeared one night at his flat carrying a cage containing the mynah bird that Lee ended up calling Chronus. Vi's theory had been that if Lee had something to look after he'd stop his self-destructive descent into addiction. And she'd been right. But it did mean that Lee rarely drank anything except Diet Pepsi, which got boring after the odd pint or five.

He wandered over to a table where some men were playing mahjong. He didn't have a clue how it worked and watching it didn't make the mechanics of the game any clearer. If you wanted to bet there was every opportunity – a craps table, blackjack, slot machines, poker schools for serious punters in the side rooms. Lee did, very occasionally, like the odd flutter, but he'd never been a gambler. Tony Bracci always said it was because Lee was shit at maths and couldn't work out the odds, which was true. But there was also the fact that gambling wasn't his poison. Everyone had their preferred addictions and Lee's were booze, fags and pills. His late father had had a raft of vices to which he'd been addicted and so did Lee's older brother, Roy. He would rather have died than be like either of them. But when Susan had said she wanted him to give up the fags, that had been a bit of a jolt. He knew he should pack them in, but he didn't like anyone else telling him to. He'd told her he'd think about it. As if to dispel that memory, Lee walked off the gaming floor and went outside for a fag. The doorman who let him out was more ox than man.

Lee stood in the casino car park and lit up. The ox-like door-man watched him impassively. In common with all bouncers, he was only interested in anyone who made trouble because it gave him a chance to show off his solitary skill, that is, he was handy in a ruck. Otherwise he was just a great slab of passivity, who was probably good to his mum and kind to kittens. Cars pulled up, mainly Range Rovers, stretch limos and Audis disgorging yet more orange women and men whose bow ties threatened to spring away like bullets from their vast, engorged necks. Lee felt like a twig in comparison, even though he knew he could best just about any of these men in a fight. Although not the ox. He was in a league of his own.

Lee smoked his fag and lit up another one. He thought about Ken Rivers and his drinking session with the old lady he'd picked up on the seafront. They'd gone to the Foresters, a pub once famed for its strippers and acerbic gay barmen, where Mavis, the old girl, had bought Ken four pints of cheap bitter. She'd been on the gin and by the time she'd decided it was time to pick up her shopping trolley and leave, Ken had been arse'oled. He'd blown her kisses and shouted at her, 'Show us your drawers!' but she'd just gone on her way, albeit with her pop socks down around her ankles. Fortunately for Lee he hadn't been able to see what Ken and Mavis had got up to underneath their table. But once the old woman had gone, and Ken was obliged to pay for his own booze, he'd left the pub and returned to the flat. Lee had won-dered at the time what Bette had thought about the state of her husband when he got home, if anything. Once again Ken had been out of the flat for hours at a stretch and Lee, not for the first time, wondered whether the old woman was even still alive.

But at least if Bette was still living, she wasn't left alone at night. Ken was not a practised boozer and those four pints in the afternoon had left him reeling along the pavement like a drunken sailor. Lee imagined the old man sleeping in a chair that smelt of tinned fish and tobacco, his mouth open, the fifty-pound notes he'd taken out of the bank that day spilling out of his coat pocket. Mean old scrote!

Two minicabs pulled up in front of the casino. The first one was full of excited girls in mini-dresses carrying enormous hand-bags. The ox let them in and then he went over to the second cab and, oddly, paid the driver. Then he held the rear door open for the sole occupant in the back.

Lee distinctly heard the ox say, 'Good evening, Mr Rivers. It's a pleasure to see you.'

But even if he hadn't, he would have known that the man in the cab was Ken Rivers by the way that he walked and the way he lit his cigarette when he got out of the car. He said, 'Good evening to you, Dale. Nice night for it, I think.'

Lee Arnold turned away and waited until the old man had gone inside before he texted his client, the solicitor Derek Salmon. He had a lot to tell him. First there was the meet with Barry Butler. Now, more importantly, there was Ken Rivers' appearance at a casino.

## 8

It was the second day that Mumtaz had spent taking stuff from her house down to the council dump in Barking. Getting a skip would have been expensive. And if she'd had a skip outside the house, she would have been nervous all the time about whether she'd inadvertently thrown some vital of piece of personal information in there that the Sheikhs could unearth and use against her. She knew that her thought processes were paranoid, but she also knew that she couldn't help it. That family had got inside her head and into her bones and, now that it looked like she was going to owe them money for the rest of her life, she wished that there was some way she could die without upsetting her mother and father and Shazia.

Mumtaz threw a pile of old curtains into the textile hopper and then went back to the car to get some boxes of papers and magazines. A last-minute bout of paranoia had her riffling through them yet again, just in case a stray passport or birth certificate had somehow become entangled in the heap. It was torture. But she had to keep it in proportion. She might be in thrall to the Sheikhs, but she was free of Ahmet, she had people who loved her and she wasn't locked up somewhere – like Ilford Hospital, for example.

Nobody had come to the Advocacy Surgery on the acute wards. Shirley said afterwards that was quite normal, especially in view of the fact that Mumtaz was new. It took service users time to get used to any member of staff, medical or otherwise. Remembering what Dr el Masri had said about the two other advocates, Mumtaz had asked Shirley if they were likely to be coming back to the hospital in the near future. 'They said they'd try to get in to meet you on Tuesday,' Shirley had said.

Mumtaz knew that the other two advocates were called Mandy and Roy and that they were both ex-service users, but she didn't know anything else about them. She was interested to hear what they had to say about the Advocacy and the hospital; hopefully she would get some time with them when they weren't with Shirley. She finally threw the newspapers and magazines into the paper and cardboard hopper and then went back to the car to get a box of general metal rubbish. It was amazing what a small car like her Micra could hold when you stuffed it to the roof. A man in unseasonal shorts hefted a wardrobe on his back and hurled it into a vast skip while everyone around him looked impressed. There weren't many times that Mumtaz wished she had a young, fit man in her life to do heavy lifting for her. But she did have a wardrobe just like that at home that could do with getting rid of. Maybe, she thought, she'd ask one of her brothers? Or Lee?

He'd called her quite late the previous night. He'd had what could be a breakthrough in his missing person job. The misper (as such people were called in their line of work) had disappeared with over a million pounds in cash and now Lee had seen the man's father playing roulette with vast wedges of banknotes at his local casino. It was the one where Lee's girlfriend worked. But the point was that an old man who should have very little money suddenly had a lot and Lee was feeling the trail of his misper hotting up. However his client, Derek Salmon, had told him to hold back on confronting the old man while he consulted with the misper's wife.

Mumtaz flung the contents of the box into a metal dustbin and then emptied out a bagful of dead batteries into a bucket. Lee was going to come back to London later on in the day. She looked forward to having him back in the office on Monday. On her own she was lonely and when she was lonely she was prey to all sorts of unhelpful thoughts. Also, Naz Sheikh nearly always knew when Lee was out of the office and would often make a point of ringing. She feared that one day he'd actually come to the office when she was alone and force his way in.

'Look, I don't want to talk about this any more, all right?' Susan said.

But Lee persisted. 'I was only . . .'

'What goes on in the casino, stays in the casino,' she said. 'And anyway, why this interest in high rollers? You're not exactly the last of the big spenders yourself, are you?'

She couldn't understand men sometimes. They'd come out for a nice walk along the seafront and all Lee had wanted to talk about were the two blokes who'd lost their shirts the previous evening. The black guy from London had lost his at the craps table while the old man she knew as Kenny had had a very bad night at her roulette wheel. To his credit, he'd taken it well, but then he always did. Kenny never won. The black guy often did and so when his fall happened it had hit him hard.

'The old bloke was so casual about his losses,' Lee said.

'Look, I've—'

'Do you think he'll come back or just not bother?'

'I don't know,' Susan said. She did. Kenny always came back. He'd been coming back religiously three times a week for over a month with his great big clumps of fifty-pound notes. Dale, the doorman, had even been given cash by the management to pay Kenny's cab fares for him. But she wasn't about to share any of that with her boyfriend. The management were very strict about confidentiality. Punters might lose their shirts in what was strictly a public place but it was up to them whether they talked about it outside the casino, not the staff.

They passed the amusement park known as Adventure Island, walking towards Southend Pier. Lee had been grumpy since she'd told him off but Susan was determined to enjoy herself in spite of his mood and the grey clouds in the sky.

'I want to walk along the pier,' she said. 'Fancy it?'

To his credit, she thought, he mustered a smile. 'All right.'

They paid three pounds fifty each to walk along the old wooden pier, which creaked and had gaps between the planks underfoot through which the grey water below could be seen. It stretched out into the Thames Estuary for a mile and three quarters, it was old – Victorian – and in spite of several fires and shipping accidents it was still, just about, in one piece. Susan loved the pier for its resilience and for the views it offered of both the Kent and Essex coasts. She'd been born and brought up in Southend and, although the place often got on her nerves with its on-going identity crisis (was it still a traditional seaside town or was it changing into something more classy?), she couldn't imagine living anywhere else.

'They're gonna build a hotel where the old gasworks used to be,' she said, pointing back at the Essex coast.

'A hotel? Who for?' Lee said.

'I dunno. Council seem to think there's gonna be conferences and that sort of thing held here.'

Lee shrugged.

'Up and coming, is Southend,' Susan said. 'Don't knock it.'

'I wouldn't dare.' He kissed her.

Susan took his arm and snuggled into his side. 'You ever think about maybe leaving London and going somewhere else one day?' she asked.

'What? Like Southend?' He looked alarmed.

Susan, aware that she might have sounded too keen, said, 'No. Just outside London.'

'No. Not really,' he said. She felt a little crushed. He looked out to sea and Susan wondered whether he was thinking about fags. They'd gone that morning to get a packet of nicotine patches from Boots. She knew she'd have to make allowances for his mood if he was giving up smoking, but she had hoped he'd be more enthusiastic about Southend now he'd spent some time there – doing whatever it was he did. But then maybe she'd started off on the wrong foot with him when he first arrived? Being naffed off that he'd talked about an old colleague on the phone the previous evening hadn't done her, or him, any good. Even if the colleague was a woman. An *old* woman . . .

'But then I suppose it would depend upon why I left London,' Lee continued. 'I mean if I left to take a better job or to be with someone, then that might be different.'

'Oh.'

'It would depend,' he smiled again and then he kissed her. Aroused, Susan pushed her body up against his and ground her hips into his crotch.

She said, 'Here, Lee, you ever had sex on a pier?'

\*

Rashida couldn't believe it. When her mother unlocked her bedroom door to give her her dinner, there was a man standing behind her. It was the old Pakistani imam from the end of the street.

'What's he doing here?' Rashida said as she pushed the food back at her mother, spilling most of it on the floor. 'Did you get him to help you stop me from getting out? I'm not going to, you know. I'm on hunger strike, why would I?'

Salwa pulled the door away from her daughter and shut and locked it, leaving Rashida alone once more. She looked at the pile of rice and chickpeas on the floor and walked back to her bed.

'If you are a good Muslim girl, you should do as your elders tell you,' she heard the old man say in his thick sub-continental accent.

Rashida lost it. 'Don't tell me how to be a good Muslim!' she yelled back at him. 'My father joined a revolution for the faith back in our country. A revolution of brothers and sisters who worked as equals in the fight.'

'Islam, for women—'

'Real Muslim women are strong and brave and they let the will of Allah guide their lives, not the will of their mothers who want to marry them off to atheists!'

She heard a brief, muffled conversation take place between Salwa and the old man and then he said, 'You mother says that the boy is a good Muslim.'

'Then my mother is lying,' Rashida said. If her father had still been around none of this Cousin Anwar stuff would have happened. Cousin Anwar came from her mother's family and she knew that her father hadn't liked him. She missed her baba so much!

'Your father wants you to marry the boy,' the imam said.

'Is that what my mother said? She's lying! Baba can't stand Anwar.'

'Rashida, you can't stay in your room forever,' her mother said. 'You must stop this starving! You must come out. You must go to school . . .'

'To school? Omy, don't be ridiculous, you won't let me go to school. Anyway, you put me in here.'

She heard the old man ask her mother whether that was true.

Salwa said, 'Of course I had to restrain Rashida. But I do want to let her out. I want her to go to school.'

Rashida shook her head in frustration.

'Your mother says—'

'My mother is a liar,' Rashida replied. When they'd got home from her father's lock-up, Salwa had taken away Rashida's keys and locked all the doors and windows. If she didn't agree to the match, Rashida would be on the first flight to Cairo. But Salwa had misjudged her daughter's resolve. 'If you try to come in here, I'll kill myself.'

'Oh no, killing yourself is a sin!' the imam said. 'Don't do that!'

'A bigger sin than marrying an atheist and having his children?' Rashida asked.

For a moment he seemed stumped and so she said, 'Don't answer that. I don't care what you think.'

'Rashida!'

'Oh, Omy, shut up and take him away, will you? If Baba wants me to marry Anwar then I will, but I know he doesn't. Let me talk to him on the phone or go to see him in Belmarsh.'

'You can't go to a prison!'

'Oh, well, then I'll have to die in this room, won't I?' she said. 'And it will be all your fault, Omy.'

Lee didn't feel too well. Before he'd left her, Susan had insisted on cooking him a bloody great roast beef dinner with all the trimmings and he'd felt duty-bound to eat the lot. Unaccustomed to pushing down big meals, especially at night, Lee felt sick and bloated. Now he was driving through Dagenham, trying to remember where the old 'village' was without having to resort to the sat nav. His phone needed charging and he couldn't do that and use the route finder. When he was a kid, a couple of his cousins had lived on what had once been the largest social housing estate in Europe, which was what Dagenham had become. Nowadays most people had bought their properties, as evidenced by PVC double-glazed windows, storm porches and concrete lions sitting on front walls. Kids of a vaguely menacing type lurked and smoked on street corners. Lee, gagging for a fag, envied them.

What was known as old Dagenham village was actually a small collection of buildings centred around the parish church of St Peter and St Paul on Church Lane and the Cross Keys pub next door to it. The church had a large graveyard that provided a rare green space in the middle of the housing estate. Lee turned left off Siviter Way and onto Church Lane. If he remembered correctly, Crown Street, the pub's address, was somewhere on the right.

He saw the church, a square-towered squat building surrounded by trees. Beyond it, on the right, just as he'd thought, he saw the lights from the pub. He pulled up in the car park and looked at his watch. It was only just past eleven o'clock and so he'd have to wait for Barry Barber. Some drinkers were already leaving, laughing their way from the old white coaching inn towards their cars. Lee wanted a cigarette more than anything else he could think of. He poked the nicotine patch on his arm with a finger and resented his girlfriend. Two Subaru Imprezas, one with 'Arsenal' emblazoned on the side, roared off into the night, followed by a pimped-up Golf GTI.

Lee took his phone off charge, chucked it onto the passenger seat and got out of the car. His memory of Barry Barber was dim. About his own age now, mid-forties, he'd looked a bit like his father but with less paunch and no cauliflower ears. But that had been years ago and Barry had been inside since then.

'Got a light, mate?' The voice was young and local.

Lee instinctively looked down at his pockets. 'Oh, yeah . . .'

The first punch floored him.

'What the fuck!'

Then he got a boot in the groin and the world became pain and bright silver stars in that order. As far as he could tell there were two of them, one kicking him, the other one landing punches on his head in quick succession. He moved his arms, but they were useless. Then there was a crack somewhere and he knew they'd broken something but couldn't say what. When he tried to yell, he found out. His jaw was fucked. Then one massive blow came, delivered by something that felt like a concrete block, and split his cheek. Amazed he was still conscious he tried to speak again, but couldn't. They picked him up and slammed him back onto the ground again in a wrestling move and Lee heard laughter. Then he passed out.

# 9

She wasn't in the mood for another day all on her own. Mumtaz's weekend had been physically hard and emotionally draining, then Shazia had kicked off about not having enough money to buy her lunch at college.

'I don't want another cheese sandwich!' she'd said when Mumtaz had suggested she make herself something to eat from the fridge. 'I had cheese sandwiches all last week. They're boring.'

'Shazia, until I get paid . . .' Mumtaz had started.

'Oh, I'll go hungry!' the girl had said and then stormed out of the house. And now Lee hadn't turned up. He was probably just late but it annoyed her.

Mumtaz listened to the answerphone messages and made notes for call-backs. A woman wanted her son followed to find out if he was dealing drugs, while a representative from an insurance company just wanted to speak to Mr Arnold about 'something'. Organizations rarely went into detail on the machine while individuals, like the woman, almost gave a full biography. She left Lee notes on his desk and then began opening the post. The first one was an electricity bill.

The phone rang.

'Arnold Agency. Good morning.'

'Hello, Mumtaz?' It was a man's voice and she recognized it, but she couldn't put a face to it. 'It's Tony Bracci.'

'Oh, DS Bracci. Hello,' she said. He'd been looking after Chronus while Lee was in Southend.

'Listen,' he said, 'don't want to alarm you, but Lee's in hospital.'

'What?' She felt her face redden instantly.

'He's OK,' Tony Bracci went on, 'but he's had to have surgery and he's still pretty out of it.'

'What happened? Is he sick?'

'All I know is . . . Well, a bloke found him in a churchyard in Dagenham in the early hours of this morning. Someone had done a right number on him.'

'He was beaten up?'

'Broke his jaw, bruised his ribs, knocked him out. When he was found he was unconscious. But he'll be all right. He's lost a few back teeth—'

'Oh my God.'

'At the moment he's doped up to the eyeballs so talking to him is a bit like trying to have a conversation with a haddock.'

The policeman's attempt at levity left Mumtaz cold.

'Mumtaz, do you know what Lee was doing out in Dagenham last night?'

'I don't. He was due back from Southend yesterday. That's all I know.'

'Me too,' Tony said.

'Does Mrs Arnold know that he's in hospital?'

'His mum?'

'Yes.'

'Yes, she's here,' he said. 'Here being Newham General.'

'Oh, good, so he's close to home. Can I visit him?'

'I wouldn't for the moment,' Tony said. 'Like I say, he's well out of it. They had to operate on his jaw and so he's off his ti— off his head on morphine at the moment.'

'How did you find out?' Mumtaz asked.

'I've a cousin on the force over in Dagenham,' he said.

Although she didn't know him well, Mumtaz was aware of the enormous Bracci family, which seemed to have branches all over east London.

'Listen, Mumtaz, did Lee have a diary that he kept with him? I don't mean his desk diary.'

'No,' she said. 'He has all his appointments on his iPhone. When he comes into the office he puts them into the desk diary too, but he hasn't been into the office. Look on his phone.'

'If I could find it, I would.'

'Oh.'

'Far as the plods in Dagenham could see, that was all that was missing. He still had his credit cards, bank card. No cash, but then that's hardly surprising. Cash always goes even if the beating's not about money.'

'You don't think that it was?'

'I don't know. But seeing as how they left his cards in his wallet and his car in the car park of a local pub it seems unlikely. Do you know what he was working on?'

'A missing person,' Mumtaz said.

'You know who?'

She couldn't remember the name but she could have looked it up. Instead, she said, 'I think you should ask Lee when he comes round, DS Bracci.'

'OK. Although if he was putting himself at risk . . .'

'Not that I know of,' Mumtaz said. Unless Lee told her to disclose information, she would keep the details of his cases and clients confidential. Those who used private investigators had to have confidence that their personal details, except in very exceptional cases, would be withheld from everyone, and that included the police. 'Do you have his girlfriend Susan's number?'

'Yeah, Lee give it to me in case I needed to get in touch, cos of Chronus. I had his number, her landline and her mobile. You know how he is about that ruddy bird.'

Mumtaz did. Chronus was Lee's baby.

'I've spoken to her,' Tony said. 'He didn't leave her place until ten and she thought that he was going straight home. She tried to call him early this morning but of course she couldn't get hold of him.'

'She must've been worried,' Mumtaz said.

'Yeah.'

When she eventually put the phone down, Mumtaz just sat. How could she concentrate on anything while Lee was lying in hospital after being attacked and beaten unconscious? And why had whoever it was done it? She couldn't believe that it had just been for his phone and a little bit of cash. Lee didn't carry much money around with him because he didn't have much. For a moment she wondered whether the Sheikhs had beaten him up as some sort of warning. But then she took hold of herself. That was paranoia speaking. And how would the Sheikhs know where Lee had been when no one else had? Mumtaz chided herself for being so self-centred. Her own mother had always said to her 'the world doesn't revolve around you'. And she'd been right.

The phone rang again. This time it was Shazia, saying that she was sorry for the argument they'd had over her lunch. Mumtaz didn't tell her about Lee.

*

Shirley knew her thoughts were irrational. The only reason she was standing in front of the door to Sara Ibrahim's old room was because the service user who had come in afterwards had been discharged. The room was empty and quiet so she could easily imagine she could hear whispers from the conversations she'd had with the girl in the past.

To think that, had she been at work the day Sara died, maybe she could have done something to save her was nuts. Sara's other confidant, the male nurse who'd turned out to be a terrorist, had been on duty and he hadn't saved her. Admittedly, he'd been on the chronic ward. Maybe Sara had been an al Qaeda supporter too? She hadn't seemed as if she was that way inclined. She'd been a very western type of Asian girl. In some respects. Shirley closed her eyes. Sara had been so young and so sick. She'd had psychotic episodes where she heard voices and had experiences that weren't real. Sometimes her voices told her to kill herself, sometimes she experienced hallucinations, imagining taking an overdose or slashing her wrists. How could anyone have relied upon her testimony when she made complaints about the hospital and its staff?

Shirley opened her eyes and looked through the doorway and into the room. There had been one time when Sara had asked for her when she'd almost taken her complaint forwards. It had been first thing in the morning and Sara had refused to get up or eat any breakfast unless the staff went and got her an advocate. Hatem el Shamy, the nurse she usually chose to confide in, wasn't available and so Shirley assumed she was the next best thing. She could see Sara's small, thin body on that bed as she gazed into the room. As soon as she'd entered, Sara had said, 'Someone had sex with me last night.'

Then she'd cried and Shirley had waited for her to stop before she'd asked her who had had sex with her. For a while the girl had said nothing and so Shirley had reiterated her question. Sara had pushed her bedcovers off and Shirley had seen that she had blood between her thighs.

'See what he did to me?' Sara had said. 'I was a virgin!'

'You're not on your period?'

'I'm not stupid!'

Shirley could see the fury in Sara's eyes even now.

'Who did this to you, Sara?' she'd asked.

And the girl had looked as if she might say a name for a moment but then her face had clouded and she'd said, 'If I told you, you wouldn't believe me. I wonder if I made it up myself.'

'I would believe you. God almighty, that blood is real, isn't it? Tell me.'

But she'd shaken her head. Shirley had asked her if she would tell Hatem el Shamy, but Sara had said nothing. Then the staff nurse, Michelle, had come in with her morning meds and Sara had covered herself up. When Michelle had gone, Sara had said, 'I'll have to go and wash now. I need to get him off me.'

And Shirley had given Sara an opportunity. 'If you wash,' she'd said, 'all the evidence will disappear. If somebody has raped you, Sara, you need to stay as you are until the police get here.'

That had been the right thing to do, even though she'd known to the core of her soul that the girl wouldn't proceed with her complaint.

'No.'

She'd taken a sanitary towel from her locker, put it between her legs and then she'd stood up.

Shirley had said, 'Why did you call me, Sara, if you didn't think I'd believe you?'

'Because you're *supposed* to do something.'

That had hurt.

Then the girl had smiled. 'But it'll all come out in the end, Shirley, and then you'll be able to tell them that I wasn't making it up, because you saw my blood.'

Sara had gone to the bathroom and Shirley hadn't tried to stop her.

And now she was dead and it still hadn't come out. She owed the girl something, but what?

'Mrs Mayfield?'

Shirley turned around. It was that new, young doctor, Golding.

'Hello.'

'What are you doing?' he asked.

'Oh,' she smiled. 'Nothing really. Just remembering a patient we used to have here.'

'The girl who threw herself from the window?'

Dr Golding hadn't been employed until after Sara had died. How had he known? He saw her confusion and smiled. 'The patients told me where her room was,' he said. 'A lot of them still seem very disturbed by it. I wanted to see it.'

'A suicide upsets everyone.'

'Especially the suicide of a young person,' he said. 'Did you know the girl well, Mrs Mayfield?'

She paused and then said, 'A little.'

'She was particular friends with the nurse who tried to blow the hospital up, wasn't she?' he said.

'Yes.'

'What was he like?'

'I didn't know him well,' Shirley answered.

'Were you surprised that he set a bomb here?'

Shirley didn't want to talk about Hatem el Shamy. Her mind was on Sara. 'I don't know,' she said. 'I didn't know him well.'

'Dr el Masri—'

'Yes, he knew him,' she said. She was tired of this conversation. Dr Golding seemed like a nice man but he had interrupted her private thoughts and she wanted him to go. 'Ask him.'

'Thank you. I will.'

As he left, slowly, Shirley had such an overwhelming urge to tell him what Sara had told her that she felt herself begin to sweat. But she didn't say anything. Anyway, she thought to herself, he was more interested in Sara's nurse. Golding went about his business and she walked into Sara Ibrahim's old room and cried.

Lee hurt in places he hadn't even thought about before. Like just behind his ears. Now that he could only speak in a whisper, he and Vi Collins were a right pair. He looked at her sitting beside him on his bed and wondered when she'd go. It wasn't that he didn't want her visiting him, but he didn't want her going all copper on him.

'What were you doing in Dagenham?' she asked for at least the third time.

'I was going to see a bloke about this misper I'm investigating, I told you.'

'Didn't tell me who the bloke was.'

'None of your business,' Lee rasped.

'You told Dagenham.'

'I had to,' Lee said. 'Get off my case, Vi.'

He hadn't got a good look at either of the men who had

attacked him, but he was sure neither of them had been Barry Barber. He couldn't have described his assailants in detail to save his life, but one thing he had known was that they had been young. The one who'd kicked him had worn steel-toed work boots. The plods from Dagenham already knew all that and he didn't want to go over it again for Vi. She knew most of it, anyway. It wasn't only Tony Bracci who had a contact or two at Dagenham nick. Vi would come across the name Barry Barber in the fullness of time. But Lee wasn't going to help her.

A small elderly woman walked down the ward towards Lee's bed carrying a plastic cup. Vi got off the bed.

'This is supposed to be coffee but I can't see how it can be,' Rose Arnold said.

'Mum, you don't have to stay here,' Lee said. 'I'm all right now.'

Rose Arnold, a small plump woman in a pink tracksuit, sat in the chair beside her son's bed. She took a sip from the cup and then said, 'Oh, well, it's wet and warm.'

With the exception of Tony Bracci and a copper from Dagenham, Lee had been surrounded by women ever since the hospital staff had got his pain under control. First his mum, who had almost taken root, then Susan, who'd torn down from Southend all tears and tits, and then Vi. He appreciated each one of them in their own way but he was tired and drugged up and he was really more interested in finding out what Barry Barber had to say for himself. Could Barry have ordered a couple of thugs to beat him up? He could, but why would he? If he hadn't wanted to speak to Lee about Phil Rivers he could have just said he had nothing more to add and left it at that. But he'd arranged to meet him about something. Unless he'd lured him to Dagenham with the sole purpose of getting him thumped. But again, why?

'Well, I'd better be off,' Vi whispered. 'Supposed to be resting.'

'It was good of you to come,' Lee said. He was glad she was going.

'No problem,' she said. As she left he noticed that the scar on her neck was big and ragged. But it was still early days and Vi was a very thin woman. When she'd gone his mother, who remembered Vi from Lee's old coppering days, said, 'She's looking rough.'

'She's just had surgery to remove a goitre,' Lee told her.

Rose Arnold went quiet for a moment and sipped her coffee. 'Roy would've come but he had to go out,' she said.

She'd told him before but she'd started to repeat herself in recent years. And Lee knew his brother Roy would be 'out'. He was always out, usually in some pub or other.

'It's all right, Mum,' he said. He wished she'd go too. He was trying to think about whether he'd left his iPhone in the car when he got out or whether it had been in his pocket. Whoever had beaten him up had taken his remaining cash, which hadn't even amounted to twenty quid. But the phone was another matter – it had his diary and contacts on and he wanted it back.

His mother finished her coffee, said, 'Ugh,' and then took out her knitting. She knew as well as he did that when Roy got back to her house he'd be arse'oled. He could see why she'd rather stay in the General with him than go home to his brother.

'Lee?'

He recognized her voice immediately and looked up. 'Mumtaz.'

'Oh my goodness,' she said. 'Your poor face.'

She put a hand out to touch it but then she saw his mother and withdrew it.

'Hello, Mrs Arnold.'

'Hello, love.' She carried on knitting.

Mumtaz sat down on his bed. Lee wished she'd touched his face. He had a mad notion she might have healed him.

'Mumtaz, you didn't need to come.'

'Oh, don't be silly,' she said. 'I wanted to see you. What were you doing in Dagenham?'

He told her. She shook her head. 'You should've told me about the appointment,' she said. 'Then you wouldn't have lain in a churchyard for hours on end. You could've died of hypothermia this time of year.'

Rose Arnold looked up from her knitting and said, 'He's always been a bit of a div.'

'Mum!'

She went back to her knitting.

'You tell me where you are all the time and I'll tell you,' Lee said to Mumtaz, knowing that she wasn't always as straight with him about her appointments as he would have liked.

She looked a little ashamed and said, 'Point taken.'

He hadn't wanted to upset her, but he'd managed it. He changed the subject. 'What's going on?'

She told him about some potential new business and what she'd got up to at Ilford Hospital. 'I'm in tomorrow for the day,' she said. 'So the office will be empty again.'

'Don't matter,' Lee said. 'I'll be out of here tomorrow.'

Rose looked up again. 'Tomorrow? In that state?'

'Tomorrow night, Mum.'

'Don't care when it is tomorrow, they can't let you home yet, not after what you've been through.' And then she stood up. 'I'll go and see that doctor of yours, have a word . . .'

'No, Mum.'

But she waved his objection away. 'Shut up, Lee.'

Rose walked down the ward towards the nurses' station. 'Here, you . . .'

Mumtaz smiled. 'My mum would do exactly the same,' she said. 'Only difference is she'd have all my aunties in tow.'

He was so glad to see her. Mumtaz, in spite of her own considerable troubles, nearly always brought a calmness into his life that no one else seemed to be able to do. Maybe faith in Islam gave her some sort of inner peace that she could draw on when needed? Lee didn't know. But whatever it was she had, he was grateful for it.

She leant towards him. 'Now, look, I can get some of the freelancers in. I know Amy's free. I want you to promise me you'll only leave hospital when your doctor tells you that you can. OK?'

Like all the other women who'd come to see him, she was chiding him.

'I'll go when they tell me I can,' he said.

'Don't hassle them, Lee.'

He thought *too late* but he suspected she knew that anyway.

'I won't.'

Mumtaz smiled. 'You know, for a private detective you're not a very good liar,' she said.

## 10

Her mother had a visiting order from the prison. This meant Salwa could visit her husband. Before she went, her mother took the kids to school and then got the old Pakistani imam's wife over to make sure Rashida didn't somehow burrow out of her room. The old woman didn't speak any English and very little Arabic, so communication between them was impossible. But Rashida didn't care. She was still on hunger strike, even though she had scraped off the rice that had dropped on the floor and eaten it and she still had a large stash of chocolate under the bed. She had to keep her strength up if she suddenly had to make a dash for freedom. Where she'd go was quite another matter. Most of her friends at school were Asian girls who came from traditional families like hers. She couldn't go to any of their houses. But then there was Kerry, who was white and crazy and MJ, who came from a funky and unconventional Hindu family. MJ's mum was really cool and wore tight fake leopardskin and mad high heels. Rashida frowned. She couldn't put nice people like that in a difficult position. Mrs Joshi, MJ's mum, had always been really good to her even when her dad went to prison and the family were all over the newspapers.

If she left, Rashida knew the only place she could go would be to Social Services. One of the girls at school had an older sister who had run away to Social Services when her parents had tried to take her to Bangladesh to get married. She'd been put into care and the family had declared her dead to them. Rashida couldn't bear that.

Downstairs, she heard the television. It was loud and she could easily make out that the old woman had it tuned to *Homes Under the Hammer*. If she wanted to, Rashida knew that now was a time when she could try to get her bedroom door unlocked and leave. The old woman was half deaf, and with the TV blaring away she could try to kick her door down and make a run for it. Alternatively, if she could attract the woman's attention she could try to make her understand that she wanted to go to the toilet, and then when the door was unlocked she could dash down the stairs and out of the house. What was some frail old Pakistani going to do about it? Rashida was ready to act.

But what about her dad? If she left, what would he have to say about it? She couldn't believe what her mother had said about him. He wouldn't approve of Cousin Anwar, not in a million years! Her father hated football thugs. Didn't he?

Rashida sat down on her bed. She'd thought that her father hated violence until he'd given her that key. It had been just before the police had come to arrest him. He'd given it to her and said, 'Keep this safe, Rashida. Don't give it to anyone.' She'd asked him what it was a key to, knowing full well what it opened because she had followed him to the lock-up one Saturday afternoon. He'd just said, 'You don't need to know.'

She'd looked inside once and, although the light had been dim, she'd worked out what was in there. If all else failed and she was given a ticket to Cairo could she make good on the threat she'd made to her mother? Her father or herself, who would she choose? Really? Rashida began to cry. When she'd finished she miserably ate a bar of white chocolate and then lay down on her bed. She wasn't even at school any more. Nothing in her life made any sense.

'Last time we had a staff conference it was summer and Dr el Masri tried to look down all the women's tops at the buffet,' Mandy said. She was about forty but looked a lot younger, even though she smoked. With her short punky blonde hair and tiny frame it was hard to believe that Mandy had three teenage children.

'He's a dirty old sod,' her companion said. This was Roy. About the same age as Mandy, but very obviously on heavy medication, which meant that his speech was slurred, his attention sometimes wandered and, on occasion, he drooled. Like Mandy he had spiky hair and some face piercings. He wore a Marilyn Manson T-shirt and both of his forearms were heavily scarred.

She'd first met the other two advocates in the project office with Shirley. But Shirley had taken a call from the forensic ward and had to go over there so Mumtaz had been left to get to know the others on her own. Talk had quickly turned to who was and wasn't to be trusted in the hospital. Mumtaz hadn't even had to drop any hints.

'And you wanna be careful of Timothy Pool,' Mandy said. 'He's ward manager on the Forensic. He's a vicious bastard, hiding behind all his Christianity.'

'I fucking hate him,' Roy said.

'Norman on Chronic is mental.'

Roy nodded his head. 'Much more mental than the patients.'

'Reckons that aliens come into the grounds at night. He sees all sorts of lights and orbs and what not,' Mandy said. 'Been on there too long, see. Gone bonkers.'

Mumtaz said, 'So have you – the Advocacy – done anything about these people?'

'No.'

'But isn't that the purpose . . . ? '

'Supposed to be,' Mandy said. 'Shirley'll tell you it is. But she won't do nothing when staff're involved.'

'So why do you stay?' Mumtaz asked.

'Because we've got mates here.'

'Service users,' Roy clarified.

'Things happen in places like this, Mumtaz,' Mandy said. 'When people are vulnerable. Everybody'll tell you that you shouldn't take anything that mad people say seriously. If Shirley could hear me and Roy now she'd make sure she got you on your own later and then tell you not to take any notice of what we'd said.'

'She's done it to all the other advocates.'

Mumtaz looked at Roy, who was rolling a cigarette with one hand.

'All the other advocates have left,' Mumtaz said.

'Because Shirley won't let 'em do anything.'

'She's subtle about it,' Mandy said. 'Just takes over anything that might cause bother. Then nothing happens.'

'Nothing,' Roy agreed.

'You could say we're taking a risk talking to you now,' Mandy said. 'You might go straight off and tell Shirley we've been dissing her.'

'I won't.'

Mandy smiled. 'I know,' she said. 'Don't ask me how.'

'Mand's a bit psychic,' Roy put in.

'Me mum says I am. We can trust you, Mumtaz, can't we?'

'Yes, of course. I want to help.' What Mandy and Roy had told her only mirrored what she'd heard Shirley say about being wary of issues involving staff and passing anything 'difficult' on to her. Maybe the story that Hatem el Shamy had told his wife was true? Maybe the Advocacy, in the shape of Shirley Mayfield, was in league with the hospital management?

'I'll tell you a story,' Mandy said. 'A bloke I know on the chronic ward, really schizophrenic, you know, well he kept on saying he was related to this famous old-school film star. On and on he went about how if the hospital phoned this man in Hollywood he'd come over and see him. Nobody believed him. But then one day this bloke came onto the chronic ward to see him and he was that film star. You can't write people off just because they're mad. Not everything they do or say is delusional.'

'Same bloke also says they inject him against his will every night, the staff do,' Roy said.

'So that could be as true as the film star relative,' Mumtaz said.

'It could,' Mandy said. 'But nobody's going to investigate it.'

'Because he's . . .'

'A nutter, yes.'

'We stick around so service users know that someone still cares,' Roy said. 'They know Shirley don't. Well, she might do, but she cares about paying her mortgage more. Nutters might be mad but they ain't stupid.'

'No.' Their candour and apparently absolute trust in her made Mumtaz bold. 'Do you remember anything about that girl who died? The one who threw herself out of a window?'

'What, the Asian girl?' Mandy looked at her with what Mumtaz interpreted as some slight suspicion.

'I'm not any sort of relative or friend,' she said. 'I just remember the story.'

There was a silence. Mumtaz wondered whether she'd gone too far too fast. And then Roy said, 'She was very pretty. I saw him looking at her.'

'Dr el Masri?'

'Yeah. How'd you know?'

'Because you told me he ogled young girls.'

'He ogled her.'

'And . . .'

'Just that,' Roy said. 'He looked at her.'

'Do you know why she killed herself?'

Mandy shrugged. 'No. But she was on fifteen-minute obs, so the staff must've been worried about suicide.'

'Oh my goodness, what have you all been talking about, looking so glum?'

They all looked up as Shirley came into the room.

'Sorry about that, folks,' she said. 'Client on the forensic ward.'

'What happened?' Mandy asked.

Shirley sat down at her desk. 'Oh, someone kicked off the other day and then blamed a member of staff.'

'Timothy Pool,' Roy said as a statement of fact rather than a question.

'Yes,' Shirley said. 'But it was groundless. Timothy's a very good nurse and there was no evidence to support what his accuser had said.' She smiled. 'So, how have you three been getting along?'

As soon as Tony Bracci opened the front door, the bird went mad.

'Geoff Hurst! Bobby Moore! Bobby Moore! Bobby Moore! Bobby Moore!'

Lee Arnold, following on behind, shouted, 'Chronus! Pack it in, for Christ's sake!'

Tony helped Lee into the living room and sat him down in his chair, which was next to the mynah bird's perch. Lee looked at the bird and the bird, quiet now his master was at home, looked back at him with rapt attention.

'You daft bleeder,' Lee said and then stroked Chronus's head. If the bird had been a cat he would have purred.

It was only midday and although Lee's mother had been assured he wouldn't be leaving the General until that evening, he'd hassled and hassled until his doctor had discharged him. His jaw hadn't been too badly broken and they'd needed the bed. Tony Bracci had told him to phone whenever he was ready to go home and he'd taken him at his word.

'I'll make you a cuppa if you like but then I'll have to get back to the nick,' Tony said.

'Oh, don't bother with that, Tone, you head off,' Lee said. 'Just leave me a couple of fags.'

'You out?'

'Susan had me put one of those patches on before I left South-end. It must've fallen off when I got me face decorated. Anyway, sod it, I need a fag.'

Tony gave Lee a packet of cigarettes and a lighter. 'Sure you don't want a cuppa?'

'Sure.'

Tony put a hand on Lee's shoulder. 'I'll be back later, mate.'

'All right. Thanks for everything, Tone.' He put his hand in his pocket and pulled out his iPhone. 'Specially this.'

A particularly awake plod had found it under the front pas-senger seat of Lee's car and had sent it over to Forest Gate nick, care of DS Bracci.

'Pleasure.'

And then he left.

Lee had a fag, felt a bit sick, put it out, had another one and felt much better. Chronus made small appreciative noises and then crapped on the newspaper below his perch. In spite of an automatic urge to clear it up, Lee found himself drifting off to sleep.

When he woke up his mouth was dry and he had drool on his chin. Desperate for a drink, he began to make his way towards the kitchen. But when he passed the spare bedroom, he stopped. The duvet was creased and the pillows were awry. There was a mug on the floor and it was dirty. Lee bent down to pick it up, felt a bit dizzy and stood up again. He could smell that it'd had coffee in it once. Tony Bracci always drank coffee. Lee shook his head. It wasn't that he minded that Tony had slept in his flat without asking him, he knew he was unhappy at home, but why hadn't he mentioned it? Did he think that Lee would mind? Lee felt a little hurt; he'd hoped that Tony had known him better.

Once he'd made himself a cup of tea, Lee went back to the living room and gave Chronus some banana. The bird growled appreciatively. Lee looked at his miraculously undamaged phone and then selected Barry Barber's number from his directory. At first he thought it would just ring out but then a familiar voice said, 'Hello?'

'Hello, Barry. It's Lee Arnold.'

There was a pause. 'Oh.' Then there was another pause. 'I've had the coppers round,' he said.

'About me getting my head kicked in. Yes, I imagine you have.'

'I don't know nothing about that. I told them. You never turned up, as far as I was concerned. I waited in the car park and when no one came I went home.'

'You didn't notice there was a car still in the car park when you left?'

'Why would I? People leave their cars there all the time. It's Dagenham.'

He had a point. Once the home of the Ford car plant, Dagenham was one of the most car-dense boroughs in London and people parked where they could.

'Well, anyway,' Lee said. 'You told me you had something to pass on about Phil Rivers.'

'Yeah. I'm back at the pub next Sunday so if you—'

'Barry, I'm not being funny but to say I'm not in a hurry to go back to Dagenham is a bit of an understatement. Know what I mean?'

'Oh.' Barry Barber did another one of his silences.

'Tell me what you know about Phil now,' Lee said.

Still nothing.

'Barry?'

Lee heard him sigh and then he said, 'Just a minute.'

The sound of a door closing. Barry lowered his voice. 'Look,' he said, 'Phil was, is, whatever, an iron.'

'He's homosexual?'

'Unless you can think of anything else that rhymes with iron hoof.'

A lot of gay men were into body-building. Still, Lee needed to press the point. 'He was married. To a woman.'

'So was Elton John. Get real,' Barry said.

'Does his wife know?'

'Course not!'

'So how do you know?'

'How'd'ya think?'

It all became clear. The meeting in the middle of the night at Barry's place of work, the reluctance to talk on the phone.

'You're . . . ? '

'We had a thing for about six months, years ago,' Barry said. 'I've got Janice and the kids now. For me it was just . . .'

'An experiment?'

The silence again and then he said, 'More'n that, but . . . Long time ago. I don't feel that way no more. It was just Phil, see. No other men.'

'And Phil?'

'Oh, he played the field,' Barry said. 'Proper tart. I dunno what he done with Sandra but I doubt it was the same as what he got in massage parlours up west.'

'Do you think he could have asked his wife for a divorce because he was gay?'

'I don't think he would've wanted to hurt her,' Barry said. 'But I s'pose that had to be at the bottom of it, whether Sandra knew or not. I'm surprised they lasted so long.'

'Sandra Rivers is rich,' Lee said.

'That's cynical.'

'What else am I supposed to think?'

'He loved her, you know.'

'Did he?'

'Yeah.'

An account of Phil Rivers agonising over deceiving his wife and his parents about his sexuality made Lee feel even more tired than he had been before the conversation. If he'd loved his wife that much he would have told her. He just wanted to have his cake and eat it.

Barry Barber claimed not to know where Phil was or who had

beaten Lee up. And, as things stood, there wasn't a lot of arguing with that. He certainly hadn't been amongst the men who had thumped him but that didn't necessarily mean that he didn't know where Phil was. When Lee ended the call he made a note to contact Barry Barber again some time in the near future. Then he called Derek Salmon.

'The police contacted me this morning,' the solicitor said. 'Are you all right?'

'Nothing heavy pain control can't help,' Lee said. But he was aware that his joke was like whistling in the dark. Being back, albeit just for a short time, on opiate medication again was nerve-wracking and he wondered how he'd cope once the pain went away. Last time he'd been in this situation he'd found himself hooked for years. He lit another cigarette and threw half the co-codamol tablets he'd been given in the wastepaper bin.

'You still in hospital?' Derek Salmon asked.

'No. I'm back at work.'

'You twat. Look I'll understand if you want off the case.'

'Nah.' Lee told him about his conversation with Barry Barber.

'Barry reckons Sandra Rivers doesn't know,' Lee said.

'You wanna ask her?'

'You're the client, what do you think?'

'Well, someone's got it in for you for some reason, Lee, and so I think we play our cards close to our chests until we find out who that is,' Derek said. 'Can you think of any old lags who might have issues with you?'

'Only dozens,' Lee said. 'So keep Sandra in the dark for now?'

'I think so, yes.'

'I'll try and find out whether he was seeing anyone when he sold the house.'

'Are you going back to Southend?'

'As soon as I can.'

'Do you plan to confront Phil's father?'

'I don't see I've got a choice,' Lee said. 'He was throwing a lot of money up the wall, Del. Phil's rolling around somewhere with a load of dosh, why not give some to his dad?'

'Mmm. Agreed. But try not to startle the old couple too much.'

'Old couple?' Lee shook his head. 'I haven't had sight of the old woman.'

'Doesn't mean she's not in the flat.'

'No, but . . .'

'Just go carefully, Lee,' Derek said. 'We don't know where the old man got that money from.'

'No, but we know where it's going.'

'Be that as it may. Just go easy.'

The solicitor ended the conversation. For a moment, Lee didn't know what to do next. With Mumtaz out at Ilford Hospital he felt he should go into the office and pick up any answerphone messages. But he was really too tired to move. In the end he put the television on and fell asleep to a programme about antiques.

Mumtaz had got into her car and was just about to start the engine when she realized she'd left her watch in the toilet. She'd taken it off to wash her hands and had forgotten to pick it up. She walked back into the hospital admin block and ran down the corridor towards the staff canteen and the toilets. She'd only been in there at most five minutes before and so there was a good chance her watch would still be on the sink. She found it immediately.

Relieved, she walked sedately out of the toilets and put her watch on outside the staff canteen. She heard raised voices. Both male, one sounded foreign.

'Look, this is your first job,' she heard the foreigner say. 'Suck it up, man!'

'I can't,' an English voice replied.

'This sort of thing goes on all the time,' the other man said. 'You have to learn to wait. It's a hierarchy here. It's institutional.'

Could the foreign voice belong to el Masri?

'It shouldn't be.'

'I know that!' the foreigner said, 'I like you. I want . . . You think I like it?'

'No. '

'We all do what we do to survive. For now, for you, that means that you just work and forget everything else. Your time will come. You understand?'

There was one small porthole window in the canteen door and Mumtaz tried to look through it. But she heard footsteps moving towards her and she began to walk away. When she got to the end of the corridor she turned. She saw someone leaving the canteen, but she couldn't see who it was.

## 11

'Tone?' Lee could hear the voice through the receiver rasping like a cartoon snake eating sandpaper.

Tony Bracci rolled his eyes and mouthed, 'The guv'nor.'

They were both sitting in Lee's kitchen after their first night as flatmates. It hadn't been easy for Lee to raise the subject of his messed-up spare bed or the coffee cup, but when Tony had come back the previous evening he'd owned up immediately. After almost thirty years of marriage, his wife had thrown him out and moved a younger model in. Until Lee had gone to Southend, Tony had been sleeping in his car. And although he'd got accustomed to living alone since his divorce and had started to prefer it, Lee hadn't been able to just chuck his old mate out.

'Yes, guv,' Tony said. He put a finger in the ear that wasn't on the phone and took out a small plug of wax. Lee, nervously, watched him roll it into a ball.

He heard Vi say, 'What's going on?'

'Not a lot.' Mindlessly Tony squashed the ball of wax into one of the legs of his trousers. Every nerve in Lee's body screamed. How could he do that?

'Lee Arnold out of hospital?'

'Yes,' Tony said. 'He's at home resting.'

She laughed. 'Expect me to believe he's resting?'

'I don't know, guv,' Tony said. 'That's what he told me.'

'So what's he been working on that got him beaten up?'

This time Lee rolled his eyes. Vi was a good copper and a great mate but she was also never off for a second, which was wearing.

'I don't know, guv,' Tony said. 'In relation to the assault, Dagenham have it, ask them.'

'I can't ask them!'

'Then I can't help you, guv.'

'What're you doing?'

'Never mind. You're off sick.'

'Tony!'

Against his better judgement, Lee took Tony's phone out of his hand. He couldn't bear to see him suffer any longer.

'Vi,' he said. 'Lee.'

'Oh.'

'In answer to your question, I'm watching cheap chat shows on the telly today and Tony's trying to do his job in spite of you.'

'I was just—'

'You were meddling, Vi,' Lee said. 'You're sick, be sick. Like I am. And leave Tony alone.'

There was a pause and then she said, 'What's Tony doing at your place, Arnold?'

The lie came out smoothly. 'He brought my car back from Dagenham. All right? Now butt out, Vi.'

Lee ended the call and gave Tony's phone back to him. Tony looked down at the floor. 'Thanks, mate. I'll make sure you get your car back today.'

'Cheers. Does Vi know about your situation?'

'She knows I'm having marital problems,' Tony said.

'She doesn't know you've been chucked out?'

'No.'

Tony had a big mortgage on the house he'd once shared with his wife and children and so Lee knew he couldn't afford rent on top. He also knew that Tony was very proud and wouldn't feel able to tell his family about his troubles. Again, the words just slipped out of Lee Arnold's mouth. 'You can stay here as long as you like,' he said.

'Ta, mate. I'll pay you.'

He sounded genuine but Lee just couldn't do it. 'No, just buy some food, the odd packet of fags and we'll be quits.'

Tony's big face smiled. 'You'll hardly know I'm here, mate. Promise.'

If the untidy bed and the dirty coffee cup he'd left in the spare room were anything to go by, Lee doubted that.

Shirley Mayfield looked at what she'd just written again. She put a line through it and chucked it into the bin. It was a lie. For all his madness, Dylan Smith knew when he'd been hit and by whom. Timothy Pool's arrogance was growing. And she, amongst others, was allowing that.

She'd wanted to spend the previous morning with the new advocate so that she could, to some extent, control her first exposure to Roy and Mandy. Roy especially could veer off into his own obsessions and she didn't want Mumtaz Huq to be put off. But Dylan Smith had sent a message from the forensic ward and so she'd had to leave them to it. When she'd got onto Forensic, Dylan had been sitting in his room, holding his face. When he looked up his left eye was half closed. By the next day it would be all the colours of the rainbow. His story, supported by no one, was that Timothy Pool had just hit him for no reason. Timothy, supported by every member of staff on shift, said that

Dylan had attacked him. The black eye had been inflicted in self-defence.

Timothy usually came across with self-righteous indignation whenever he had issues with service users. But this time he had been smug too. However, what was more significant still was that his staff, usually unconditionally supportive, had looked uncomfortable. None of them had wanted to talk much and she noticed that a couple of them couldn't actually return Dylan's damaged gaze. The ward manager was turning into an increasingly vicious autocrat and nobody was going to do anything about it. Shirley remembered little Sara Ibrahim again, even though she tried very hard not to. Dylan's smashed-up face and Sara's sweet one melded in her head. How could she have told the advocates that Timothy Pool was innocent?

She'd have to get a new job. She'd looked at the *Guardian*'s charity work vacancies page online but didn't find much. There was one mental health job, coordinating a befriending project in Hackney, but everything else was voluntary work. Shirley often felt desperate. Her husband had left her years ago and the kids had gone so now she had to pay all the costs on her house herself. That meant all the bills plus the mortgage. She had to work. But it was costing her in ways that had nothing to do with money.

Things hadn't been right before Sara's death. There had been rumours – about what happened at night, about what certain members of staff did and why. Timothy Pool was vicious. Roy had ended up on Forensic for a bit a few years back and always claimed that Pool had once punched him until he'd passed out. Dr el Masri was a lecher whose eager hands, it was said, sometimes got the better of him. And then there had been Sara. Who had raped her? Had it been Dr el Masri? It was well known that he hadn't been on friendly terms with the other Egyptian in the hospital. Nurse Hatem el Shamy, later known to all staff as 'the bomber', had been a particular friend to Sara Ibrahim. But had he taken advantage of that?

Shirley had only ever worked in the community before coming to Ilford. She'd been advocate in residence at a day centre in Barking. There the patients needs were complex – they frequently required support when visiting the Jobcentre, help with housing, going to their GPs – but they weren't trapped in an institution where personalities became larger than life, enmities festered and nights were long and drug-addled. What was real and what wasn't had become blurred, although the line drawn by the management and the clinical lead, in the person of Mr Cotton, was clear. Patients were generally deluded and staff told the truth. Shirley had bought into that via her deeds but never in her mind. Years before she'd done a short Open University psychology course. She didn't remember a lot about it but one thing that had stuck was the notion of cognitive dissonance. This was where a person did one thing whilst thinking the opposite or vice versa. Her whole working life had become a classic example of cognitive dissonance.

What could she do? The thought of going through the process of getting a new job again frightened her. She was the wrong side of fifty and she had the odd health issue. Realistically, she was best off staying at Ilford until it closed and then taking early retirement. Except that the thought of doing that made her feel suicidal. There was another option, however, and Shirley considered it.

She could do her job the way it was supposed to be done. But that was the scariest option of all.

*

Mumtaz left a message.

'Shazia,' she said, 'it's Amma. The solicitor called and we've got a moving date. It's Monday the twenty-second. That gives us just under three weeks. Our new landlord says it's fine to move in that day and so it's all settled. Hope you're having a good day.'

She ended the call and spent a few moments feeling content. Things were far from perfect but at least once the move was over she could tick it off her list of things to do. And once she'd got Shazia away to university, she could think about tackling the Sheikhs – or not. Maybe being in debt to them forever was her fate?

The entry phone buzzed.

'Who is it?'

A woman said, 'It's Amy.'

'Oh, hi,' Mumtaz said. 'Come in.' She opened the door.

Amy Reid was a young ex-policewoman who worked for the Arnold Agency from time to time on a freelance basis. Lee had a small stable of people he used in this way and they'd almost all been in the police. Recently married, Amy had a spring in her step, which was obvious from the way her feet clattered rapidly on the iron stairs outside.

'Hi, Mumtaz.' She almost ran into the office and Mumtaz smiled. Blonde and fit, Amy was always good company and she enjoyed seeing her. But then her smile froze on her face.

'So, this is the office,' Naz Sheikh said.

'Oh, Mumtaz, I met this gentleman outside,' Amy said. 'I think he wants to use our services . . .'

Mumtaz cleared her throat. Aware that her face was hot she said, 'Ah, well, sir, maybe you'd like to make an appointment. I'm afraid we don't see people without one.'

'Oh?'

He was a good actor. But then so was she. 'I've a meeting now so maybe you can give us a call later?' She handed him one of her cards.

'Well, thank you, I will,' Naz said. 'Soon.'

She smiled, widely. 'You do that.'

Amy looked at her a little strangely. Had she gone a bit over the top with the fake bonhomie?

'I will,' Naz said. 'You can count on it.'

He left and Mumtaz shut the door behind him. She heard his feet run down the iron staircase.

'He was cute,' Amy said.

'Was he?'

Amy sat down in front of Mumtaz's desk. 'Yes,' she said. 'Couldn't believe it when I saw him outside the office.'

'Where was he?' Mumtaz sat down before she fell down. Having Naz in the office even for just seconds had been stressful.

'Oh, he was at the top of the staircase,' Amy said. 'Nervous about ringing the bell. I don't know, maybe he's got some really embarrassing problem. Unfaithful wife or something.'

At the top of the stairs. How long had he been there, on his own, listening to her making calls through the office door? Mumtaz felt her skin go cold. He knew his money was coming and so this stunt had to be a mind game. Naz liked those.

'So what's the job?'

Mumtaz hardly heard her. 'Eh?'

'The job, Mumtaz. You said something about a Polish woman . . .'

'Ah yes. A Mrs . . .' she looked down at a piece of paper on her desk – 'Brzezinski. She's worried her sixteen-year-old son is dealing drugs on her estate.'

She passed Amy the photograph the boy's mother had pushed through the letterbox. He was blond, spotty and clearly cultivated a moody look.

'Where do they live?'

'The Keir Hardie Estate in Canning Town.'

'Some of that's quite desirable these days,' Amy said.

'Not where they live,' Mumtaz said. 'And the boy, Antoni, isn't working or at college. He's just hanging about the streets, according to his mother. She wants him followed.'

'OK.'

'Also because Lee's likely to be off sick this week I was wondering if you could be in the office for me on Friday?'

'Yeah,' Amy said. 'That's fine. Hey, Mumtaz, is Lee OK? God, whoever beat him up must have been an animal. Lee's really hard, you know.'

'It was two men,' Mumtaz said.

'Ah, well, that makes sense. Poor old Lee, though. Harsh.'

When Amy finally left, Mumtaz felt exhausted. Just trying to be normal after an appearance from Naz had taken it out of her. And then her mobile phone began to ring and she saw that it was him. She switched it off, but then the office phone rang and she had to answer that. It was Naz, but all he said was, 'Like your girlfriend. Like blondes.'

And then he cut the connection.


The fridge was full of stuff Susan wasn't sure Lee could eat. When he'd called first thing and said he'd be back the next day, she'd gone out to Sainsbury's and bought a load of food. She'd been a bit of a mare to him when he'd visited her before and she wanted to make up for it. But with a broken jaw, albeit repaired, what could he actually get down?

She was pretty certain that the steak had been a mistake and she'd had a bit of a funny moment when she'd bought the vegetarian lasagne. Not in any way Lee's sort of thing. But she had also got a load of cakes and she knew he liked those. Although whether he could get his battered mouth around a doughnut was another matter.

In the hospital he'd looked so vulnerable in that bed with his face all bruised and swollen. Like a wounded soldier. His mother had been a pain in the bum, not giving them a second to themselves, but then Susan recognized that she must've been worried too. And anyway, now Lee was out of hospital, he was coming to see her, not his mum, even if it was for work.

Susan didn't know what Lee was working on in Southend. She suspected it had something to do with her casino, although Lee had denied it. But if it wasn't anything to do with the casino then why had he been so interested in their high rollers? He'd said it was because he found the behaviour of gamblers fascinating but that sounded to Susan like a speech he'd picked up from Mumtaz. She had a degree in psychology or sociology or something.

Since Lee's beating, the old man who'd lost a lot of dosh the previous week, Kenny, had been back twice. Probably desperate to try to win some of his money back, he'd lost big again on both occasions. Usually he didn't behave as if he cared, but Dale the doorman had said that when he'd put him in his cab to go home the second time, Kenny had been visibly shaken. But then he wasn't rich, was he? Dale always got him a cab to or from his home, which was at the far end of the Golden Mile. Nobody with any money lived round there, unless Kenny was an eccentric millionaire with a liking for working girls and candyfloss. Which was always possible.

Susan closed the fridge. If the worst came to the worst she could always make Lee macaroni cheese or some soup. And if he didn't like either of those options she'd buy him a Chinese. Noodles were dead easy to eat, especially with a big splash of soy sauce. She went into her bedroom to get ready for another night at the American roulette wheel. Maybe she'd see poor old Kenny again, although Susan hoped that she didn't, for his sake.

## 12

Rashida knew the signs. It always started with an inability to speak anything but Arabic and then progressed to obsessive cleaning. Her mother didn't know what to do and, without her father, her mind fell apart. She'd had a phone call from Rashida's school.

'I should've bought you a ticket and put you on a plane as soon as I found you at the lock-up,' Salwa said.

'It's the middle of term, Omy,' Rashida said. 'If you take me out of school now they'll know you've sent me back to Cairo. Then they'll come for you.'

Salwa chewed her bottom lip. 'Who?'

'Immigration,' Rashida said. Without her husband, Salwa had to rely on men like the local imam, people who were strangers. She didn't always trust what they told her. Frightened, she was relatively easy to manipulate. Rashida inwardly blessed her school and all her teachers.

'Immigration?'

'Of course,' Rashida said. 'It's against the law to keep a child out of school in this country. Remember how Baba was so careful to take me in the holidays for my operation? They'll deport you and the children and then Baba will be here all alone.'

'Oh no.' Salwa sat down beside Rashida on her bed. 'Oh no, we can't have that, that would break him. And what about the private detective and her investigation? What shall we do?'

Her mother had the key to Rashida's locked bedroom door in her pocket. If she felt so inclined, Rashida knew that she could easily overpower Salwa and just take it. But what good would that do her? She had nowhere to run to and her mother had probably primed the imam and all his followers to keep a look out for her in case she escaped. What she needed was time – to think and to plan.

'Let me go back to school,' Rashida said.

'No.'

'So get arrested,' Rashida said.

'I told them you were sick,' Salwa said. 'Now I think I must get you an air ticket.'

Rashida rolled her eyes. She was going to have to play this very carefully. Her mother was frightened but she wasn't a fool. 'Now? Omy, if I disappear now, they will know you've sent me away to get married. They're always suspicious about girls who suddenly leave before the end of term. One of the Pakistani girls left a week into last term and everybody knew why.'

'Did they catch her?'

'No. But that was because her whole family went to Pakistan too,' Rashida said. 'For good.'

Salwa shook her head. 'Maybe you are just saying that to trick me, Rashida. How do I know that if I let you go back to school you won't just run away?'

'Run away? Where?'

'Or maybe you'll do something worse,' Salwa said. 'What you said about betraying your father. Although for what I can't . . .'

'I didn't mean it. I was upset.' Rashida realized that she'd used the biggest lever she had too early on in her negotiations with her mother. Now she had to be as sincerely sorry for that error as she could be. What she needed was time, and being at school until the end of term was one way of getting some.

Her mother shook her head. 'I can't trust you,' she said.

Rashida leant back against her pillows. 'Even if I swear on the Holy Koran?'

One thing Rashida knew was that her mother was entirely convinced of her daughter's adherence to her religion.

'Swear what on the Holy Koran?'

'That I won't run away and I will stop my hunger strike,' Rashida said.

Her mother, frowning, said, 'Until the end of term?'

'Unless you want to send me away now and get deported,' Rashida said.

Salwa shook her head. 'No.'

'No?'

She stood up. 'You think I'm stupid, Rashida? If I let you go back to school you will spend the rest of the term looking for ways to get out of marriage.'

'I will swear on—'

'No!' Salwa stood up. 'Today I will go to the travel agent and I will buy you ticket for Egypt.'

Rashida began to cry. 'But, Omy, they will . . .'

'I will take my chances with the British immigration people,' Salwa said.

Rashida wanted to yell, 'Then I'll starve myself to death in this room!' But she couldn't. She'd been sure that offering to swear on the Koran would work. And she wouldn't have broken her promise. She wouldn't have run until the day that term ended. Hopefully by that time, she would have worked out where she might go.

As her mother left, she said, 'You'll be in Cairo by Sunday.' Then she locked Rashida's bedroom door behind her. The girl cried and then she pulled herself together. There was still a back-up plan, even though it was very unlikely to succeed.

The pub, which was called The Butterfly, was more than half empty. And of the patrons who were drinking, most were elderly men like Ken Rivers.

Lee Arnold bought himself a Diet Pepsi and sat down opposite the old geezer. There wasn't going to be any easy way he could introduce himself. He put one of his business cards on the table. 'Mr Rivers?'

The old man looked up, squinted and then looked down at the card.

'My name's Lee Arnold, I'm a private detective. I've been engaged by your son Philip's wife . . .'

'Sandra?'

'Yes. I've been engaged by Mrs Rivers to track Philip down.'

Ken Rivers shook his head. 'He done a terrible thing to her, taking all her money,' he said. 'She wants it all back off him, I s'pose.'

'No. She just wants to talk to him.'

'So she says.'

The old man picked up Lee's business card. 'Why should I believe you?' he said. 'You could be anyone.'

'So phone Sandra.' Lee found her number on his phone and gave it to Ken Rivers. 'Go on.'

He looked at it for a few moments and then said, 'Nah. I'll call her later.'

'Mr Rivers, do you have any idea where your son is?' Lee asked.

Ken drank his glass dry and then said, 'I could do with another.'

The ambiance wasn't nice. The Butterfly was one of those pubs where the carpet was forever sticky and the beer looked and probably tasted like piss. Lee looked at the old man and raised his eyebrows. So this was a bribery situation.

He picked up Ken Rivers' glass. 'What you having?'

'Pint of Stella.'

Even when Lee had still been drinking, he'd never bothered himself too much about lagers. Although far from being a fully paid-up member of CAMRA, he had always been more of a bitter man. He went to the bar, bought the beer and sat down again.

'Well?'

The old bloke supped, slowly. The way he behaved made Lee feel vindicated. Susan had been sorry for 'Kenny' when he lost so much money at the casino, but ever since Lee had first spotted him he hadn't been able to shift the idea that Kenneth Rivers was a nasty piece of work.

'I haven't seen Phil since last Boxing Day,' the old man said.

'Did he come down to see you?'

'Yeah. We had a couple of pints and then he went back to the Smoke. He never said he was selling Sandra's house.'

'Have you heard from him since?'

'Shit!' A lone twenty-something put some coins in a slot machine and lost the lot.

'No,' Ken Rivers said.

'Did you try to contact him?'

'No.'

'Why not?'

'We wasn't close,' the old man said.

Sandra Rivers had told him that Phil often went down to Southend to see his mum and dad. But in view of what Barry

Barber had told him maybe Phil had been visiting men for sex rather than going for tea with his folks.

'And your wife?'

'She don't know which way's up,' Ken Rivers said. 'Didn't Sandra tell you that?'

'She told me your wife was suffering from dementia.'

He shook his head, drank and then said, 'You don't know the half.'

'You look after Mrs Rivers?'

'Who else is there?' he said.

So the old woman was in the flat. Somewhere. Lee remembered all those silent, apparently empty rooms he'd seen through the windows.

'What do you do, Mr Rivers, apart from looking after your wife?' Lee asked.

He shrugged. 'No much. Get out for a pint when I can. Have a cuppa somewhere . . .'

Lee couldn't help himself, he wanted to know. 'Who looks after your wife when you go out?'

There was a long silence before Ken answered. And when he did, his cold blue eyes burnt into Lee Arnold's face. 'You said you come here about Phil,' he said. 'Not my old woman.'

'I was just—'

'Well, don't "just" nothing,' the old man said. 'I ain't got nothing to tell you about Phil and I ain't got nothing to tell you about my old woman neither.'

He turned his head away. Lee waited for him to turn back, but in vain. Ken Rivers remained silent until Lee got up and left. He said, 'Look, call me if you do see Phil, will you, Mr Rivers? Bottom line is his ex-wife is worried about him. Money's not important, she just wants to know he's safe.'

But Ken Rivers didn't so much as twitch.

Out on the rainy seafront, Lee walked back to his car. His meeting with Ken Rivers hadn't gone as well as it could, but at least he was now almost certain the old man hadn't seen him at the casino. Lee had been careful not to make any sort of eye contact with him but then Ken Rivers had only had eyes for the roulette wheel. It was doubtful he knew anything about his surroundings once he was playing.

Where had Ken's money come from? He'd frittered away thousands on the one occasion Lee had seen him gamble. Was Phil putting cash into his dad's account? The old man had said that they hadn't got on, so if Phil was giving him money, then why? But then Sandra Rivers had been sure that her husband had been to visit his parents often and that they were close. Had Ken been lying to her about that? If so, why? Had Ken been covering up his son's infidelities? Had Phil's mother also colluded in the deception? And where was the old woman anyway?

When he got back to his car, Lee called Derek Salmon.

'I'd go back into the shadows for a bit if I were you,' the solicitor said. 'If Ken Rivers is that hostile just watch him for the time being.'

'OK.' Then Lee called a man he'd first met when he'd been on the force. He was called Leslie and he could go places that other people only dreamt about.


'Miss Huq?'

Mumtaz turned. She'd never really got used to 'Mrs Hakim', which was useful now.

Dr el Masri smiled. 'Hello,' he said. 'I was hoping to see you.'

'Oh?'

She was on her way to meet Shirley and Mandy in the advocacy office. She had to pass the doctor's offices to get there.

El Masri leant out of his open door and smiled. Behind him, Mumtaz could see an embarrassed expression pass across his secretary's face. 'You know, I think that you and I may have got off to a bad start,' the doctor said.

'Really?'

He looked at her with soft eyes. Mumtaz knew all too well when a man was flirting with her.

'I believe I was a little harsh about your qualifications,' he said. 'And, in fact, when I thought about what you said, I realized that you are probably the most qualified advocate we've ever had.'

'Thank you.'

'A conversation between us might be both useful and enjoyable,' he said.

'Maybe.'

'Maybe?'

'I found what you said about advocate impartiality, particularly as pertaining to ex-service users, really offensive,' she said. Only afterwards did she think that might not have been the best thing to say. But at their first meeting he'd made her cross.

He looked down at the floor. Was he a little cowed?

'I'm sorry for that, Miss Huq,' he said. 'Sometimes I speak before I think.'

She waited for him to raise his head again so that she could see his eyes.

'Well . . .'

He looked at her and smiled. 'An old doctor's lack of manners and understanding,' he said.

And there, covering his face like a sheen, was lust. Everything inside Mumtaz cringed. But it was an opportunity and she had to take it.

'A conversation about psychology would be very pleasant,' she said.

'Excellent.' He rubbed his hands together. 'Have a word with Sylvia –' he waved a hand in the direction of his secretary – 'and she will book you in. Late afternoons are generally best for me.'

'Very well,' Mumtaz said.

Dr el Masri bowed. 'Then I will see you,' he said and he went back inside his office and closed the door.

'Wear metal pants.' A hand landed on Mumtaz's shoulder. Mandy.

'He's always trying his luck,' she continued as they walked towards the Advocacy office.

'Did he ever try it on with you?' Mumtaz said.

'Nah.'

'Why not?'

Mandy snorted. 'What, an ex-service user? Yeah, right. No he only tries it on with "sane" advocates.'

'Is that why some of the others left?'

She laughed. 'I dunno. Rattled your cage, though, didn't it?'

Mumtaz shook her head. 'You are terrible.' Then she said 'What about actual service users?'

'On the wards?' Mandy shrugged again. 'I don't know. When I was on Acute One, I was too ill to know what my name was. But there have been stories.'

'About el Masri?'

'About doctors, nurses, everyone. When you're off your nut you're fair game because nobody is going to believe you. They might say that they do, but they don't. Me and Roy told you about Shirley, didn't we?'

'Yes.'

They reached the Advocacy office door. 'You have to make up your own mind, Mumtaz,' Mandy said. 'If you think that what a service user's saying is true then you have to do something about it even if Shirley don't want you to.'

'Yes, but you—'

'Me and Roy can't do nothing off our own bat. We're ex-service users and so nobody will believe a word we say. The hospital only listens to people like you and even then it's hard.'

Mumtaz went to open the door, but Mandy stopped her. 'Shirley won't help you,' she said. 'But if you take the lead, me and Roy will always be behind you.'

'Did you try to be behind the advocates who left?'

'Yeah. We did but they all left anyway.' Mandy looked sad. 'As you will.'

Mumtaz put a hand on her shoulder. 'I won't,' she said and instantly regretted it.

Mandy shook her head. 'You will. This place is its own little world with its own rules,' she said. 'One way or another, in the end, it won't let you stay.'

Something hit the window. Rashida looked down into the street and saw a girl wearing a torn vintage dress over a pair of mad candy-striped leggings. MJ.

Tentatively, Rashida tapped the window. Her mother was downstairs somewhere and, although she had the television on, she had good hearing. MJ didn't respond and so Rashida tapped again, a little harder. MJ's round, pierced face looked up at her and smiled. Then she gave a thumbs-up sign and mouthed what Rashida reckoned was 'I'm doing it'.

Rashida's heart beat so fast it made her dizzy. Still looking at MJ, she sat down on her bed. She waved and MJ waved back but then there was a knock at her door and Rashida's breathing stopped.

'Who is it? What do you want?' Her own voice sounded husky and thick.

'I did it,' a much smaller voice said from outside the door.

Rashida flew across the room and pressed herself against the doorpost. 'Zizi!'

'MJ's outside,' her younger sister said.

'Yes, I know,' Rashida whispered. 'You told her what to do? Exactly what I told you?'

'Yes,' the little girl said. 'Rashida, Baba wouldn't be cross with me if he found out, would he?'

'No, Baba would be proud of us,' Rashida said. 'But, Zizi, we have to keep this a secret from Omy and the boys. And we mustn't talk of it again. Understand?'

'Yes.'

'Promise?'

'I promise.' There was a pause and then the little girl said, 'I'm going to play now.'

'All right, you do that,' Rashida said. 'And forget all about MJ and everything else, Zizi.'

She heard her sister walk down across the landing to her own room and shut the door. Rashida went back to her window and saw that MJ had gone. Then she heard the house phone ringing downstairs and began to smile.

# 13

Susan had hoped that Lee would go to the casino with her but apparently that wasn't possible. He had to go and meet some bloke out of town on business. He'd said he'd be back later in the evening and would join her at work then, but he hadn't said when. Susan had told him not to bother and just to let himself back into the flat when he got back. Lee had looked hurt.

She listened to him trying to sing. Why he had to take another shower just to go and see some bloke on business she couldn't imagine. She didn't trust him. She picked up his phone and looked at the list of calls he'd made that day. Two of them had been to Vi Collins. One a few minutes before he'd returned to the flat. He obviously hadn't wanted Susan to hear it.

Susan picked up her own phone and put Vi's number into her directory. She didn't know what, if anything, she was going to do with it, but she knew she had to have it.

When Shirley returned to the Advocacy office it was dark and she was still shaking. When she'd finished her meeting with Mandy and Mumtaz, instead of joining them for the Advocacy Surgery on the acute wards, she'd gone on to Forensic. Against all her self-preservation instincts, she'd marched into ward manager Timothy Pool's office and told him that they needed to talk. At first he'd ignored her. But then Shirley had shut his door, plonked herself down in front of him and said, 'We need to talk about Dylan Smith.'

'He went crazy and attacked me,' Timothy had said. He was small but stocky and when he spoke his short hands balled into fists. 'The Lord is my witness.'

'Be that as it may,' Shirley had said. 'Your staff aren't so sure, are they?'

'What do you mean?'

'Oh, come on, Timothy,' Shirley had said, 'you must have seen the way they looked anywhere but into my eyes when I talked to them about it. Not one of them can so much as talk to Dylan . . .'

'Because he's a vicious boy who needs to be taught a lesson!' Timothy had countered. 'Nothing to do with being mentally ill, he's a bad character and he must be curbed.'

'By violence?'

'No!'

'Oh, Timothy,' she'd said, 'I think you're lying. In fact, I know it. Service users complain about you all the time.'

He'd looked at her out of the corner of his eye and he'd said, 'So why, if that's the case, haven't you brought my "bad behaviour" up in front of Mr Cotton and the hospital management? That's your job, isn't it?'

She'd leant forward in her chair and said, 'Ah, but you know exactly why I haven't, don't you, Timothy?'

'No.' But he'd looked away from her as he'd said it.

'Yes, you do.'

Then he'd looked at her. 'Why's that? Tell me.'

And so she had. She'd talked about the culture of automatically disbelieving service users, of wards run like medieval fiefdoms, where patients had to watch what staff wanted them to watch on TV and where the withholding of privileges was used for the most minor infractions of often imaginary and senseless rules.

As she'd talked, Timothy Pool had looked at her with cold, impassive eyes. Then he'd said, 'But I ask again, if it's so bad here, why haven't you reported it?'

'And I tell you again, Timothy, that you know exactly why I haven't.'

He'd gone quiet at first. Then he'd lost it. Trembling with rage, he got to his feet and yelled, 'What's got into you, woman? Why do you come to me with this?'

'Because I'm going to make a formal complaint about you to the hospital management on behalf of Dylan Smith.' She'd said it very calmly and quietly.

Timothy fell back in his chair and, for a moment, Shirley had thought that he was in shock. But then he started laughing. 'You?' he said. 'You complain about me? Some do-gooder woman thinking she can help these "poor" people somehow?'

What he'd said had hurt. Middle class and middle-aged, Shirley knew that she probably looked like a classic 'do-gooder' but she also knew that even at that she had failed so far.

'Yes, I am a do-gooder,' she'd said, 'and so I'm going to do good. I'll start by stopping you, Timothy.'

For a moment he'd looked a tiny bit afraid, then he'd smiled again. 'Ah, but I have a far greater power than you on my side,' he'd said.

'What? The management and the staff?'

'No! God's truth, woman!'

It was at that point that Shirley had risen from her chair. 'I'm not going to stay here while you bang on about the Lord,' she'd said. 'Apart from anything else, religious talk in a clinical setting is totally inappropriate. Just know that I'm supporting Dylan and you'll be hearing from me, formally.'

Then, after a short conversation with Dylan, she'd left the ward. However she hadn't stopped shaking since. She'd heard the stories almost as soon as she'd come to work at Ilford. Staff like Timothy Pool – in fact any senior member of staff – were sacrosanct. Doctors were untouchable, and even junior nurses, if they were liked by senior management, were pretty hard to make complaints about. Cleaners and some care workers were expendable. The Polish girl who had opened the window for Sara Ibrahim had been dismissed.

Shirley sat down at her desk and wondered again why she had actually gone ahead with a crazy idea that would almost certainly see her losing her job. Had it really been for the look of gratitude on Dylan Smith's smashed-up, sewer-mouthed face? There wasn't much to love in a young man who called one of the other service users on the ward a 'fucking Paki' and routinely stole from other residents too delusional to know what day it was. But that was irrelevant. He was a powerless service user and it was her job to first of all believe him and then to help him obtain justice. But in supporting Dylan she'd made a powerful enemy of Timothy. She looked at her phone and wondered when it would ring to summon her to a management meeting or an audience with Mr Cotton. But it remained silent.

Shirley put Dylan's file away in her desk and locked it. She looked in her handbag to make sure her car keys were accessible and then counted how many fags she had left. Not enough. She'd have to stop at the garage and buy some more on the way home. Shirley put her coat on.

When she got to the office door she pulled the handle down

but nothing happened. It was old and it did stick sometimes and so she tried to ease it out while kicking the bottom corner, which sometimes worked. Not on this occasion. She banged it with her fist, which also sometimes worked too, but that failed. Shirley bent down to look at the small gap between the door and the doorpost to see if she could locate the problem. Her skin went cold.

The door was locked. Someone had got a key, turned it and trapped her in her own office. Could the caretaker have thought the office was empty and locked it? As far as she knew he was a lazy bugger who rarely moved from his small room down by the old disused laundry block. Why would he lock the door? He wouldn't. Shirley spoke out loud to herself, 'It's OK. There are still people about.' She took her phone out of her bag and called Acute 2. All the doctors and their admin staff had gone, but the wards would be manned.

No one answered. She tried the door again and then called Acute 1. An over-friendly voice responded and it took Shirley a little while to realize that it was in fact a bipolar patient, who sounded very high, on the end of the line. 'Get Dawn, you know, the ward manager,' Shirley said. But the woman said she didn't know any Dawn and put the phone down.

Shirley tried the door again, but it wouldn't budge. She called out, 'Hey, my door's locked! Can you give me a hand?' but was met with silence. For a moment, Shirley stepped back from the door and looked at it. She saw the gap between the door and the doorpost go black and realized that someone had turned off the lights in the corridor. The paranoia began. Timothy Pool had done this to frighten her. Shirley ran back to the door and crouched down to call through the gap. 'Hello? Who's there? Can you help me, please? I think I'm locked in here.'

But again, silence. Shirley began to sweat. She stood up and pulled at the door handle until her hand hurt. Old and splintered, it rattled and shook but when she stopped there was another noise that sounded like someone sniffing. 'Who's there?' She looked at her phone again and brought up the number for the forensic ward. As she waited for someone to answer she muttered, 'Think you can frighten me? You can't.'

But no one answered. And then something new happened. The door began to rattle from the outside. Shirley dropped her phone on the floor, her whole body in a spasm of terror. At first the movement was minimal but, as whoever was out in the corridor put more pressure on the handle, the rattling became ever more intense. And although Shirley wanted to run away and hide somewhere she could no longer move. She heard someone on the end of the phone say, 'Hello? Hello?'

And then suddenly the door sprang open.

Shirley screamed.


It was 'Elvis Nite' at the Riverside Caravan Park. Apparently, vodka was on special offer and the big chalet that was called the Clubhouse was heaving. But Lee Arnold ignored such delights and walked down the side of the building. Finding a caravan wasn't as easy as finding a house; especially at night they all tended to look the same. Except that Lee knew Leslie's didn't. When he'd answered Lee's call he'd told him that his caravan was 'down near the River Crouch with Spider-Man in the window'.

Lee walked on into darkness as he closed in on one of Essex's lesser-known riverbanks. The closer he got to the smell and sound of the water the more the caravans thinned out, until only one remained. Lit up like a Christmas tree, the caravan had a life-sized model of Spider-Man in one window and a heavily bearded human face in another. It had a name plate which said 'Fortress of Solitude'.

'It's Superman's secret hide-out,' the man said as he opened the caravan door, grabbed Lee and pulled him inside.

'What?' Lee shook his head. 'What is?'

'Fortress of Solitude – it's Superman's secret hide-out. In actuality, of course, it isn't in Essex but in the polar regions . . .'

'Yeah, Leslie, great.' Lee didn't find it easy dealing with nerds even when they were ex-cons. He looked around the caravan for somewhere to sit but found only boxes of comics and many computers. 'Leslie . . .'

'Oh, chair, yes,' he said and then left the caravan for who knew where.

Alone, Lee wondered whether he'd made a mistake tapping up Leslie Baum. He might be a genius but he was also mental and sometimes that combination was hard to take. Convicted fifteen years previously of hacking into systems that belonged to several notable scientific research laboratories, Leslie's aim had been to put a stop to the Human Genome Project. Although both his parents had been ultra-orthodox Jews, Leslie's objections to the Project had not been religious. He had been afraid that once the code was known, humans would be able to animate robots who, with their superior strength and durability, would make slaves of mankind.

'Here we are,' Leslie said as he struggled through the door with a deckchair. 'I'm afraid I've no teabags and the milk's gone off.'

Lee took the deckchair from Leslie and assembled it, as best he could, opposite the stool where his host sat. 'That's OK,' he said as he very gently lowered himself into the contraption.

'Refrigerators are not what they once were,' Leslie said. 'What do you want, DI Arnold?'

Lee knew that it was pointless trying to get Leslie to drop his old police title or even to call him Lee. 'I want to find out where someone's getting money from,' Lee said.

'Easy enough.'

'Someone who doesn't have either a computer or a mobile phone,' Lee said.

Leslie shrugged. 'A little more problematic, but possible,' he said. 'Why do you want this information?'

'I think the money's hot.'

'Stolen.'

'Possibly.'

'Mmm.' Leslie rubbed his beard with long, thin fingers. The computer screen he sat in front of was, like all the others in the caravan, covered in what was, to Lee, incomprehensible code.

'So, just to get this straight, DI Arnold, you're not asking me to do anything that could possibly result in financial or any other kind of gain for yourself or myself?'

'No.' Leslie always asked that question. But then, putting aside the fact that he'd had a terrible time in prison after his conviction, he was a very moral person.

'Good.' Although Lee knew that some of the people who could loosely be described as Leslie's 'friends' were usually not so scrupulous. 'So tell me about the client.'

Ken Rivers' life was laid as bare as Lee thought Leslie needed. While he spoke, Leslie typed the salient details into a laptop in a language that was unknown to the private detective. Lee hoped it was Hebrew but feared it might be Klingon.

When Leslie had finished he said, 'I will need expenses. I'll have to go to Southend once at least and so that'll mean bus fare.'

Lee took a twenty-pound note out of his wallet and put it on Leslie's phone, which was shaped like the cartoon cat Garfield.

'And I will need help.'

'I don't wanna know.' Lee put down four fifty-pound notes. He'd seen some of the types that Leslie hung about with. Mostly kids. They'd want at least a computer game or a bunch of puerile apps for their trouble.

Leslie did something on the screen in front of him, something else on the laptop and then said, 'Leave it with me.'

'Thanks, Leslie, I appreciate it,' Lee said. It wasn't easy getting out of the deckchair, mainly because Spider-Man was in the way. But he did it.

Leslie, still staring at his computers, said nothing. When Lee had arrested him back in 1997, Leslie had been living in a flat in East Ham. Rejected by his wealthy religious family in north London for being an atheist, Leslie had been on benefits when he was nicked. And because his crime had been so clever, with implications for cyber-security that went way beyond just hacking a few science labs, the judge who'd tried him had thrown the book at him. The prison system had not been kind. When he did get out, only a sudden rush of generosity by his parents had saved Leslie from homelessness. They'd bought him the caravan at the Riverside and for many years no one, including Lee Arnold, had heard a peep out of him. Then rumours began to circulate about a mad super-geek somewhere in Essex who could get into anything, anywhere. Lee had tracked him down. He'd also kept him to himself.

Lee opened the caravan door and walked down the few metal steps to the ground. 'You not going to Elvis Nite then, Leslie?' he asked.

'I'd rather have a colonoscopy performed by a lunatic using a fence post,' the brilliant mind of Leslie Baum replied. 'Good evening to you, DI Arnold.'

Rashida sat between her two little brothers and ate her soup in silence. From across the table, sitting beside Zizi, her mother watched her. It was the first time that Rashida had eaten with her family in almost a week.

Eventually her mother said, 'Remember how many copies of the Holy Koran you swore your oath on, Rashida? If you run away from school tomorrow you will burn in Hell.'

'I won't,' Rashida said.

She felt Zizi's eyes on her, full of mischief and some fear.

Salwa raised her arms and shrugged. 'I have never known such schools as they have in this country,' she said. 'If a parent says that a child is sick, then a child is sick. How can they not believe? What's the matter with them?'

No one said a word. The boys because they didn't know any better, Zizi because she knew that her sister had done something bad but didn't really know exactly what and Rashida because she was still in shock that her mother had actually believed MJ's impression of Mrs Rose, the headteacher.

'How can a school give a child a medical?' Salwa continued. 'It's not decent.'

'But they won't do it now I'm going back, Omy,' Rashida said.

Her mother shook her head.

'And I won't go anywhere but school,' Rashida continued. 'I've sworn an oath and I will keep to it.'

'You will go to Cairo when term is over,' Salwa said. 'And know this, Rashida: it's your father's will that you marry Anwar.'

Rashida didn't believe her but she said, 'Yes, Omy.'

The younger of her two brothers, Gamal, said, 'Is Rashida getting married?'

His mother stroked his hair. Rashida knew that Gamal was her favourite. He was a boy and, unlike her other brother, Asim, he wasn't sulky.

'Yes, she is,' Salwa said in the baby voice she often used to Gamal. 'Her time has come.'

'Why?'

'Because she was prepared a long time ago and she needs to marry before it is too late.'

'Too late for what?'

Gamal was always asking questions. Asim stopped eating and slumped back in his chair. He hated too much talk and was much happier alone with his computer. Rashida stifled a smile. She'd caught him looking at online pictures he shouldn't.

'Before she gets too old,' Salwa said.

'Too old for what?' Gamal asked.

'For any man to want her. Men only like to marry girls when they are young and guaranteed to be pure. It is the Islamic thing to do.'

Rashida boiled. Her mother was so ignorant! The tradition of child brides and their ghastly 'preparation' was not Islamic but an evil folk-custom that affected all peoples of the Middle East, including those who weren't Muslims. But she kept her opinions to herself and carried on eating.

'When I grow up, will I have to get married when I'm still at school?' Gamal asked.

This time Rashida's sister, Zizi, replied, 'No,' she said. 'Don't be silly. You won't get married until you're really old.'

'But will my wife be young?'

Salwa kissed him on the head. 'Oh yes,' she said. 'Don't worry about that, my little darling. Omy will find a young and tender bride for you. She will be as beautiful as a rose.'

Rashida put her spoon down and stopped eating. Suddenly she felt nauseous.

# 14

'Hello?'

Mumtaz put a professional smile on her face. She'd packed kitchen equipment for hours when she'd got home the previous evening and was exhausted. 'Mrs el Shamy, it's Mumtaz Hakim from the Arnold Agency,' she said.

'Oh. Do you have news about el Masri? Have you seen him having relations with his patients?'

Like all clients, she wanted instant results.

'No,' Mumtaz said. 'But I have heard rumours about inappropriate behaviour on his part. I've also made an appointment to see him next Tuesday.'

'About his behaviour?'

'No.'

'Why?'

Mumtaz sighed. She'd explained this. Now she was going to have to explain it again. 'Mrs el Shamy, I'm gathering information about Dr el Masri. I'm not in the hospital as myself. As you suggested, I am working with the Advocacy. So I am undercover. I'm doing this so that I can collect intelligence on Dr el Masri for you. A few rumours about a doctor's behaviour is not enough to interest either the police or the BMA, which is the organization that is responsible for disciplining doctors.'

There was a moment's silence. 'I pay you a lot of money to do this.'

'I know,' Mumtaz said. 'But in order to make that investment worthwhile, you must let me do what I can to find out the truth. Wanting el Masri to be an abuser doesn't make him one.'

'But he is! Hatem said he was!'

'Mrs el Shamy, I am not disbelieving your husband,' Mumtaz said. 'I'm working on it. It's looking promising. Just give me time . . .'

'You have two weeks, that is all!' the Egyptian said and then cut the connection.

Mumtaz put her head in her hands. Of course money was an issue, she understood that more than almost anyone. But if Salwa el Shamy wanted to know the truth she would have to wait. Working to some arbitrary deadline was impossible. Anyway, even if she'd wanted to call her client back, Mumtaz couldn't speak to her again that day. When she'd been packing away the kitchen equipment she'd had Naz Sheikh on the phone, twice. The first time he'd offered to help her move, for a price, and the second time he'd talked about her continuing 'debt'. She'd ended up in tears. Luckily Shazia had been up in her room doing her homework and was none the wiser. But it was wearing Mumtaz down. As hard as she tried, throwing herself into her work, although helpful, was not blanking out the horror of her own situation. Once the house was sold she didn't strictly owe the Sheikhs a penny. It was debatable whether she had ever really owed them anything. However it was too late for thoughts like those now. They'd issued her with a contract for a new 'debt', and although she still hadn't signed it, she knew she'd have to.

At one time she had thought about trying to talk to others who were in debt to the Sheikhs. She'd heard rumours about a

Turkish kebab restaurant and a widow who had a fabric shop in East Ham. But how could she even begin to talk to them about it? The Sheikhs had houses that they rented out all over east London. She had once followed Rizwan Sheikh as he went on a rent-collecting trip around Canning Town and although she had tried to talk to one of his tenants afterwards, the man hadn't been able to speak any English. A lot of the Sheikhs' tenants appeared to be Middle Eastern and, from what she had seen of them, they all looked poor and frightened. Mumtaz strongly suspected they were in the country illegally. Not that she could use her suspicions to her advantage. If she tried to harm the Sheikhs by going for their poor tenants she'd find it hard to live with herself.

The office phone rang.

'Hello, Arnold Agency.'

'Hi, Mumtaz.'

It was Amy, the freelancer. She was watching Antoni Brzezinski, whose mother feared he was dealing drugs.

'How's things on the Keir Hardie Estate?'

'Quiet. Antoni didn't get up until eleven, when his mother got in from her cleaning job,' Amy said. 'Then they had a row and he left the flat in a strop. Now he's hanging around the shops on Freemasons Road with an Asian boy and a white lad, both wearing black hoodies. They're smoking cigarettes and the white lad and Antoni are drinking cheap cider, but nothing more.'

'Some kids just get drunk, they don't do drugs.'

'I know, but it's early days,' Amy said. 'How's Lee?'

'Working.'

'Working?'

Mumtaz shook her head. Lee had gone back to work far too

soon. 'On a case down in Southend. But you know how he is, Amy, you can't tell him anything.'

'I know.' And then she said, 'Hey, did that cute guy I found on the stairs come back or call?'

Naz. Mumtaz's face dropped. 'No,' she lied, 'he didn't.'

'Oh, that's a shame,' Amy said.

'Yes. Isn't it.'

The bloke knocking on Ken Rivers' door was so big, Lee was concerned he might pop the buttons on his jacket. It was a very nice jacket, light grey with an attractive sheen. But it was too small for him. Lee sank down a little behind his steering wheel. A good minute passed before the old man came to the door. He looked angry and when he spoke he sounded it. 'You can't come in,' he said. 'She ain't well.'

Lee didn't hear what the big man said but then he heard Ken say, 'I can give you a cheque now, or I've got a ton in cash and I'll give you the rest later.'

Lee still couldn't hear the big man talking. He risked lowering his passenger side window a little more. Briefly Ken appeared to look over but then he heard him say, 'Well, that's the way it is, take it or leave it.'

'I can't,' the big man said. 'You know that.'

Ken Rivers shrugged.

'Tomorrow without fail,' the big man said. 'How's that?'

Ken muttered something that Lee thought was probably an agreement. Then the big man said, 'So, where's Cindy? You know?'

The old man shook his head. 'Went out in her car with the baby. I dunno where they went.'

'Well, tell her I called.'

'Yeah. Yeah.'

The man began to turn, 'Don't forget, tomorrow? OK?'

'OK.' Ken Rivers shuffled back inside the house and slammed the door behind him. The ape-like creature lumbered down the path and got into a BMW. He made a phone call and then drove away.

Ken Rivers owed money to someone. It was more than a hundred pounds and whoever the large and scary man had been, he hadn't seemed to like cheques much. Lee took a punt and drove up to the leisure centre where he parked his car. He headed to the High Street and waited in a shop doorway diagonally opposite NatWest Bank. Just over an hour later he saw Ken Rivers walk slowly up the High Street eating a meat pie from a Greggs bag. Lee wasn't surprised when the old man went into the bank. When he came out again he was tucking something into the inside breast pocket of his raincoat. What Lee wanted to know, however, was whether he'd got money out to pay his debt, or to piss up the wall at the casino.

Mr Cotton, the chief psychiatric consultant, looked down at his notes and then looked up at Shirley. He coughed hard. His face went red, and for a moment, Shirley felt alarmed. But then he stopped.

'You've no staff corroboration,' he said. 'Not even anything from other patients.'

'I'm working on that,' Shirley said. 'When Dylan originally complained I only spoke to him. Now I'll need to speak to other service users.'

'Yes, but even if you do, you know as well as I do that they can sometimes experience things that haven't actually happened.'

'Yes,' Shirley said. 'But that doesn't mean that they shouldn't be heard.'

'Of course not,' he said. 'I am merely pointing out to you the simple fact that any resolution of this complaint may well hinge upon the balance of probabilities that exist between the stories of Dylan Smith and Timothy Pool.'

'I know.'

Shirley was aware of the slight catch in her voice. When her office door had finally slammed open the previous evening she'd screamed in shock, but she'd seen no one. In spite of her fear she'd run out into the corridor and looked both ways. Nothing. Now though, still shaken, she was determined to stay her course. She'd also put in a request for the caretaker to look at the lock on her door. There was always the possibility that there was something wrong with it. Although Shirley didn't really believe that.

Mr Cotton folded himself back into the depths of his big leather chair. Shirley thought he looked like a roosting vulture. 'I must say, I'm finding it hard to believe that a man like Timothy Pool would be violent to one of his patients,' he said.

Shirley wanted to say 'Where the hell have you been?' but she didn't. Although it was eighteen months ago, the consultant had had cancer and was still under treatment to monitor his health. He had to be at least partially distracted. 'There have been other complaints about him in the past,' she said.

'But none of them have ever come to anything.'

Shirley said nothing.

He leant forwards. Hunched up, he looked even thinner

than he usually did. 'Mrs Mayfield, when this Dylan Smith thing first happened, I thought you and I were on the same page,' he said. 'We usually are.'

He was right. They generally were. Not this time.

'Mr Pool is one of my longest-serving and most reliable members of staff,' he said. 'He has a spotless service record. All his nurses support him a hundred per cent and he's—'

'What he is, is a bully,' Shirley said. As soon as she said it she felt her face flush.

For a moment he just stared at her and then he said, 'You do know that you will have to back that assertion up, don't you, Mrs Mayfield?'

'Yes.' Her heart was pounding now and she felt a bit sick.

Mr Cotton sighed.

'Timothy Pool has been ruling that ward by fear for years, maybe decades,' she said. 'You must know!'

'In what way does Nurse Pool use fear?'

'I don't know, exactly,' she said. 'Maybe he threatens staff with the sack . . .'

'No, no, no, that couldn't happen. There'd have to be an investigation and if malpractice was so much as suspected, heads would metaphorically roll. Anyway, why would Nurse Pool threaten his staff? What would be the purpose of that?'

'I don't know,' Shirley said. 'To preserve his power?'

'His power? Timothy is a deeply religious man. Power means nothing to him.'

'Doesn't it? I'm not so sure about that,' Shirley said. 'Listen, Mr Cotton, Timothy is always talking to service users in ways that he must know are inappropriate. Going on about the Lord and God and what have you. Nobody who works here is supposed to try to influence service users about politics or religion.'

'I know Timothy can be a bit—'

'He's out of order,' she said.

'Do you have anything against Christianity?'

'No! But it's wrong to push it down people's throats. Mr Cotton, I think that Timothy is a fanatic. One of my old advocates left last year because he thought that Nurse Pool was just plain wrong and he couldn't work with him. And before you ask, that volunteer was not an ex-service user. Pool punishes his patients. He makes moral judgements about them not just in terms of their index offences but also their everyday behaviour.'

'What do you mean?'

She said, 'Well, there's the smoking, which he doesn't like, and Dylan told me that Nurse Pool sometimes tells his staff to watch out for anyone who might be masturbating at night.'

'Oh, that's preposterous!' he said.

'Is it? How do you know? Mr Cotton, I know that you want your hospital to run smoothly and I know you have the best interests of everyone here at heart, but you have to accept that staff can mess up.'

'I do accept that.'

'No, you don't. Every time there is an incident involving a member of staff you tell me how great you think they are and how much confidence you have in them. And I know you don't mean to put pressure on me to favour your staff over the service users but that is how it feels and that is what I've done in the past. And it's wrong.'

His eyes were very blue she noticed as he stared at her.

'What I mean is that it has been wrong of me,' Shirley added. 'To be influenced.'

Mr Cotton put his pen down. 'Be that as it may,' he said. 'I have never sought to unduly sway you.'

He had but she said, 'No.'

'You do know I imagine that this case will almost inevitably involve your word on behalf of Dylan Smith against Timothy Pool's.'

'Maybe.' Shirley knew that he was almost certainly right. The chances of any other service users coming forward to support Dylan were practically zero. When Timothy was on the ward, all the patients flinched. She'd seen them and passed by on the other side. But no more.

Shirley got to her feet. 'Well, if that's all . . .'

'Sadly it probably is,' he said. He was like a vulture again, hunched up in his chair.

'It gives me no pleasure to do this,' Shirley said. 'But it is part of my job.'

'I know,' he said. And then he smiled. 'But let's hope we can resolve this amicably, shall we?'

'I do hope so.'

'And so do I, Mrs Mayfield,' he said. His face looked strained again. 'For my part I would like to get my hospital back to normal again as soon as possible.'

But Shirley doubted whether that would happen. Not if she had anything to do with it.


If he was honest, even Leslie Baum's voice drove Lee Arnold mad. It was posh, obsequious, tetchy and slightly common all at the same time.

'I beg to differ, DI Arnold,' Leslie said as Lee tried to eat a sea-front hotdog while holding his phone to his ear, 'but I don't think you can have consulted the Land Registry.'

'Leslie, I did,' Lee said. 'It said that the property was purchased by Mr and Mrs K. Rivers.'

'And then purchased just six months ago by a Mr S. Warner. When did you look at the registry?'

'I dunno, a couple of weeks ago . . .'

'Maybe it did take them time to update their records. But I doubt it,' Leslie said. 'You really do have to be meticulous, DI Arnold.'

'Ken Rivers is still living in the flat.'

'Doesn't mean that he still owns it,' Leslie said.

Disgusted by the amount of grease on his hotdog onions, Lee threw what was left of it into a bin. The bloody awful slot-machine place he was walking past was playing an electronic version of 'Greensleeves' at him. Lee wanted whoever was in charge of that dead.

'Leslie, why were you looking at the Land Registry anyway?' he asked. 'I told you to investigate Rivers' finances.'

'And his property isn't part of his financial portfolio? DI Arnold, when I do a job, I do it properly or not at all. I'm the best there is at what I do, as Wolverine rather clunkily puts it.'

'I wanted to know about Rivers' bank account.'

'I'll get to that. But if he's splashing a lot of money about then it could be cash he's made from selling his flat to Mr Warner,' Leslie said.

There were schemes whereby people could sell their homes, still live in them and pay rent. Equity release. It was something that mainly elderly people did, usually to prop up a small pension. It was often dodgy and the person who released the equity in their home generally regretted it. But it was generally done by companies rather than individuals.

'Do you know who this S. Warner is?' Lee asked.

'No, but I can find out.'

Lee remembered the big bloke who had come to Ken Rivers for money that morning. Could he be S. Warner or was he just his muscle? Probably the latter. He'd asked about a girl called Cindy when he'd spoken to Ken – the girl with the old-style Mini and the baby. Was she a tenant of his too?

'OK, Leslie, I'm gonna leave it with you,' Lee said. 'Get back to me when you've got some junk on S. Warner.'

'I will consult with my colleagues,' Leslie said and then he hung up.

Lee had seen a few of Leslie's colleagues and wondered if they had actually been in his caravan, hiding in the bedrooms and stinking of spot cream, when he'd called. If they had, he had a nasty feeling they'd all been reading comics. He didn't really care. What was exercising Lee's mind was whether or not Ken Rivers had sold his flat and, if he had, whether he was using the money from the sale to gamble. It wasn't Lee's business but if it was the case, and Ken had his own money to burn, it could rule out any need for contact between father and son.. Maybe Ken and Phil really hadn't got on?

His phone rang again. Lee moved away from the slot-machine place. 'Hello?'

'Lee, Vi,' she rasped.

'Wotcha. How's it going in cut-throat land?'

'It could be better,' Vi said.

'Sorry. What can I do for you? Stick of Southend rock? Large sugar dummy on a ribbon?'

'Think I'll pass,' she said.

He heard her take a deep breath. It was something bad.

'What is it, Vi?'

'I think it's yer girlfriend,' she said.

'Susan? What do you mean? What's she done?'

'I think she's been calling me and then hanging up,' Vi said. 'Twice this morning, three times this afternoon. About an hour ago I called the number back. I thought it was some weird mistake. You know how it is with mobiles. But it went straight to voicemail. Told me to leave a message for Susan Castle. That's her surname, isn't it?'

Lee slumped against a wall. 'Yeah.'

'I mean I'm not saying it was definitely her but . . .'

Lee asked Vi to read out the phone number. It was Susan's.

'Did you leave her a message?' Lee said.

'Yeah, I asked her why she was calling me. I suggested she might have been given my number in error by somebody else.'

'That isn't likely, is it?'

'It's possible.'

'Yeah, but . . .'

He'd never given Susan Vi's number. Why would he? She'd made it clear that she didn't like her the first night they'd met and he'd been careful to make all his calls to Vi well away from Susan. She must've looked at his phone sometime when he was in the flat. A lot of people spied on their partners via their mobiles.

'I'm sorry, Vi,' he said.

'Not your fault, or even hers,' she said. 'Women get possessive.'

He knew that. What Susan was doing, though common, was fucked up. Phoning Vi and then just going silent on her was creepy.

'I'll have words,' Lee said.

'All right.' She paused for a moment and then she said, 'You feeling OK, are you?'

'Jaw's still sore and I've got some bruises the size of dinner plates on my belly. But I can't complain.'

Vi croaked a laugh and Lee could hear that in spite of her doctor's orders she was drawing on a fag.

When he got off the phone, Lee had some thinking to do. He liked Susan but if she was going to behave like a nutter around him he didn't want to know. To look at his phone, which she must've done, was a complete betrayal of his trust. At the same time, he was keen to go to the casino that night, so he'd have to keep her sweet for the time being. Ken Rivers had taken money out of his bank and Lee wanted to know what he was going to do with it. Lee hoped Ken didn't think that he could pay his rent from his winnings, but he strongly suspected that he did.

## 15

It was cold and windy and so Rashida clung tightly to MJ's side. Her friend was so fearless and confident, not even a gale could knock her down.

MJ drew on one of her mother's gold-collared menthol cigarettes. 'We have to get you out of there, Rashida,' she said. 'I've spoken to my mum. You can come and live with us.'

Much as she loved MJ and her mum, Rashida couldn't think of it. 'No, you'll all get into trouble and—'

'My brother's a barrister,' MJ said. 'He's the straightest man I know but he has his uses. Krish will sort it all out legally. Don't worry.'

'MJ, you've done enough already,' Rashida said. 'Now I'm back at school, I'll be OK.'

But she knew she was lying. MJ knew it too.

'Rash, don't be so silly,' she said. 'Your mum'll just wait until the Christmas holidays and then take you to the bastard in Cairo. You have to leave, girl. You have to get out of there and tell Social Services what your family have in mind for you. Come stay with us, eh?'

The Joshis had money. Rashida had been to their house (without her mother's knowledge) twice. They lived in a big modern place overlooking Wanstead Flats. MJ's late father had been a surgeon and had left the family a lot of assets and a big pension. Mrs Joshi spent it liberally – on her house, her two children and on herself. The first time she'd met Rashida she'd just had plastic surgery. 'A tummy tuck,' she'd said. 'Not for some man, you understand. I was simply sick of looking at what looked like a jelly at the top of my thighs.' Rashida had blushed. It had been bad enough that Mrs Joshi had greeted the girls wearing nothing but a short leopardskin kaftan and a pair of sky-high wedges, but details about her actual body had been too much. On the plus side, MJ's family were kind. Like her other friend Kerry's mum and dad and her numerous siblings, who lived in a stinking dump on the Barking Road, they were good people. That was all the more reason not to involve them.

'I can't,' Rashida said.

MJ sighed. 'So what will you do? Look, if it's like a Muslim thing, you can do whatever you want at our house. You can pray, you can cover, you don't have to be like me and Mum.'

'I know.'

Rashida felt bad. Mrs Joshi and MJ were great but the way they lived was not her way and she was nervous about it. What if MJ's brother turned up one day when she was alone in the house? What if Mrs Joshi had a man round? Rashida knew that she did from time to time because MJ had told her. Weirdly, she'd been all for it. 'Mummy's an attractive woman,' she'd said. 'Why should she spend the rest of her life mourning Daddy? He's gone.'

Somewhere, she couldn't remember in what book, Rashida had read that Hindu women threw themselves on their dead husbands' funeral pyres. But maybe that had been a long time ago? She'd certainly not heard of it happening since she'd been in London and Mrs Joshi clearly hadn't done that.

They arrived at the end of Rashida's road. In a lot of ways, MJ was like a boy. She even sometimes walked her friends home. She put her hands on Rashida's shoulders. 'Look, just think about it,' she said. 'You and me together, we got you back to school.'

'You did.'

'We both did,' MJ said. 'Don't throw it all away, Rash.'

MJ kissed Rashida on both cheeks, which always made her feel uncomfortable. But she smiled.

'See you tomorrow,' MJ said and then she ran off back the way they'd come. Rashida watched her as she disappeared into the distance behind a cloud of menthol cigarette smoke.


'This is my Uncle Bob,' the boy said as he pushed the middle-aged man across the threshold of Leslie Baum's caravan.

Leslie viewed the man, who stank of cigarettes and was clearly terrified, with suspicion. He knew the boy, who called himself 'Gollum' after the character from the Lord of the Rings trilogy, but Uncle Bob was new to him.

'What are you doing?' Leslie asked.

The boy pushed the man down into the old deckchair Leslie had left out since Lee Arnold's visit and said, 'Just sit there, I'll sort it.'

Leslie wasn't good at children's ages but he reckoned that Gollum was probably about fifteen. He still wore school uniform – Southend High School for Boys – but he'd grown a lot since they'd first met three years before. Gollum, for all his youth, was man-sized. He was also one of Leslie's many informants.

Unnerved by the presence of another middle-aged man in his caravan, Leslie looked at his computer screen and said, 'What is it, Gollum? Why have you brought your uncle . . . whoever he is?'

'Bob.'

'Yes?' the other man said. Then he looked at the boy. 'What's going on, Pat? Who's Gollum?'

'Pat?'

Gollum whispered to Leslie, 'Sorry. He's a bit, you know, mental.'

Leslie flinched away from the boy. 'What do you want?'

Gollum took his phone out of his pocket. 'You texted,' he said. 'Information about an S. Warner? Might be a bit dodgy?'

Leslie always contacted his many acolytes when he had some sort of job or investigation in hand. Sometimes it concerned the secret rulers of the world, sometimes it was about alien abduction, and on a few occasions it was a favour for DI Lee Arnold.

'Do you know an S. Warner?'

'No, but Uncle Bob does.' He looked at Bob and smiled. 'Don't you?'

'Shane Warner? He's a nutter,' Bob said. 'Don't wanna have nothing to do with him.'

Leslie turned to look at this Bob who, now he came to regard him properly, did look a lot like some of the 'mentals' he'd come across in prison.

'He's your real uncle?' Leslie asked Gollum.

'Dad's brother,' Gollum said. 'Bob, tell Spider-Man what you told me about Shane Warner.'

Bob flinched. 'Spider-Man? Where's Spider-Man? What you talking about, Patrick?'

The boy shook his head impatiently. 'Sorry,' he said to Leslie. Then he turned to Bob. 'Look, I told you we all have other names. I'm Gollum and he's Spider-Man.'

'Why?'

'Why what?'

'Why do you have other names?' Bob said. 'What's this? Some

sort of paedo ring or something? You don't want to get into nothing like that, Pat, it's sick. There's blokes over Shoebury way they say have them interests . . .'

'Bob, we're not paedos,' Gollum said. 'I brought you here to tell Spider-Man what you know about Shane Warner. Remember?'

Bob looked as if he was thinking hard for a few moments and then he said, 'What, my Shane Warner?'

'Yes. Tell Spider-Man about him.'

'He buys things,' Bob said.

Leslie frowned. 'What things?'

'Anything. Cars, women, hooky booze, property, drugs. Mainly drugs. He helps out people in trouble,' Bob said. 'He's helped me out.'

'At a price?'

'Always at a price,' Bob said.

'So who is he, this Shane Warner?' Leslie asked. 'Do you know where he lives?'

'No,' Bob said. 'He used to come in a big posh car but he sends his blokes to do business now. I ain't seen him for a long time.'

'What "business" did you have with this man?'

Bob put his head down.

Gollum got close to Leslie again and whispered, 'This bloke or his people used to buy drugs from Bob. Psychiatric stuff . . .'

'Largactil,' Bob said. 'I got fags and packets of biscuits with the cash.'

'We didn't know he was doing it for years,' Gollum said. 'Then he lost it and ended up back in hospital. The doctor said that you hadn't been taking your medication, didn't he, Bob?'

'Yeah.'

'But if he doesn't . . . ?' Leslie asked.

'I can't get by,' Bob said. 'There's bills and rent and food and fags and everything. Some people like to take medication and they'll pay for it. Or they used to. Shane Warner.'

'So he's a drug dealer?'

'Yes,' Gollum said.

But Bob said, 'No. He used to buy meds. Not now. But he owns a lot of property from York Road down to the seafront.'

'York Road, Southend? The red-light district?'

Bob said, 'Yeah. I live there.'

'He's got a bedsit,' Gollum said.

'So this medication . . . ?'

'Largactil? I have to take it,' Bob said.

'He's got schizophrenia,' Gollum told him..

'So they say.'

Leslie looked at Bob and Bob looked away. The 'mentals' used to sell their meds when he was inside. The heavy stuff, the medicine he imagined schizophrenics would take, zoned people out and made the time pass more quickly. There was a market for it on the outside too.

'Did or does Shane Warner deal in non-prescription drugs too?'

'What like dope and coke?'

'Yes.'

'Yeah. He does everything,' Bob said. ''cept not prescription meds any more. Don't buy them now. So they say.'

'Why not?'

'Dunno.'

'Is he your landlord?' Leslie asked.

'No,' Bob told him. 'But he owns a lot round my way. His blokes go round collecting rent. They're all massive.'

'And Shane? Is he massive?'

Bob shook his head. 'Nah. Tiny he is. Sort of pale and he's got thin hair and he's skinny. He's got a mean face. Know what I'm saying?'

'No.'

'It's sort of caved in on itself and the chin's pointed,' Bob said. 'Like a rat. But he's always surrounded by pretty women. He's got money. Money talks.'

Leslie didn't like Bob. He didn't like anybody if he was honest. Emotion was a place he didn't go. But there were times when he wished he could do something to put a stop to some of the horrific abuse that took place in the world. He'd tried to destroy the Genome Project because he knew that people would only mess with it and make it a bad thing – which they had. Higher intelligence, like Leslie's, was required to control such things. With drugs, vast minders and possibly violence involved, this Shane Warner thing was clearly a job that only a superhero could do. He'd have to tell Lee Arnold to back off. Only a Man of Steel could take this job forward.

While she'd been getting ready to go to work, Susan had kept glancing at her phone. Now she was at the roulette wheel she seemed to have forgotten about it. Lee was seeing her through fresh eyes since his conversation with Vi. There was no doubt that Susan had called her because he had recognized her number. But why had she done it? Why had she stolen Vi's number from Lee's phone? He knew that women could be jealous but he hadn't thought that Susan was capable of being quite that jealous.

Vi could occasionally be a pain with her demands on his body. But he understood Vi. He wasn't sure he understood Susan. Did Susan want a live-in lover, or even a husband? She had made a point of asking him if he ever wanted to move out of London. Did that really mean anything?

The more Lee looked at Susan the more he fancied her. She was voluptuous and very dirty in bed. What wasn't to like? Well, except that possessiveness allied to a clear propensity to involve herself in his private stuff. Lee drank his Diet Pepsi and wondered when and if Ken Rivers was going to put in an appearance. That afternoon he'd received a call from an old informant about the primary focus of his investigation, Phil Rivers. The snout, who lived in Manor Park, claimed to have seen Phil on the Romford Road buying fruit and veg from some Turkish mini-mart. Lee really needed to check that out, although quite what Phil would be doing back in the East End he couldn't imagine. Surely too many people still knew him there?

Lee finished his drink, put his glass on a table and reached for his fags. Just in time he remembered he couldn't smoke inside anywhere that was a public place any more and put the cigarettes away.

Then he heard Susan say, 'Good evening, Kenny, nice to see you.'

Ken Rivers' now familiar voice replied, 'Good evening to you too, Susan. Let's see what Lady Luck can do for me this evening, shall we?'

Lee turned his face away and moved into the shadows at the edge of the room.

The door to his room opened and then closed again. Dylan pretended to sleep. If it was Harman it was best to let him do what he needed to. After all, he never touched him. But Dylan curled into a foetal position, his back to the wall, just in case. There was a pause and then, to his horror, fingers wound themselves around the back of his neck. Dylan tried to speak but first something was stuffed into his mouth and then a hood was pulled roughly over his head.

Fuck! What was this? Had Harman tired of wanking and wanted to go further? But then he remembered that Harman was fat – and weak. A strong, bony fist punched him once in the stomach and all the breath in Dylan's body disappeared. Before he had time to recover, a second blow, a rabbit punch to the kidneys, made him want to cry out in pain, but his voice wouldn't work.

The blows kept coming, in silence. Breathing was almost impossible. Dylan skirted around the edge of consciousness. His head was full of light that sparkled brightly every time he was hit and there was a smell of piss he knew was his. But he noticed something else too, something more important. Only his torso was taking a pounding. Whoever was thumping him didn't want his bruises to show and there was some comfort in that, because it meant that his attacker didn't mean to kill him.

This was a warning and, in spite of feeling as if he was about to pass out, Dylan had taken note.

As quickly as the assault had started, so it stopped. One final, deep, thrusting blow to the ribs then nothing. But Dylan couldn't move. He could barely breathe. Liquid bubbled out of his nose. It tasted salty and metallic. He didn't hear anyone leave, but as he pulled the blood-soaked pillowcase off his head he heard first what he thought was a sob and then the sound of his door closing.

Dylan switched on his bedside lamp and saw his blood- and saliva-soaked T-shirt. He knew he'd have to look at the damage inflicted on his skinny body sometime, but took a few moments to prepare himself. There were still a few oxygen starvation lights going off in his head and his hands were too shaky to do much. Eventually, Dylan sat up. Then, when he felt able to, he lifted up his t-shirt. The flesh on his belly was every shade of purple from almost black to pale violet. When he moved it hurt so much he wanted his attacker to come back and kill him. Dylan let his T-shirt drop again. If he thought about what damage might have been done inside his body he couldn't handle it and so he made himself think about who might have done it. Timothy Pool was not on shift and he had fingers like wanker Harman's, thick and fleshy, not bony like his attacker. But it had been a message from him, albeit delivered by an unknown fist. Mrs Mayfield, the advocate, was finally taking Dylan seriously and Tim couldn't do much about her. But he could nobble Dylan. And he had. How could he go on with his complaint if this was where it was going to lead? He couldn't call for a doctor because no one would listen. For all Dylan knew he could be dying already. Suddenly he was frozen again – in terror.

Then a sound from outside his door gave him hope. It was a single sob again, just like the one he'd heard before his door closed.

'Can I buy you a drink?'

Ken Rivers looked up into Lee Arnold's face and said, 'You.'

'Yes, and in answer to your next question,' Lee said, 'I have been following you. Now, Ken, what's your poison?'

Slumped on a bar stool in his best suit, his bow-tie hanging off at an angle, Ken Rivers looked like a caricature of a gambler who had just lost his metaphorical shirt.

'I'll have a Scotch, double,' he said.

Lee caught the barman's eye and ordered. Back on the casino floor, life had returned to normal after Ken's big loss. All the bullet-headed men and perma-tanned women had moved on.

'Here you go.' Lee put the whisky in front of Ken and then paid the barman. Ken Rivers drank most of it down in one.

'I told you I don't know where Phil is,' he said. 'Why you still following me?'

'Because you could have been telling me porkies,' Lee said. 'And because I'm curious how a bloke like you can keep on coming here and losing.'

He'd lost three thousand pounds in the space of two hours and, this time, his customary *joie de vivre* appeared to have deserted him. Still working at the roulette wheel, Susan looked over from time to time, frowning, but Lee ignored her.

Lee moved in closer to the old man and whispered. 'Your son got away with one point two million quid, Ken. You're a bright man, you can see where I'm going with this.'

The bar was made of some sort of dark granite and the lighting was low but Lee could see the old man's face reflected in the highly polished surface and it wasn't amused.

'If I knew where the bastard was then don't you think I'd be tapping him up?' He finished his whisky and then ordered another one. He didn't offer Lee a drink. 'That's just about cleaned me out,' he said.

'So why'd you do it?'

For a moment Lee thought that he was going to throw Scotch in his face, but Ken Rivers just turned his nose up. 'Know what it's like to look after a person with dementia, do you?' he said. 'She started going funny in the head almost as soon as we left London.'

'Your wife?'

'Yeah.'

'So you gamble to take your mind off your troubles?'

He didn't answer.

Lee said, 'If you didn't get the money from Phil then where did you get it?'

'Mind your own business.'

Lee brought Leslie Baum's latest email up on his phone and said, 'Not from the sale of your flat to Shane Warner then?'

The old man drank the rest of his whisky.

'I know Warner owns it,' Lee said.

'Then why ask?'

'And I know he's also a drug dealer and a thug. I saw his gorilla round your place, rent collecting. Did the girl upstairs sell her flat to Warner too?'

Still he kept silent.

'What was the plan then, Ken?' Lee said. 'Bring your three grand here and win a bucketload so rent's not an issue for a bit and you can carry on gambling? As plans go, I have to say it's not one of the best I've heard. I've seen you lose before, Ken, and you lose big.'

Ken, his head down, said, 'She always said I was a Jonah.'

'Your wife?'

'Said I couldn't win a game of Snakes and Ladders and she was right.'

'So why'd you do it then, Ken?'

Over at the craps table there was a roar of triumph.

'Look, I told you I ain't seen Phil and I ain't,' he said. 'I never got no money from him. If I could've I would've done. Now I'm buggered. Leave me alone.'

Ken Rivers wasn't a likeable man, but that didn't mean that Lee couldn't feel sorry for him. And his wife, wherever she was.

'I want to help . . .'

'You got the three grand I lost tonight? The four I lost last week?'

Lee said nothing.

'No, I thought not.'

He made as if to get down from his stool but Lee stopped him. 'Ken, before I was a PI I was a copper, Forest Gate. I know you know the manor.'

'So what?'

'So if I'm right and you've just lost all your cash then you could be out on the street. What does Warner charge you in rent, eh? Five hundred a month? Six?'

'Five-fifty. I've got me pension, the wife's . . .'

'Can't be a lot.'

'It'd be enough if . . .'

'If?'

Ken Rivers shrugged.

'You owe Warner more'n just your rent, don't you?'

There was a long pause before the old man said, 'They say gambling's a disease, don't they?'

'Ken, you need to tell someone everything,' Lee said. 'And that might as well be me.'

'You won't like it.'

'Doesn't matter what I think.'

He sighed. 'All right,' he said. 'But not here.'

'Where?'

He thought for a moment and then he said, 'We can go to my place.'

# 16

Mumtaz had been fretting about Naz Sheikh all day. Ever since Amy had reminded her that the gangster had come to her office, she'd been trying to think of ways she could stop him doing it again. But she had nothing to threaten Naz with. Not really. So she phoned him. It was late and she hoped he was either in bed or in some club, drinking and womanising while his father and his brother weren't looking.

'Ah, Mrs Hakim,' he said when he answered. 'What can I do for you?'

'If you ever come to my office again I will find a way to kill you,' she said.

He laughed. She'd expected him to.

'If you think I won't serve time in prison for you, then you're wrong,' she said.

He laughed even harder. 'You know, I can remember your late husband making similar threats,' he said. 'I don't think I have to remind you how that ended.'

What she said next, she said because it was true. And because she couldn't stop herself. 'I won't have any money once the house is sold. Your extra "fees" will effectively kill me.'

There was a pause. She wondered whether she should check

the front and back doors. Shazia was in the house and what she'd blurted out, in anger, could have put her at risk. It was always Shazia that they threatened. She expected more of the same and at first she thought that was what she was getting.

'Well, if you can't pay, there are other ways,' he said.

'Touch my daughter and you're dead,' she said.

'Who said anything about Shazia?'

Mumtaz cringed. She hated it when he used her daughter's name.

'We've been thinking. It occurs to us that there is another way you can pay part of your debt to us without involving the girl.'

She imagined herself spread-eagled on a bed waiting for Naz, his brother and his foul father to take turns raping her. Better her than Shazia.

'When you've moved, we'll talk,' he said.

'Will we?'

'I think it will be to your advantage,' Naz said. 'You see, Mrs Hakim, our business is growing and, although we have a lot of friends in all sorts of places you probably couldn't imagine, we always need more.'

'I'm not about to become your friend. Forget it.'

He laughed again. 'Oh, I'm not about to invite you over for tea, Mumtaz. But there are ways in which people can be friends that don't involve being sociable. Friends do things for each other, you know?'

He wanted something. Whether it involved her body or not, Mumtaz wasn't sure. But whatever it was had to be unpleasant because it was Naz.

She said, 'Don't involve Shazia and don't come to my office again. Or hang out round my home.'

'If you agree to talk about my proposition, I can do that,' he said. 'You know we're not animals, Mumtaz. We understand that you're in a very unfortunate position, partly of your own making, but you know, as fellow Muslims—'

'Oh, spare me the lecture about the value of the umma,' she snapped. 'You don't care who you extort money from.'

There was a pause. She heard him suck on his shisha and then he said, 'But aren't you forgetting something, Mrs Hakim?'

'What?'

'Your husband was a bad man,' he said. 'That was why he met an untimely end. That was why, if you remember, you failed to give the police any sort of useful description of the man who ended Ahmet's life. I don't think that sometimes you remember the very great debt you have to us. A debt that goes far beyond mere money.'

And then he cut the connection. Mumtaz closed her eyes. Every day, in her mind, she saw Ahmet fall and bleed out on the rough ground of Wanstead Flats. She saw Naz, his silver trainers shining in the dying evening light, running away from them. And she still, sometimes, saw her husband's blood all over her hands as she tried, too late, to call 999 on her mobile phone.

It was a typical converted Edwardian house. The grand front door led into a small hall with two scruffy chipboard doors, one leading upstairs and one into Ken Rivers' flat. There was a bit of dirty old rug on the floor and an overwhelming smell of damp. It was nothing that Lee Arnold hadn't been expecting.

The old man opened the door into his flat and switched on the light. 'It's a bit of a mess,' he said.

He wasn't wrong. If Lee had to sum up the hallway, he would

have used the word 'dingy'. Narrow and dominated by the colour brown (walls, heavily stuffed wooden furniture), it looked like the sort of place TV companies made misery documentaries about. Ken Rivers led the way.

'You'll have to excuse the state of the place,' he said. 'Since she went doolally it's been hard keeping on top of it all.'

Lee felt his shoes stick to the hall carpet. His stomach turned. Old as he was, hard up as he was, even Ken was capable, surely, of scrubbing an old carpet with a bit of washing-up liquid. Other smells mingled with the damp – some organic, others less easy to place. Ken was effectively a man on his own so anything was possible. Lee knew where he was coming from. After his divorce, when he'd existed on booze and painkillers, his flat had been a shithole.

'I'll make a cuppa if you like.' Ken pointed at a door. 'Go in and make yourself comfortable.'

The door handle was greasy. Of course it was.

'Switch the light on,' Ken said. 'On your right.'

He found it. That was greasy too and, oddly, it had a group of flies round it.

The lightbulb was one of those energy-saving things and so it took a while for Lee to be able to see what he was looking at properly. But even straight off he could tell that it wasn't a sitting room. There was a dressing table, a linen basket and, most significantly, a massive brass bedstead right in the middle of what was not a very big space.

He turned. 'Ken . . .'

There was just one blow, but it was to his head and it was hard. Lee Arnold hit the deck, smashing his face against brass as he fell.

*

'Help me.'

Dylan's voice was a ghost. It hung in the air for a moment and then disappeared. No one would be able to hear him. But he kept on saying it because he was in pain. A shot of morphine or even a couple of old school DF118s would do it. He didn't want a doctor. None of them would help him.

He looked at the clock on the wall. They'd taken his bedside clock away because he'd tried to cut up with the hands. Fucking bastards. Said they didn't want him to die, but they were happy to make his life hell. Didn't they realize that he didn't want to die either? The cutting wasn't about that. It was all a game. In reality they didn't give a shit about him. But if he died they'd have to answer questions and maybe even take some responsibility and that was all too much hassle.

The clock on the wall, so high up you needed a ladder to reach it, said three thirty-two. A long way to go until morning. But then what did morning bring that was so good? Tim Pool on duty and tea that tasted like gravy.

'Help me.'

Tim Pool. He'd watched him for tells. He had a bunch. When he felt he'd got one over on you he puffed his chest out like a pigeon and tapped his forefingers and thumbs together. When he liked someone he dragged his fingers through his hair. Happiness was a foot twirl and when he was frustrated he clicked his tongue against his teeth. Good job he never played poker.

'Help me.'

The left side hurt more than the right. He was sure he had at least one broken rib. Earlier on he'd wondered who had worked him over, but he knew he wouldn't find out. One hard, bony fist was all he'd seen. The only thing he *knew* was who had sent it.

And the only thing he had to work out was whether or not he was going to give in to the threat.

His door opened. Instinctively, Dylan pulled his bedclothes up to his chin. At the end of the corridor, somebody yelled out 'Di!' It was Yates, calling to the wife he'd murdered twenty years ago. Eaten up with remorse, he did it every night.

Because the bedside lamp was on, Dylan could see the woman who came into his room. Small and blonde, she ran over to his bed and put something in his hands. 'Co-dyramol,' she said. 'You must be in pain.'

Dylan had never seen her before but he took the tablets.

The woman hurried back to the door. Before she left she said, 'What they did to you was wrong.' And then she was gone.

Dylan, on reflection, didn't care who she was or what she'd said. He just waited for the drugs to kick in. Then, finally, he went to sleep.

Susan was furious. Lee had sodded off and left her. Two-thirty the casino had closed and he'd just abandoned her with no transport. She'd had to get a lift with Dale and listen to him droning on about his body-building regimen all the way home. He'd also told her that he'd seen Lee leaving with that Kenny who'd lost big.

When Lee had first started asking her about high rollers, Susan had wondered whether he was investigating someone at the casino or even the establishment itself. Was he private detecting – whatever they called it – old Kenny? Or had the two of them simply gone on somewhere else for a drink? But then, Lee didn't drink.

Susan looked at Lee's coat on the end of her bed and went through his pockets. She didn't know what she was looking for, she just felt spiteful. She found a packet of fags. The bastard. Then Susan remembered the last time she'd been in Lee's pockets and she felt guilty. She'd called that rough copper woman more than once but she'd never had the courage to speak to her. Then the woman had left a message on her phone. Had she tumbled who she was? Had she connected her to Lee? Did he know about it?

If he knew she'd called the old bird, he would be angry. He was mild and thoughtful and all those other things she'd been so attracted to, but he was also a bloke. A bloke who had women around him. Not just the old boiler but also that Mumtaz, too – not that she was any sort of threat. Those covered-up Muslim women were like nuns, except when they blew themselves up in Iraq.

What she called 'normal' Susan, didn't like 'jealous psycho' Susan. But she had to live with her. There was no getting rid of her. Whenever she started a new relationship, up she popped like the proverbial. And even though part of Susan's mind was occupied with worrying about whether Lee might be safe, jealous psycho Susan was wondering who he was with and what he was doing to her.

He knew this. He'd had it enough times. What he'd never had before was a KO that gave him hallucinations. Lee looked at the bluebottle flies on his arms and they seemed to look back at him. That was madness.

As he sat up, the room moved away and then tipped sideways. But it was OK because it was only concussion and it would soon pass. But there was a smell that was turning his stomach. It was familiar and not in a good way. Panic added to concussion was not a good mixture and so, in spite of the foul miasma that engulfed him, Lee took a few seconds to breathe. Something was rotting in that room and, in spite of the fact that he felt he knew what it was, he ran through a whole gamut of possibilities that included dogs, cats and even goats. When he'd first become a copper he'd found the mummified body of a dead goat under the floor of an old widow's house in East Ham. It was possible.

What he needed was fresh air. He knew he couldn't stand up in case he fell, so Lee shuffled over to the door on his knees. He put his hand on the doorknob and turned. Nothing. Several dozen bluebottles landed on his arm. He was locked in.

He cleared his throat. 'Ken.'

It was a weak cry and so he tried again, 'Ken!'

He waited but nothing except silence came from beyond the door. He looked back into the room. Then his face started to hurt and he put a hand up to it. Blood. He checked inside his mouth for broken teeth but couldn't find anything obvious. There was a lump in the bed, as if it was occupied. Was Ken's 'old woman' asleep in this disgusting room? Or was it someone else? Was someone dead in there?

Lee kind of knew the answer to that. But he distracted himself by looking for his phone. When he found it, over by the dressing table, he saw that it was smashed. So he was locked in this room with God knew what and his phone was fucked. Great.

'Ken Rivers, you shit!' he yelled.

The sickness came on him suddenly and the next thing Lee knew he was looking at a puddle of stale Pepsi on a carpet with a pattern that made your eyes cross. Exhausted, he let himself lie down although the floor was filthy.

It was then that he saw the hand hanging out of the far side of the bed. It was very white and it was moving.

## 17

'He doesn't want to see you,' the ward manager said.

Shirley had experienced Timothy Pool's smug face many times before.

'I'll be the judge of that,' she said. 'He in his room?'

She tried to walk past him but he shot an arm out and barred her path.

'He won't see you. He told me.'

'Nurse Pool, if you stop me going about my business I'll report you to the hospital management,' she said.

For a moment they locked eyes. He knew something she didn't.

He clicked his tongue against his teeth, slowly moved his arm out of her path and said, 'You know where he is. He's laying down.'

She walked past him and made for the corridor. Most of the bedroom doors were open for cleaning. But one was closed. She knocked on it. 'Dylan? It's Shirley. Are you in there?'

A service user she knew a little, a man convicted of stalking, walked past her, rolling a cigarette with one hand. That was quite a skill.

'Dylan?' She knocked again.

'Leave me alone,' he said.

Every alarm in Shirley's head went off. He sounded broken and that wasn't Dylan.

'We need to talk about your complaint,' Shirley said. 'We have to get it written up.'

'I'm not going to go ahead with it.'

Shirley opened the door. Dylan was lying on his bed holding his stomach. His face was grey.

'I didn't say you could come in here!' he said. 'Fuck off!'

'What's happened to you?' Shirley walked towards him. 'Dylan . . .'

He cringed away from her. 'I changed me mind.'

She knew why. She'd seen it all before. Patient makes a complaint, patient is beaten up and/or intimidated, patient withdraws the complaint. From the look of him, someone had given him a good kicking where it wouldn't show.

'You should go,' he said. 'You can't do no good here.'

'Dylan, did someone . . . ?'

'I'm fine!'

She looked into his eyes, which were bloodshot and close to tears. Things were supposed to change. Dylan was going to be the patient who made up for all those others she'd fobbed off in the past. Was that selfish of her? It was but if it got the job done then who really cared?

Shirley said, 'Dylan, you can't give in to intimidation.'

'Who said anything about intimidation? I've just changed me mind.'

He tried to reach a glass of water that was on his bedside table but she had to help him. As he took it from her, Shirley caught a glimpse of the bruising to his chest.

'God almighty, Dylan, who did that to you?'

He drank. 'Did what?' he said. 'I'm all right. What makes you think I'm not?'

'Bruises,' Shirley said. 'On your chest. Dylan, if this is . . .'

'Yates done it,' Dylan said. 'He wanted me to have sex with him and I had to fight him off. I'm no poof.'

'Did you—'

'Look, Yates battered me but I ain't a grass so let's leave it at that,' he said.

'But if Yates beat you up that's got nothing to do with your complaint against Nurse Pool.'

'I know. I changed me mind about that, like I told you.'

'Why?'

'Can't be arsed.'

She was sure he was lying, but what could she do? Maybe Yates, who was known for his over-sexualised behaviour, *had* tried to assault Dylan. But maybe he hadn't. Most likely he hadn't.

'Dylan,' she said, 'if you don't stand up to people they will walk all over you.'

'Oh, and since when did you give a shit?' he said. 'You think I really thought you was gonna go for Tim Pool?'

'You asked me . . .'

'You're a pussy,' he said. 'Everybody knows the Advocacy don't do nothing but do whatever the hospital wants. It's a joke, man.'

Shirley was hurt but Dylan wasn't saying anything she didn't know. 'That's how it was, Dylan,' she said. 'I know. But that's not how it's going to be.'

'What do you mean?'

She shrugged. 'I'm taking them on,' she said. 'It's my job and somebody has to. I was a coward in the past but I've had a bit of a Road to Damascus moment.'

He looked at her and frowned.

'I've realized that what I was doing was wrong,' she said. 'I mean to help you, Dylan, I do.'

For a moment he looked as if he was thinking about it but then he said, 'Nah, don't think so.'

When Shirley left the ward she fancied that she heard someone laugh behind her back. She kept on walking.

Ken and Bette Rivers' living room was not much better than the bedroom in terms of clutter. But at least it didn't reek and there wasn't a dead body in there – as far as Lee could tell.

A WPC called Wren gave him a cup of tea. 'You know, you should really go to the hospital, Mr Arnold,' she said. 'Just so that they can check you out.'

'Oh God, I've spent far too much time in those places recently,' Lee said. 'I'll pass.'

To get checked out would be sensible but it wasn't for him. Not this time.

A tall, thin man of about fifty came into the living room. For a moment he looked at all the dusty dolls that sat on the filthy mantelpiece and then he said, 'Mr Arnold, I'm Detective Inspector Cobbett, Southend CID. All right if we have a chat?'

'As long as you don't mind if I smoke,' Lee said.

Cobbett shrugged. 'Knock yourself out.'

The policeman asked Lee how he'd come to be in the flat and Lee told him everything – who he was, what he was doing and why. He'd eventually managed to break the bedroom door down in the early hours of the morning, waking the girl upstairs. Ken Rivers was long gone by that time. Lee had just been grateful to get out of that room. Then the coppers had turned up. They'd offered to take him to hospital several times but all he'd wanted to do was talk to whoever was in charge.

'From your knowledge of him, do you have any idea where Mr Rivers might have gone?' Cobbett asked.

'No,' Lee said. 'Like I told you, I'm looking for his son Phil, on behalf of Phil's missus. I've yet to follow up on a supposed sighting in Manor Park but that's nothing more than just a rumour at this point. The family originally came from North Woolwich and Phil used to work for an old car thief and clocker called Brian Barber. He also had an affair with Brian's son Barry, years ago.'

'Did this Phil's missus know he was gay?'

'No,' Lee said. 'And I don't know whether his old man did either. I never got around to asking him. Ken denied that he was in contact with his son but he could've been lying. He's either buggered off because I was getting too close to Phil, because of his debts, or possibly because he killed the old woman . . .'

'We don't know who that corpse is at the moment, Mr Arnold,' Cobbett said.

'Yeah, right.' His stomach turned.

'But the deceased has been dead some time,' he said. 'Are you sure you don't want medical—'

'No. But I do want to give you my statement while it's fresh in my mind,' Lee said quickly. 'And I will need to call my assistant.'

'That's OK, we can arrange that.'

'The SIM in my phone is undamaged, so all I have to do is get a new handset,' he said.

'Use my phone for now.' He handed Lee a smartphone.

'Will you need me to stick around?' Lee asked as he dialled his own office number into the handset.

'You're not leaving the country, are you?'

'No.'

'Then you can probably go back to the Smoke tomorrow,' Cobbett said. 'You'll have to make yourself available . . .'

'Sure.' And then Mumtaz answered. 'Hiya,' he said. 'It's me. You know that old saying about lightning not striking twice? Well, guess what . . .'

Her mother threw the telephone at its stand. It missed and hit the floor. Being careful not to meet her mother's eyes, Rashida picked it up and carefully replaced it.

'That private detective woman is always on another call!' Salwa yelled. She was getting the younger children ready for school, pulling Zizi's hair into a ponytail so tight it made her cheeks red. Rashida knew that once she was put in charge of her two brothers and her sister she'd loosen that elastic band, which would hopefully let Zizi continue her day in comfort. Her mother was always like this when she was angry. Spiteful.

'Why all these Pakistani women round here say she's good, I don't know,' Salwa continued. 'Maybe they just tell me that because I'm outsider and they want to laugh at me, eh? Foreigners! That Polish man in the shop that sells all those disgusting sausages made of pig, he tries to cheat me if I have to go in there to get milk. Everyone is cheating us! Because they think bad things about your father . . .'

'Not everyone knows who we are, Omy,' Rashida said.

'Then why do they all try to cheat us? Eh?'

'They don't.'

Salwa finished fiddling with Zizi's hair and pushed her away. 'Get your coat on.' She said to Rashida, 'So it's me being stupid, is it?'

'No, but—'

'But what? Eh? Rashida, don't make excuses for these foreigners. You do it too much these days. I've seen you with that white girl and that Indian.'

Rashida put her head down.

'The one wears an instrument of death around her neck while the other worships demons in the shape of elephants and women with a hundred arms.'

Kerry did wear a cross on a chain around her neck, true, and MJ was Hindu, but hardly the most devout Hindu in the world. And even if she had been, that would not have changed the way that Rashida felt about her. She'd been able to turn to MJ and ask her for help when she'd had nobody else and was all out of hope. That particular 'foreigner' had come through. But she knew better than to challenge her mother over it. It was obvious that Salwa already felt that the girls were too close. And of course she did have a point. Kerry and MJ did worship idols and false gods; they were infidels. But did that make them bad? Rashida knew that on the one hand they had to be beyond the pale but on the other, they were probably the kindest girls she'd ever met.

'Now take these children to school while I try to ring that detective again,' Salwa said. She walked towards the phone. 'If I am left with my sanity today it will truly be one of Allah's greatest miracles!'

Rashida met her brothers and her sister in the hall. They looked up at her for some sort of reassurance. It had been one of 'those' mornings for all of them. Their Omy could be such hard work.

'Come on, you lot,' Rashida said. 'Let's get out of here.'

*

Shirley at the Advocacy wanted to see her as soon as was convenient and Salwa el Shamy was all for cancelling her contract,
judging by the answerphone messages she'd left. But all that
Mumtaz could think about was Lee – and Naz Sheikh.

Lee had been hit on the head, again, although this time by a
known person. The father of the man he was trying to find. And
then he'd found himself locked in a room with a corpse. As Lee
had told her, there was more to the massive fraud perpetrated by
Phil Rivers than met the eye. He just didn't know what it
was – yet.

Ever since she'd spoken to Naz Sheikh in the middle of the
night, Mumtaz had been fretting about what he'd meant. On
the one hand, some way of paying him off without using money
was intriguing, while on the other, it was terrifying. If he didn't
want money, what did he want? Usually he talked about Shazia
when money became an issue for her, but this time he hadn't.
Trying to second-guess what was in Naz's mind was impossible,
but Mumtaz gave it a go anyway. What had all that stuff about
being a 'friend' meant? Her life sometimes, she thought, felt like
a Bollywood version of *The Godfather*.

The office phone rang again.

'Arnold Agency. How can I help you?'

'Mumtaz, it's Tony Bracci.' He sounded breathless. 'I've just
had a phone call from Lee.'

'Oh, so you know . . .'

'What the fuck – 'scuse me – what the hell is he doing?'

'It's his missing person case, DS Bracci,' she said.

'This geezer whose missus don't want the law involved?'

'Yes.'

'Well, sounds as if the law's going to have to get involved if he
keeps on getting thumped on the head,' he said.

'Southend police have to investigate the family now a body has been found in the flat where Lee was attacked,' Mumtaz said.

'Do they know who it is?'

'Not yet, although Lee suspects very strongly that it was the old man's wife. She had dementia . . .'

'And he killed her?'

'I don't know, DS Bracci. Lee is hoping to be back tomorrow and so maybe you can ask him then.'

She knew that Tony was staying at Lee's flat and she knew why but Mumtaz just said, 'Are you all right for food for Chronus, DS Bracci?'

'Oh, er, yes, you know I'm, um . . .'

'Very kindly looking after Lee's baby, yes,' she said. 'If I wasn't moving I would have brought him to my house and taken care of him. But it's so chaotic . . .'

'He's fine here, at Lee's, you know.'

'Yes.' She looked at her watch. If she was going to get to Ilford Hospital in time for the meeting Shirley had asked her to, she'd have to get a move on. 'I'm sorry, I have to go.'

'That's OK. See you soon, Mumtaz.'

'Yes, and if I hear anything else, I will call you.' Then, just before she ended the call she said, 'Oh, and how is DI Collins now? Is she any better?'

She heard him sigh. 'Well, her voice is getting stronger, sadly, and she can eat now. But she's also, well, she seems a bit down. Know what I mean?'

Mumtaz picked her bag up from her desk. 'Could be post-operative depression,' she said. 'That can sometimes set in after surgery.'

'Could be. I dunno. Maybe she just needs another woman to talk to. It's all men in the guv's life, you know.'

Mumtaz smiled. Vi Collins was really a man's woman and she couldn't imagine her either wanting or needing a heart to heart with another female but she said, 'I'll go and see her, DS Bracci. Maybe she'll open up to me.'

'Be great if you could, Mumtaz, thanks,' he said.

There was a note of desperation in his voice that made her believe that he really meant it. But then if Vi had been using him as a sounding board for her personal angst he was probably exhausted, especially given his own vexed situation.

'Must go,' she said.

'See ya.'

She ended the call and took her car keys out of her bag. Shirley had sounded panicky on the phone. She didn't want to make her wait.


DI Cobbett finished reading Lee's statement and put it down on the table in front of him.

'That's all I know,' Lee said.

'Shane Warner is known to us,' Cobbett said. 'And if the old chap was in deep to him he was in trouble.'

'Ken Rivers had always been a gambler and so when his wife was suffering from dementia he decided he'd have some fun,' Lee said. 'He sold the flat to Warner and then rented it out from him so he could stay here.'

'Happy days.'

'Until gambling took a hand,' Lee said.

Cobbett shrugged.

'And I tell you something, DI Cobbett, I've seen a few punters lose at craps, cards, the gee-gees or whatever over the years, but I've never witnessed anyone lose as easily and comprehensively as Ken Rivers. To say it's a talent is an understatement. Money fell out of his hands.'

'And still he believed that he could beat the house?'

'He went along last night with his last three grand and lost it.'

'No doubt attempting to double it.'

'Yes, of course,' Lee said. 'His rent is due today. That gorilla I saw outside his house yesterday was going to come back.'

'Which he hasn't, for obvious reasons,' Cobbett said.

'You lot don't tend to be popular.'

'You must remember it well.' Cobbett smiled.

'I'm not exactly flavour of the month now,' Lee said. 'If you do think about becoming a PI when you retire, DI Cobbett, don't expect to make friends or influence too many people.'

Cobbett looked down at the statement again. 'Did you ever meet Bette Rivers?'

'Not that I know of,' Lee said. 'As I said in my statement, I knew Phil Rivers' old boss, Brian Barber, but I never came across Phil himself.'

'Mmm. We'll have to talk to the ex-wife,' Cobbett said.

'Sandra Rivers just wants Phil back. She doesn't want him prosecuted,' Lee said.

'Sandra Rivers will have to lump it,' Cobbett said. 'I've got a dead body and a missing man who is guilty of assault. If she knows something she's not telling anyone . . .'

'She wants Phil found,' Lee said. 'She's not hiding anything.'

'Maybe not deliberately.'

'What do you mean?'

'I mean, Mr Arnold, that even though Mrs Rivers might have no direct knowledge of her husband's homosexuality she might know some of the men her husband befriended over the years. She probably thinks they were just mates. We need to speak to her.'

'To tell her that her husband is gay?'

'What's the point of not doing so?' Cobbett said. 'It could have a bearing on her husband's crime or her father-in-law's disappearance. I'm interested in the latter and I'll use every bit of intel I can get my hands on to throw some light on that.'

Lee recalled Sandra Rivers' fragile fatness and he wondered how long Cobbett's information would take to destroy her.

Cobbett stood up. 'Anyway, I'm doing it,' he said. 'As for you, Mr Arnold, if you can stay in the area tonight I should be in a position to send you back to London tomorrow. In the morning we should be able to have some sort of idea about who the corpse is and how they died.'

When he got outside, now armed with an old handset provided by one of the Southend constables, Lee rang Derek Salmon and told him everything. Most of the time the solicitor just listened in seemingly stunned silence. But when Lee got to the part about what the police wanted to tell Sandra Rivers he squeaked, 'You what? They can't do that!'

'They can and they are.'

'But it could send her over the edge,' he said. 'You've seen the state of her! She'll probably eat her own weight in chocolate and then stuff down a couple of sixteen-inch pizzas. She'll end up bloody diabetic! I'll have to be with her when they come.'

'Well, you are her solicitor.'

'She'll need me.'

'Derek, did you know that Phil Rivers was gay?' Lee asked.

'Me? No! Why would I?'

'I don't know. The police may ask you.'

'Well, they can ask what they like, it's news to me,' he said.

'I was just saying. '

Derek sighed. 'I know. God, Lee, this job has turned out to be a bloody can of worms, hasn't it?'

'Sandra should have just gone for the jugular,' Lee said. 'Then she'd know where Phil was.'

'Behind bars.'

'Where he should be.'

There was a pause and then the solicitor said, 'Just keep me in the loop, OK, mate?'

'Will do.'

Lee ended the call. What he hadn't told Derek or anyone else was that the pain he was experiencing was giving him more than just discomfort. When he'd been in hospital the doctor had given him a load of codeine-based painkillers to take home. He'd thrown a lot away. So far he hadn't taken any of those that remained. Like any addiction, abstinence was a day-to-day struggle and opiate meds were seductive. Two co-codomol and he could be out of pain and off his nut in less than half an hour. He hadn't indulged for years and so the high would be tremendous. Lee put his hand in his pocket and then, just as quickly, he withdrew it. Weak he may be, but he wasn't stupid. He also had yet to go back to Susan's place. She had to be worried, particularly as she appeared to be so keen on him. Why he hadn't phoned her, he didn't really know.

## 18

'Dylan Smith has been beaten black and blue,' Shirley said.

'That's Tim Pool for you.'

They all looked at Roy, who continued, 'Deprived me of a couple of teeth.'

'But you said nothing.'

'Course not.'

Mandy took Roy's hand. She said, 'You don't. So if Dylan Smith's withdrawn his complaint you'll have to respect his wishes, Shirley. We're there for the service users. We do what they want.'

'Pool'll do something worse if Dylan goes ahead,' Roy said.

Mumtaz didn't know what she could contribute to the discussion. Shirley had asked her to come in and she'd come. But to do what? Shirley looked genuinely upset that she couldn't take this service user's complaint any further. When Shirley went to the toilet, Mandy spoke up.

'I think that Shirley's changing,' she said. 'Don't know why. She's always been for a quiet life but now it's like she's on a mission. All of a sudden.'

'You don't know why?'

'No. If she upsets too many people Mr Cotton'll get rid of her. And she's got a mortgage.'

'But representing the service users is her job,' Mumtaz said. 'She must've known it carried risks when she took it?'

Roy shrugged.

Shirley returned. 'I'm not going to give up on Dylan Smith and I'm not going to let those service users on Forensic live in fear any longer.'

'Who you gonna get to help you?' Roy asked. 'Batman?'

'No, but I'd like to introduce you to someone who can help us without the aid of a silly costume,' Shirley said. Then she called out into the corridor, 'Would you like to come in now?'

She was little more than a girl. Blonde and small, she wore a baseball cap and a thick woollen scarf that obscured half her face.

'Denna has been doing nights on Forensic,' Shirley said.

'I've not seen you here before,' Mandy said.

'I've only been at Ilford, on and off, for just over a month,' Denna said. She had a light, boyish voice. 'I'm agency.'

'But she's seen enough,' Shirley said.

'Smith got beaten by another patient,' Denna said. 'On Pool's orders.'

'How do you know that?' Mumtaz asked.

'The patient, Moran, was allowed to go outside for a smoke in the early hours of the morning,' Denna said. 'That just doesn't happen, especially not on Tim's shifts. He hates smoking.'

'I can see that's unusual, but what does that prove?' Mumtaz asked.

'Moran is a very violent man. His index offence is murder.'

'Him I do know,' Roy said. 'He killed his flatmate and then cut him up and put him in dustbin bags.'

'When I saw him outside I noticed that Moran's knuckles were swollen,' Denna said. 'At dinner time they hadn't been.'

'So? Maybe he thumped a wall,' Mandy said. 'Self-harm.'

'Yeah, I'd accept that,' Denna said, 'if Moran hadn't spoken to me. His cigarette lighter wouldn't work and so I lent him mine. I could see he wanted me to ask him how he'd managed to get extra smoking privileges from Tim. They're as rare as hen's teeth and are trophies on the unit. He kept me on tenterhooks as long as he could. Then he said, "I'm here because I helped Mr Pool out with a problem." And then he smiled at me and I just felt sick. I'd heard one of my colleagues, can't say who, sobbing earlier outside the patients' rooms. I confronted her.'

'And?'

'She told me that Smith was in a bad way. She didn't say why and I didn't ask her. As soon as I could I went to see Smith who was in a right state,' Denna said. 'I gave him a couple of painkillers for his pain – it was all I could do in the short time that I had.' She looked at Shirley. 'Then I came to see you. I can't tell you whether I'll make a formal statement yet. I'll have to think about it. But I want to.'

Staff members were in an invidious position when it came to whistle-blowing. If they weren't believed, they found work elsewhere hard to get.

'It's OK,' Shirley said. 'I've made a request for one of the doctors to examine Dylan Smith. Dr el Masri has agreed to do it.'

The sudden mention of el Masri's name brought Mumtaz up short. He was the real reason she was at Ilford Hospital. It was so easy to get distracted in this toxic environment. She looked at her phone and saw that she had an appointment with el Masri at five-thirty.

'He won't find anything,' Mandy said. 'They never do.'

'Then I'll get an independent doctor from outside,' Shirley said. 'We're entitled to do that.'

'Only if Dylan agrees to be examined, which he won't,' Roy said. 'Shirley, he don't want us to help, so we can't. It's great that Denna's come forward and that but you can't do nothing unless Dylan lets you.'

'We'll see about that,' Shirley said.

Mumtaz remembered what Mandy had said about Shirley being 'on a mission' and couldn't help wondering if she realized just how dangerous the game she was playing might get. If Timothy Pool could get one patient to half kill another one, and if Dr el Masri could plant a bomb in Hatem el Shamy's locker – assuming those incidents had really happened – then almost anything was possible.

Susan hadn't taken it well. Lee could have left bringing up her silent phone calls to Vi Collins for another time, but he'd decided to go ahead. At first she'd denied it. But she'd left her phone where he could get it. He'd shown her what she'd done.

'You went behind my back!' she said.

'Pot? Kettle?' Lee said. He was much more relaxed then he'd been for weeks but he also wasn't in the mood for any crap. 'Where'd you get Vi's number, eh, Suze? Oh, off my phone, wasn't it?'

She looked down at the floor. 'I was so worried when you didn't turn up this morning, Lee.'

'Don't change the subject,' he said. He'd already told her where he'd been and something about what had happened. 'This thing with Vi, what's it about, eh? You jealous of her or something?'

Susan said nothing.

'Because if you are,' he said. 'You don't need to be. Vi's a mate. We worked together in the police. We flirt a bit, we always have.'

'She's got it bad for you, Lee, believe me,' Susan said. 'Women know these things. What I did was wrong, but I just couldn't help it. I don't trust that woman.'

She was right not to. Lee knew that. Vi would sleep with him whenever she could. Although he hadn't slept with her since he'd been with Susan. Should he own up to ever having had sex with her? Lee knew the answer to that.

'Me and Vi are just friends. We always have been. We've never been anything more.' He was a private detective, he knew how to lie.

'You sure?'

'What, that I've not slept with Vi? Suze, even I'd remember if I had.'

He sat down at the kitchen table. It was a wise move because he was dizzy and, although he'd expected it, it had made his stomach lurch. He'd lost so much of his tolerance. But when he thought about it, the guilt rolled in. 'You don't need to phone Vi again and I'd be grateful if you didn't,' he said.

She stayed silent for a moment and then she said, 'I won't.' She looked up. 'I'm sorry.' Then she frowned. 'Lee, you're ever so white. You OK?'

Back in the old days he'd called it the 'codeine white-out' when the drug finally relaxed you and your face temporarily drained.

'Just tired,' he said. 'And of course I hadn't planned to spend most of the night with a dead body.'

'Ugh.' Susan sat beside him. 'To think that Kenny . . .'

'We don't know what Ken did or didn't do at the moment,' Lee said. 'We don't even know the identity of the body.'

He hadn't seen its face. But he had seen that hand, hanging out of the bed, moving to the rhythm of its maggots. He told himself that that was the reason why he'd taken the tablets, even though he knew it wasn't true.

'So are you staying?' she asked.

'If you'll let me,' he said.

She kissed his cheek. She was a beautiful, sexy woman and he was lucky to have her. When she'd phoned Vi it had been done on the spur of the moment, it had been an aberration. Except that it hadn't. Susan had phoned Vi several times and, much as he liked and fancied her, he had to keep that in his mind. The last thing Lee needed was a stalker, especially when the first person he always called when things went wrong or he needed support was Mumtaz. Sod the dead hand of whoever had been in Ken Rivers' bed, it had been that realization that had tipped him over the edge. The codeine washed down his spine and relaxed it and Lee Arnold vowed never to take opiate-based painkillers ever again.

Derek Salmon arrived at Sandra Rivers' house before the police. As soon as he was through the door she was asking him questions.

'Have they found Phil?' She nibbled on a chocolate eclair; a sure sign to Derek that she was stressed. 'Is he all right? If they have found him, I don't want him prosecuted. And why Southend Police? That's where his dad and mum live. Where's Lee Arnold and why hasn't he—'

'Sandra, Sandra, Sandra.' Derek took one of her wrists in his hands and sat her down. 'Listen, the police are coming to see you about your father-in-law,' he said.

'Ken?'

'Yes, he's gone missing.' He told her about Ken's gambling,

about what he'd done to Lee and he told her what the police had found in the flat.

Sandra rapidly finished the eclair. 'It wasn't Phil . . .'

'No,' he said. 'But Ken's gone AWOL. He hit Lee Arnold over the head and then locked him in that room with that body. Obviously something's up, Sandra.'

'But, Del, I don't know anything about this!'

'I know, I know,' he said. He made calming motions with his hands. 'But the police suspect that Ken may be with Phil. I think it's unlikely but it is possible. Lee found no current connection between Ken and Phil but if Ken is as skint as we think he is, then if he knew where Phil and all his money were he'd go there. He might be there now. But the point is, Sandra, that the police are going to tell you something that you won't like.'

Her eyes widened.

'I should say up front that I don't think for a moment that it's true but . . . Sandra, there's been a suggestion that Phil might have been gay.'

She didn't look shocked so much as confused.

'I think their reasoning is that they think that when Phil defrauded you he went off with a gay lover. Sandra, they're going to ask you about any friends or acquaintances . . .'

'He didn't have any friends,' she said. 'He spent his time with me, or training or with his mum and dad. He used to go down the pub with Barry Barber, but that was years ago and Barry Barber's married.' Her eyes filled up. 'What's going on, Del?'

He put a hand on her shoulder. 'I don't know,' he said. 'I sent Lee Arnold down to Southend to keep an eye on Ken and Bette and see if they made contact with Phil and then this happens.'

'Bette! Where's Bette then?' Sandra asked. 'Oh, Del!'

'The dead body could be Bette,' he said. 'But, Sandra, before you start imagining all sorts, you must remember that Bette was old and she had dementia. The police still don't know if whoever it is died of natural causes or not.'

'If it isn't Bette, then who is it?'

'I don't know.'

Sandra shook her head. 'How could anyone think that Phil was gay?' she said. 'He loved women. He loved me – once. Why do the police think that?'

'I don't know.'

'But he wasn't,' she said. She stood up.

'Sandra . . .'

'I need to go to the kitchen,' she said. 'I'm sorry, Del, I should've offered you coffee. Would you like some coffee?'

'Sandra, don't . . .'

'I'll make you coffee,' she said.

She walked into the kitchen, a large woman in a large Mary Portas dress in egg-yolk yellow. Derek felt wretched for her. But he sat and waited for his coffee, knowing what she was really doing.

The doorbell rang. Sandra had left the security gates open after Derek arrived. The police were at the front door. There was a pause. Had Sandra even heard it? Derek called out, 'Sandra!'

But no one answered. The doorbell rang again. He walked into the kitchen. 'Sandra there's the—'

Derek Salmon stopped. On all fours, her considerable back-side sticking up in the air, Sandra Rivers had her head inside her fridge. When he did finally manage to get her attention and she turned to face him, Derek saw that, from the mouth downwards, Sandra was covered in cream.

'Oh, love,' he said, 'you're gonna have to give this Phil thing up. It's killing you.'

*

'Nature or nurture?'

Mumtaz smiled. 'Well, both,' she said. 'Any behavioural phenomenon has to come about via an interplay of genetic inheritance and experience.'

Dr el Masri, though physically unpleasant, had a certain charm that Mumtaz, to her surprise, found herself warming to.

'That's a very rational answer,' he said. 'But do you believe it?'

'Why wouldn't I? Nothing else makes sense.'

'I mean, as a devout Muslim,' he said. 'How do you reconcile a scientific approach that allows for change with a faith of predeterminism like Islam?'

She put the ball back in his court. 'I might ask you the same question,' she said.

He smiled. 'You might, and that would be valid, but not in relation to Islam.'

'You're not a Muslim?' She had thought that even avowedly secular followers of President Mubarak would not openly deny also being good Muslims too.

'I am a Copt,' he said. 'A Christian by upbringing. Not that I believe in all that.'

The Copts and their troubles in the new post-Mubarak Egypt had been in the press a lot. They claimed that instead of life getting easier in the new Egypt, for them it had become harder. The new rulers of the country, the Muslim Brotherhood Party, that Hatem el Shamy was a supporter of, were trying to make them conform to an Islamic way of life and there had been attacks on their places of worship. It was the sort of thing that made Mumtaz feel sad, sorry and uncomfortable all at the same time. Muslims all over the world had been put down, enslaved and attacked for centuries. Why were they doing the same to others? Had they learnt nothing?

'Well?' el Masri said. 'You're an intelligent woman, I want to hear what you think.'

'About Islam and science? I take a view,' she said.

'Which is?'

'I think that Muslims lost their way,' she said. 'Back in medieval times amazing work was taking place. In Andalusia we had al Zahrawi the surgeon, whose techniques were so advanced they look modern. And what about ibn Sina, the Persian who described the different forms energy can take and the properties of light? In Christian Europe people were still touching the dead bodies of saints to effect cures and buying Indulgences to limit the time they had to spend in Purgatory.'

'Scientists like ibn Sina came into conflict with their rulers.'

'Just like the Christian, Galileo,' she said. 'But we were on a trajectory, Dr el Masri. Islamic scientists were moving forwards.'

'And then they stopped.'

'Yes. It would be too simplistic to say that progress stopped because so many Islamic lands were colonised by non-Muslims. We had the Ottoman Empire, we didn't just grind to a halt. But colonisation was a factor, together with low levels of education, which were exploited by corrupt rulers keen to consolidate their power. They used and continue to use religion as a weapon and a tool to crush dissent. I have read the Koran many times and I believe it to be the true word of God. But I also do not and cannot believe that God doesn't want us to be curious about the world He has made available to us. I think it is our duty as Muslims to question and explore.'

He frowned. 'But Islam means submission . . .'

'To God, yes,' she said. 'I submit to God's will every day of my life. I accept my lot. But I also work to make my own life and those of others better. To not do that would be to deny the education my parents worked so hard to give me.'

'Your headscarf,' he said, 'is that an outward sign of your submission to God?'

'In part,' she said.

'You feel it offers you protection?'

She saw a light in his eyes.

'From men?' he added.

'I like to cover my head,' she said. 'But I am not a fool, Dr el Masri. I know that if a man wants a woman, a piece of cloth will not save her. That kind of man doesn't care what type of woman he assaults. That's why the whole notion of women in short skirts tempting men is flawed. Men either assault women or they don't.'

'Maybe.'

'There's no maybe about it!' Mumtaz shook her head. 'But I'm sorry, Dr el Masri,' she said, 'I'm ranting.'

'That's OK.'

Rather than focusing on el Masri, the conversation had made Mumtaz think about her dead husband again. Ahmet had raped her covered or uncovered. He'd even raped his own daughter.

'I am a great believer in the power of catharsis,' Dr el Masri said. 'It's good to release emotions and tension; I encourage my patients to do that whenever they can.'

Mumtaz made herself concentrate. 'So, you use psychoanalytic techniques . . .'

'I refer to any school of thought I think may help my patients,' he said. 'But as a psychiatrist, as I am sure you know, Miss Huq, my principal job is to medicate and then rehabilitate. These days we have wonderful drugs that can turn a person's life around. But the wrong drug prescribed to the wrong person can be a disaster. I am paid well to try to prevent such things happening.'

She wanted, somehow, to get around to the subject of Hatem el Shamy, but that was difficult because they'd moved on from Egypt. Mumtaz let the conversation run and it was, she had to admit, enjoyable. Only once, when he'd talked about her headscarf and she'd seen that light come into his eyes had she recognized the lecher that Salwa el Shamy had described. And even then it was very slight. It was only as she was leaving that Mumtaz brought the subject of el Masri's homeland up again.

'Did you ever practice in Egypt, Dr el Masri?' she asked.

'For a while,' he said. 'But, to be truthful, it was difficult.'

'Why?'

He shrugged. 'You won't want to hear it.'

'Please?'

'The Muslim Brotherhood, even before they came to power, made life difficult sometimes for people like me. Don't get me wrong, I come from a wealthy family and my people don't live anywhere near to the seats of the Brotherhood's power. But I wanted to work with the poor, that's what I do here.'

'Why couldn't you in Egypt?'

'Because elements within the Brotherhood don't believe in psychiatry. They certainly don't believe in a Copt practising psychiatry. For a while I kept my head down and tried to just do my job without attracting attention. But it was too hard. Now all I can do with regard to Egypt is send money to my old hospital whenever I am able. I have provided accommodation for several members of my family who have wanted to leave Egypt over the years. One does one's best. I imagine you know that we had a member of the Muslim Brotherhood working as a nurse here?'

'Yes. Didn't he plant a bomb?'

'A bomb was found in his locker, yes,' he said. 'Whether he put it there will be for a jury to decide.'

'Did you get on, as fellow Egyptians?' she asked.

He sighed. 'On the face of it he was a good nurse,' he said. 'But I had some doubts about him that went beyond the fact that he hated me because I am a Copt and a supporter of Hosni Mubarak.'

'Did you hate him?'

'No,' he said. 'But I didn't trust him. I can't say any more than that because his case has not yet come to court. It's difficult for me, Miss Huq. I cannot approve of him but at the same time I cannot, as they say here, badmouth him either. Do you see?'

She did. When she left, Mumtaz thought about her conversation with Dr el Masri in detail. On the face of it he seemed a very reasonable man. He hadn't condemned Hatem el Shamy and had even left the door open to the idea that he might not have planted the bomb in the locker.

Why hadn't Salwa el Shamy told her that el Masri was a Copt? It was well known that the Copts and the Brotherhood were often at odds and although Mumtaz had known that the issue between the two men was in part personal, she hadn't been aware to what extent. In Salwa's world, el Masri had set her husband up, but why would he? El Masri was a successful psychiatrist doing what he wanted and, by his own admission, getting paid well for it. Why would he bother with Hatem, however much he hated the Brotherhood?

Her phone rang.

'Ah, Mumtaz,' her father said, 'about this house move . . .'

'Baba, it's fine,' Mumtaz said. 'It's ten days away and we're almost packed.'

'Good. Your brothers and I will move you,' he said. 'Your cousin Aftab has a van.'

Mumtaz rolled her eyes. She already had the move organized. 'Baba, I have a van,' she said. 'I've paid for men to move us.'

'Then un-pay them,' her father said. 'Did you really think that your family would just let you move all alone? Two ladies moving alone – ridiculous!'

'Baba, I can't un-pay the men I've engaged to move me.'

'And I can't un-ask your cousin Aftab,' he said. 'If we turn down his generous offer now he'll be offended. And he's family.'

The great Bangladeshi family. Mumtaz had known when she'd booked the van from Forest Removals that she should have consulted the family first. But if the Sheikhs turned up, she didn't want her father or her brothers anywhere near them.

'Ron and Harry who run the removal company are very nice men,' Mumtaz said. 'Ron's a neighbour. If they don't get another job for Saturday week they'll be out of pocket and that isn't fair.'

'So maybe they will get a job?'

She walked out of the hospital and into the car park. A small group of service users smoked in the lee of the old laundry block. While Mumtaz had been in with Dr el Masri it had got dark. She pulled the collar of her coat close around her neck.

'And if they don't get another job?' Mumtaz asked. 'What then?'

'Well then, I will pay them,' her father said. 'If it's so important to you. We can't have Aftab inconvenienced. He uses his van for his shop and so this is a very big favour he is doing.'

She shook her head. 'Yes, Baba.'

'Tell your men I will pay them,' her father said. 'Your Ron and Harry.'

She sighed. Resistance was pointless. 'OK.'

'Good!'

He finished the call, leaving Mumtaz stressed at the thought of the Sheikhs seeing her family with her. They knew who the Huqs were, of course they did, but she still preferred to create some distance between her tormentors and her blood relations.

As she got into her car, Mumtaz saw one of the smokers looking at her. He turned to one of his companions and said, 'Do you think she's got any tobacco?'

The other man said, 'No. They don't smoke.'

'Who?'

'Covered-up women.'

Although she'd never smoked in her life, Mumtaz was almost tempted to pick up a dog-end and give it a go. Few people smoked more than her Auntie Asma who lived in complete purdah in a village fifty miles from Dhaka. When her friends visited her for tea they all arrived completely swaddled from head to foot. But once in her salon, off came the niqabs and out came the cakes and the cigarettes. Then they all danced.

## 19

Salwa couldn't sleep. Mumtaz Hakim's call had upset her. So what if el Masri was a Copt? How did that change what he had done to Hatem? If anything it made it worse. Everyone knew that Copts were just worshippers of the old Egyptian gods in disguise. Why would they have almost total control of the ancient temples otherwise?

And then the Hakim woman had gone on about how *nice* the psychiatrist had been! Hatem had told her that el Masri was cunning, but she hadn't thought for a moment that the so-called private detective would fall for his lies. And they had to be lies. Salwa looked at her clock. It was two a.m. so to leave the house would be madness. All sorts ranged around in the night – drunks from the local pubs, drug addicts, perverts. Salwa put a hand in the drawer of her bedside cabinet and took out a set of keys. Such a fight she'd had to get them from Rashida! Now she could go to Hatem's lock-up any time she wanted. If she wanted.

Salwa didn't know what was in the lock-up any more than she hoped her daughter did. She had some ideas, but they were disloyal and she tried to suppress them. This time she failed. What if Hatem was not the man she thought he was? She'd never forget how guilty he'd looked when she'd first found him at the lock-up. She'd been on her way home from taking the children to school and suddenly there he'd been. Underneath those arches, a bunch of keys in one hand and a sack containing who knew what in the other. He'd been furious. He'd put the sack just inside the door of the unit and then locked up. He'd shouted at her to mind her own business and stop following him, and although Salwa had tried to make him understand that she hadn't been following him, he hadn't been convinced. From then on, until his arrest, he had looked at her with suspicious eyes. That had to be why he'd given the lock-up keys to Rashida.

Had Hatem known that Rashida wouldn't look inside? He couldn't have done. Salwa knew her daughter wanted to. She'd almost done it when she'd caught her there, skipping school. But then Salwa thought Rashida must have looked, because if she hadn't, why would she threaten to reveal what her father had inside? What was in there? Her palest fantasy was about Muslim Brotherhood leaflets. Her darkest was guns, ammunition, explosives. Even thinking about it made Salwa cringe. How could she think that Hatem had explosives in that lock-up? He was a man of peace. Or, at least, he had become one.

There had been a bomb, long ago. Designed to blow up Mubarak's car it had detonated in a garage in the suburb of Manshiyet Nasser. When Hatem and his brother Muhammed had opened the door it had gone off, luckily not wounding either of them. After that, so Hatem said, he had been too frightened to make any more bombs. Salwa had to believe him. But if the lock-up didn't contain bomb-making equipment then what did it contain? And why was Hatem so adamant that no one should know what was in there?

*

'You're a fucking shitbag,' Lee Arnold said. 'And you're a stupid one.'

Muttering to himself, he was glad that it was a dark autumn night in the rain on a deserted Southend seafront. If anyone had heard him talking to himself, he was sure he'd be sectioned. But Lee needed a good talking to, even if it was only from himself. The codeine had felt so good it had made him weep. There were no words for the relief it had given. He'd forgiven Susan for stalking Vi and then he'd made love to her and, with the codeine on board, he had felt completely involved in the act. That was rare.

Stunning as she was, Susan's was not the kind of body Lee dreamt about in the deepest, darkest places of his soul. He wouldn't even give those desires a name. If he did he knew he'd disappear down a black hole from which he'd never emerge. Wasn't he down a black hole now? Lee took the packet of co-codamol out of his pocket and counted the number of tablets he'd taken. Four was nothing when you had been on twenty a day. But four tablets after years of abstinence were making his head woolly in a very good way. And if his past addiction had taught him anything, it would get a whole lot better before it got worse. If he could catch it just before it went bad on him . . .

That was fucking ridiculous. Nobody ever managed to do that. He'd left Susan sleeping in bed to come and rant at himself on the seafront because he knew that was bollocks. If he stopped now he'd never have to go through all the headaches that nudged the codeine-dependent back to addiction. All he'd have to contend with was being a bit pissed off that he had to deal with reality in the raw. That was if he didn't succumb.

Lee walked past the old Foresters pub. Devoid of lights and with boards advertising strippers, it looked like an old caravan park toilet block. Caravans brought to mind Leslie Baum; Lee wondered if he was playing Dungeons and Dragons with a group of boys half his age or whether he was having a lonely wank. Ending up like Leslie wasn't hard to do. Tens of thousands of men did it every year. Lee lit a fag. As he watched it burn, he wondered whether he should ask Susan to marry him. He knew she'd be up for it and he'd never be lonely again. And he'd have good sex.

If only something happened in his head when he thought about her. Lee's feeling of unease with Susan, exacerbated by her behaviour towards Vi, had only been assuaged by the addition of codeine. And now that it was wearing off a bit he was beginning to feel pain again, both mental and physical. What was it about Phil Rivers and his family that made this job so bloody dangerous? When he'd gone to meet Barry Barber at that pub in Dagenham, he'd got beaten to within an inch and now Phil's dad had almost put him back in hospital. It was unlikely that Barber had had anything to do with that first assault. He'd wanted to talk to Lee about Phil. But if he hadn't smacked him up, who had? Someone had to have been following him to know he was going to that obscure part of Dagenham. That thought made his skin creep. To go to so much trouble just to give him a slap seemed like madness. Unless they'd intended to kill him. But why? Phil had had it away on his toes with a lot of money and he may or may not be a gay boy, but were either of those things worth killing for? But then it was one point two million . . .

'It's got to be here somewhere. Where are you, you little bastard?'

In the summer the seafront was heaving with people even in the wee hours of the morning. But once winter came it was given back to the homeless. What looked like a bundle of rags scrabbled after a bottle of something or other, presumably alcohol, as

Lee walked by. He'd just pulled level with one of those slot-machine places, now mercifully silent, and he would have carried on going if the tramp hadn't started crying. And if he hadn't recognized his voice the second time he spoke.

'Oh, fuck! Where's that fucking bottle. Somebody? Please?'

Lee didn't even look for the bottle but he did bend down and look into the man's face. It made him go cold. 'Ken?' he said. 'Is that you?'

'No, you can't examine me. Fuck off!'

Dylan pushed the doctor away.

'Mr Smith . . .'

'What're you doing, coming in here in the middle of the fucking night?' Dylan pulled his blankets up to his chin and pushed himself back into his pillows. 'And with him!'

Timothy Pool blinked as Dylan jabbed a finger at him.

'Dylan, I am your ward manager . . .'

'Leave me alone!' Then he looked at el Masri. 'And you, you're not even on-call here tonight. What you doing here?'

'Dr el Masri has come to examine you,' Pool said. 'Mrs Mayfield from the Advocacy made a request for you to be examined by a doctor because of these injuries you seem to have sustained.'

'I never asked her to do that!' Dylan's eyes bulged. It was all very well shouting at Tim Pool but dobbing him in, after what Dylan had been through, was quite another. 'She made a fuss about it all, not me!'

'Mr Smith, I can see bruises on your arms,' el Masri said. 'Why don't you just let me have a look at you?'

'No!' Dylan turned away.

'These issues between patients can be intractable, as you

know, Dr el Masri,' Pool said. 'It's like prison culture, you know. Nobody "grasses". What can I do?'

Bastard! Dylan wanted to smack Timothy Pool's lying mouth. Dylan might not know who'd smashed him up but he did know who'd ordered it. And anyway, why should he tell a perv like el Masri about what had happened? Word was that he shagged female patients when they were asleep. Why should he trust someone like that?

El Masri said, 'I don't need to know who assaulted you, Mr Smith. I just want to make sure that you are all right.'

'I am.' If el Masri examined him, he'd have to write something in his notes and give some sort of account of himself to that bloody Shirley. What was she doing suddenly meddling in things she'd always avoided before? Why did she suddenly give a shit?

'What's going on?'

Someone had told Dylan that Dr Golding was going to be on call. But he hadn't expected to see him, not with el Masri in the room. Now he stood at the end of his bed.

'Mrs Mayfield from the Advocacy expressed some concern about this patient's physical wellbeing,' el Masri said. 'I am offering him an examination.'

'In the middle of the night?'

Golding's tone expressed precisely what Dylan had felt. 'They woke me up!' he said.

Golding frowned. He was the doctor on-call that evening, and he hadn't heard anything about this. 'Dr el Masri,' he said, 'can I speak to you about this in private, please?'

'Yes. Of course.'

They left. But Timothy Pool didn't go with them. Dylan tucked his bedclothes tightly around his body. Pool looked him in the eyes, 'It's OK, Dylan,' he said. And then he smiled.

Then he left.

Dylan shivered. He knew exactly why el Masri hadn't turned up until just after midnight. That was when Timothy Pool was on shift and the doctor wouldn't examine him without Tim. The Egyptian might be a highly qualified psychiatrist with years of experience, but at Ilford he knew his place in the pecking order and that was below Timothy Pool. Unfortunately, as he was sure it would turn out to be for somebody in the end, nobody had told Dr Golding what the score was. Dylan had seen Tim Pool's face when Golding had suddenly turned up and intervened. It hadn't been pretty.

Even though he was ex-job, Lee was surprised when DI Cobbett offered to let him watch Ken Rivers' interview. Behind a one-way mirror, Lee sat with a constable called Frith and a cup of bad cop-shop coffee. The codeine had almost worn off and he felt wide awake again.

Ken Rivers, who looked like a crumpled collection of charity shop donations, sat next to a knackered-looking duty solicitor. He told Cobbett his name, his age and his address without sounding much more than a bit tipsy. Even when he asked him about Lee, Ken answered immediately.

'I hit him,' he said.

'Why?'

'He was nosing in my business,' the old man said.

'You made him go into a room with a dead body before you hit him, though, didn't you, Mr Rivers?' Cobbett said.

There was a long silence. When Ken spoke again he sounded as pissed as a parrot. 'Dead what? What? Dunno what you . . .' He looked at the solicitor. 'Can I get a drink, can I?'

The solicitor shrugged.

Cobbett looked down at some notes and said, 'When Mr Arnold called us from Miss Franks' flat, which is the one above yours, he said that there was a dead body on the bed in the room where you, Mr Rivers, had locked him after your assault.'

'Don't know nothing about that.' Lee could see the old man trembling. 'He must've put it there,' Ken said.

'What, Mr Arnold?'

'Yeah.'

Cobbett consulted his notes again. 'Mr Arnold called us at three forty-five yesterday morning,' he said. 'Our forensic team sealed off the crime scene, which contained a dead body. The corpse has been examined by a pathologist whose findings so far are interesting. Want to know what they are, Mr Rivers?'

Ken shrugged.

'She – we know it's a female – has been dead for at least a month. A considerable amount of her had liquified into the mattress she was lying on, apparently.' He looked up. 'An elderly lady, the pathologist reckons. Where's your wife, Mr Rivers?'

Ken didn't answer, but he continued to shake.

'Elizabeth, or "Bette", Rivers? Know where she is, Mr Rivers?'

Again, Ken said nothing.

'You were married for a long time, weren't you, Ken?' Cobbett said. 'Forty years or so? Then there was your son. Philip, thirty-five years old.'

'He's missing,' the old man said. 'And the old woman too.'

'Your wife is missing?'

'She's got the dementia,' Ken said. 'She just wanders off. I try to keep hold of her but she's away with the fairies.'

Cobbett leant onto the table between them. He wore an expression Lee knew well. It said: *You know and I know that you are full of shit.*

'So how long has Bette been missing, Mr Rivers?'

Ken pretended to think. Then he said, 'About a month.'

'So you've reported her disappearance?'

'No.' As soon as he'd said it, Ken put his hand up to his mouth. Closing the stable door after the horse had bolted.

'Why not?'

There could be no reasonable answer. Ken looked at the floor.

'I mean, I don't know, but I imagine you've still been collecting Bette's pension since her disappearance,' Cobbett said. 'Given your dire financial straits. When did you sell your flat to Shane Warner? There's no point lying to me, Mr Rivers, because that I can find out easily.'

Lee finished his coffee-like drink and Constable Frith said, 'Would you like another, sir?'

'No thanks.'

Behind the glass, Ken Rivers said, 'Four months ago.'

'When you sold to Warner?'

'Yeah.'

'Why?'

He shrugged. 'She was off her nut. I thought I might need to have her put in care, you know.'

'But you didn't, did you, Ken?' Cobbett said. 'Far as I can see Warner gave you a shit price, you agreed to some ridiculous rent and then you decided you'd have some fun trying your hand at being a professional gambler. How much did you lose? And again, don't lie because we know where you gambled and we can make the casino show us their records.'

He took a deep breath in. For a moment he said nothing and then he murmured, 'All of it.'

'All of what?'

'All of the money I got for the flat.'

'Which was?'

'Fifty grand.'

Nobody said a word. Frith pulled a face. Even though Ken lived in a shit part of town in the middle of a recession, he lived in a two-bedroom flat, which had to be worth at least double what he'd been paid.

Cobbett broke the silence. 'Warner saw you coming.'

Even the solicitor shook his head.

'But even so, to blow fifty grand in what, four . . .'

'Three.'

'Three months, is impressive,' Cobbett said. 'So did you have fun doing it or—'

'They always ordered me cabs,' Ken said.

'The casino?'

'Yeah.'

'Well, I suppose they would. You being such a massive loser. Christ, Ken, it was the least they could do! Make you feel special, did it?'

Lee remembered what he'd been told by Sandra Rivers and Derek Salmon about Ken, how hard he had taken his redundancy from the docks. Then Bette had got sick. Had the gambling given him some sort of purpose? The illusion of being a man who was successful enough to lose money and still come back to high roll again?

'So what do we have so far?' Cobbett said. 'You, Ken, sell your flat to a gangster who gives you half its value. I assume you owned the flat with your wife and I imagine, knowing him, that Shane Warner had her sign on the line to approve the sale using all the charm and guile I know that he has.' He smiled. 'Not. After that you spend as if your life depends on it and a month or so ago Bette went missing. Am I right so far?'

He still looked at the floor. 'Yeah.'

'Good. Only fly in the ointment, however, is the woman melting into your bed,' Cobbett said.

'Well, him, Arnold, he must've killed her. Yeah?'

Cobbett didn't answer immediately. Lee saw Frith cringe and wondered what would happen next.

'Mr Arnold couldn't have killed her, she'd been dead for a while,' Cobbett said in a low, almost growling voice. 'She was long dead when he found her. In your flat. On your bed. Now, Mr Rivers, our pathologist doesn't yet know how the elderly lady Mr Arnold found – who, by the way, was wearing a bracelet with the name "Bette" engraved on it – died. Hopefully we'll find that out later on today. But we'll assume that the woman was your wife. So you'd better stop prattling on about her "going missing" and tell me what really happened.'

This time there was a very long pause. Then Ken Rivers said, 'She died. I weren't ready. I needed a big win to sort meself out. Know what I mean?'

## 20

Shirley said that Mandy had 'let her down'. She'd got very upset about the Dylan Smith situation the previous day and probably needed to rest. Now Mumtaz was covering for Mandy on the chronic ward where, as usual, Terry had issues.

'They scatter ashes around my bed to send me out of my mind,' he said.

It was the same old thing with the aeroplanes and the cremated ashes of his father. Except that this time the staff were apparently not just failing to stop the planes from dropping the ashes, but were actively throwing them around his bed. Terry was intensely agitated and, if anything, sicker than the first time Mumtaz had seen him.

'Terry, no one wants to send you out of your mind,' Mumtaz said. 'You know what the aim of the hospital is, don't you? It's to get you back into the community.'

'Into the community? I don't want to go back there,' he said. 'I just got shit out there.'

'I think you need to try to relax.' Even as she said it, Mumtaz felt stupid. She'd always thought of chronic wards as places where most of the patients were almost in medication-induced comas. But at Ilford they were all more active than she had expected. How anyone could relax around so much activity and agitation was impossible to imagine.

But Terry ignored her. They were standing outside the ward so that he could smoke. It was drizzling lightly and the sky was grey. Mumtaz couldn't help feeling that the weather was appropriate.

'What are you going to do about it?' Terry said. 'You're the advocate. You've got to get them to stop doing it.'

She tried to replicate Shirley's speech about how some people saw the world in different ways and how that was valid, if not necessarily the way things really were, but she just couldn't. It was true but it was patronising too. In the end Mumtaz said, 'I'll have a word.'

Terry finished his fag and then went back on the ward. Mumtaz silently wondered how much longer she could keep up her nice Miss Huq persona. She'd spent the previous evening with Vi Collins, who'd almost driven her to distraction with her moaning about ageing and the menopause.

'Hi, Mumtaz. How's it going?'

It was Kylie, the care assistant Mumtaz had met on her first day at Ilford. On that occasion she'd been smoking a cigarette. She'd also been in a lighthearted mood. This time she was still smoking but she looked grave.

'OK,' Mumtaz said. 'You?'

Kylie leant against the ward door. The drizzle had made her hair go flat and she looked exhausted. 'I've just got off Forensic,' she said.

'Busy?'

Kylie shook her head. 'Mental,' she said. 'When I got in Dr Golding and Mr Pool were having a row about something in Mr Pool's office. All the patients were agitated. One of them told me that it was all to do with Dylan Smith. He'd kicked off or something in the night and Dr el Masri was called. I dunno what it was all about. But Mr Pool should've gone home hours ago.'

Shirley had made a request for Dylan to be examined and Dr el Masri was the one who had agreed to do it. Had he done it? Or had he just gone out to see the patient in the middle of the night because he'd become agitated or violent? And why had Dr Golding got involved?

Kylie finished her cigarette and then lit another. 'I've been here a year,' she said. 'And so I know most people. But I still don't know how this place works or what's really going on.'

'What do you mean?'

'Well,' Kylie said, 'take Dr el Masri. Everyone says that he's a bit of a lech, you know. When that girl threw herself out the window, over on Acute, people were saying that el Masri'd be questioned by the police, that he'd forced her to have sex with him and blah, blah, blah. They all went on about how he'd put her on fifteen-minute obs because he was frightened she'd top herself after what he'd done. But he never put her on obs. Her mate did that.'

'Her mate?'

'That other Egyptian, the nurse who's in prison.'

'El Shamy?'

'Yeah,' Kylie said. 'He put her on suicide watch.'

'If he was worried about her, he would,' Mumtaz said.

'Yeah, but then why would he lie about it later?' Kylie said. 'The nurse who tried to save the girl, Michelle something, she said that when she looked at the girl's obs notes after she'd died she saw that someone had crossed out el Shamy's name and put Dr el Masri's in its place.'

If that were true, then it was strange and illegal. And why had it even been done? To frame Dr el Masri in some way?

'Who told you all this?' Mumtaz asked.

'Oh, Daria,' Kylie said. 'She's a cleaner.'

'And how does she know?'

'She overheard Michelle talking about it to one of the other nurses,' Kylie said. 'Mind you, Daria don't speak English too well. Interesting, though, innit?'

Lee wasn't surprised when he got the call from Derek Salmon telling him that Sandra Rivers wanted to give up looking for her ex-husband.

'The whole homosexual thing just blew her brains out,' Derek said.

Lee, who had left the police station to have a cigarette said, 'I can understand that. But I'm still sort of involved because of Phil's dad.'

'What did the stupid sod lump you one for?'

'He says the plan was to knock me out and then do a runner,' Lee said. 'Trouble was he got pissed instead.'

'Arsehole.'

'I can go home, but I'll have to stay in touch. Hopefully we'll find out who the body on the bed was soon. I'm sure it's Ken's wife. Who else could it be?'

'Did he kill her?' Derek asked.

'Don't know yet. He says not. He also says he doesn't know where Phil is.'

'What a fucking mess. But look, Lee, when you get back swing by my office and I'll pay you what you're owed. All right?'

'Yeah. Cheers, mate.'

Lee ended the call. Giving up on finding Phil was probably best for Sandra Rivers if it was distressing her so much. It was a bit of a pain for Lee – her money had been limitless and freely available. And there were niggles. The biggest one was why he'd got beaten up when he'd gone to see Barry Barber in Dagenham. Who'd done it? Had it been ordered by Phil Rivers himself? Maybe he'd been watching his parents' place and had identified Lee as a threat?

Lee got the front-desk sergeant to let him back into the station. Cobbett was waiting for him and he was holding a piece of paper.

'Mr Arnold, thought you might like to see this,' he said.

Lee took it from him. It was a letter from Phil Rivers' bogus solicitors, Myerson & Jackson. It was addressed to Ken and it told him that his son Philip didn't want to see him or his wife any more. Worded in cold and efficient legalese, the letterhead was decorated with a ton of industry award marks and logos. It must have hurt Ken and Bette a lot.

'Found it in his coat,' Cobbett said. 'Thought you might be interested.'

'Did he say anything about it?' Lee asked.

'Only to tell me that it proved what he'd told you about not knowing where his son is.'

Lee shook his head. 'All irrelevant now anyway,' he said. He gave the letter back to Cobbett. 'My client doesn't want her husband found any more.'

'Philip Rivers should serve time for what he's done,' Cobbett said.

'But if the wife has paid off the victims and won't make a complaint herself . . .'

'Nothing we can do.'

'No.'

Later that day Lee was packing his clothes away at Susan's flat when his mobile rang again. It was Cobbett.

'Just thought you'd like to know,' he said. 'The corpse in the bed died from natural causes.'

'So Ken's off the hook.'

'For murder, yes,' Cobbett said. 'But if that is his wife's dead body, he kept it for at least a month, during which time he carried on collecting her pension. And he hit you over the head.'

Sulky, spotty but not bad-looking, Antoni Brzezinski was either not the brightest star in the sky or he was working hard to appear that way. His mates, an Asian boy whose name Amy hadn't yet been able to catch and a white kid called Puffy, hung around the shops at the end of Freemasons Road near Custom House station. She noticed they made a point of not lurking around the off-licence, which was their ultimate goal. Instead they stood outside the baker's and hassled older girls from the estate, usually with babies in tow, to go and buy cheap cider for them. Sometimes the girls complied and sometimes they didn't. But the boys got moderately pissed and then sort of grunted at each other, noises that she imagined passed for speech. Amy had seen them do it before. But then something different happened.

A boy, well-dressed, lanky and dark, pulled up in a BMW sports car. A few years older than the others, he had a swaggering vibe, which made people look at him. When he yelled at the boys to 'Get in, you fuckers!' he had an accent Amy couldn't place. The boys did as they were told. They jumped into the car while their driver said, 'Careful of the paint! Be careful of the fucking paint!' Then he put his foot down and roared towards Victoria Dock Road. When he got to the bottom of Freemasons, he turned left. Amy, in her Renault Clio, followed at a much more sedate pace.

*

Shirley wasn't prepared to give up without a fight.

'He's sectioned,' she said. 'Dr el Masri didn't need Dylan's permission to examine him.'

'The patient wasn't complaining of pain or discomfort and Dr el Masri had not been asked to perform a medical,' Mr Cotton said. 'Our hands are tied.'

She'd been summoned to the chief consultant's office as soon as she arrived for work. Dylan Smith was still, as far as she knew, in bad physical shape and not being treated. In a way, Shirley wished she'd stayed at home.

'And if Dylan collapses?'

'That's another matter entirely,' he said.

'When did Dr el Masri try to examine Dylan?'

Mr Cotton looked down at some notes. 'Six-thirty yesterday evening. Just before shift handover.'

'To Timothy Pool?'

'Yes,' he said. 'Prior to that. I know it's not what you want to hear, but Dylan Smith also told Dr el Masri that he doesn't want to have any more input from the Advocacy.'

Dylan had already made that very clear to Shirley. But it was still hurtful to hear it from a third party.

'I will, of course, have to report the entire incident to the Trust,' Mr Cotton went on.

Which meant that, depending on how he reported it, the Advocacy could be sanctioned or perhaps even shut down. Shirley said nothing. So much for her one and only attempt to do some real representative work. She felt as if he'd just stuck his boot through her head.

The walk back to the Advocacy office seemed endless. But when she found Mumtaz waiting for her, Shirley made herself smile.

'Hi, Mumtaz. Thanks so much for coming in. How'd it go with Terry?'

'He's very agitated,' Mumtaz said.

'He often is.'

'I'd say he needed a medication review, if that were my place,' Mumtaz said. 'His meds don't seem to be doing much to alleviate his condition. In fact, to me, all the chronics seem agitated. I'm not saying they should all be medication zombies, but they shouldn't be as distressed as Terry and some of the others appear to be.'

'It's hospital policy to try to reduce medication.'

'Which is admirable. But maybe they're going too fast?'

Shirley didn't reply.

Mumtaz said, 'Shirley, I've heard something this morning I think you should know.'

'What?'

'About Dylan Smith. Dr el Masri had to be called out to him in the early hours of the morning, apparently,' Mumtaz said. 'Dylan "kicked off" for some reason. I don't know whether the doctor sedated him.'

Shirley breathed in deeply to try to calm her nerves. Mr Cotton hadn't mentioned any sort of incident. 'How did you find this out, Mumtaz?' she asked.

'It's only hearsay,' Mumtaz said. 'Someone told one of the cleaners over there.'

'Who is?'

'They might not want me to say.'

'Dr el Masri went over to Forensic to examine Dylan physically at my request yesterday evening,' Shirley said. 'That's why I was seeing Mr Cotton this morning. Dylan refused the examination.'

'Maybe that was what it was about?'

'But it wasn't in the middle of the night,' Shirley said. 'It was six-thirty in the evening, just before Timothy Pool came on duty. I was assured by Mr Cotton that was the case.'

'So maybe Dylan kicked off later on.'

Shirley frowned. 'Even if he had, Dr el Masri wouldn't have been called. Dr Golding was on duty on Forensic last night.'

'Was he? Apparently Dr Golding and Timothy Pool were having an argument about something in Pool's office this morning. Maybe it was about why Dr el Masri was called out to Dylan and not Dr Golding.'

'Maybe. If that's true.'

'If it is.'

'I can't see why Dr el Masri would have been called out instead of Dr Golding,' Shirley said. 'Unless Dylan suddenly wanted to be examined after all. But then, if that had happened, Mr Cotton would have told me about it.'

'You think he would?'

'Yes.' But Shirley wasn't sure. Mr Cotton had never enjoyed advocacy intervention in his hospital and, because she was beginning to pursue matters properly now, he was feeling under threat. Had she picked up some satisfaction in his voice when he'd told her he was going to report her actions with Dylan Smith to the Trust?

The BMW roared along the Royal Albert Way, past the University of East London campus, and at Gallions Reach it turned into one of the entrances to the new Gallions housing development. This was a maze of apartment blocks in what Amy always thought of as 'loud' colours, most of which cost more than the average Newham resident could even imagine. She knew the development a bit, mainly because it pissed her off. Right at the middle of the site was the old Gallions Hotel, a graceful Edwardian building which, surrounded by the new apartments, looked as if it was being hassled by a gang of incomprehensible children's TV characters.

The whole site was controlled by double yellow lines, which meant that only the residents, who had underground parking facilities, could leave their cars in safety. Visitors risked a ticket. But that didn't seem to bother the driver of the BMW. He just dumped the car by the side of the road and he and the boys got out. They all went into a white apartment block to the left of the old hotel. Amy drew up on the opposite side of the elegant Edwardian pile and kept watch both for the boys and for traffic wardens.

She had a long wait. Her only consolation was that because it was winter and the old hotel was empty, not many visitors drove into the area, and that included traffic wardens. She just had to cope with the boredom. Beyond the hotel, there was nothing to see at Gallions. Through a forest of empty transparent box-like balconies, she could just see the end of the Royal Albert Dock. But if she got out and went to have a look, she might draw attention to herself. Most of the flats were probably empty because their owners were at work. Antoni and his mates were in the white block – somewhere – and those places had a lot of windows.

Amy sat. Every so often she'd look over at the BMW and then just stare into space. All she knew about Gallions Hotel was that it had once provided accommodation to people going abroad on the ships that left for far-flung parts of the British Empire from the Royal Docks. She'd heard that it had even had its own railway station, once. Not a station like the Gallions Reach Docklands Light Railway station, but a real steam-train terminus where people walked from the bar straight out onto the platform. How many modern drunks would have appreciated that when they went one over the eight in the middle of the night? Amy smiled. When she'd been in the police she'd pulled more Friday and Saturday night shifts than she could remember. Turfing pissed boys out of the Beckton Arms in Canning Town and pushing aside outraged Muslim men to pick up intoxicated white girls off the pavement outside pubs on the Barking Road. Booze was a bloody menace and, ever since she'd worked the streets of Newham as a copper, Amy had all but given it up.

Amy wondered whether Antoni and his mates were getting pissed in one of the flats. Maybe the driver of the car had taken them to his place for a booze-up. Although if he did live at Gallions, why hadn't he put his car away in the underground car park? Unless the driver had been desperate for a drink? But he hadn't struck Amy as that sort of bloke. His skin was unblemished and his car was too good. To her, he'd looked much more like a drug dealer than a boozer.

Time began to feel like slow-running treacle. Ten minutes ticked lazily into fifteen and as the drizzle stopped and the sky began to lighten, Amy began to feel her eyes get heavy. She was bored and the car was stuffy, so she opened a window and took a swig from the flask of coffee she kept underneath the passenger seat. She couldn't drink too much in case it made her want to go to the toilet.

She'd just put her flask back when she heard a muddle of loud, boyish voices. There was laughter and she heard the BMW driver say, 'I told you!' But in the middle of the talk and the hilarity there was an incongruous sight. One of the boys, the white kid who called himself Puffy, was having to be supported by Antoni and the Asian boy. His eyes were closed and his feet dragged along the pavement. He looked practically unconscious.

Amy photographed the trio. The driver said, 'Just put him in the back. He'll be OK.'

The kids clearly found Puffy a heavy load and it took longer to put him in the car than the driver wanted. 'Come on!' he snapped. 'What you like, eh? Weak little girls?'

Once Puffy was in, Antoni and the Asian boy jumped into the car. Then it sped off, again at some ridiculous speed. Amy followed. At Gallions Reach, the BMW headed back towards Custom House along the Royal Albert Way. But then, just beyond the old derelict post office on the side of the Royal Albert Dock, the car suddenly stopped. Unless she wanted to blow her cover, Amy had to drive on by. But as she passed she saw Antoni and the driver pull Puffy out of the BMW and lay him on the pavement. She noticed that his face was a bright, almost translucent white. Amy pulled over as soon as she could and dialled 999.

It was weird being back in the East End. Lee had got used to the smell of cockles and vinegar as well as the relative emptiness of Southend. Maybe Susan had been onto something when she'd talked about him moving out of London? But then perhaps she hadn't. She wanted him in any way she could get him and he now knew, for certain, that he didn't feel likewise. When she'd got Vi's number off his phone, she'd shot herself in the foot. But he hadn't ended their relationship. He wasn't up to any emotional scenes and he suspected that Susan would make a few. Besides, he was a coward when it came to women and he knew it.

'Lee!'

He'd just left the car in Morrisons supermarket car park and was walking along Stratford Broadway towards Derek Salmon's office.

'Lee Arnold!'

It was a woman's voice, which he didn't immediately recognize. But then he looked down. Rosie Sweeney had always been small.

'Where you striding off to like you're on a mission from God?' Rosie said.

She'd never been pretty even as a teenager when they'd been at school together but there had always been something about Rosie that made lots of blokes want her. Lee had never got it. But then he liked curves and Rosie was a bit light on those.

'I'm just off to see your old man,' Lee said.

He saw Rosie's face drop even before she spoke. 'Well, be careful, he's got a stinking cold and he's not "my" anything, Lee,' she said. 'Not any more.'

Lee frowned. Rosie and Derek Salmon had been childhood sweethearts. They had two kids, both now at university, and what he'd always imagined was an idyllic lifestyle in the posh Essex village of Ongar.

'But Derek never . . .'

'Said anything?' Rosie snorted. 'Fucking coward! He wouldn't, would he?'

'I don't . . .'

Rosie put her four heavy supermarket bags down at her feet and straightened her back a little painfully. She looked down. 'Shopping for Mum.' She looked up. 'She's still at Shipman Road.'

Lee remembered the house. When he was a kid it had been typical Custom House fare, all cheap furniture inside, broken-up old tat in the yard outside.

'So are you and Derek . . . ?'

'We're so fucking over it isn't even funny,' Rosie said.

'I'm sorry to hear that, Rose, truly.' But she just shrugged. 'What happened? You two were always solid.'

'What happened? If I knew I'd tell you,' Rosie said. 'Eleven months ago he comes home one evening and tells me it's all over. Luckily the kids were both away at college when it all kicked off. Although of course I had to tell them when they came home for Christmas because Del had buggered off by that time. He's renting a flat and I've had to put the house up for sale. Not that there's any more than a gnat's fart of equity left in it. We're skint.'

Lee didn't understand. Derek had always been very successful. In fact, his new posh offices gave the impression that he was doing very nicely. 'But . . .'

'No, I don't know what my husband has been spending our money on either,' Rosie said. 'I didn't know he'd taken out a second and then a third mortgage on the house. Christ knows how he managed to trick me into those.'

Lee felt for her. Rosie had always been a decent sort. Why had Derek Salmon dismantled their lives in this way? He couldn't believe it was just to fund his shiny new offices. Was there someone else?

Rosie said, 'But anyway, that's not your problem. Just make sure that if he owes you money, you get it, OK?'

'Del's always paid me on time and in full in the past,' Lee said.

She shook her head. 'And he probably will again. The business is probably fine. I'm just bitter. If I knew why he'd ditched me and the kids, I wouldn't be so fucking livid. But he won't talk to me, and so what can I do? He calls it "irreconcilable differences" but that can mean anything. As far as I was concerned, we agreed on most things.' She picked her shopping up. 'Anyway, must get back to Mum's. Might be living with her soon, so I can't afford to piss her off.'

Rosie left and Lee went to see her soon-to-be ex-husband. He didn't tell Derek he'd met Rosie but he did look at him with different eyes. As far as he could see, Del was just Del. The solicitor seemed sad that the Phil Rivers case had come to nothing, but happy to hand over a big fat cheque from the missing man's wife. He didn't say a word about Rosie.

## 21

Amy had followed the ambulance to Newham General Hospital. Even before it had arrived, Antoni and his mates had got back in the BMW and sped off towards Custom House. She'd put Puffy in the recovery position, but he'd stopped breathing.

The paramedics got him going again, which was a relief, and although Amy only owned up to being a disinterested passer-by, she followed the crew to the hospital anyway. As soon as they'd taken Puffy inside, she called Mumtaz.

'I don't know what those boys did in that flat,' she said. 'But when Puffy came out he was all over the place.'

'You think he took something?' Mumtaz asked.

'That would be my best guess. But I don't know what,' Amy said. 'The others seemed straight.'

'But we can't assume that.'

'No. I didn't tell the paramedics who I was and I haven't told the medical staff anything yet,' Amy said. 'But I'll have to fill them in.'

'Of course,' Mumtaz said. 'Tell them anything they need to know. I'll tell Antoni's mother what's happened.'

'OK.'

Amy finished the call and walked into Accident and Emergency. She told the nurse at reception that she'd come in with the boy who'd collapsed on the Royal Albert Way. She was told to sit with the other patients in what was a very full waiting room. Someone would come to speak to her. The first hour was the worst, especially when a couple of alcoholics decided to have a wheelchair race.

It was never easy talking to someone you didn't know well. Ever since he'd started at Ilford, Shirley had felt that Dr Golding was a bit aloof and unhappy. But then she'd had that brief conversation with him in Sara Ibrahim's old room and she had felt something she had interpreted as sympathy for the dead girl. She came across him in the staff canteen. Dr D'Lima had just left and so Golding was alone. Not knowing how long she'd have him to herself, Shirley sat down opposite Golding and smiled.

He smiled back. Shirley looked at the door, which remained closed.

She said, 'Dr Golding, I don't know whether you remember me . . .'

'You're Mrs Mayfield from the Advocacy,' he said. 'Of course I do.'

He was very good-looking and so Shirley blushed a little. She said, 'Can I ask you something, Dr Golding?'

'You can.' He put the sandwich he'd been eating down. 'Don't know if I'll be able to answer, though.'

Shirley looked at the door one more time and then she leant forward. 'Were you called out to Dylan Smith on Forensic in the early hours of this morning?' she asked.

He didn't answer for a moment. Watching him, Shirley felt he was considering her question very carefully.

She'd just about given up hope of ever getting an answer when he said, 'Yes. Yes, I was.'

'Why?'

'I can't tell you that,' he said.

Patient confidentiality. Shirley understood. 'I see,' she said.

'Sorry.'

Shirley looked at the door yet again. Anyone could come in at any minute and she wasn't even sure that she could or should trust Golding. But she felt she could. Was that good enough?

'Well, can you tell me if Dr el Masri was there?' she asked. 'He tried to perform an examination of Dylan at six-thirty in the evening and . . .'

'Dr el Masri and myself were with Nurse Pool in Dylan Smith's room in the early hours of this morning,' he said. 'Unless Dylan decides to tell you more about that meeting, I can't say anything else, Mrs Mayfield.'

He looked disgruntled now and although Shirley wanted to push her case further, she didn't. Her information had come via a cleaner who had been listening to gossip. So Golding had been in Dylan's room with el Masri in the early hours of the morning? So what?

Dr Golding stood up and began to walk towards the canteen door. Shirley said, 'Don't you want your sandwich?'

He turned, looked at the sandwich and then said, 'No.'

'OK.'

He made as if to carry on walking out, but suddenly reversed and came back to Shirley. With one furtive look at the canteen door he said, 'I can't tell you what happened last night. But I can tell you one thing, which is that Dr el Masri didn't even attempt to perform an examination of Mr Smith until the early hours of this morning.'

And then he left, quickly.

Shirley was stunned. Mr Cotton had assured her that el Masri had tried to examine Dylan at six-thirty. But if Golding was right then it had actually happened right in the middle of Pool's shift. Dylan hated Pool – he would have been terrified if he'd been in attendance. No wonder he hadn't consented to the examination. But why had Mr Cotton lied to her?

If being back in the East End was weird, then sitting behind his desk in his office was even weirder. It seemed as if he'd been away for months and yet, in reality, it had only been a few days. Lee allowed himself a smile. The place was still as cramped and dark, and the ever-present damp hadn't deigned to go away, but he was glad to be back, even if he was on his own.

He'd called Mumtaz, who was working her Ilford Hospital gig. Apparently Amy was at the General with some kid who was a friend of the Polish boy she'd been following. The kid had collapsed and so Amy was going to have to blow out the case in order to possibly save the boy's life. Which was a pain in the arse. But at least he'd just put a nice wedge of cash in the business account, courtesy of Derek Salmon. He flung Derek's paperwork on Mumtaz's desk. She'd file it for him later. Money was always an issue and whenever it came in, Lee just banked it and then moved on.

Lee's mobile rang. It was Susan. He ignored it. He wasn't ready to talk to her. But was that fair? He thought about Derek Salmon's wife, Rosie, and how wrung out she'd looked when he'd met her in Stratford. And why was she in such a state? Because Derek had given her her marching orders but not given her a reason. Lee looked at his phone again and was just about to pick it up when it stopped ringing. He shook his head. Why did he find dealing with women he was romantically attached to so difficult? Or was he making too much of his recent experiences? Was it just Susan?

His phone rang again and this time he picked it up. He expected Susan, but in fact it was DI Cobbett from Southend.

'Thought you'd like to know the result of the inquiry on the body in the Rivers' flat,' he said.

'Yeah.'

'Ken Rivers finally admitted that the body in his bedroom was that of his wife, Bette. According to Ken she'd died suddenly in their bed and he hadn't known what to do.'

'You said natural causes before – do you know any more?'

Cobbett said, 'The poor lady had an aneurysm. No sign of foul play.'

'Good.'

'But he still failed to get medical attention for his wife,' Cobbett said. 'Admittedly there would have been little anyone could have done for her, but he didn't report her death and he carried on collecting her pension. He also attacked and imprisoned you.'

'True. Why did he lump me one?'

'He's sticking to his story that he was trying to do a disappearing act,' Cobbett said. 'You'd caught him gambling and you knew he was in debt up to his bollocks. Quick as a flash, he reckoned that if you were found with the body of Bette he could do a runner and you'd take the blame for her death. He's not the brightest tool in the box.'

'He is a tool, though.'

Cobbett laughed. 'And now Shane Warner, his landlord, has given him notice to quit,' he said. 'There's not a lot anyone can do about it. Warner, as well as being a go-to bloke when it comes to drugs and women, also has a very good solicitor. Ken's tenancy is very clear: if he doesn't pay rent to Warner for three consecutive months, then he's out. And it's watertight.'

Lee shook his head. Ken Rivers wasn't a nice man but he wasn't a completely rotten one either. Just stupid.

'So is he in his flat now?' Lee asked.

'He's got two weeks to get out. If we can't find his son or some other relative he'll be a candidate for the homeless shelter,' Cobbett said.

Lee told him that his hunt for Phil Rivers was over.

'Well, we'll see if we can find him,' Cobbett said. 'If only to hand over responsibility for Ken to him. I never understood your client's interest anyway – it's a strange world when a woman wants to find her ex-husband to see if he's all right and doesn't care about the vast amount of money he's ripped her off for.'

It was odd, but then there was no blueprint for relationships. When he'd finished talking to Cobbett, Lee went outside the office and had a fag. A couple of schoolgirls were lurking around the end of the back alley smoking cigarettes too. One looked like a Goth while the other one had her head covered. For a moment he thought she might be Mumtaz, until he saw her face.

When she'd phoned him they'd talked mainly about Amy and her Polish kid whose mother had, it seemed, been right to worry about the company he kept. Mumtaz had said she had news about her own assignment too. But it would have to wait for the next morning. She'd finish at Ilford at five and then go home to do some more packing. Lee, meanwhile, also had to go home.

Normally that thought would have filled him with joy. To go home and see Chronus, put the telly on and get a bit of cleaning done. But Tony Bracci was also in the flat and he left coffee cups on floors and didn't think that pairing socks was important.

MJ offered Rashida the joint again.

'It's only weed,' she said. 'It won't do you any harm.'

Rashida shook her head. 'No, it's un-Islamic to take drugs,' she said. 'It's OK for you.'

'What, because I'm a Hindu? Not really,' MJ said. 'But so what? It's just cannabis, girl. Honest to God, there are things that are *so* much worse out there and it will help to relax you.'

But Rashida carried on shaking her head. 'All drugs are bad,' she said.

MJ smoked. 'Weed's not. It's not like heroin or that mad stuff gangsters in Russia make out of petrol and Mr Muscle.'

'Petrol and Mr Muscle?'

'They call them legal highs because you can't get arrested for having them. But they're lethal. Then there's coke, that's bad, and there's even some prescription drugs on the street that can really fuck you up.' She puffed again. 'Weed just relaxes you a bit and you laugh at stuff.'

It also made you say things. Rashida had been around MJ long enough to know that when she was stoned she just gabbled away about anything. That was OK for her. MJ didn't have secrets. Rashida thought about her father's lock-up and she moved even further away from the joint.

MJ laughed. 'Fucking hell, man, it won't bite you!'

But Rashida said 'No' once again because she knew that it could.


It took a while to track Daria the cleaner down. Like a lot of the other girls who'd been brought in by the cleaning contractors to work at the hospital, it was rumoured that she was probably an illegal immigrant. Whatever her status, she worked all and any hours God sent. She was cleaning the toilets in the admin block when Mumtaz found her. But how to open a conversation with Daria, who she didn't know, about a dead patient?

Mumtaz washed her hands and thought how she might start a dialogue when Daria walked over to her. About forty, Daria was very dark – some people had said they thought she was a gypsy – and very, very thin.

'You are Muslim woman?' she said to Mumtaz. She pointed to her headscarf.

'Yes.'

'Me also,' Daria said. 'Albanian. Kosovo.'

'Ah.' Most Albanians in the UK were Kosovan Muslims. The women, particularly, tended to be poor. Daria conformed to this Albanian norm. She wore big, baggy shalwar trousers that looked as if they were made of curtains, and an oversized, very threadbare man's suit jacket. On her feet she wore flip-flops. By comparison, Mumtaz looked like a catwalk model. How could she, in all conscience, ask this woman to do anything for her without offering her something in return? But what? If something illegal had happened to Sara Ibrahim's medical notes, and Mumtaz gave Daria money, then the whole investigation could be put at risk. It could be argued that she'd paid Daria to fabricate evidence.

'You know we are forgotten Muslims,' Daria said. 'In old days we are ruled by Turks and then they go. Then Serbs come and kill everyone. Because we are European Muslims nobody cares.'

That wasn't strictly true. Although the international community had not done enough to protect the Kosovars during the ethnic wars of the 1990s in the former Yugoslavia, they hadn't totally abandoned them. Nobody had been "forgotten". But Daria was poor and so how could she see any kind of parity between herself and almost every other person she met – and that included the service users. Mumtaz suddenly felt stupid and manipulative. How could she ask this woman to give her anything? Even information.

But she'd given it to Kylie. Why? Was Kylie her friend, or did she think that she was? Maybe she should have asked Kylie to introduce them. Maybe she could still do that.

'Well, I'm Mumtaz,' she said. 'What's your name?'

'I am Daria.'

'Oh?' The deception came quickly and easily. She creased her brow as if trying to remember something.

'Oh? What you mean?'

'I've heard your name,' Mumtaz said. 'I've got a friend called Kylie . . .'

'Ah, Kylie, yes!' Daria's face lit up. 'She my friend too! Sometimes we go to pub!'

'Do you?'

Mumtaz didn't think there was any implied criticism in her tone. But Daria must have picked some up. 'I don't drink,' she said. 'Just have conversation.' And then, unexpectedly, she gave Mumtaz an opening. 'You must come! Pub is only at end of road. Me and Kylie, we go tonight. You must come.'

Amy saw Mrs Brzezinski drag Antoni up to the reception desk. 'I have brought in my son to see Dr Banerjee. Antoni Brzezinski.'

'Oh, yes.' The receptionist took them straight through to the treatment area.

Dr Banerjee had been very understanding when he'd met Amy. Some medics, just like some coppers, automatically sneered at PIs. But he'd totally got why Antoni's mum had employed the agency. He'd said, 'Parents can't be too careful, especially not on estates.'

Amy still didn't know what was wrong with Puffy. Unless he'd suddenly developed a previously undetected condition out at Gallions, she assumed it had to be drug-related. As far as she could tell, Puffy was still alive, or rather nobody had come to let her know that he wasn't. And the doctor had said that he would keep her informed.

A man wearing a traffic warden's uniform walked up to the reception desk. His face was red and he was out of breath. The receptionist looked at him as if she wanted him dead. A lot of people had that sort of reaction to traffic wardens. 'Yes?'

'You've, er, got my son 'ere,' the man said. 'He was brought in from Royal Albert Way. His name's Paul Hall.'

'Oh, right.' Her demeanour changed immediately. 'Come through here, Mr Hall, doctor's waiting for you.'

So that was Puffy's real name, Paul Hall. Plain and boring. No wonder he'd embraced a nickname. It was hot in the waiting room and, after a while, and in spite of argumentative mothers of asthmatic kids, howling alcoholics and a very suspicious bloke who claimed that the police had banged a nail into his knee and then super-glued his eyes shut, Amy went to sleep. What turned out to be a considerable time later, she was woken by Dr Banerjee. 'Can we have a chat?' he said.

She followed him to a small office at the end of the admission ward. 'I know I've asked you this before,' he said, 'but did you see the boy take anything?'

'No,' she said. 'I saw the group go into a flat at Gallions Reach and when they came out the boy they all called "Puffy" was falling about. The rest you know.'

'Do you know which flat they went into?'

'I'd know the block, but not the flat,' Amy said. 'Does this mean that drugs are involved?'

'If only it were that simple,' he said.

'Then . . . ?'

'I can't be specific. We're still treating the boy. But I can tell you that Antoni Brzezinski is fine.'

She'd thought that only Puffy had indulged. But in what? If it wasn't some sort of illegal substance, then was it one of those legal highs she'd heard about? Some of those were lethal. Some, like a thing called 'krokodil', which rots the skin on users' bodies from the inside out, had been developed in Russia to mimic the effects of expensive illegal drugs like heroin.

'Will the sick boy be all right?' Amy asked.

'I don't know. Time will tell. But he isn't out of the woods yet,' the doctor said. 'You've been watching Antoni and his friends for some time, have you ever seen them take anything before?'

'No. They just drink cheap cider. Or they did until today.'

'What changed?'

'Another boy turned up,' Amy said. 'Older, with the car that Puffy was in when he got sick. I've got the registration number.'

The doctor shrugged. 'Antoni has told us that neither he nor his friends took anything at the flat in Gallions Reach. He said it was just the boy Puffy. None of the others, he claims, saw what he did or when.'

'Then why did they abandon him?'

'A good question. But I'm not the police and neither are you. And as I say, illegal drugs are not the issue here.'

'So will you call the police?' Amy asked.

He thought for a moment and then he said, 'I will. But quite what they'll do about it, I can't predict. Especially if the boy doesn't wake up.'

## 22

It was well past seven p.m., but Shirley couldn't go home. She sat at her desk, staring out into the corridor and the darkness beyond the windows. Long ago, Ilford Hospital had possessed even more extensive grounds that at one time had also included a small farm. Back then, patients had been encouraged to work outside, growing vegetables and tending to a flock of chickens. But since the ultimate aim of treatment at the unit had changed, and was now focused on returning people to their communities, such elaborate rehabilitation had ceased. Now residents had little to divert them and Shirley found herself wondering whether the old days had not been better in some respects. Of course, there had been a very large down-side, exemplified by barbaric restraints like straitjackets and manacles. If only abuse had been stamped out along with those instruments of torture. Shirley thought about Dylan and wondered how he was getting on.

Had he complied with Timothy Pool and let whatever injuries he had sustained remain a mystery? And had Dr el Masri in some way colluded with that? She had heard that el Masri was a sex pest, but she'd never heard anything about actual cruelty. The doctors had limited contact with the patients, so it wasn't usually an issue. But other staff members, who worked on the wards day in and day out, were much more liable to take their frustrations out on those in their care. Like Timothy Pool, for instance. But how could she, or anyone, stop it?

The major problem was that unless perpetrators of cruelty were actually dismissed, or suspended immediately from duty, there was always the chance that they could silence a complainant. If a service user complained, his or her life could be made hell; the abuse could escalate. If it was a member of staff making an allegation, they could be putting their career on the line. She thought about Nurse Denna and wondered where she was. She'd not seen her that day. Of course, she was agency, so she could be almost anywhere. Shirley knew she had to keep whatever was happening at the hospital in proportion.

She had her office door open because she was afraid she'd get locked in again. She still didn't know who had trapped her in there or why, although the caretaker had said that the door did stick. But even if she told herself very firmly to be rational, she was still sure that someone had locked it from the outside. And then unlocked it. At the time she had reasoned it had been done to frighten her. She'd just had an altercation with Timothy Pool and she wouldn't put such a cruel and childish prank beyond him. He wasn't subtle, after all. Shirley was sure that with his staff under his thumb, Timothy felt he was untouchable.

Shirley was about to pack her stuff away and leave when she heard voices in the corridor outside. Or rather, whispers. And whoever was there sounded angry. For a moment she just sat, straining to try to make out individual words – but she couldn't. It was spooky and it made Shirley want to stay where she was, in case they, whoever they were, found her. But eventually her curiosity got the better of her. Slowly, in case she inadvertently scraped a chair leg on the wooden floor, she stood up. The voices, which both sounded male, got a little louder, She moved towards the door. When she reached the Advocacy's filing cabinet she stopped.

Although she still couldn't hear any words, she noticed that the voices were getting louder, the anger had increased. The hairs on her arms stood up and Shirley licked her dry lips. Then she did hear something very clearly.

'I'll fucking kill you!'

Lee was so pissed off he was almost tempted to go back to the office. But he was also tired and the fridge needed defrosting. He'd taken all the food out and put it in a box on the worktop when Tony Bracci had come in. First of all he'd taken the milk out of the box to put in his coffee, which was reasonable, then he'd just left the bottle on the side of the sink, which was not. But Lee had ignored it. Tony had gone out to get fish and chips, which they'd eaten together, and then Tony had gone to his room. When he'd come out, he'd brought five filthy coffee cups with him, which he had just flung in the sink. Then he'd gone into the living room and put on the TV. As Lee refilled the fridge, all he could hear was the sound of Bruce Forsyth patronising some blonde woman and Tony farting. He couldn't go back in there!

But if he didn't, when Chronus woke up he'd start screeching. If it was evening and the lights were on, he expected to see Lee. If he didn't, he showed off. Lee put the last piece of cheese back in the fridge and took his courage in his hands. As he walked in, Tony said, 'It's just the *Strictly* catch-up. You don't mind, do you, mate?'

He should have said 'yes' but it wouldn't come out. 'No.'

'Ta.'

Lee picked up Tony's copy of the *Sun*. But it too was full of *Strictly Come Dancing* nonsense, as well as a load of other reality TV garbage. He put it down. Vi was still not fit enough to return to work and so he didn't have anyone he could talk to about this situation. He liked Tony Bracci and he didn't want to fling him out on the street. But he had to have some feeling of control in his own home. The dirty coffee cups were symptomatic of a general slackness towards life that Lee couldn't take. Tony noticed nothing. Things didn't niggle at him. He could walk into a room full of shite and just lie down and go to sleep. He was a nice bloke, but Lee could see why his wife had had enough.

'I'm just going to have a bit of a tidy up in the bedroom,' he said to Tony.

'All right, mate.' Tony waved a hand in the air but he didn't look away from the telly.

Lee closed his bedroom door and sat down. On top of the whole flatmate thing, the abortive Phil Rivers case was still bugging him. How could someone just get away with 1.2 million quid of somebody else's money? How could they be allowed to do it? And what had that letter to his father from Phil's nonexistent solicitor been about? According to Ken they hadn't been close and Lee was inclined to believe him. So why bother with the letter? It was as if he was making sure his parents didn't contact him. But if they didn't know where he was, how could they? Then again, maybe stupidity ran in the family. How Ken had thought that anyone would have been able to connect Lee to Bette's long-dead body in that bedroom was a mystery. How he had ever imagined that he was some sort of modern man who broke the bank in Monte Carlo was another puzzler. Professionally as well as financially, Lee wished he'd been able to find Phil Rivers and bring the whole business to a successful conclusion.

But if Sandra Rivers didn't want him to then nothing more could happen. One thing was for sure, Phil Rivers, wherever he was, didn't have to sit in his bedroom like Nobby No Mates listening to a middle-aged bloke farting in front of his telly. Money bought you out of experiences like that.

The Barley Mow was one of those pubs that had been taken over by a large brewery chain. The pubs this chain bought up tended to then be 'ruralized' – bits of old plough hanging on the walls, a surfeit of straw and horse brasses around faux fireplaces. But this one was excessive. There were even, Mumtaz noticed, plastic milk churns in the beer garden. But Kylie liked it and Daria seemed to think it was some sort of palace.

'If this was Kosovo, everywhere would be full of smoke from men's cigarettes,' Daria said. 'This is so clean. I still can't believe it.'

When Mumtaz had walked in with Daria, she'd seen the look of alarm on Kylie's face. She was almost certainly wondering whether she'd told Daria what Kylie had told her about Hatem el Shamy and Dr el Masri. And it was bothering her. Did this mean that Kylie had lied? She was certainly slurping down her beer as if her life depended on it.

'The toilets have soap that smells like heaven,' Daria said. She got up from her seat. 'I go now to use it.'

When she'd gone Kylie said, 'You know I told you what she said to me in confidence. I hope you haven't . . . ? '

'I've said nothing,' Mumtaz told her. 'But, Kylie, I have to find out whether that story is true.'

'Why? What's it to you?'

'I'm with the Advocacy.'

'Sara Ibrahim's dead. You can't advocate for her, can you?'

'No, but . . .' Mumtaz leant forward across the table. 'I don't know, but I'm sure that you've had your fair share of problems with el Masri in the past.'

Kylie frowned. 'What? Looking down me top and that?'

Mumtaz knew she had to make this seem as if she was engaged in some sort of investigation on behalf of the Advocacy into Dr el Masri's sexist behaviour. In a sense that was the case. She just wasn't doing it on Shirley's orders.

'We want it to stop,' Mumtaz said.

'I don't like it but . . .'

'I need to know whether Daria's story about el Masri changing Sara Ibrahim's medical notes is right,' Mumtaz said. 'Because if he's doing that, then who knows what else he's up to?'

Kylie shrugged. 'So what?' She drained her beer glass. 'That girl's dead. Her notes will've gone to the basement, nobody ever looks at old cases.'

'Yes, but if what Daria heard about what was done is true then I could get those notes brought up and—'

'And what? So he changed the notes, he—'

'It's illegal!'

A man over at the bar gave Mumtaz what she could only describe as a 'funny look'. You didn't get too many covered women in pubs. And they certainly didn't usually get into heated discussions. Mumtaz lowered her voice. 'As you said yourself, there are a lot of things that happen in the hospital that none of us understand. The job of the advocates is to uncover things that disturb people and combat things like cruelty and sexism.'

'And have me lose me job? No,' Kylie said. 'And don't you go questioning Daria neither! She's my friend, we go drinking together.'

As far as Mumtaz could see, Daria took Kylie out and bought her drinks – she hadn't seen Kylie return the favour yet.

'Then how do I know if what you told me about her is true?' Mumtaz said.

'You don't.' Kylie put a stick of chewing gum in her mouth. 'Just forget it. Dr el Masri'll screw up some other time, you'll just have to wait.'

They sat in silence for a moment and then Mumtaz said, 'Kylie, why did you tell me that story about Daria if you didn't want me to take it further? You know what I do at the hospital.'

Kylie looked down at the table. 'I dunno,' she said. 'Just gossip. You know how it is.'

'Yes, but if you didn't want me to challenge Daria . . .'

'I know! I know!'

Mumtaz saw Daria walking back from the toilets at the same time as Kylie. 'Just don't tell her! All right?' Kylie said. 'I need her.'

For her money? Mumtaz couldn't help looking at Kylie with a cynical eye. But she agreed. She could hardly do anything else. By that time she'd had an idea that, on the face of it, was probably much better than trying to get accurate information out of an Albanian woman with poor English language skills.


Drink was Susan's poison of choice, but it wasn't doing enough. She'd never been into drugs but she had friends who were. She knew dealers, too; some were regulars at the casino. But this was her night off and she was supposed to be enjoying herself, not giving a shit about work. She was distracted and she wasn't having anything like a good time. Lee had gone back to London and she feared he wasn't coming back. She asked herself whether she could blame him and decided that she couldn't. Why had she made those calls to Vi Collins? Why did she do mad, strange things like that to any man who came into her life?

Susan put her bottle of Stella to one side and opened the gin. She poured herself a large one and splashed a bit of orange juice on top. Then she drank most of it. The truth was that no man had ever cheated on Susan before she'd started the stupid jealous behaviour. But as soon as she got a bloke, it was as if she couldn't help herself. She had to know where he was going, what he was doing and who he was seeing. Where such insecurity came from she didn't know. Her dad had always been faithful to her mum, it wasn't as if there was some sort of childhood trauma. Just an innate insecurity.

She looked at her phone and wondered. Should she call Lee? He had to come back to Southend at some point because of Kenny. Should she invite him to stay at her place? She was being ridiculous. Susan drank more gin. Or should she phone that Vi Collins and apologize to her? Surely that'd make Lee happy?

She still had the number. She looked at it. Best would just be to leave a message but then Vi might answer and she couldn't end the call like she'd done before. That would be weird. But could she talk to the woman if it came to it? She knew she couldn't. What about texting? Susan poured herself some more gin, this time without orange. Texting was a good idea. She composed all sorts of elaborate phrases before she came to the conclusion that it was probably best to just say 'Sorry'. Vi would know it was her. So she sent it. Then she regretted it.

Then Susan cried.

## 23

Salwa had had enough. Rashida had come home smelling of smoke. Things had to change. She was going to book flights to Egypt for the first day of the childrens' school holidays and then she was going to dismiss that private detective. She'd do it in writing so there could be no misunderstanding. She'd deliver the letter to Mrs Hakim's office herself. She'd done nothing and Salwa was angry. Why hadn't Mumtaz Hakim tried to tempt el Masri herself? She was a good-looking woman, he had to want her. But she hadn't. She'd said something about how it wasn't right to 'trap' someone like that. But he was a criminal! Salwa couldn't understand it. Surely if el Masri was a criminal it didn't matter how he was unmasked? And why hadn't she broken into his house to find his explosives? He had them, Hatem had said so. Why couldn't Mumtaz Hakim just go in there and find them?

She put the computer on and while it booted up she thought about how she'd never understand this country she'd come to so many years ago. On the one hand, the British seemed to do everything they could to protect the guilty and prison sentences were really short. On the other hand, they had just assumed that Hatem was guilty right from the start. Was it because he was a Muslim? It seemed so. And yet they allowed her to visit Hatem and he was going to be tried in court, albeit using made-up evidence.

Salwa made her way to the British Airways site. Four returns and one outward journey. Once Rashida was married to Anwar she'd forget all about smoking and her father's lock-up.

She looked at the screen for flights that left at a reasonable hour. She wished Hatem was coming too. The new Egypt was Islamic and exciting, everything Hatem had ever wanted, but it was still poor. Her family were poor. Rashida's wedding would be a cheap affair and she'd have to live in a house with no bathroom. She would hate it. But what could Salwa do? When Hatem had gone to prison the family had funded them, and now the family wanted Rashida for Anwar. What could she do but agree to the match? Salwa would return for Hatem's trial, which wasn't until February. Now she had a few weeks to get into el Masri's house and find his explosives herself. She just had to discover where he lived.

Mumtaz took her headscarf off and put it into her handbag. The basement was underneath the admin block, and although she didn't know whether she'd be able to get in, she did know where the stairs were. It hadn't been easy deciding whether to try to get in as herself or as someone unknown. As soon as she took the scarf off she was a different person as far as the world was concerned. She suspected that the hospital receptionist, who had a liking for celebrity magazines, would barely raise her head whatever Mumtaz did.

On her way from the car to the admin block, Mumtaz had a moment of anxiety when she found herself walking towards Roy, her fellow advocate. But he didn't appear to recognize her.

Mumtaz entered the admin block and the receptionist briefly looked in her direction. She was about to say she was on her way to the finance office when a man came in carrying multiple bunches of flowers. The receptionist looked over at him and smiled. 'They from the crem?' she asked.

The man said they were. Mumtaz moved towards the door to the staircase.

The receptionist picked up two bunches of lilies. 'Ah, aren't they lovely?' she said. 'These from that Thelma who used to be on Chronic?'

'Yeah,' the man said. 'There's bloody loads of them.'

'Oh, it's nice of her family to send them to the patients.'

Mumtaz slipped through the door and down the stairs. This was supposed to be her day off. She'd told Shazia she'd just pop out to the hospital and then she'd spend the rest of the day packing. And if the door to the basement was locked, that was what she would do. If it was unlocked she'd have a task on her hands that would take some time. She didn't even know how or where the records of deceased patients were stored. Loads of stuff was, she had been told, put down in the basement. Defunct employment records, old equipment, rat poison, out-of-date accounts – the basement apparently held it all, along with the records of the dead.

'Puffy's in a coma. Mrs Brzezinski – Antoni's mother – says Antoni won't tell the police the names of the other boys in the car,' Amy said.

'Kind of confirms her worst fears,' Lee said.

'We keep the customer satisfied once again.'

Amy took a cigarette from Lee's packet and lit up. They were sitting on the metal stairs outside the office. Amy had forgotten it was Mumtaz's day off and had come in to update her on Antoni Brzezinski, but she'd found Lee instead.

'You took the reg of the car the kids used?' Lee asked.

'I gave it to the doctor who passed it on to the police, yes,' she said.

'So the driver'll be tracked down eventually, provided the car wasn't nicked.'

'I imagine if he hasn't already ditched it, he will do,' Amy said. 'Those kids must know what Puffy took and exactly where he got it. They all just strode into that block of flats. They went there for a purpose. What I don't understand is, why just Puffy? Why didn't they all take what he took?'

'Maybe he was the only one brave enough to try whatever it was,' Lee said.

'Or they used him as a guinea pig. He's a bit of a sad lump of a kid. I got the feeling he followed the others around.'

Lee's mobile rang.

'Hello, mate,' Vi Collins rasped.

'Hiya, Vi.'

Amy put her fag out and walked back into the office.

'Listen, got a text off your Susan last night,' she said.

Lee felt his heart sink. 'Oh, Christ, I'm so sorry, Vi!'

'Not a problem, love. She just wrote the word "Sorry". I assume it was for giving me the silent treatment. Just thought I'd better let you know.'

'Thanks.'

'I don't know where you two are up to or . . .'

'Neither do I,' Lee said. 'She's a nice girl and all that, but . . . Shit, Vi, I can't be checked up on at my age. All that jealousy stuff . . .'

'Depends if you love her,' Vi said. 'You know what people put up with if they're in love.'

'Oh, I don't know about that,' Lee said. He knew he wasn't in love with Susan, but he also knew that he wasn't sure he could give her up. Was it just the sex?

'Well, I just thought I'd let you know,' Vi said. 'All being well, I'm back at work in a couple of days.'

'That must be a relief.'

'Just a bit. You ever watched daytime telly?' Vi put the phone down and Lee smiled.

When Vi was back at work she'd be happier and, maybe, she'd be able to help him sort Tony Bracci out. Lee didn't want to make Tony homeless, but he did want him to leave. When Tony had finally gone to bed the previous night he'd left his cup in the living room, together with an empty crisp packet and a light dusting of crisp particles all over the chair. Lee had had to clean there and then but he'd had to do it quietly. It pissed him off and made him wonder if his life was spinning out of control again. But then he knew the answer to that. That little incident had resulted in another dose of co-codamol. Soon he'd be swinging between co-codamol and co-dydramol, just like the old days.

Lee got up and walked into the office. 'I s'pose I'd better bite the bullet and write me report for Derek Salmon. Then I'd better do some paperwork,' he said to Amy.

'Unless you want me to do it,' she said.

'I'd have to pay you.'

'True. But, come on, Lee, I've just lost Antoni Brzezinski and I've got to pay for my roof to be re-tiled.'

Derek Salmon had just given him what for the Arnold Agency was a vast wedge of cash. And Mumtaz had got seriously behind with the paperwork since she'd been working up at Ilford Hospital. And Lee was a soft touch.

'OK,' he said. 'Make a decent cup of tea for me and you're on.'


There were things in that basement that didn't bear close inspection. Electrical and other contraptions that Mumtaz suspected had once been used to try to cure patients. There were also some suspicious scuffling noises that, at first, had alarmed her. Was she alone in there or not? After she saw her first rat she realized that she wasn't by herself. She found several tins of unopened rat poison, which she did consider using, but she didn't know what she was doing with the stuff and so she decided against it.

Mumtaz very soon discovered that the job she'd set herself, to find Sara Ibrahim's medical records, wasn't going to be easy. There was no system. Not just in the storage of medical records but in any part of the basement. Medical notes were jumbled up with accounts, letters to and from the hospital management were in turn tangled up in old equipment. The tins of rat poison were complemented by dozens of mouse-traps, some of which were also mixed up in paperwork. But in spite of what she'd told Shazia about doing more packing, Mumtaz knew that she wasn't in a hurry. Sara's notes had to be in there somewhere and if she didn't find them this time, she'd look again another day. Her only fear was that someone might lock the basement door, not knowing she was in there. But it was a risk she'd have to take if she wanted to know whether Dr el Masri and/or Hatem el Shamy had changed Sara Ibrahim's medical records. Why either of them would have done such a thing she couldn't imagine. But if she had the proof in her hands she could at least go back to her client and tell her she had something. Depending upon what she found that could incriminate el Masri, Hatem el Shamy or both. For Hatem's wife, whatever Mumtaz found could be a mixed blessing. But at least it might just move her nearer to the truth.

'Oh, good God, you frightened me!'

Shirley was still nervous after the previous night's experiences. Then to have Roy apparently creep up on her . . .

'Are you supposed to be in today?' she asked him. 'I thought Mandy was coming on her own?'

'She's still not well,' Roy said. 'Panic attacks.'

Shirley sat down behind her desk. Put next to somebody threatening to kill somebody else, a few panic attacks were very small potatoes. But she also knew how badly Mandy could suffer. She said, 'I've got a couple of appointments on Acute One so if you can do the chronic ward that'd be really great, Roy.'

'Yeah, OK.'

Roy had been an inpatient on Acute and Forensic at Ilford many times. Although only thirty-four, he'd got to know most of the regular patients who came in and went out of residential care. Unlike Mandy, who was always wary of the chronic ward, he regarded the psychotics, sex addicts and other apparent incurables on the ward as his friends.

'Anything I need to look out for?' Roy fiddled with the pens on her desk, which irritated Shirley. But she didn't say anything. Roy fiddled. It was what he did.

'Only the usual,' she said.

'Staff still telling them off when they light up in the bogs?'

'We know that smoking's banned everywhere inside the hospital, but you can't make someone who's been an inpatient for thirty years just stop,' Shirley said. 'Staff can tell them to take their fags outside, but shouting at them and bullying them is out of order. Ask the service users about their experiences.'

'Except for Melvin,' Roy said.

'Oh, yes,' Shirley said. 'That's just common sense.'

Melvin lived in a world that was controlled by immense violent rodents. Whatever sense of reality he may once have possessed was long gone. Even his food had to be mushed up and fed to him with a straw because that was how the rodents wanted it to be.

'Ask Len,' Shirley said. 'He's generally got more of a hold on what's happening than most of them.' Then she remembered something that Mumtaz had said about Terry, the man who lived in fear of planes. 'Also, let me know if you think they're particularly agitated on Chronic, if you will, Roy.'

'OK.'

He didn't ask why she wanted to know this, or how he was supposed to assess their agitation. But Shirley knew he'd know if the residents were particularly distressed because he'd been one himself.

Roy left and Shirley began to prepare herself for her meetings on Acute One. But at the back of her mind those words wouldn't go away. *I'll fucking kill you!* People did say things like that all the time, and they rarely meant anything. But in this case, she wasn't so sure. There had been so much malice in the tone. What had it been about and why had one of them wanted to kill the other? Had they been service users or staff? And had they realized that the door to the Advocacy office had been open?

Shirley had what she knew was an irrational fear about one or other of the protagonists coming to 'get' her at some point. Rationally she knew it all stemmed from being locked in her office that night. But if one of them did kill the other, it could happen. Then again, she hadn't seen anyone and no one had seen her. But Shirley still felt her hands shake as she put the papers she needed into her briefcase.

Millie had just been given her first course of electroconvulsive treatment when Mumtaz heard a noise. It wasn't a rat, she was used to them by this time. Someone had come into the basement. She sat, frozen to the pile of wood she was using as a chair. Footsteps followed, and then some whistling. This wasn't good. Mumtaz took her headscarf out of her handbag and put it on. The footsteps came closer. Then she saw him.

He was an elderly man, carrying a load of heavily-filled cardboard files. Whistling and muttering to himself, he would see her if he just turned his head. If she moved he'd definitely hear her. Mumtaz became stone with a pounding heart.

For a moment he appeared to be searching for the right place to put the files, even looking up and down a rack of shelves to try to find where his documents might fit. But then he sighed, shrugged and just dropped the whole lot on top of another stack of files on the floor. She heard him say, 'Bloody state!' and then he left. The door closed behind him but she didn't think that she heard the lock turn. When he'd gone, Mumtaz breathed out. She'd been certain he'd see her and she still couldn't quite believe that he hadn't. She took her headscarf off and began to follow Millie's story again.

Committed to Ilford Hospital by her family in 1955, Millie had been pregnant out of wedlock. She'd received all sorts of diagnoses including depression, schizophrenia and 'moral weakness'. In 1959 she'd been given electroconvulsive therapy to 'alleviate her symptoms' but that had been 'unsuccessful'. Mumtaz couldn't find any record of what had happened to her baby. Why was she reading Millie's notes anyway?

Mumtaz put the notes down on the floor and began shuffling through another pile. Sara Ibrahim's file had to be somewhere and, logically, because she had died recently it shouldn't be too difficult to find. Unless someone had removed it. Getting involved in other people's stories hadn't helped Mumtaz, but each file led to a life she had only previously glimpsed through the eyes of her lecturers at university. Tales of life before the Mental Health Act, when pregnant women could be put away by their families and sexually active women were tricked into having hysterectomies. Men suffered too, but there were so many more female than male records. Women whose bodies had been under the total control of those who cared for them, at the mercy of those who pretended to care. She realized now that Salwa el Shamy's husband had been a side issue. As soon as she'd been told that a young woman had taken her own life, and what might have happened to her, Mumtaz had been determined to get into Ilford Hospital. Was it because her own abuse was impossible to resolve? Was she trying to solve the problem of what had happened to Sara Ibrahim and why because she couldn't deal with her own life?

Where was Sara's file? Did it no longer exist? Surely even if someone didn't want it found they wouldn't actually destroy it, because that could arouse suspicion if the documents were ever requested. But then suddenly Mumtaz had an idea. She went over to where the old man had dumped the files he'd been carrying and squatted down on the ground. She moved the recently discarded files away and looked at the slightly dusty ones underneath.

*

Lee took the letter from the woman's gloved hand. She'd announced herself as Salwa el Shamy over the entry-phone but she could have been anyone. Wearing the niqab made women just shapes. Lee said, 'What's this?'

'I want that Mrs Hakim doesn't continue her investigation,' the woman said.

'At Ilford Hospital?' He opened the letter, which was terse and damning.

'She don't do nothing.'

Lee felt his face redden. 'She's been working flat out,' he said.

'Then why she have nothing against man who tell lies about my husband?'

'Maybe because she needs more time,' he said.

'I don't have time.'

'Then I don't know what to say. Investigations like the one Mrs Hakim is conducting for you are complex and difficult.'

'I have no more time. Tell me what money I owe. But don't do more,' she said.

'If that's what you want.'

'I do.'

She left. Lee turned to Amy. 'Is it me or do people want everything yesterday?'

'In general, yes. Lee, I've nearly finished,' Amy said. 'Do you want to check through what I've done before I go?'

'No, just bung it all on my desk when you've finished and I'll deal with it,' he said. The business had gone from doing well to doing very little at a stroke, with only a couple of potential clients in the pipeline. It was all very well for coppers like Tony Bracci to talk about being a PI as if it were some sort of soft option. Not that he'd said anything like that recently.

'There you go,' Amy said. She put a large pile of papers on Lee's desk.

'Thanks, Amy. I'll pay you what you're owed for today, and for the Polish boy, and hopefully I'll have some more work for you soon.'

'Cheers, Lee.'

When she opened the door to leave, he could see that it was already dark outside. Mumtaz would be at home, packing. He wondered whether he should call her about Salma el Shamy but he decided against it. She'd know about that soon enough, when she came to work in the morning.


Even though she knew it shouldn't be a shock, it was. It had been so badly done. Hatem el Shamy's name hadn't even been properly concealed. Just crossed through and replaced with 'Dr el Masri'.

Sara Ibrahim's notes told a story of a girl who had struggled with life. Born into a poor Anglo-Pakistani family in Canning Town, her father had been an invalid while her white mother had struggled with five children, almost alone. The mother, a semi-literate convert to Islam, had been too tired and ground down to worry about why Sara always seemed so sad. Until Sara tried to slit her wrists. Patchy treatments, ranging from talking therapies to drugs, had followed. But in the end, Sara had been admitted to Ilford. What lay behind the girl's unhappiness was never, as far as Mumtaz could see, ascertained. As often happened in these circumstances, professional opinion was divided on what diagnosis to give Sara. El Masri, she noted, was inclined to believe that she had a personality disorder. That made her, to him, manipulative and attention-seeking. Dr D'Lima, who had been called out to Sara one night in the previous summer, claimed to have witnessed Sara hearing voices which pointed towards a diagnosis that was more in line with some sort of psychotic disorder. Sara had either been knowing or delusional or maybe both. What she had certainly been was sick. Her notes detailed a long list of instances of self-harm, plus two suicide attempts.

What Mumtaz hadn't expected was a copy of Sara's post-mortem report. She'd thrown herself from the second floor of the acute ward and so her injuries were extensive. She'd broken her neck and had sustained injuries to her internal organs. And then there was something else that Mumtaz hadn't expected. But maybe she should have done. She folded Sara's notes up and put them in her handbag.

## 24

'Mrs Mayfield!'

Shirley turned. Mr Cotton was looking particularly arrogant. She just wanted to go home.

'Yes,' she said.

'I've forwarded my report regarding your activities with Dylan Smith to the Trust,' he said. He coughed hard.

'Thank you for letting me know.'

She wanted to tell him that she really didn't give a shit what he did, but she stopped herself. Whichever way she looked at it, she'd have to find a new job soon and she may still need a reference from Cotton. If he'd deign to give her one. If being under investigation by the Trust didn't automatically preclude her from employment elsewhere.

'Good night, Mrs Mayfield.'

'Good night,' Shirley said.

He walked past her and she saw him leave the building. It was cold and dark outside and she'd had a bad day with two patients on Acute who were clearly too delusional to know what was real and what wasn't. One of them was insisting that she contact some no win no fee legal firm about an accident that couldn't have happened. In a way, Shirley relished the idea of presenting a firm of ambulance chasers with a story about her client, the singer Madonna and a poorly secured dustbin. On the other hand, she didn't feel she needed it.

She locked her office door and began to walk down the corridor. There was an odd smell underneath the usual disinfectant and piss that she couldn't place. It wasn't pleasant.

Mumtaz watched Shirley leave. Most of the lights were off in the building now. If she remembered correctly where el Masri's office was, it was dark. But would it still be open? Probably. Because the whole building would soon be locked, not everyone who worked there was particularly scrupulous about locking doors. But filing cabinets and computer equipment were another matter. They would be carefully stowed away. There was an argument that poking around el Masri's office was pointless. What did she hope to find?

According to the post-mortem, the foetus Sara Ibrahim had been carrying when she died had been DNA-tested. There was no copy of the results in the file and she had no idea whether they were even relevant. But what was evident from the paperwork was that the DNA test had been requested by Dr el Masri.

Given the rumours about him, had el Masri suspected that he was the father of Sara's child? If he had, why had he falsified her records to make it look as if he had ordered her observations? A senior nurse could do that, and Mumtaz felt that if el Masri had got Sara pregnant he would want his name disassociated from hers in any way possible.

She walked into the building, past the now unmanned reception desk and up the stairs to the corridor that led to the doctor's offices. If anything connected to Sara Ibrahim was accessible in el Masri's office, she was going to find it. Hatem el Shamy and his guilt or innocence were now not much more than details. It was Sara and her baby that mattered.

Lee didn't want to look over the paperwork Amy had done, but he knew he had to. Some of it needed his signature. He divided it into two piles, one for signing and the other for filing. Scanning through he realized just what a good month they'd had and he made a note in his diary to ring up the garage and organize appointments for the company cars to be serviced. The gig he'd got from Derek Salmon had been particularly lucrative. He looked at the figure on the bottom of Derek's receipt with pleasure. That was one for the filing, but the more he looked at it the more he couldn't seem to put it away.

The phone rang.

'Wotcha.'

It was his new housemate, Tony.

'Hiya, Tone.'

'Just letting you know I may not be back tonight,' he said.

'You get lucky?'

'Me? Lucky?' he snorted. 'Nah, work, mate.'

'Oh.'

'Yes, "oh",' he said. 'Back of a van with a Coke bottle for a bog.'

He was on a stakeout. 'Welcome to my world,' Lee said.

'You think?'

Lee said, 'Thanks for letting me know, Tone. I'll leave the chain off the door.'

'Ta.'

Lee put the phone down and looked at Derek Salmon's receipt again. It had been printed on his company stationary, which Lee had seen many times before. Derek liked to display all the quality marks the firm had earned on his paper as well as all the badges of organizations he'd joined over the years. Only the address was different. Lee recalled the shiny new office on Stratford Broadway with an unruffled Derek, newly single, sitting at its biggest, most opulent desk.

But the new office wasn't the reason why he was looking at Derek's stationery. He knew that something, even though he didn't know exactly what, was troubling him about it. And then it came to him. His face cold with tension, he picked up his phone and dialled.

Everything was either locked away or absent. Only el Masri's desktop computer stood out against the unbroken emptiness. There were no photographs of a wife or child, no stray cardboard files, no naff nick-nacks from the land of the Pharaohs. Mumtaz thought the word 'anodyne'. And yet, to her, el Masri had seemed exotic. Had he used his difference to gain Sara Ibrahim's confidence?

Young, troubled girls were vulnerable to doing things they didn't like. Even her own stepdaughter, Shazia, had sometimes complied with her father's sexual demands without complaint. She'd told Mumtaz it had been easier that way. It saved her a beating; besides, Ahmet had driven her self-esteem into the ground.

Had Sara felt like that too? Mentally ill, hearing voices that frightened her, taking refuge in self-harm, she'd been such easy prey. Her family were, by all accounts, barely functional and so she'd probably not had the familial support she deserved. But none of that meant that el Masri had abused her. He'd altered her medical records. There was no proof he'd ever had sex with her.

Mumtaz had to decide whether or not to log into el Masri's desktop. It was highly unlikely that anything to do with Sara Ibrahim would be on the computer, but then again people could be very stupid. An inordinate number of paedophiles seemed to leave incriminating material on their systems. She hesitated for a moment and then she switched the machine on. The doctor's home screen was pleasingly Egyptian. The god Anubis reared his jackal head up at her and said something she couldn't understand. But it sounded menacing. It was also loud. Mumtaz looked behind to make sure she wasn't being watched and then located the machine's speakers and turned them off. Although Shazia had an Apple laptop, Mumtaz wasn't familiar with them. The system asked for a password, and Mumtaz had to decide whether she'd try to wing it or not. In the end her courage failed her and she turned the computer off. Looking at its blank screen she wondered whether she should have taken a punt. But it was too dodgy.

Mumtaz sat back in the doctor's chair and looked around the room. All the filing cabinets were locked, she'd checked them. She got up. There was no point staying. She walked towards the door. Then she stopped. Between two filing cabinets was a door. She imagined it led to el Masri's secretary's office. But she didn't remember a door like that in the secretary's room. She turned the handle. It opened towards her and, as she moved the door, she noticed that it smeared some liquid across the floor. Mumtaz found herself looking not into an office but a cupboard. Stuffed with coats and umbrellas, it smelt musty. Somewhere between metal and wet dog.

The liquid on the floor was coming from the cupboard. As far as Mumtaz could see, it came from a massive pile of coats right in the middle. She put a hand down to touch the wetness. When she looked at her fingers they were red.

Cobbett was out on a job, and nobody would tell Lee where or what it was. Nobody would riffle through his evidence either. This was unsurprising, if frustrating. All Lee wanted to know was what the letter Ken Rivers had received from his son Phil's solicitors, Myerson & Jackson, looked like. If he remembered correctly, all the trade association and quality mark logos were on an uneven right-leaning slant. He'd noticed it immediately when Cobbett had shown him Ken's letter. Was it the same on Derek's stationery? He looked at Derek's letterhead again. It was. Had it been on the slant like that only since Derek had moved office or was he making that up? Did Del have his stationery printed elsewhere or did his people do it in-house? He didn't know. Maybe he should ask him?

Even in his head it sounded weird. 'Hello, Derek, you know your stationery? Do you get it printed or do it in-house?' He couldn't ask that. Lee looked at his watch. And anyway, it was almost seven p.m. If Derek Salmon was at his office, he almost certainly wouldn't be answering calls.

If the printing fault on the Ken Rivers letter was identical to Lee's receipt from Derek Salmon, what did that mean? At its most basic level it could be that Derek and Phil Rivers' hooky solicitors used the same printing company. It didn't mean they necessarily knew each other. Ken's letter had stuck in Lee's mind because of the wonky logos. If Derek's stationery hadn't looked the same, he would have forgotten all about it.

He'd left a message for Cobbett on his mobile, although that didn't mean he'd necessarily get back to him. If Derek Salmon and Myerson & Jackson had used the same printer what did *that* mean? The letterheads and addresses for each company were different but if they used the same printer perhaps they had a connection of some sort. And if they had a connection then, potentially, Derek Salmon would know who they were.

So why had Derek hired Lee to find Phil Rivers? But then *he* hadn't. Sandra Rivers had asked Derek to hire someone to find her ex-husband. Derek had told him that if he found Myerson & Jackson along the way then all well and good, but the target had been Phil.

Lee still had Sandra Rivers' phone number on file. He took it out and dialled. He knew he shouldn't; she was an ex-client, she wouldn't want to be bothered.

'Hello?'

He apologized for disturbing her. Profusely. Then he asked her about Phil.

'You want to know why I gave you the heave-ho?' she said. 'Fair enough. And I'm sorry, Lee, I know that's your living. But I was getting myself in such a state over it all. Derek persuaded me it was for the best.'

'What, to give up looking for Phil?'

'Yes,' she said. 'I do still love him, Lee, but Del was right. Carrying on was just hurting me. I'll never get over Phil, but I do have to move on. He's gone.'

*And he was gay!* Lee thought, but he didn't say it. He also didn't say that he wasn't surprised that Derek Salmon had advised Sandra not to carry on looking for Phil. He wished it had surprised him, but it hadn't. By the time he put the phone down, all he could think about was how much Phil and his mates had paid for Del's new offices. He also found himself wondering how

Derek and Phil had got together, who their associates were, and what, if anything, that had got to do with Salmon's separation from his wife.

Her mother often looked determined, but not like this. By the time Rashida had got home from school, dinner had been cooked and her mother had the kids in their nightclothes ready for bed.

'I have to go out tonight, Rashida,' she told her. 'You must put the children to bed. You understand?'

'Yes. Where are you going?'

'It's not your business,' Salwa said.

Rashida hoped that it wasn't. Her mother had promised not to take them all to Egypt until the Christmas holidays, but she had seen her on the computer. She'd been on airline sites. Was she going out this evening to ask the neighbours to watch the house while they were away? Panic took hold of Rashida. She'd thought she'd have until the end of term; she didn't have a plan. MJ had said that she could go and live with her family, but that would just get them into trouble.

'Will you be long?' Rashida asked her mother.

Salwa pulled a coat around her shoulders. 'I don't know. As long as it takes.'

'What?'

'What do you mean "what"?'

'I mean, what are you doing, Omy?'

'It's my business,' Salwa said. She walked towards the front door.

But just before she left, unable to stop herself, Rashida called out, 'Omy, you're not going out to do something about going back to Cairo, are you?'

Her mother turned. Her face was ugly with anger. 'I told you, we are going back,' she said. 'You know this.'

'Yes, but not now, not—'

'We will go back when I say,' Salwa said.

'Yes, but that won't be—'

'That will be when I say, Rashida. Now please go to your room and do your homework. I will be back when my business is finished.'

And then she left. Rashida sat down on the hall floor and cried. She couldn't trust her mother. And if Rashida was out of the country and married to her cousin in Egypt, Salwa would not care what the school said. They couldn't do anything.

For a moment she just sat and listened to the kids playing upstairs and then she made a decision. Rashida ran into the kitchen and grabbed a pile of clothes from the radiator.

Up close the smell was unmistakable. The iron cut into your nose. Whoever or whatever was hidden underneath those coats had been walking around in the not-too-distant past. Mumtaz took a moment to compose herself and breathe. If it was an animal underneath the coats – although why it should be, she couldn't imagine – that was one thing, but if it was a person it could be a crime scene.

Was it el Masri in there? She peered into the dark cupboard, but she couldn't see anything distinctly. She knew she didn't really want to. What she had to do was call someone. Blood was seeping from this cupboard and it was on her hands and she needed help. As so often happened, she didn't have a tissue to hand and so she took off her scarf and used it to wipe the blood off her fingers. When she'd got it all off, she took her phone out. There was no point messing about calling Lee, she'd just have to get the police out.

She didn't hear so much as a footstep moving in her direction. So when the blow did come, it caught her entirely by surprise.

## 25

'Lee, do you know where Amma is?'

'No.' As far as Lee had known, Mumtaz had been at home, packing.

'Only, it's late,' Shazia said.

'Is her car there?'

'No,' she said.

'Do you know if your mum went off anywhere?'

'I know she went to the hospital, but that was this morning.' She paused for a moment and then she said, 'There's a man outside the house.'

Lee was liking this less and less. 'What kind of man?'

'Young, Asian. I've seen him before,' Shazia said. 'I saw him talking to Amma once. She didn't look happy. He creeps me out.'

'Did you ask your mum who he was?'

'No,' she said. 'Lee, can you come, please? I'm scared.'

Lee put all the correspondence from Derek Salmon into his desk drawer and locked it. 'On my way,' he said.

'Thanks.'

'Don't open the door to anyone but me, all right, darlin'?'

'Yes.'

Lee slipped his phone into his pocket and put his coat on. He made one more call to Cobbett on the landline but he was still otherwise engaged. Then he left. Del Salmon's letterheads would have to wait.

Rashida had just zipped up her bag when Zizi came into the living room.

'What do you want? Get back to bed,' she said.

'Where are you going?' the little girl asked.

Rashida felt her face get hot. 'Nowhere.'

'Then why've you got that big bag?'

It was in full view and it was stuffed to bursting. Rashida sat down on the sofa. 'Come here,' she said to her little sister.

Zizi almost tripped over her nightie as she ran across the room but Rashida caught her. She sat her down on her knee.

'Where are you going?' Zizi reiterated.

She was a bright kid who knew a lot more about the world than anyone, with the exception of Rashida, gave her credit for. Rashida could lie to her brothers, but not her sister.

'I have to go away, Zizi,' she said. 'Mum wants me to marry Cousin Anwar and I just can't.'

'Does Baba want you to get married too?'

Apparently he did, although Rashida couldn't bring herself to believe it. 'I don't know,' she said. 'But I can't marry Anwar. He's horrible.'

'He fights people at football matches,' her sister said. 'And he smells.'

He did. Although her mother hadn't recognized Anwar's smell, Rashida had. Whenever he wasn't fighting he was smoking cannabis. When he fought he took cocaine.

Rashida stroked her sister's hair. 'I can't marry him, Zizi,' she said.

Zizi shook her head. 'I don't want to get married. There's a lot of washing and cooking. It's boring.'

'So I have to go.'

Upstairs their two brothers fought and laughed.

'Where?'

'I can't tell you,' Rashida said. 'And you mustn't tell Omy or the boys. You have to promise me that.'

'Will you go to MJ's?'

MJ had to be her first port of call, there was nowhere else she could go. But she said, 'No.'

'So where will you go?'

'I don't know yet. But if I don't get out now I may never be able to go,' Rashida said. 'You do understand that, don't you, Zizi?'

She nodded her head. But Rashida saw that her sister's eyes were wet. Zizi was a tough kid who could easily hold her own with her brothers, but, like Rashida, she found their mother difficult. She put her arms around Rashida's neck. 'I don't want you to go.'

'And I don't want to leave you, but I have to.' She put Zizi on the sofa beside her and stood up. 'I'm sorry.'

The little girl cried. Rashida felt her heart break. But if she didn't leave soon her mother would come back and then she'd be trapped. 'Zizi, I have to go.'

'But I'll never see you again!'

'You will. You will. I promise.'

'But how?'

It was a good question, which Rashida couldn't answer.

Upstairs it sounded as if the boys were trying to break the walls down. They were such a pair of little thugs.

Then Zizi said something that had never occurred to Rashida. 'What if Omy makes me marry Cousin Anwar?'

Rashida looked into her sister's seven-year-old eyes and became very still. She hadn't thought of that. If her mother had promised a bride to Cousin Anwar and she didn't deliver one, then it would bring shame on Salwa and on Hatem. And although her sister was too young to marry just at that moment – she hadn't even been cut yet – she could be that pig's wife in less than a year. They would cut her almost immediately. Called a 'circumcision' or 'operation', Rashida still remembered hers with horror. Her own grandmother had laid across her body as some witch-like old woman from Aswan had stuck a knife into her private parts and cut them away. For years she'd tried to put it from her mind but if her sister was at risk she couldn't.

She had no idea how long her mother was going to be out and so Rashida had to act fast. 'Go and get your shoes and your coat on,' she said to Zizi.

She wiped away a tear. 'Am I going with you?'

'Yes,' Rashida said.

Zizi jumped down off the sofa and began to run towards the door. 'I'll go and get Barbie and Spongebob.'

Rashida grabbed her. 'No!'

'No!' The little girl's face crumbled.

Rashida pulled her back. 'No toys,' she said. 'If you go upstairs the boys will hear you. I'm sorry but if we're going, we just have to go. There's no time.'

For a moment she wondered whether Zizi would leave without her favourite toys but then she said, 'All right. But will you buy me another Barbie and Spongebob, Rashida?'

'Yes,' she said. 'Now come on, let's go.'

The girls' brothers were still fighting upstairs when they let themselves out of the house. Once in the cold, wintry street Zizi said, 'So where are we going then?'

Rashida put her bag on her back and picked her sister up. She said, 'To a crazy place. But it'll be fun.'

Zizi laughed. 'I hope it's with MJ,' she said. 'I like her.'

It was totally black. Her head didn't just hurt, it shrieked. The darkness combined with the pain was like being inside her own headache. Mumtaz wanted to massage her temples but she couldn't move her arms. Somehow she was confined. And there was that smell too, blood and – distinct now she really got her nose around it – faeces.

Slowly she sifted through events in her mind to try to make sense of what had happened. She'd been in el Masri's office and she'd opened a cupboard. There had been blood and, although she hadn't seen a dead body, she had feared that one had to be close. She still had that feeling. Was she in that cupboard? She couldn't see anything and, because she was unable to move her arms, she couldn't check out where she might be by touch. And there was no sound.

Mumtaz tried to move her legs but they too were restrained. She had a notion that they were in a bag of some sort. There was a feeling of coarse material against her legs, which she tried to kick off until she realized that her ankles were tied together. She had an urge to scream but knew she couldn't. Someone had tied her up and put her in this darkness, which meant that they didn't have her best interests at heart. Screaming could provoke them. But at the same time, she couldn't just lie where she was and wait for death or whatever else whoever had hit her had in mind. She tried to move onto her side. Trussed up, she felt like a beetle on its back. Then her heart began to pump. Adrenaline overload was great if it allowed her to get the strength she needed to free herself, but Mumtaz knew that was unlikely.

And then, suddenly, the floor beneath her dropped. Twice. Her prison fell and fell again. Not far, just centimetres. Mumtaz's breathing became almost non-existent and her head felt as if it was made of wool. Something underneath her body began to vibrate. With no visual cues to help her, Mumtaz had no idea what was going on. But then her prison began to move and she almost laughed. Could it be that she was in that crime film cliché, the boot of a car?

'He went,' Shazia said.

'When?'

'About ten minutes ago. But he was really out there, Lee, I'm not making it up.'

'I know you're not, love,' Lee said. Mumtaz owed money to people she wouldn't name. But if those people were staking out the house he'd have to get Mumtaz to talk. Shazia was trembling with fear. That was unacceptable.

'You've tried your mum's mobile?'

'Just goes to voicemail,' Shazia said. 'Have you tried?'

'Yeah. Same.'

'So what do we do?' She sat down on a beanbag that was squashed between two piles of cardboard boxes. She looked shattered and defeated. 'Why does Amma just go off and do things without telling anyone, Lee? Why?'

Mumtaz Hakim had really taken to private investigation work. Lee had hired her initially on the strength of her psychology degree. He'd thought, correctly, it pointed at an enquiring mind.

He had underestimated how enquiring and hadn't bargained for quite such an independent nature. She was almost his twin when it came to going off alone to pursue her own agenda.

'So the last place you know she went . . . ? '

'That hospital.'

'Ilford.'

'I guess.'

'So let's ring them and see if she's there.' Lee looked around for somewhere to sit but then gave up.

Shazia said, 'Do you want the beanbag?'

'No.' He Googled Ilford Hospital and phoned reception but he just got an answerphone message. 'I'm gonna have to go over there,' he said.

Shazia stood. 'I'll get my coat,' she said.

'No, Shaz . . .'

'Don't even go there, Lee!' She held up a slim, manicured hand. 'This time I'm coming with you.'

The last time Mumtaz had gone missing, she had been held hostage by the husband of a client. Shazia, along with Mumtaz's parents, had had to watch the progress of the siege on television.

'And anyway, you can't leave me here in case that man comes back again,' she said.

Young and Asian was how she had described him. Lee knew that Mumtaz owed money to her late husband's creditors, who were likely to be Asian. He'd wondered for a long time which particular gang she was in hock to. He knew a few and they knew him.

'Well, come on!' Shazia had her coat on and was wearing a pair of massive, platform-soled Goth boots.

Lee looked at her and shook his head.

'What?' she said.

'The boots . . .'

'Oh, God, you sound like Amma. The boots are fine, come on, let's go.'

She walked towards the front door. Lee, head down, feet weary, followed her like a besotted father who'd been nagged, against his will, into taking his child to a dodgy nightclub.

## 26

There'd been an article in the local paper about these flats even before they'd been built. People had been worried the ground they were going to be built on was poisoned. Salwa hadn't understood, but Hatem had told her it was because there used to be a gasworks and a chemical factory nearby. Then a woman at the mosque, a white convert, had told her about the estate she lived on, which was just to the north of the flats, at Beckton.

The woman had said, 'We used to find all sorts in our back yard when we first moved into our place. Bits of metal and stuff my husband said was poison. Sometimes the rotary dryer for the washing would sink into the grass, the ground was so bad.'

Salwa walked up to the front entrance and then looked at the address she'd written down on her hand. It was amazing what the imam's son could find out about people on Facebook. She pressed a buzzer at the top of the display and waited for someone to answer. She had her story all ready in her best English. But no one responded. She pressed the buzzer again.

It was cold and Salwa wanted to go home. But she couldn't. She'd come to confront el Masri. He had explosives in this flat of his. She knew it. When he let her in, she would find them, even if she had to kill him to do it. She'd sharpened the paring knife from the kitchen. If he gave her any problems, she'd stick it in him. Getting in was the difficult part. She had a story prepared about being from a charity that collected for poor people at Christmastime. El Masri had told Hatem many times how he always wanted to help the poor. And he was a Christian. But he wasn't answering his door. She looked up at the building and wondered whether he could see her from wherever he was. Reluctantly, she uncovered her head. Then her phone rang.

'Omy?' It was the younger of the two boys, Gamal. Her favourite.

'Yes, my soul. What is it?'

'Rashida and Zizi have gone,' he said.

For a moment she didn't understand him. She made him repeat what he'd said in Arabic. Then she understood.

'Gone? Gone where? To the shops? What?' she said. 'When?'

'We don't know,' Gamal said.

'Is Asim there?'

'Yes, Omy.'

Gamal put his older brother on the phone.

'Do you know where your sisters have gone and why?' Salwa asked.

'No.'

Salwa's hand shook. 'Why not?' she shrieked. 'What were you doing that you didn't see them go?'

'Omy . . .'

Her face was hot. She threw her headscarf on the ground. It was just getting in her way. 'I'm coming home,' she said. 'Stay where you are. Don't move.'

She'd walked from Beckton bus station, which had been a long way. She started to run back, even though she knew that she couldn't do it for long. What was Rashida doing? The girl wouldn't have just gone to the shops and, if she had, she wouldn't have taken her sister with her. Had Rashida found out about the Cairo tickets? Her heart went mad. What if the girls had gone to Social Services? What if Rashida told them everything? What if they found out she'd been cut? Nobody did that in Britain and so they didn't understand. They thought it was wrong. Illegal.

It began to rain. As her clothes got wet, Salwa felt herself being pulled down towards the poisoned ground. If Rashida had gone for good then everything was going to unravel. Salwa began to cry.

She'd been travelling for ten or maybe fifteen minutes when the vehicle stopped. She heard voices but she couldn't make out any words. Again, it moved down, which had to mean that someone else had got in. Then they were off again. Going round corners was frightening. Roundabouts were even worse. Mumtaz didn't have anything she could hang on to and so her body was just thrown about like a doll.

She wasn't alone in that boot either. When the car turned there was a clanking noise like the sound of tools smashing against each other in a bag. And there was something else. Large and heavy, it pressed against her legs when the car changed direction and she feared it was whatever or whoever she hadn't managed to see in Dr el Masri's cupboard. How could she have been so foolish as to go to that office on her own after dark?

Hadn't Lee said that she had to keep him in the loop? And what would Shazia do if she died in this car boot or was shot in some country lane miles outside London? If she'd been working solely in her clients' interests, Mumtaz could justify it. But she hadn't been. What she'd done had been more about Sara Ibrahim than Hatem el Shamy. If anything, she was more suspicious of el Shamy than she'd ever been. When Lee found out he'd lose his mind. If she survived whatever this was, he'd probably sack her. There was no way she could keep on paying the Sheikhs if she was on benefits. Mumtaz began to cry. Then she stopped herself. That wouldn't do any good.

The car turned right and the heavy object at her feet forced her body up against some sort of protuberance. She tried to kick it away with her hobbled feet but it just wouldn't go.

Even if he hadn't known her registration number, Lee would have recognized Mumtaz's car. Even old Micras weren't usually that battle-scarred. He tried the doors but they were all locked. Lights were lit in very few of the buildings on what was a big site. With unmaintained and ill-defined pathways, it was a difficult place to negotiate in the dark, especially if one was wearing platform-soled boots. Shazia went over on her ankle twice. Lee had to swallow old-man comments like 'I told you not to wear those.'

A building shadowed by a clock tower was helpfully signed 'Reception'. But it was locked and dark.

'So what now?' Shazia said.

Below the sign was a piece of paper. Scrappy and indistinct, Lee peered at it. It said, *In case of Emergency call* . . . then detailed a mobile phone number. Lee called it. It rang for so long that he thought it must be wrong until somebody said, 'Yeah?'

Lee explained enough to get the caretaker, who was a disgruntled middle-aged man with a paunch, out from wherever he usually hid and into reception. He claimed to know Mumtaz.

'Yes, nice lady,' he said. 'Her car still in the car park, you say?'

'Yeah.'

'Well, she's probably on one of the wards then.'

It seemed unlikely, but it could explain why Mumtaz's phone was off. 'Can you check?' Lee asked.

'Yeah, all right.'

He strolled over to the reception booth and made his calls. Shazia said, 'Would she still be seeing patients now? She's only ever seen people in the day when she's been here before.'

Lee shrugged.

The caretaker returned. 'Not on none of the wards,' he said. 'No one's seen her.'

'But her car's here,' Shazia said. 'So she must be here.'

The caretaker shook his head. Then he said, 'Unless she's up in one of the offices, but all the lights are off.'

'Well, can we look anyway?' Lee asked.

He thought for a moment and then he said, 'That's doctors' offices up there. All sorts of confidential stuff.'

Lee had pegged him as lazy but not as a jobsworth. He said, 'Listen, we don't want to look at any files or computers or anything. We just want to see whether Miss Huq is up there.'

'What, on her own? Alone in the dark?'

'Yes. Maybe.' Angry now, Lee said, 'Listen, mate, for all you or I know she could be being held hostage by a patient in one of them offices.'

He saw Shazia give him a dirty look. He didn't say anything. It was all very well being politically correct about mental health but there were forensic patients at Ilford and some of them had killed.

'Come with us,' Lee said. 'Make sure we don't look at anything we shouldn't.'

The caretaker thought for a moment and then he lit up a fag. 'All right,' he said, after the first couple of drags. 'But if you do anything funny, I know where the alarm buttons are.'

'Are we there yet?'

Not only had Rashida forgotten to bring her Oyster card, she hadn't taken any money from the house. Walking from Manor Park to posh Aldersbrook wasn't far, but with a bag on her back and a tired Zizi in her arms it felt like trekking to the Arctic.

'No,' she said. 'Look, can you walk for a bit?'

'I can . . .' But she didn't look happy about it.

Rashida ignored it. 'I need you to,' she said. 'If you can walk we can be there all the sooner.'

'Where?'

'Where we're going,' Rashida said. She didn't want to tell Zizi where they were headed until they got there, just in case their mother should come flying around the corner suddenly, demanding to know what they were doing. She didn't want to get MJ into trouble.

The little girl walked slowly by Rashida's side. 'Are we ever going home again?' she asked.

There was a way that they could and there was another way that meant they couldn't. Rashida knew that if she left the door open by not telling Social Services about her upcoming forced marriage, her mother would take her to Egypt and leave her there. Everyone would be happy except Rashida. But MJ's mum would call Social Services and they might discover that Rashida had been cut. MJ would tell them. She'd been horrified.

'Who circumcised you?' she'd asked Rashida when she'd first told her. 'God, you could prosecute that person!'

Rashida hadn't told MJ her grandmother and the woman from Aswan had done it. She hadn't told her she'd almost died either. She'd been so focused on her own problems she'd forgotten that another visit to Egypt probably meant that Zizi was due to be 'done'. She looked down at the child, who was walking with difficulty and who looked cold. How could anyone, let alone her own mother, want to hurt her? Both Rashida's mother and her father had explained it all to her, about how purity was so important in Egyptian society. But Rashida had told them she'd never have sex with anyone outside marriage. They'd said they believed her but that a prospective husband might not. That unless she was cut and sewn up he would always have doubts and that was a bad thing. She'd have to tell Social Services, even if MJ didn't. For Zizi's sake. What she wouldn't tell them about was the lock-up.

MJ's house was illuminated by lots of white lights. It was the Hindu festival of Diwali some time soon and so that was probably why. In the drive there were three very big posh cars and a little sports car.

'Is this where we're going?' Zizi asked.

'Yes.'

'Oh, it's like Disney World,' she said.

Rashida pressed the front doorbell, which played a tune of some sort. Then a young Asian man opened the door. This was Krishna, MJ's brother. 'Hello?'

'Hello,' Rashida said, 'is MJ in? I'm her friend . . .'

'Rashida, yes we've met,' Krishna said. He looked down at Zizi and smiled. 'And this is . . . ?'

'My sister, Zizi.'

'So you finally did the right thing.' MJ pushed her brother to one side and took Rashida's hand. 'Come on.'

Rashida, finally exhausted, cried. 'Oh, MJ, I didn't have a choice.'


Lee almost missed it. A corner of green material was sticking out from underneath el Masri's desk. When he looked at it he could see that it was Mumtaz's headscarf. Shazia was talking to the caretaker. In spite of his protestations about security, he was being very indiscreet.

'Egyptian, Dr el Masri,' Lee heard him say. 'Money. He drives one of them massive great Mercedes.'

'My dad used to have one of those,' Shazia said.

Lee knew that scarf well. He put it in his pocket. There was a ferrous smell in that office that could be blood, but he couldn't see any.

'Lives out in one of them new flats down by the Royal Docks,' the caretaker said. 'Who wants to live down there?' He shook his head. 'Half a million quid to live on top of a load of coke from the old gasworks. Where's the sense?'

Lee patted his pocket. Just because she'd been in this office didn't necessarily mean that anything had happened to Mumtaz. But for her to be without her scarf was unusual.

'Do you know if Dr el Masri's gone?' Lee asked.

'Saw his car go about an hour ago,' the caretaker said. 'Maybe your lady friend's car broke down and so she left it here. I've seen her have trouble starting it, especially now it's cold.'

That had always been an issue with the Micra. But if the car had broken down Mumtaz would've told Shazia. Lee hadn't seen any other evidence of Mumtaz's presence in the other offices. El Masri had been her main target. If the doctor had gone he needed to find out where. A good start had to be to discover exactly where he lived. But the caretaker wouldn't go away.

'I'm gonna have a look in the toilets,' Lee said. 'They're not locked, are they?'

'No,' the caretaker said. 'But if you're finished in here . . .'

'I'm not,' Lee said. 'Shazia, can you wait with this gentleman while I go and check the lavvies?'

She looked a bit doubtful for a second but then she caught a look in his eye that told her he really needed her to do this. 'OK.'

Lee went across the corridor towards the Ladies and then sprinted down the hall to the reception desk. As he'd suspected, all the registration numbers of vehicles allowed to park freely on the site were pinned up on the wall for easy reference. He found el Masri's, wrote it down on the back of his hand and then ran back to the men's bogs opposite the chief consultant's office.

When he got back to el Masri's office, Shazia was sitting on the doctor's desk. The caretaker was telling her about the time when a patient on Forensic had held a nurse hostage with a plastic knife. He had subsequently absconded and had got as far as Cornwall. 'Bloody good effort,' the caretaker said. 'He only got caught because some holidaymaker from up here was down there for a few weeks and recognized him from the local rag.'

The car stopped and this time so did the engine. Mumtaz heard voices outside, low, almost whispers. She tried not to move. If they opened the boot, should she play dead? She had no idea what might be in store for her but she couldn't believe that it could be good. Someone had done something that had resulted in blood staining el Masri's office. She'd been hit over the head. Whoever it was didn't play nice.

She heard a click and then saw a sliver of light. Mumtaz shut her eyes. Cold air flooded into the boot and then she felt warm breath on her cheek. Someone's face was very close to hers. A hand picked up her wrist and held it between slim fingers.

'She's alive.'

Mumtaz didn't recognize the voice. It could be any middle-aged English man.

'Let's get him out first.'

Grunting noises followed. There were a couple of abortive attempts to remove what sounded as if it had to be a body at her feet.

They got it out and then they came for her. Cold air was soon replaced by a slightly warmer atmosphere and the sound of feet on floorboards. Then there was the sound of a door closing. They were inside somewhere. She was laid down on the floor.

She heard footsteps walking away. Did she dare open her eyes? The footsteps had faded out to her right but, because she didn't know where she was, that didn't do her much good. Wherever she was smelt musty and a little acrid. When she moved her fingers against the floor it was gritty. Her heart churning, she opened her eyes.

Except for some light from a window high up in the wall opposite, she was in darkness. Muffled male voices still drifted towards her from somewhere, but they were getting fainter. Were the men going back outside? In spite of the darkness, she looked around. Some light was getting in and so soon her eyes would adjust. She just needed to stay calm.

Her legs came into view. Stuck out in front of her, her feet held together with thin wire. To her left there was a pillar, which was slim and had some sort of scrollwork at the bottom. It was close and she could see that it was ornate. In the distance were others. Mumtaz had the impression of a building that was old and well built. Then she looked to her right.

The expression on his face showed very clearly that he had not died easily. His eyes were still open and his mouth was pulled back over his teeth; it made him look as if he was about to eat her. For a moment, Mumtaz wondered whether he was in fact alive. She wanted to prod him with a finger just to make sure, but her hands were tied.

He had to be dead. There was so much blood. Where his throat had been slashed, there was a black wound. Dr el Masri's blood had started to coagulate as soon as his heart had stopped. He was no danger to anyone now.

## 27

'If your mother is there and she sees you, she'll have my guts for garters,' Lee said.

Shazia, sitting calmly beside him in the passenger seat, said, 'So deal with it. I'm coming with you and that's that.'

It had only taken Lee one phone call to find out the address where Dr el Masri's car was registered. It was in one of those blocks of flats that looked as if they were made of Lego at Gallions Reach. The same area Amy had staked out when she had followed Antoni Brzezinski. Drugs had been involved. Nice neighbours, Lee thought.

'When Amma was being held by that crazy Khan in East Ham, I had to watch it all on the TV,' Shazia said. 'I'm not doing that again.'

It had happened just before the Olympics. Mumtaz had taken a job for a young woman called Nasreen Khan, who had feared her husband, Abdullah, was not all he seemed. She'd been right. Her husband had not been a conventional, prosperous lawyer but an enforcer for a powerful crime firm. He'd had debts and a past that he found impossible to accept. Eventually his violent lifestyle had pushed him into a corner, and he had taken his wife and Mumtaz hostage at his house in East Ham. For almost twenty hours footage from outside the house had been broadcast during TV news bulletins. Shazia had watched it all with her heart in her throat.

'I'm nearly seventeen, Lee,' she said.

He thought how young that was but didn't say anything. Now on the A13 headed towards Beckton, Lee was trying to deal with the variable speed limits on the road and not descend into morbid fantasies about what might have happened to Mumtaz. Her headscarf had been stained with blood.

'Try your mum's phone again,' he said to Shazia. 'She might've got a taxi home or something.'

He didn't really believe that. But it gave Shazia something to do while Lee wondered what the hell Mumtaz had been doing at the hospital on her day off. What had been so urgent that she'd stopped packing and driven to Ilford?

'Still no answer.' Shazia put her phone in her lap. 'She's in trouble again, isn't she, Lee?'

'I don't know, love.' Why would she have gone off with el Masri of her own accord? And what did the headscarf on the floor mean? Lee put his hand in his pocket to make sure it was still there. Shazia hadn't seen it and he wasn't about to show it to her.

'You know why Amma always has to prove herself, don't you?' Shazia said.

Lee turned left onto the slip road leading to Woolwich Manor Road.

'Why's that?'

'Because of my dad,' Shazia said.

Even at the Asda roundabout the road was almost empty. Two buses came out of Beckton bus station. Lee didn't know what, if anything, he should say. He knew Ahmet Hakim had left his wife and daughter with debts. There had been some cruelty in that marriage too. Mumtaz had never told him so, but he'd seen enough abused women in his time to know the signs.

'He treated her like she was stupid,' Shazia said. 'He did that to both of us.'

'I'm sorry.'

'Not your fault,' she said.

'You must still miss your dad, though.'

She said nothing and then turned to look at him. Even out of the corner of his eye, Lee knew he didn't like what he saw. Her expression made him wince. He changed the subject. 'When we get to Gallions you stay in the car. Agreed?'

'If you say so,' Shazia said. Then she smiled and, to Lee, she came back to herself again. 'If you must leave a young girl alone in a car in the dark . . .'

'I'm not coming home, Omy,' Rashida said. Snuggled deep in one of MJ's luxurious sofas she felt warm and safe. Zizi was so relaxed she'd gone to sleep.

'You're at that dirty girl's house, I know it!' Salwa said. 'I'll call the police and those people will get into trouble.'

MJ's brother came into the room, put a cup of hot chocolate down in front of Rashida and then left. Rashida said, 'Call them and I'll send them straight to Baba's lock-up.'

'You wouldn't do that!'

Rashida knew that her mother was right, but all she needed was the threat. 'You had me cut, Omy,' Rashida said. 'And that isn't allowed here.'

'What? Why are you bringing that up now? You had your operation in Egypt, it's none of anyone's business here.'

'And you'll get Zizi cut.'

'I've said nothing about—'

'When we go to Cairo for my wedding to that pig Anwar you'll get her cut,' she said. 'She's the same age as I was. It's the perfect opportunity. Why wouldn't you?'

Salwa didn't answer for a moment and then she said, 'Where do you get these ideas from that everything we do is bad? You have always been a good Muslim girl. Modest. What will your father say when he finds this out? My daughter, I am telling you, you have been corrupted. Your sister must be cut or no man will ever want her.'

MJ had already had sex and what she'd told Rashida about it hadn't sounded unpleasant. She hadn't been cut.

'Your father is a freedom fighter,' Salwa said. 'Wrongly imprisoned in this country. Will you abandon him now when he needs you most? Baba needs us all to do our duty as his family and as Muslims. You want to be a good Muslim, don't you?'

'Of course.' Rashida didn't say anything else. But she wanted to. What she'd seen in her father's lock-up, try as she might, couldn't be unseen. With or without marriage to her cousin Anwar, and her little sister's circumcision, she couldn't go back in time to a place where she unquestioningly idolized her father.

'Rashida?'

'Omy, we're safe, but in the morning I will call Social Services.'

'They will take you away!'

She'd thought about it. She'd spoken about it to Krishna. She knew that they could end up in care. But she was almost sixteen and, if MJ's family agreed to let them stay, which MJ said they would, there was a chance the sisters could remain together.

'Where are you? Tell me.'

'No.'

'They won't put me in prison,' Salwa said. 'If that is what you want!'

'I don't want that,' Rashida said.

'So what do you want?'

She'd never thought about it much. She did now, and then she said, 'I want people to trust me. I want you to trust me.'

Salwa said, 'Girls can't be trusted, Rashida. They tempt men, they can't help it.'

'So men are just helpless?'

'Yes!'

Rashida shook her head. She could talk to her mother until the end of time, she'd never change how she thought. 'Goodbye, Omy,' she said. 'I'm sorry.'

Her mother tried to say something but Rashida ended the call. It had been all very well being a small girl who was pious and unquestioning. But when her grandmother had held her down and cut her, that had been when questions she was still asking has started to occur to her. As a woman she was no longer trusted like she'd been as a little girl; every time she spoke English older family members in Cairo looked at her with disapproval. She'd searched the Koran to find something that helped her make sense of what had been done to her. But she found none. She'd nearly bled to death because of a folk custom and yet nobody would admit that.

MJ came in with a bowl of crisps. 'You OK?' she asked.

'Mum'll fight to get us back,' Rashida said.

MJ sat down beside her. 'Then we'll fight her,' she said. 'Simple.'

*

There was only one vehicle parked in the vicinity of the Lego-like flats. An old Ford Sierra, it was in such a state it had probably been dumped. There were double yellow lines everywhere. Underneath the buildings were vast car parks. OK for the residents so why should anyone care about visitors or workmen? Lee found modern developments like this self-absorbed. Most of the residents, he imagined, were single with lots of disposable money they could spend on the type of car that has to be put in a garage. Fortunately it was probably too late for traffic wardens. He pulled over beside the old Gallions Hotel.

'That looks a bit creepy,' Shazia said.

It did. A bit faux Tudor, a bit stucco overload, Gallions was all late Victorian splendour and it was dwarfed by the Lego flats.

'No one knows what to do with it,' Lee said. 'When I was a kid it was probably the roughest pub in the whole borough.'

'What is it now?'

The entire building was dark and silent. 'Just empty,' Lee said. 'Now look, I'm gonna go and see if I can track down this doctor's flat. You stay here.'

He could see she didn't want to. He headed off towards the block to his right. Whoever had built these flats had put them in front of the old hotel so they got the best views of the Royal Albert Dock and the River Thames. From a developer's standpoint it made sense. Views sold. He looked down at his phone, which was where he'd made a note of el Masri's flat number. He wouldn't be able to see what any of the blocks were called until he got closer. Why did so many blocks have names you could hardly read? Or was it just his eyes?

Vi used to tell stories about Gallions. Her uncles had been patrons of the pub and when the American film director Stanley Kubrick had filmed *Full Metal Jacket* on the site of the old Beckton gasworks, Vi had escorted some members of the production team into the building. They hadn't wanted to shoot any scenes inside it, they'd just been curious to find out what it was. Then, back in the 1980s, it had been not much more than a ghost. Now it was a tarted-up ghost. Lee looked up at the block whose name he still didn't know and lost count of the number of bicycles on nearly every balcony. Money with a green conscience.

He turned to make sure that Shazia was still in the car. It was then that he saw the Mercedes S-class. Aware that it was the latest model, he also recognized the number plate. Why hadn't el Masri put it in his garage space?

The footsteps grew louder. Mumtaz forced herself to stop looking at el Masri's face and shut her eyes. But her deception had been spotted. Silently, hands that were remarkably gentle unwound the wire from her ankles and a soft voice said, 'You're going to have to walk now.'

For a moment she tried to pretend that she hadn't heard. The voice said, 'Do stop playing games, Miss Huq.'

She opened her eyes.

'Wrong place, wrong time,' Mr Cotton said. 'Or was there something more to your peculiar research today, eh?' He held her handbag up and said, 'Well?'

The other man, whose face she couldn't see, dragged el Masri's body away by its feet.

'Where is he being taken?' she asked.

'Somewhere he won't be found. But I asked you a question first,' Cotton said. 'What have you been doing today wandering around the hospital, sometimes covered with your headscarf, sometimes not?'

Mumtaz didn't answer. He must have been watching her all day. Had she been that obvious? What was he doing here, wherever here was? And had he killed el Masri?

'Sara Ibrahim was dead long before you came to us,' he said. 'Why so much interest in her?'

Mumtaz didn't answer.

Without untying her wrists, Cotton lifted her to her feet. 'Unlike el Masri you can walk, and so you'll have to.'

But she didn't move. 'What are you doing?' she asked.

'Me?' He shrugged. 'I'm taking you for a walk, Miss Huq.'

'What are you doing here?' she said. 'Why is Dr el Masri dead? Did you kill him?' Hysteria was beginning to get the better of her. Mumtaz made herself pause for breath.

'So many questions. And yet you still haven't told me why you're so interested in Sara Ibrahim. Not related, are you? When you breezed into the Advocacy with all your qualifications I admit I had my suspicions.' Still carrying her handbag, he pushed her forwards. 'But in answer to one of your questions, at the moment I'm walking with you. Later I won't be.'

That didn't sound healthy.

He put a hand on her shoulder. 'You'll need to go to the left,' he said. 'Just a bit. Then there are some stairs.'

He was talking so softly, Mumtaz wondered whether they were somewhere they could be overheard. If they were, should she scream? She didn't know where she was. This musty building could be in the middle of nowhere.

The stairs didn't look very safe. She hesitated. With her arms tied behind her back, if she fell she wouldn't be able to save herself. But he took her elbow and led her down. An even dustier and darker space than the one above yawned.

He pointed towards a space in front of her that was so completely black it looked like a void. 'We go down there.'

Although she'd been frightened as soon as she'd seen Cotton, Mumtaz was now almost overcome with terror. 'No.'

For thirty seconds there was no sound or movement except the ever-increasing beat of her heart.

Then he said, 'Do you want me to carry you?'

She turned her head and looked into his eyes. He put a hand on her body and her skin shrank from it. Had he touched his patients when they hadn't wanted him to? He pushed her very gently and she stumbled over something.

'I'm sorry,' he said.

She looked down. It was a plastic sack. There were others behind it.

He moved them out of her way. 'Mustn't damage the goods,' he said.

Did he mean the sacks or her? He put his hand on her body again.

Was this all about sex? Angry, she said, 'Men! You're just led like sheep by your sexual needs, aren't you?'

He pushed her into the darkness. 'Oh no,' he said, 'no sex here, Miss Huq. This is business.'


He hadn't been inside Gallions Hotel for decades. In fact, when Lee thought about it, he realized that he probably hadn't even seen the place since he was a child. His dad had taken him and his brother one Saturday night when their mum was away. That had been in the days when it had been called the Captain's Brothel. He and Roy had run around inside between the dockers and their women while their old man had got plastered and then vomited down his shirt. Lee's main recollection of Gallions was that its basement had been a stable. No longer used for horses when he'd sneaked down there, it had retained the old stalls and some riding equipment. There'd also been a door that some old drunk had told him led to the Albert Dock. He'd said that if anyone opened the door the whole place would flood. That had given him nightmares. Forty years on, that story still gave Lee the creeps. And now there were sounds coming from the old place. He put his ear to a crack in a door and tried to work out whether he was just imagining that he heard voices. When he leant against it, the door moved.

He went back to the block of flats where el Masri lived and rang his bell, number thirty-five. He got no answer. Why had el Masri parked his car beside the old pub? He looked at it again. Had he forgotten his key or code or whatever he used to get into the garage under his flat? Lee rang again. What he needed was another resident with a key he could follow in. But the place was deserted.

He had no evidence that Mumtaz had gone anywhere with Dr el Masri. She was missing, but she was an adult and so the police wouldn't class it as a disappearance for twenty-four hours. If the doctor was in his flat alone and he didn't want to answer his door buzzer, that was up to him. But the new Mercedes S-class worried at him. He looked at it again and it was then that he saw a very faint light pass across one of the lower windows of the old hotel.

Lee ran back to his car and said to Shazia, 'El Masri's not in his flat. There's something going on in the old building.'

She began to get out of her seat.

'Oh no. You stay where you are,' Lee said. 'El Masri's car's round there and he isn't in his flat so I'm going to have a bit of a poke around.'

'You think he might be in that old place with Amma?'

'I don't know,' Lee said. 'That's why I'm going to have a look. I won't be long.'

'I want to come!'

'Well, you can't.'

'I'll be scared here all on my own!'

There was a side to this kid that was manipulative and wilful and Lee knew it.

'Then lock the doors,' he said as he began to head back to the hotel.

The van he'd seen earlier moved closer to the flats.

## 28

The ground beneath her feet was tiled. Cotton had a torch, which meant Mumtaz could see the pattern on the tiles was ornate. High Victoriana. She wondered what the passage was and where it was going. There were no doors leading off it and no lights. Made of vaulted brickwork, it was stuffy, like being in a tube tunnel. One of her big fears had always been getting stuck in a tube train and then having to walk along the tracks in the darkness.

Why was she complying with him? Cotton hadn't directly threatened her. He'd not hurt her or held a knife to her throat. Her hands were still tied but if she turned and kicked him she could get away. The other man had disappeared with el Masri's body and Cotton was neither young nor strong. She turned her head and looked at him. His eyes were dead. She turned back. If she was going to do anything to get out of this place she had to do it soon. The words burst out of her, 'If you're going to kill me, I need to know why,' she said.

'Why do you think I'm going to kill you?'

'You killed Dr el Masri.'

'Did I?'

She turned and looked at him again. Light from the torch lit his thin face from below.

'Somebody did,' Mumtaz said.

'And you believe, without any evidence, that that person was me?'

The air in the tunnel cooled slightly. 'You asked that other man to put his body, to use your words, "where it can't be found". What am I supposed to think?'

'Maybe the other man killed him,' he said. 'Maybe *I* am helping *him*.'

There was a roaring sound that was familiar but also unknowable in that context. 'Where are we?'

He pushed her forwards. She stumbled but managed to stay upright. The air around her was cold now and, as Mumtaz looked up, she saw lights and water and then she saw a plane take off.

The lock on the refurbished door was probably original because Lee had it open in under a minute. As he let himself into the old hotel, a plane from City Airport skimmed the roof. People paid hundreds of thousands of pounds to live in flats next door to a flight runway. The whole living in London thing at any price was fucking crazy.

Lee let his eyes adjust to the darkness, then he used the torch on his phone to look around. The place had been gutted. The bar had gone, ditto all the furniture, which had been rough even the last time Lee had been there. Outside it had looked well renovated, but inside it was a playground for spiders and, given its proximity to the water, probably rats as well. There were no voices now. But Lee was certain he'd heard them. And when he looked at the floor he could see footprints in the dust. He wasn't alone.

Because he hadn't been in the place for so long, he had only the vaguest sense of its layout. He moved left. The bar would have been on his right. The main entrance was to his left, which was where, back in Victorian times, there had been a train platform to provide transport for travellers staying at the hotel into London. Somewhere there were stairs down to the old stables. But where? If he went back into his seven-year-old head they were right at the far end of the building. There had been stairs down and also stairs up to where the rich colonial travellers used to stay, back in the day. When it had been the Captain's Brothel, rooms upstairs had been rented by the hour. He thought about that other knocking-shop he'd recently seen in Southend and then he remembered Susan. He hadn't phoned her for days. Last time he'd looked he'd counted six missed calls to his mobile from her. He switched his phone to silent.

Walking from one end of the building to the other, he couldn't find any stairs. He began to trace his steps back again when he saw a lot of plastic sacks stacked on the floor. He squatted down and looked at one. Fertilizer. Hadn't Salwa el Shamy had a theory about Dr el Masri making a bomb to frame her husband? Lee couldn't remember what kind of bomb had been found in Hatem el Shamy's locker, but the use of fertilizer was common in homemade devices. He opened the bag and put his hand inside. It felt like such innocuous stuff, soft and squishy. There had to be about fifty other bags. Why have so much fertiliser? His hand hit on something hard. He pulled it out. It was a small box. Even using the torch he couldn't read what was written on it because he didn't understand it. Then he heard a noise. He looked to his left and there was a rat – and the stairs. Lee put the box down and stood up.

There was nobody in the bar. He'd seen no lights in the rooms upstairs. The stables, as he remembered them, were almost without light. You had to open the double doors that had led out into a courtyard now long gone. But at least, if the doors remained, he'd have an escape route. He left the bags of fertilizer and walked down the stairs. As he put his feet down on the treads they creaked and splintered. He saw footprints.

The stables were still recognizable. Once he'd determined he was alone, Lee held his torch over his head and then scanned it round the space. Knackered but still intact, the stalls remained as he remembered them. There was even the occasional glint from a metal artefact that some Victorian horseman had left behind several lifetimes ago. Lee felt strange. With a drunk for a father, his childhood had not been happy and yet there were still things about it that he missed. Back then, ordinary stuff that ordinary people needed had been cheap. Basic food and booze was affordable, and everything medical, dentistry included, had been free. The world had been grey in many ways but what it hadn't been was so confusing. Why had a doctor come to live in a flat in a place like Gallions Reach? Why had any of these people with their thousand-pound bikes and secure underground parking?

The old double doors were shut, secured by a padlock. There were a couple of windows high up that Lee didn't remember and then there was a gap. An arch-shaped hole in the wall at the bottom of the stairs. Was it the door the old alkie had told him would, if opened, let water in from the dock? Lee went over to it. He tripped over something, but managed to stay upright. Another bloody fertilizer sack! He moved towards the arch. There wasn't a door. But it was an entrance. He trained his torch inside and saw a vaulted tunnel with a tiled floor. There were fresh footprints in the dust.

\*

It was too creepy. A woman wearing one of those furry head-bands had come along and looked at her through the car window. Then a man in cycling gear with a thin face had knocked on the window and asked her what she was doing. It had just come out. 'I'm waiting for my dad,' she said.

'And where exactly is he?' the man had asked. He was prob-ably only twenty-five, but he talked like an old person.

Shazia had said, 'In one of the flats.'

'Doing what?'

'Mind your own business!' she said.

As she rolled the window up, she heard him say, 'You know you're not allowed to park here, don't you?'

He left. Pushing his bike towards the block on the right, she could see that he was angry by the way he walked. Like he was marching into war.

Then there was the white van. When Lee had gone round the back of the old building, it had driven up in front of the flats. People were in it, even though it had its lights off. But then so did Lee's car. She wondered whether the people in the van were watching someone or waiting for something. Maybe they were watching Lee? Watching her?

That Lee had left her in the car had annoyed Shazia at the time. Now it pissed her off even more. She was cold, it was dark and weirdos kept looking in at the windows. She couldn't listen to the radio in case the noise attracted even more attention and she'd left her iPod at home. She didn't want to move to that tiny little flat Amma had chosen. She knew the move wasn't Amma's fault – her father had left them with a lot of debts – but she still resented her. She didn't understand – sometimes she'd seen Amma with strange people, like the young man who'd sat in his car outside the house. But Amma had never mentioned such people and how was she supposed to ask?

Shazia rubbed her hands together. Lee had taken the car keys so she couldn't get any heat. How long was he going to be? He'd said he wouldn't be long but he was taking forever. Bored and cold, she got out of the car and closed the door. It was freezing outside. For a moment she stood by the side of the car, shaking. Nobody was about now.

What if Lee and Amma were in trouble in that old building? He'd told her to stay where she was, but what was she supposed to do if he didn't come out again? Should she call the police or would that ruin whatever Lee and Amma were investigating? She'd just have to go in and find out for herself. She made sure that her phone was on vibrate and then she put her gloves on. She walked towards the old building, her footsteps echoing loudly around the almost amphitheatre-like environment created by the blocks of flats. Lee had told her not to wear those boots.

What the noise from her boots also drowned out was a van door opening and then closing. Just after she walked past it, a figure jumped out, grabbed her from behind and pulled her into the vehicle.

She was standing beside the Royal Albert Dock. Another plane took off from London City Airport. Its runway, between the Albert docks and the George V docks, trembled. Water lapped at the entrance to the tunnel and at Mumtaz's feet. How had she come to be here?

A man was curled into a squat beside the bundle she

recognized as el Masri's body. Cotton pushed her down roughly onto the wet shingle. Then he tied her feet together. Mumtaz watched him go over to the other man.

He said, 'You wanted an "in", David. Now you have one.'

'I didn't want anyone to die.' The man raised his head.

Mumtaz wasn't shocked that Cotton's accomplice was Dr Golding, but she was surprised. She'd had him pegged as a good guy.

'Have you put stones in his clothes?' Cotton asked.

'Yes,' said Golding. 'But I just can't . . .'

'Push him in,' Cotton said. He shook his head. 'You have to take responsibility.'

Golding stared at him. 'You killed him,' he said.

'And you were happy, because it meant that you could take his place.'

'I caught you.'

'Then why didn't you call the police?' Cotton said.

Golding carried on staring.

'Because you wanted to make money,' Cotton said. 'And that is no criticism on my part.'

Cotton pushed el Masri's body with his foot and watched it as it began to sink. Then he threw Mumtaz's handbag after it. She gasped. There went her proof that Sara had been pregnant. Cotton spoke to her. 'When Nurse el Shamy made him cover up that mess he was in with the Ibrahim girl, el Masri's revenge was ruthless. Might as well have killed him.'

What 'mess' had Hatem el Shamy got into with Sara? Mumtaz could guess. Had Hatem el Shamy been her unborn baby's father?

Cotton pushed el Masri's body further into the dock. Bubbles began to appear. The chief consultant kept looking, but Dr

Golding's eyes were on Mumtaz. She wondered what he was thinking and how he'd got involved in this. He'd found Cotton killing el Masri and then he'd helped him dispose of the body. From what Cotton said, it hadn't sounded like a case of Cotton threatening Golding with dismissal if he didn't help him. There was a business here and money, as Cotton had said. But what kind of business?

At last el Masri sank below the water and Cotton turned to Golding. 'Too much disturbance to the water surface may attract attention,' he said. 'We'll leave her a while.'

Golding looked at Mumtaz again. He stood up. 'I suppose we have to . . . ?'

'Unless you want to go to prison, yes.'

'I haven't killed anybody.'

'You've helped.'

Golding spoke with a voice that was cold. 'I could say I was afraid of you. I could say that you coerced me.'

Cotton just smiled. He put his hands on Golding's shoulders. 'I've arranged for her car to be driven away from the hospital and dumped. I will be depositing what would have been el Masri's share into your bank account. I know you know what that figure is. Now, do you still want to tell the police that I made you do all these terrible things that have so disturbed you?'

Golding said nothing.

Mr Cotton stood just inside the tunnel and lit a cigarette. 'It wasn't even as if you liked el Masri,' he said. 'You hated him.'

'He was an unprofessional lecher,' Golding said.

Cotton smiled again. 'And you, David, are what the police call an "accessory". None of us are perfect.'

*

The tunnel went straight out from underneath the building and then began to curve gently upwards. What was it? It wasn't what the old alkie had told him years ago. A door holding back millions of gallons of water was bollocks. This tunnel didn't have a door. He'd been just a kid when he'd swallowed that story. And alkies lied.

Lee heard voices. The air in the tunnel was fresher now. He was going to come out somewhere. But Christ knew what he'd find when he did. Now there was light up ahead he switched off the torch on his phone and hoped he didn't trip on anything. He heard a man whisper, 'I'm going to give her something.'

Peering through the darkness into the light, he saw two figures. The tunnel was amplifying sound. Lee took his shoes off and began to creep.


'What are you doing here?'

'What are *you* doing here?' Shazia countered.

Tony Bracci rubbed his eyes. 'I don't have to tell you. You have to tell me,' he said.

It was cramped and stuffy in the back of that van but Shazia was relieved it was the police. When someone had grabbed her, she'd thought she was being kidnapped.

'What's Lee Arnold doing poking about round here?' Tony said. 'That's his motor, isn't it?'

'Ask him.'

One of Tony's colleagues cleared his throat.

Shazia said, 'What?'

'PC Jackman is clearing his throat so he don't say anything he shouldn't about stroppy teenagers,' Tony said.

Shazia looked at Jackman, a PC in his late twenties who blushed easily. 'That is *so* out of order!'

'Shazia, what the hell is Arnold doing here?'

For a moment she thought she might come up with a sarcastic answer and then she said, 'We're looking for my amma.'

'Your mum?'

'Yes.' She sighed. She was worried and needed to tell someone and Tony Bracci was nice really. 'She's been working at Ilford Hospital,' she said. 'I don't know what she's been doing. But Lee thinks she might have gone home with some doctor who works up there. We found her car in the hospital car park but she wasn't at the hospital.'

'Why did you come here?'

'Because Lee found out this doctor lives here.'

'Do you know where?'

'In one of the flats.'

'These gaffs here?'

'Yes,' she said. 'Lee tried to get him at his flat but no one was in. Then he saw a light or something in that other place, that old hotel. And the doctor's car is down by the old hotel.'

'That S-class Mercedes belongs to the man Lee Arnold's looking for? The one your mum might be with?'

'Yes,' Shazia said.

Tony looked at PC Jackman. It made Shazia uncomfortable.

'What is it?' she said.

'It's OK.'

'Not it isn't! There's something wrong. Tell me!'

'Jackman, call the station. And get a WPC for the young lady.'

'Guv.' Jackman made a call.

But Shazia wouldn't be deterred. 'You want a WPC for me? Why?' she said.

'Because I think you should get out of the area,' Tony said.

'Out of the area? I'm not a kid! What's going on?'

Tony said nothing. Jackman spoke softly into his phone.

'DS Bracci,' Shazia said, 'if you don't tell me I will . . .'

'Keep your voice down!'

' . . . keep my voice up until you do!'

He didn't answer. Then he said, 'Look, the man who owns that car is, we think, a bit of a villain.'

Suddenly Shazia wished she hadn't asked. 'Does he kill people?'

'Not that we know of, but he does do a few hooky things and we have to assume he could be dangerous,' Tony said. 'If he's in the old Gallions Hotel with Lee and your mum they could be in danger. And it's a much bigger place to search than you might think.'

'Oh no.' On the verge of tears Shazia said, 'Oh dear.'

PC Jackman got off the phone and said, 'They're on their way.'

'Good.'

Then Shazia asked, 'What do you mean it's bigger than you might think, DS Bracci?'

'Gallions has a lot of rooms on its upper floors where people travelling on ships going abroad used to stay,' he said. 'There are stables in the basement and then there's the tunnel, if it hasn't been bricked up or fallen down.'

'What tunnel?'

'Used to go from the stables underground to the Albert Dock,' he said. 'It was for posh people, so they wouldn't have to get wet when they went to get on their ships.'

Under normal circumstances, Shazia would have found that story fascinating. But now it just made her sick. The old hotel had creeped her out as soon as she'd seen it. Now that she knew it had a tunnel it made her even more afraid. Whether Amma was inside or not she didn't know, but Lee was and she liked Lee.

## 29

They were talking, but Mumtaz couldn't hear what they were saying. Trying to disentangle the wire Cotton had tied her wrists with, all she was doing was cutting herself. Someone was going to take her car away from the hospital and so even if Lee did go looking for her there, he wouldn't find anything. Shazia would have called him by this time and so they were searching for her almost without a doubt. But they'd be looking in all the wrong places.

Whatever happened, she'd go down with a fight. She couldn't let them throw her into the dock and drown. That was no end to a life. A roaring noise above her head obscured the men's whispers and her thoughts. A plane landed at City Airport, tearing down its short runway, braking hard. Compared to other airports, where a plane could often taxi for up to half an hour before coming to a halt, passengers disembarked quickly at City. Like tiny model railway people, their small size made Mumtaz realize how large the dock was, how far away the airport. Even if she had been able to wave at the plane as it landed, nobody would have seen her.

More silence punctuated by whispers. Irritation overwhelmed her. 'You're going to kill me, so why whisper?' she said. 'What are you trying to do? Save my feelings?'

Cotton stepped out of the tunnel. 'Yes, actually,' he said.

'Oh, because you're a doctor? Is that it?'

'You're an unwitting and unfortunate victim, Miss Huq,' he said. 'If you hadn't found el Masri's body . . .'

'I didn't find it,' Mumtaz said. 'I found some blood in a cupboard. Then someone hit me. I didn't know Dr el Masri was dead until I found myself lying next to his body.'

'But you would have found him,' Cotton said. 'And then you would have called for help.'

He took something out of his pocket, which he held behind his back.

Mumtaz felt her face drain. 'What've you got there?'

He said nothing. She thought, He's a doctor, he's going to drug me.

'Whatever it is, I don't want it,' she said. 'Throw me in the dock. Do what you have to.'

'Drowning is not an easy death,' Cotton said. He looked sad. Was it genuine or just his bedside manner? Did it matter?

'For you watching, maybe.'

He looked away. She'd hit him below the belt and she was glad. But it wouldn't change anything. He took his hand from behind his back and she saw the syringe. Although her first urge was to close her eyes, she kept them open.

'It won't hurt,' he said.

She watched him knock the liquid up into the syringe. He undid the buttons of her coat. As he leant forward she thought she might try to bite him but she was distracted by something else. Someone else. Or rather the absence of someone. Dr Golding had disappeared.


Tony Bracci pointed his torch down at the floor. His colleague, a young woman, nodded. Footprints. Lee Arnold had left the door open after he'd broken in. Gallions Hotel widened its Dickensian mouth and swallowed Tony and four others, folding them into its silence. Tony was riveted. He'd thought about getting inside and finding what remained of Gallions former glory, but he never thought he'd get a chance.

'Guv?'

'Take Jackman and Hall and get upstairs,' Tony said.

The young woman, DC Rose, said, 'The stairs?'

'I dunno. Look for 'em.'

Alone with DC Rock, a man of Tony's own vintage, he whispered, 'Done every training course on everything, can't find the fucking stairs.'

Rock shrugged.

Footsteps over their heads told Tony that DC Rose had found the stairs. He swept the beam of his torch close to the floor. Keeping it low meant that it was less likely to be seen from outside. The place was pretty much empty except for a pile of sacks. He walked over to them and found the stairs himself. Rock said, 'Looks like fertilizer, guv.'

'Ah.' Tony knew what that could mean. Explosives. He stopped for a moment, looked at the bags and, seeing nothing that looked like a detonator, he ploughed on. At the top of the stairs he paused. 'Follow me down.'

When they got into the basement Tony wished he'd brought his camera. An almost completely preserved subterranean Victorian stable. The amateur historian in his head went into overdrive. How would *this* look on his Newham: Old and New website? How unprofessional would it be to take some shots with his phone? He took it out of his pocket.

'Guv, there's a tunnel.'

Rock was behind him. Tony turned. The DC was shining his

torch into a rounded brick-built cavity. On autopilot, Tony photographed it.

'What you doing?' Rock said.

'It still exists,' Tony whispered. 'Can you believe that?'

Bracci's eyes shone. Rock said, 'Guv, I can hear voices down there.'


He must have seen something change in her expression because he said, 'What?'

Not waiting for her answer, Cotton turned his head and saw that Golding had gone. He looked back at Mumtaz.

'Hadn't you better find him?' she said.

He lifted the syringe again. Mumtaz looked him in the face. Then she saw two large hands circle Cotton's neck.

'Put it down, mate,' Lee Arnold said. 'And I don't mean in the lady's arm.'

Cotton didn't move

'I'm an ex-copper,' Lee said. 'I know how to kill you if I want to. Do it.'

He put the syringe on the ground.

'Put your hands behind your back.

Cotton didn't try to resist. Lee secured his hands.

'Sorry, Mumtaz, had to use your scarf,' he said.

'Where'd you find that?' she said. 'Oh my God, Lee.'

'In Dr el Masri's office,' Lee said. 'Where's he?'

He forced Cotton on to the ground and laid him on his side.

'He's dead,' Mumtaz said.

Holding on to Cotton with one hand, Lee unwound the wire on Mumtaz's wrists. He used it to secure Cotton's ankles.

'How?'

Mumtaz flexed her fingers and then began to peel the wire from her ankles. 'El Masri's throat was cut. I think he did it.'

'This geezer?'

'Mr Cotton, Consultant Psychiatrist,' she said. 'Oh, but there's another one, Lee! Dr Golding! He just disappeared.'

She stood up shakily and looked around. 'Don't know where he's gone.'

Lee followed her gaze. 'When I was in the tunnel I heard a voice,' he said.

'No one passed you in the tunnel?'

'No.'

'Then he has to be out here somewhere,' Mumtaz said.

The ground shook as a plane prepared to take off. 'What the hell's been going on?' Lee yelled above the sound of the engines.

'I don't know,' Mumtaz said. 'You'll have to ask him.' She pointed at Cotton.

The plane took off and Lee dropped to his knees. 'So what's the deal here, pal?' he asked the psychiatrist.

But before Cotton could answer, Mumtaz said, 'Lee!'

'What is it?'

'In the tunnel,' she said. 'I think I can see someone.'


DC Rock's attempts at blending in with the wall of the tunnel were hardly a success. The even larger figure of Tony Bracci stood out even more. As soon as Tony recognized Mumtaz he moved out into the light. As well as Mumtaz there was also one figure on the ground and another one squatting down. The one squatting turned his head.

'Lee!'

'Tony? What you doing here?'

Tony shook his head. 'I've just had young Shazia ask me the same thing. And like I told her, I'm the law, I don't have to tell you anything. What are *you* doing?'

'My Shazia?' Mumtaz said. 'What . . . ? '

'It's all right, she's fine,' Tony said. 'Now what's going on here?'

'I've no idea, Tone,' Lee said. 'All I do know is that this bloke here just tried to kill Mumtaz and he's got an accomplice out there somewhere.'

'One of them killed a psychiatrist called el Masri,' Mumtaz said.

Lee said, 'They're all psychiatrists. You couldn't make it up.'

'Some sort of psychiatric war . . .' Tony began.

'Don't be flippant!' Mumtaz said. 'Dr Golding has run away. You need to get after him.'

Tony called DC Rose and told her to get the rest of the team down to the basement and through the tunnel. Still shocked at Mumtaz's tone he said, 'Did you see which way this geezer went?'

'No.'

Lee pulled on Cotton's shoulder. 'Where'd he go?'

But the psychiatrist said nothing.

'Not gonna get much change out of him.'

'What does this Golding look like?' Tony asked.

'Thirties, white, dark hair, handsome,' Mumtaz said. 'And the handsome bit isn't just my opinion. Most of the women at Ilford Hospital fancy him.'

'Lucky him.'

Rose and the other plods arrived.

'All right,' he said, 'we're looking for a young bloke, thirties, IC1, dark hair, good-looking.' He watched DC Rose smile. 'Yeah, yeah, I know you've been looking for that all your life.' He looked at Mumtaz. 'Is he dangerous? Armed?'

'I don't think he's armed and I'd say he's more scared than dangerous,' she said.

'All right,' Tony said. 'I'm gonna call for back-up. You lot spread out and I'll go back and secure the pub.' He looked down at Lee. 'Can I leave you with him?' He nodded his head at Cotton.

'Yeah.'

'Mumtaz, you coming?'

'Where's Shazia?'

'I sent her back to the station with a WPC.'

'Then I'll wait here with Lee,' Mumtaz said.

Tony shrugged. 'OK.' He went back down the tunnel.

For a while, neither of them spoke and then Mumtaz said, 'How did you track me down to the hospital?'

'Shazia was worried. She said you'd gone off to Ilford in the morning and so I made that my starting point. Found your car in the car park.'

'Cotton told Golding they were going to get someone to dispose of it,' she said.

'That hadn't happened when we arrived,' Lee said. 'Were you there all day?'

'Yes,' she said. Now that she was no longer afraid, she began to feel the cold and started to shiver.

'Why?'

'I heard a rumour el Masri had changed a detail on the notes of the girl who committed suicide on Hatem el Shamy's ward,' she said. 'It won't seem much to you. El Shamy ordered fifteen-minute observations on Sara Ibrahim, what you'd call suicide watch, then after her death el Masri replaced Hatem el Shamy's name with his own. I wanted to know why and so I searched the archives for her records.'

'Did you get permission?'

'No.'

'You're learning.'

'Not very well,' Cotton said. 'I saw what she was up to.'

'Then why didn't you stop me going into el Masri's office?' Mumtaz said.

'I was otherwise engaged.'

She ignored him.

'It took time but I found them,' she told Lee. 'And I saw that the rumour was true. I also found out that Sara was pregnant when she died.' She looked down at Cotton.

He said nothing.

'These professional types don't say anything without a brief,' Lee said. 'Might as well ask the dock.'

Mumtaz looked across at the airport. While she'd been beside the water, flights into and out of City Airport had decreased. Soon they would be suspended for the night. A hard frost was developing on the ground. It made her feet feel dead.

Lee said, 'Why don't you go back to Tony, get to the station with Shazia?'

'I don't want to leave you. Not with him.'

'He can't move,' Lee said.

'No.'

'Well, at least take my jacket. You're shaking like a bloody cork in a storm.'

'No. I'm OK.'

'For fuck's sake, stop martyring yourself!' He took his jacket off and threw it at her. 'And if you have to stay here, then get inside the tunnel. You'll fucking die of cold sitting by the water. Now, look, you've made me swear twice.'

Mumtaz picked up Lee's jacket and put it on.

'And get in the fucking tunnel!'

Smiling, she began to move.

'That's three times now,' he said. 'It's not big and it's not clever you know, Mumtaz.'

As she walked towards the tunnel, Mumtaz said, 'You don't know what a relief it is to hear you swear and not apologize.'

He'd always done that and it had irritated her. She tried to be a good Muslim and she covered her head but she was also a human being. Mumtaz pulled Lee's jacket around her shoulders and sat down just inside the mouth of the tunnel. The old bricks, though not warm, did provide insulation and protection from the cold wind outside. And now that she was no longer in danger, Mumtaz felt exhausted.

The handsome doctor couldn't have got far. To her right, DC Rose had the University of East London campus, to her left, where she was headed, a group of old buildings on the shoreline. Jackman and Rock had gone off to the university while Hall had gone on ahead of her towards the new council buildings. This left Rose alone in a vast wasteland.

Even though she was only in her twenties, she could remember when all the land around the docks had been derelict. Strange and forbidding industrial structures, some not much more than piles of bricks, had reared up from time to time by the dockside, recalling times when her grandparents had made good money from British sea trade. Efforts over the years to rehabilitate the area had been partially successful. But in spite of the university, the new council offices and the airport, there was still a bleakness to the place that made it feel haunted. Maybe it was. Thousands had died in the docks in the Second World War, and thousands more had left when containerization killed traditional dock-work back in the 1970s.

What had the good-looking doctor done anyway? Bracci hadn't said. Rose had seen some strange collections of suspects and victims over the years but an elderly psychiatrist lying on the ground with wire round his ankles was a first.

Rose saw something. A darker spot in the blackness. Just for an instant. It moved so fast she almost missed it. Part of her, a side removed from her modern pragmatism, shuddered. Her granddad had told tales about the war when she was little. About bombs so powerful they made whole families disappear. Vaporized, he'd called it. Then there were the children he'd found in a house in Silvertown who'd looked as if they'd been sleeping. Her granddad had always said there had to be ghosts.


Ahmet was moving across the bed towards her. She knew what he wanted. She pulled the covers up to her chin and said, 'No.'

He said, 'You're my wife.'

As if that justified what he was about to do.

'You can't. I have my period.'

Ahmet raised his hand and she felt herself flinch. 'You think I'm going to buy that story? Again?'

Mumtaz felt him pull the bedcovers down. She slammed her legs shut but he pulled them apart and then he was on top of her. She wanted to scream but she couldn't because he had his hand over her mouth. He pushed down hard; she couldn't breathe. Was she going to die? If only she could wake up. Mumtaz forced herself to breathe and then she made her eyes open. Looking out of the mouth of the tunnel she saw that two bodies were now on the ground. A third was standing over them. It wasn't Lee Arnold.

Thick, black hair curled on the back of the standing man's neck. He said something, which she couldn't hear, and then he bent down to help one of the figures on the ground with something. She saw a scarf she recognized as her own float towards the ground.

Why had Golding come back? He'd left Cotton alone for a reason. Why had he changed his mind? It didn't matter. All that did was that he was freeing Cotton and Lee was no longer in control. Mumtaz used the bricks of the tunnel to pull herself up. Golding was having trouble with the wire around Cotton's ankles.

Golding heard her approach and he turned his head. But he hadn't untied Cotton and he moved too late. She kicked him in the head so hard she screamed. Maybe that dream about Ahmet had unleashed excessive violence? Golding collapsed across Cotton's body and Mumtaz, shaking in every part of her body, put her foot on Cotton's neck. Lee, lying beside the psychiatrists, appeared dead. Cotton's syringe, which had been on the ground, had gone. Mumtaz screamed again, 'Help! Help me!'

The young woman police officer arrived first, followed by a man.

'I think Lee's dead,' Mumtaz said. 'I fell asleep. I let him down.'

The woman put a hand on Mumtaz's shoulder. 'This man?' She pointed at Lee.

'Yes.'

She bent down and felt for a pulse in his neck. The other police officer handcuffed Cotton and then Golding, who was now beginning to come round.

'He's got a pulse,' the woman said. 'But it's weak. Do you know what happened to him?'

'No. I was asleep. But Dr Cotton had a syringe . . .'

And then she saw it in one of Golding's hands.

'There!'

The male officer shook Golding. 'What was in the syringe?' he barked.

But Golding's eyes just rolled and then his head flopped forwards again. The officer turned to Cotton, 'What was in the syringe?'

Cotton said nothing.

The female officer requested an ambulance and then called Tony Bracci. The male officer levelled a kick at Cotton's head.

## 30

The tunnel brought Mumtaz up into an old building which, she was told, had once been a pub. Outside were flats that were modern, brightly lit and which completely surrounded the old place. People had gathered round the building trying to see what was going on.

Tony Bracci took her arm. She'd watched Lee being loaded into an ambulance down by the dock and was still traumatized. The paramedics had given him oxygen.

People stared at her. One man's face was familiar but she didn't know why. He stood next to another man who coughed so hard he crossed his legs. Little things attracted her attention. Mouldings of classical figures under the eaves of the old building, children's toys on balconies of flats. She felt dazed and alienated and although she knew she was in the docklands, she couldn't recognize anything.

Tony opened the door to a police car and helped her get in. 'I'm having you taken to the General,' he said. 'Just so they can check you out. Shazia's fine, she's at your mum and dad's now, so you don't have to worry about her. OK?'

'And Lee?'

'Love, we don't know,' Tony said. 'But they will sort him out at the General.'

'Why wouldn't Mr Cotton say what was in that syringe?' she said.

'I've no idea,' he said. He began to close the door.

'You must drag the dock,' Mumtaz said. 'For Dr el Masri's body. And my handbag, too. There's evidence in there. You will do that, DS Bracci, won't you?'

'Not personally but we will drag the dock, yes,' he said. 'Now you're going to A&E. All right?'

And then the car moved away, through a tangle of buildings she didn't know. She only got her bearings when the car came to Gallions Reach roundabout. Then she put her head back and closed her eyes briefly. But Lee's white, motionless face wouldn't leave her. She wondered what the doctors at the General were doing for him and then she wondered whether she'd ever be able to trust a doctor again.

The two men were in separate side rooms, each with a police guard. Tony Bracci peered in at Cotton, who seemingly slept the sleep of the just, and then looked at Golding. Mumtaz Hakim admitted she'd kicked him in the head, but she must've given it some wellie. Golding had a fractured skull. Cotton had an egg-sized bruise on his head and Tony wondered whether she'd had a pop at him too.

He went down to the intensive therapy unit and asked for the man in charge, Dr Banergee. He just caught sight of Lee Arnold as he passed the entrance to the unit.

'Come into my office,' Banergee said. A young, smart Asian, he spoke with an Oxbridge accent.

He took Tony to a small, cupboard-like room. They both sat.

'The syringe Mr Arnold was injected with contained traces of Largactil,' Banergee said.

Tony felt a ripple of fear. 'Like the kid the other day?'

'That was tablets, this was intravenous, but the same substance.'

Paul 'Puffy' Hall, the reason Tony and the team had been on a stakeout at Gallions, was still in a coma induced by the anti-psychotic drug Largactil.

'It's a major tranquillizer and so it lowers the blood pressure and can produce cardiac arrhythmia,' the doctor said.

'And coma.'

He shrugged. 'Your colleague is stable at the moment. All we can do is monitor his cardiac function, blood pressure and breathing.'

'And what about the kid?'

Banergee looked at the floor. 'I'm afraid he has deteriorated,' he said. 'But from what his friend told us it would seem that he took a massive dose. Boys together like that, they show off.'

'What about Lee Arnold?'

'It's difficult to say how much he's had, but he does go in and out of consciousness, which would suggest to me that he hasn't had as much as the boy. You know, some trade in psychiatric drugs has always gone on but I've never seen anything like this. Ordinary tranquillizers like diazepam are one thing, but major antipsychotics can be deadly. I do hope this isn't a new trend.'

'I hope not as well,' Tony said. 'Hopefully the men we've got up on the second floor'll be able to tell us something about that tomorrow.'

'Let's hope so.'

Tony went outside for a fag. It was too cold and too dark to drag the dock for el Masri's body immediately, but he had no doubt that Mumtaz had been telling the truth. He was in the water somewhere. Had el Masri, Cotton and Golding fallen out over drugs or money or both? El Masri had been the bloke that had had some issue with that Egyptian nurse who'd turned out to be a terrorist up at Ilford. Did that have any bearing on what had happened that evening? Bracci's phone rang.

'Guv?'

It was DS Rose. She and Rock had got the building caretaker to let them into el Masri's flat.

'Hello.'

'El Masri's flat?'

'Yeah?'

'As Mrs Hakim said, he wasn't in it. But someone else was.'

Tony looked up. 'Who?' If someone else had been in the flat why hadn't they opened the door?

'Young, male, IC6.'

'Name?'

'Butrus el Masri,' she said. 'The doctor's nephew.'

Tony dragged on his cigarette. 'And what did he have to say for himself?' he asked.

'Nothing,' Rose replied. 'He's dead.'


It was just after four in the morning when Salwa el Shamy turned up at the Joshis' house in Aldersbrook. She had Gamal and Asim in tow. Both boys looked exhausted. Ignoring the bell she banged on the front door. 'Give me back my children!' she yelled. 'Kidnappers!'

Mercifully, Zizi remained asleep. But Rashida flew out of bed, put on a dressing gown MJ's mother had given her and made for the stairs. How could her mother make such an exhibition of herself? When she stepped out onto the landing and looked down, she saw that MJ's mum and her brother were already at the door.

'I will call the police!' Salwa shouted.

'Mrs el Shamy, why don't you come in and have tea and we can talk?' Mrs Joshi said. 'It's such a cold night. Why don't I make some hot chocolate for your little boys?'

'No! I want my daughters! Give me my children!'

Rashida couldn't see her mother but she could feel her passion and she wept for her. She loved her in spite of everything.

'Even if your daughters wanted to go back to you, I would have to report what Rashida has told me to the authorities,' Krishna said.

There was silence.

'I am a barrister, Mrs el Shamy,' Krishna said. 'Your daughter Rashida knows this, and in that knowledge she has told me that you wish to take her back to Egypt to marry a relative against her will. Furthermore, you also wish to take your youngest daughter to Egypt to have a circumcision procedure carried out on her. Forced marriage and female genital mutilation are both illegal in the United Kingdom.'

'She isn't forced to be married. Rashida, she wants to do this. It is what her father wills.'

'That is not what Rashida has told me.'

'She is lying.'

Rashida wanted to shout down, No, I'm not! But she knew that would only make the situation worse.

'Any attempt to take a young person out of the country to marry against their will is a criminal offence,' Krishna said. 'Mrs el Shamy, nobody wants to take your children away from you. But at the same time they must be protected according to the

laws of this country. Female genital mutilation is not legal here
and it hasn't been legal in Egypt since 2008.'

'But it is our tradition. All people do it.'

'Then they're breaking the law,' Krishna said. 'Mrs el Shamy, I
have already informed the police that your daughters have taken
refuge here as a place of safety. In the morning they will be inter-
viewed by Social Services. They will not be returned to you until
this matter is resolved.'

Either Rashida's crying or the stand-off on the doorstep woke
MJ. Crazy-haired and fuzzy-eyed, she came out onto the landing
and put her arm around her friend.

'I do love my mum,' Rashida said. 'I don't want to hurt her.'

MJ kissed her cheek. 'Honey, I know you love your mum, but
you can't marry your cousin. He's an arsehole and he'll hurt you.
And what about Zizi?'

'I know. I know. But I hate it.' Rashida nuzzled into MJ's hair.
'But what will Social Services do with us, eh? Will they put us
into care?'

Rashida knew kids who'd been in care and so did MJ.

MJ squeezed her tight. 'That won't happen, girl,' she said.
'Krish'll make it right. I promise.'


Who the man was that she'd seen in the crowd at Gallions had
come to her as soon as she'd woken up. Still high on adrenaline,
Mumtaz had only had two hours sleep since she'd got back from
the hospital. Fighting her way through the boxes in her bedroom, Mumtaz had a quick shower and then left for the office.
She was due at Forest Gate police station at nine but she had to
do this first.

When she arrived, the office was cold and the light on the

answerphone was flashing. But she ignored it. Instead she went to the filing cabinets and pulled out a cardboard folder. When she opened it she saw a photograph of the man she'd seen the previous night and she smiled. She knew she'd been right. She put the folder in her handbag, locked the office and then ran to the police station.

The nausea was only topped by the muscle spasms, which were excruciating. That he felt as if he'd just been doused in ice was almost irrelevant. But Lee was awake and weirdly he wasn't crouching down over some bloke on the edge of the Albert Dock. But he did have a mask on. It wasn't his only encumbrance.

When he tried to sit up, he couldn't. His arms were covered in stuff. Wires and needles, cuffs and clamps. What the hell was happening? A woman in a nurse's uniform came over. She looked into his eyes before she spoke to him.

'You with us, Mr Arnold?'

He couldn't speak because of the mask. He nodded his head.

'Do you feel sick?'

He nodded his head again.

'I'll ask the doctor if he can give you something for that,' she said. 'You feel as if you could drop off again?'

This time he shook his head.

'Good.'

A terrible pain gripped his left arm and Lee knew he was having a heart attack.

But the nurse smiled. 'Just the blood pressure cuff,' she said. 'It'll go off every fifteen minutes. Sorry, but we have to monitor that really carefully. How's your pain?'

He waited for the blood pressure cuff to deflate and then he shrugged.

'You getting muscle cramps?'

He nodded.

'How bad? Can you hold up your fingers?'

Lee raised both hands through a tangle of tubes.

'If one's no pain and ten's unbearable, hold up the number of fingers you think best describes what you're feeling.'

It was hard. Pain was something he had become used to and then he'd stopped having any pain again. The need for codeine or something even stronger was intense and he felt ashamed. He was in pain and it was bad but how much of it was in his drug-addicted head? Eventually he raised five fingers.

'Oh, that's not bad at all,' the nurse said. 'That's good. But I'll still get doctor to write you up for something extra. All right?'

She left. It wasn't all right. Somehow, again, he was in hospital. He had been on the ground beside the Albert Dock and Mumtaz had been there. She'd been tied up and there had been a man who he had restrained on the ground. The man had tried to kill Mumtaz. Where was he now? And more importantly, where was Mumtaz?

When the panic hit him it was like running into a brick wall. Around him monitors began to make noises like sirens and the nurse who had just left came back at a run.

## 31

Mumtaz Hakim had been and gone and now they were on to the tough stuff. A body matching Dr el Masri's description had been found in the Royal Albert Dock at first light, wedged against the side of the airport runway. Now Tony Bracci had to find out how it had got there. Mumtaz Hakim said Mr Reginald Cotton had pushed him in. According to the hospital, Dr Golding was still too sick to question. He'd gone into what they called a 'fugue state' which meant that he couldn't talk. Or wouldn't. Mr Reginald Cotton, consultant psychiatrist, on the other hand, was as cool and collected as his expensive solicitor and had already discharged himself from hospital. This interrogation was going to be a challenge. Tony knew that Vi would have loved it.

He sat down next to DC Rock, acknowledged the brief, who he didn't know, and then looked at Cotton. Tall and thin, he was the kind of middle-aged man some people described as 'distinguished'. For a moment Cotton didn't acknowledge him. He stared at Rock instead. If Tony hadn't spoken would he ever have looked at him? Tony asked him his name, his age and his profession. Cotton answered in a clear, confident voice.

'What is your relationship to Dr Ragab el Masri?' Tony asked.

'He's a colleague.'

Tony hadn't told Cotton that el Masri's body had been found.

It was interesting that he was talking about the Egyptian in the present tense.

'He's been at Ilford for ten years now,' Cotton continued.

'And how do you find him? As a colleague?'

'He's good at his job. Patients like him. He's rather too fond of the ladies . . .'

'What do you mean?'

Cotton smiled. 'I mean he appreciates a pretty woman,' he said. 'What I'm not saying is that Dr el Masri has behaved inappropriately towards women, to my knowledge.'

'What about a girl called Sara Ibrahim? She committed suicide back in March last year. She was one of Dr el Masri's patients, wasn't she?'

'Yes.'

'And what kind of relationship did el Masri have with her?'

'Professional, I imagine. What's that got to do with what happened last night?'

'Last night? I don't know,' Tony said. 'But then what did happen last night, Mr Cotton?'

Cotton turned to his brief. They had a short whispered conversation and then Cotton said, 'No comment.'

Once again Cotton was being predictable. Cool and controlled. But then what was he supposed to say? He'd been found in what had been very unusual circumstances with a colleague, a man drugged out of his mind on psychiatric medication and a woman who was making some serious accusations against him. Then there was el Masri's body – and something else, too.

'We found something interesting in the Albert Dock this morning,' Tony said.

He watched as Cotton's face reddened. Inside Tony smiled. Just like Vi always said, keep 'em scared for as long as you can.

Cotton and his lawyer had a short, whispered conversation.

The brief said, 'My client would like to know what this "something" you have found is.'

'Sara Ibrahim was pregnant when she died,' Tony said. 'Know that, did you, Mr Cotton?'

Cotton's lawyer looked at him but the psychiatrist turned away.

'You must've known,' Tony said. 'Being the chief consultant psychiatrist.'

'How do you know about this allegation?'

Cotton sounded more lawyer-like than most briefs Tony knew.

'I don't think it's just an allegation,' Tony said.

'Did that woman, that advocate—'

'Mrs Hakim.'

Cotton frowned.

'Mumtaz Huq to you,' Tony said. 'Yes, she mentioned it, but if you think it's just her word against yours then you're wrong.'

'What do you mean?'

'We've got a team searching el Masri's office right now. Know what we're looking for?' Tony said.

Cotton did not respond.

'Well, it's not a drug called Largactil, cos we got a lot of that from the old Gallions Hotel. Oh, and some methadone, too,' Tony said. 'No, what we're looking for in el Masri's office is a test result.'

'What test result?'

'DNA,' Tony said. 'A DNA test was done on Sara Ibrahim's unborn child after her death.'

'Is that what the advocate woman, whoever she is, said?'

'Yup,' Tony said. 'But I'm not just taking her word against

yours, Mr Cotton. You know, bit of advice, when you throw a woman's handbag into a body of water you really want to weight it down.'

The psychiatrist's face drained.

A woman in a long brown coat and flat shoes walked up to the front door holding a plastic folder. She rang the bell. Rashida felt sick. She and Zizi were going to have to go with this woman. She heard MJ's mum let her in and offer her a cup of tea. But the woman declined.

She said, 'I'd like to see Rashida and Zizi.'

She sounded business-like. She sounded as if she'd have no problem with putting them into a care home.

Rashida's phone rang. It was her mother.

'Bring your sister home now and we will talk no more about this,' she said.

'Will you still take us to Cairo?' Rashida said.

'I have booked flights.'

'I can't marry Cousin Anwar and I can't let you do that terrible thing to Zizi,' Rashida said. 'I don't care if it's the right thing. I nearly died. How can Allah want that? It doesn't make sense.'

'If you don't come back you will die!' Salwa hissed.

Rashida felt her heart jolt.

'You've dishonoured your family,' her mother said. 'You know what that means.'

She'd heard the stories all her life. Of girls in Port Said, Alexandria, Luxor – killed for smiling at a boy. Sometimes they weren't even guilty. Sometimes there was just a rumour put about by jealous old women or men whom the girls had spurned. But the girls had still died. Rashida's family were going to get her.

Then, although it made her voice shake as she spoke, she told her mother, 'Leave us alone or I'll tell the police what I found in Baba's lock-up.'

For a moment there was nothing but silence. Rashida said, 'You know what that was, don't you, Omy? And you know what people do with that? They make bombs. They make bombs exactly like the bomb they found in Baba's locker at the hospital. The one he made.'

'What bomb?'

Rashida looked up. The woman in the long brown coat was standing next to MJ's mum, looking concerned.

'What bomb, Rashida?' the woman reiterated.

And then Rashida had to make a choice.


Not even Lee's mother was allowed to be with him. His ex-wife had been told that she shouldn't bring their daughter up to London to see her dad. Lee needed to be calm and the monitoring regime he was under was full-on.

'They check him every fifteen minutes,' the constable who'd been stationed outside ITU said. 'It's the first two days what are crucial, so they tell me.'

Mumtaz hadn't been able to get close to a doctor or a nurse to ask how Lee was doing. Only Constable Wallace would speak to her.

'He's had this psychiatric drug overdose . . .'

'Largactil.'

'Killed a boy who had the same thing,' Wallace said. 'Died last night.'

Mumtaz couldn't think of the lad's real name. Amy had called him 'Puffy' – Antoni Brzezinski's friend. She knew he'd taken drugs but she hadn't known it had been Largactil. He must have got it from el Masri's flat. Unless more than one person was doling out psychiatric drugs from a flat in Gallions Reach. She wondered whether the police had got Antoni to identify Butrus el Masri as the one who had taken them all there. DS Bracci had told her he was dead now too. How had that happened?

'I wanted to show Lee this picture,' Mumtaz said. She took Phil Rivers' photograph out of her bag.

'Who's he?'

'A missing person we were engaged to find,' she said. 'I saw him at Gallions Reach last night. He was in the crowd of locals who came to see what was going on.'

'I don't know him,' Wallace said. 'And you can't give this to Mr Arnold now. If the guy's a misper, you could hand it over down the station.'

'The client Mr Arnold was working for didn't want the police involved.'

'And what if Mr Arnold dies?'

Mumtaz put the photograph back in her bag. She didn't like the old grey handbag she'd had to dig out but she'd had no choice. Her real bag was with the police who'd be holding on to it for some time to come.

'Yes, but Lee won't die, will he?' she said. Unless Allah willed he would, and there was always peace in acceptance. Except that didn't apply now.

'No,' Wallace said. 'DI Collins is back to work tomorrow and Mr Arnold's a mate of her's, isn't he? She doesn't allow dying when she likes someone.'

*

Tony saw Vi through the window in her office door when he left the interview room to go for a break. He went straight in. 'What you doing here?' he said without preamble.

'Nice to see you too, Tone,' Vi rasped.

Tony sat down. 'Sorry, guv. Thought you weren't back until tomorrow. How are you?'

'I've had me throat cut, how do you think?'

Tony looked at the floor.

Vi laughed. 'Oh, I'm OK,' she said. 'Just pulling your chain. Why I'm here is because of your fun and games down at Gallions Reach last night. What's all this about drugs?'

'Guv, you do know that you're not insured to be here until tomorrow, don't you?'

'Fuck off and answer my question,' she said.

'Well if I'm gonna do that, I'll need a fag,' Tony said. 'I'm in the middle of interviewing some up-his-own-arse psychiatrist and I'm on a break. Can we go outside?'

Vi got her coat and they both went out into the freezing car park. They both lit up.

'You supposed to be smoking, guv?' Tony knew the answer and when she just looked at him he shut up.

'So what's the story?' she said.

'A kid got taken to hospital with a drug overdose,' he said. 'Word was the narcs, psychiatric stuff, come out of a flat down Gallions. So I got an obbo approved. That was yesterday night. So we get in position and then suddenly there's Mumtaz Hakim's girl, Shazia, wandering about all on her own. First off I wondered if she was there buying gear herself. But then I saw Arnold's motor. I got the kid in the van and it turns out Arnold's in the old Gallions Hotel looking for Mumtaz.'

'Why did he think she was in there?'

'Long story short, Mumtaz had been working undercover at Ilford nut-house for the wife of that Egyptian nurse who was supposed to have planted a bomb in his locker. The wife said the real bomber was a doctor called el Masri, another Egyptian, who was also sexually abusing his patients. This el Masri also owned the flat I was watching. So anyway, me, Rock, Rose and a couple of plods ended up in the old Gallions Hotel where we found Arnold holding onto a consultant psychiatrist and Mumtaz screaming about another doctor having just done one away on his toes. This was all down by the Albert Dock. Do you know, guv, the tunnel what used to let passengers get from the hotel to their ships in the old days was still there so . . .'

'Tone, this ain't *Time Team.*'

'Sorry, guv.' He took a drag from his cigarette and then took a breath. 'Mumtaz's story is that the psychiatrist and this other doctor, Golding, kidnapped her and were gonna kill her because she'd found the body of that Dr el Masri in his office.'

'These doctors had killed him?'

'Cotton, the chief consultant, says it wasn't him. Says he don't know how el Masri died. Golding, the other one, is still in hospital, won't speak. He's due to be assessed by a psych himself this afternoon.'

Vi, smoking, frowned. 'This ain't really going in my head. Was it Golding who buggered off?'

'Yeah. While we was off looking for him, Golding come back to get Cotton and it was him, we think, who injected Lee Arnold with something called Largactil, a psychiatric . . .'

'Yeah, yeah. So how did you catch him?'

'We didn't,' Tony said. 'Mumtaz did. She kicked Golding's head so hard she knocked him out.'

Vi leant against the station wall. 'Fuck me.'

'I know.' He shrugged. 'We found Largactil in Gallions Hotel and methadone, all done up in fertilizer sacks. We also found more at el Masri's flat. And the dead body of el Masri's nephew.'

'Fuck. And I heard a stiff was took out of the Albert Dock this morning?' Vi said.

'We think that's el Masri,' Tony said. 'He'd had his throat cut. Just like you.'

'Fuck,' she said again. 'So which of the doctors did that and why?'

'Not sure. Could've been Cotton or Golding,' Tony said. 'Why? Drugs. At the moment we've got drugs, we've got doctors, we've got a bomber who's in prison and we've also got intel on a dead girl who may or may not have been made pregnant by someone at the hospital. That's what Mumtaz Hakim says she'd found out when she went to Dr el Masri's office and found his corpse in a cupboard.'

'Which was when Cotton and the other bloke kidnapped her?'

'Yeah.'

'So I repeat, Tone, what's it all about? At bottom?' Vi said. 'Drugs? Pregnant girls? A bomb?'

'All of the above,' Tony said.

'And what about Lee Arnold?' Vi asked. 'He'd had some of this drug or . . .'

'He's in the General, guv,' Tony said. 'He's holding his own. But the kid who originally took the drug died last night. It's evil stuff. In overdose it can knacker your heart, your breathing, everything.'

'Have you been able to visit him?'

'No. He's in ITU,' Tony said. 'If he makes it past tomorrow he'll be on the home straight but until then he has to be left alone.'

'OK.' She looked grave for a moment. She put her fag out, then lit another.

'Mumtaz Hakim gave a statement this morning,' Tony said. 'She claims Cotton threw her handbag, containing the medical records she'd got about the dead pregnant patient up at Ilford, into the docks. Whoever threw it, we got it back. It was floating on the water.'

'Benefits of a good handbag. You looked at these records?'

'They'd been tampered with.'

'How?'

'The name of the person who'd ordered observations on the kid had been altered. She was on suicide watch. She was pregnant when she killed herself and someone ordered a post-mortem DNA test on the foetus.'

'So who tampered with the records and what were the results of the DNA test?'

'Where suicide watch observations had been ordered, some-one, presumably el Masri himself, had scrubbed out Nurse el Shamy's name and replaced it with his own. But the DNA test results are missing,' Tony said. 'I've got a team up at Ilford going through el Masri's office looking for them.'

'You think he was the daddy?'

'Can't think why he might have ordered and then hidden DNA results if he wasn't. But then why put his name on the girl's records like that? I'd've thought that if he had sex with her he'd want to distance himself from her. Especially seeing as she topped herself.'

Vi shook her head. 'There ain't half a lot you don't know, Tone.'

He looked down at the ground. She was always light on compliments.

Then Vi pushed herself off the wall and smiled. 'Well, a lot for me to do tomorrow,' she said. 'In the morning, I want to know how far you've got with this Cotton and whether Dr Golding has spoken. If he hasn't I'll have to go and have a word. Oh, and Tone, I'll want to see Mumtaz too. What did she think she was doing working for the wife of a terrorist?'

'It was a job.'

'Will I be able to talk to Lee Arnold tomorrow?'

'Don't know, guv. Doubt it.'

Then Tony's mobile went off. He answered it and frowned.

Rashida got her key out. As the door to the lock-up opened, two police officers moved forward.

'It's bags of fertilizer,' she said. 'I don't know if he's got what you need to make it into a bomb. My dad's not a bad person.' Tears built up in her eyes.

A team of people in white hooded suits, their feet covered in plastic shoe protectors, went in and put the light on. Rashida moved closer to Mrs Sidney, the social worker. She'd turned out to be a nice woman and she said, 'You know you did the right thing, Rashida.'

But Rashida couldn't answer. She hadn't. She'd betrayed her own father and now he would be in prison for ever.

A police constable and one of the white-suited figures walked towards her carrying a bag of fertilizer. 'Is this what you saw?' he asked her.

'Yes.'

The policeman said to Mrs Sidney. 'You can take her away now. That's all we needed.'

He turned to go.

'What'll happen to my dad?' Rashida asked.

The policeman looked back. 'Don't know,' he said. 'This is your dad's lock-up. If it's his stuff . . .' He shrugged. 'We're gonna have to ask your mum, aren't we?'

Rashida cried.

'You used to employ a man called Hatem el Shamy as a nurse,' Tony said.

'Yes,' Cotton replied.

'An Egyptian, he had connections to the Muslim Brotherhood. A homemade bomb was found in his locker at Ilford Hospital.'

'That's right.'

Tony looked down at his notes. 'You reported the device to the police station at Ilford High Road.' He looked up. 'Who told you about it?'

'Someone heard ticking in the locker room. I narrowed it down to el Shamy's locker.'

'Who heard ticking?' Tony said.

'I don't remember now,' Cotton said. 'Probably another nurse.'

'When you gave your statement to Ilford police you said that you noticed the ticking yourself. You didn't mention no third party.'

'Then maybe I forgot.'

'Or you were protecting someone?'

'Protecting who? And why?' Cotton said. 'God Almighty, something was ticking in a nurse's locker, I was a little preoccupied at the time. I can't remember chapter and verse. And anyway, what has this got to do with why I'm still here?'

Tony smiled. 'Bear with me,' he said. 'Just to get things straight, someone told you that there was a ticking sound coming from a locker in the locker room.'

'Yes.'

'You went and you tracked the sound to Hatem el Shamy's locker.'

'Yes.'

'How did you know it was his locker?'

'I recognized the number,' Cotton said.

'How? You've got to have at least fifty nurses, care assistants and cleaners up at your place. How'd you know it was his locker?'

Cotton sighed. 'Because, as you said yourself, Detective Sergeant, Hatem was a supporter of the Muslim Brotherhood. He could be vocal about it at times and I knew that he approved of the notion of *jihad*, dying for God. I made it my business to know as much as I could about him.'

'So why'd you employ him?'

'I didn't,' Cotton said. 'That was my predecessor, Mr Singh.'

'So you distrusted Hatem el Shamy's politics. Why didn't you bring him to the attention of the police?'

'For what? Saying he approved of the Muslim Brotherhood? Don't we allow free speech any more?'

'You know what I mean,' Tony said. 'Then he set a bomb, didn't he?'

'Yes.'

'Except that he says he never done it. He's always said he was fitted up. And because of their differences of politics he has pointed the finger at Ragab el Masri.'

'El Masri is a Coptic Christian and el Shamy is a Muslim,' Cotton said. 'It is well known they didn't get on.'

'Yeah, but why would Dr el Masri fit el Shamy up?' Tony asked.

'That seems like a lot of effort to go to just to get rid of someone you could sack.'

Cotton didn't say anything.

Tony put his hand in his pocket and pulled out a plastic bag. 'Unless it wasn't about politics or religion,' he said. He put the plastic bag on the table. It contained a small packet and a bottle of liquid. 'Largactil tablets and methadone,' he said. 'Just like we found in Gallions.'

'Where'd you get that?' Cotton asked.

'From a lock-up in Manor Park,' Tony said.

Again, Cotton said nothing.

'Rented out to Nurse Hatem el Shamy. His daughter took our officers there,' Tony said. 'Packed out with bags of fertilizer, wood chips, plant food, it was. The el Shamys' garden's about the size of a postage stamp and looks like shit. So did Hatem have a little business on the side involving horticulture? You and I know he didn't. And do you know what? What el Shamy also didn't have was anything else you need to make a fertilizer bomb, like diesel and detonators. What was in the bags was drugs, not fertilizer. Just like the drugs we found in other bags down at Gallions Reach last night, in the old pub rented out by Dr el Masri. Hatem el Shamy was selling psychiatric drugs, wasn't he, Mr Cotton?'

'I don't know.'

'Of course you know,' Tony said. 'And if you don't then you're a shit director of your hospital. You, el Masri, Nurse el Shamy and possibly Dr Golding were selling drugs – psych drugs – weren't you?'

Cotton looked down at the floor.

'Mr Cotton,' Tony said, 'we are going to go through your

hospital and its accounts like a dose of the clap. And, by the way, you can stop all this pretending-Dr-el-Masri's-still-alive pony, because we found his body in the Albert Dock this morning when we found Mrs Hakim's handbag. He'd had his throat cut.'

'I don't know anything about that.'

'So why were you at the Albert last night and why did Mrs Hakim tell us that you tried to kill her?'

'She has a bee in her bonnet about the Ibrahim girl,' Cotton said.

'Does she? Odd that, because I know for a fact that Mumtaz Hakim is actually a private detective . . .'

'What! That—'

'Covered woman? Yeah,' Tony said. 'Check your prejudice, Mr Cotton. She's worked with us once or twice too. And believe me, you don't want to give her any sort of mystery to solve because she don't have a stop lever, if you know what I mean. Mrs Hakim was employed by Hatem el Shamy's wife to try and find out if Dr el Masri fitted her old man up. Story Mrs el Shamy tells has Ragab el Masri abusing his patients. Hatem found out, so Salwa el Shamy says, and Dr el Masri set the bomb in the locker to shut the nurse up.'

'That's preposterous!'

'Yes, I think so too,' Tony said. 'But I think it might have a bit of truth in it. This is only a little about sex and a lot about drugs. As you yourself told Mrs Hakim, what you and your mates have been up to is all about business.'

DC Leela Rose discovered the document in an envelope in a desk drawer in Ragab el Masri's study at his home. A DNA profile of a foetus, it wasn't alone. With it was another profile of a male

Egyptian, aged fifty, who may or may not have been el Masri. She called DC Rock over.

'Look at this,' she said.

'What am I looking at?' Rock asked.

'DNA profiles. They look different to you?'

Rock shrugged. 'This what we've been looking for?'

'Yes.'

'Then it's a result, well done,' he said.

She called over one of the scenes of crime officers and gave the evidence to him.

# 32

It was a new day and Lee Arnold had made it through the night. Vi even waved to him as she passed by the door to the ITU. Oxygen mask still on, he waved back.

Vi followed Tony to the side room where a bored-looking plod tried to snap to attention as she passed.

'Golding's physically all right and the psych who saw him yesterday reckons he's faking all this "fugue" pony,' Tony said.

'So I just need to frighten the bejesus out of him,' Vi said.

She pushed the door open and saw a good-looking, dark-haired young man lying on a hospital bed. As she walked over and sat down beside him, his eyes rolled.

'Fucking hell,' Vi said. 'I would've thought that as a psychiatrist you'd be able to fake being mad a bit better than that. But maybe you're a bad actor.'

He said and did nothing.

'So I suppose I'll just have to talk to you and hope you're listening. At least I'll've done my duty,' Vi said. 'Now, your old colleague Dr el Masri is dead. Someone cut his throat and your boss, Mr Cotton, says he don't know who that might be. But know what I reckon? The three of you had a falling out over the drugs you'd been ripping off from Ilford Hospital. There was some sort of altercation, which left you and Cotton with the job of disposing of el Masri's body in the Albert Dock. Sadly for you, an advocate at Ilford saw you and so you took her to the Albert Dock too, with the intention of killing her as well. But she had a friend who tracked her down. You or Cotton managed to put her friend, Mr Arnold, in ITU here at the General, but you didn't kill him and so it's all gone a bit tits-up for you, hasn't it, David? I mean, when I do get to speak to Mr Arnold I wonder what he'll say? Someone gave him a big dose of psych drugs. But only you, Mr Cotton and Mr Arnold were there when that happened. And Cotton ain't talking.'

'That's the shortened version,' Vi continued. 'If I told you we don't now believe Nurse Hatem el Shamy planted a bomb in his own locker, we'd be here all day. Suffice to say, old son, you're in a bit of bother and your boss ain't gonna be in your corner when push comes to shove. Know what I mean?' She stood up. 'I'm gonna sod off now and give you a bit of time to think about that and then I'll be back and maybe you'll've stopped pretending you're a RADA drop-out. Come on, Tone.'

They left. David Golding rolled his eyes and lolled out his tongue.

Lee's mother, as his next of kin, knew about her son's condition. But Mumtaz wasn't so sure whether his girlfriend, Susan, knew. She hadn't phoned the office and she didn't know whether she'd tried to ring Lee's mobile. Shazia had told her to forget about it. But she couldn't.

Susan had just got up. 'Hello?' she said wearily.

'Hello, Susan, it's Mumtaz Hakim, Lee's business partner,' Mumtaz said.

'Oh.'

'I'm afraid I have to tell you that Lee is in hospital again,' she said. 'I can't give you any more details than that but he is making a recovery, and hopefully you will be able to visit him in the next couple of days.'

There was a pause and then Susan said, 'I'm sorry to hear he's not well. But Lee won't want me visiting him.'

'I'm sure he will,' Mumtaz said. 'When the doctor says he can have visitors. Not even his mother has seen him yet.'

'Have you seen him?'

'Me? Only through a window,' Mumtaz said. 'He's in ITU. But when he gets out we'll all be able to see him. I'll let you know as soon as they tell me.'

Again there was another pause. Susan said, 'Better not.'

'Better not?'

'Me and Lee are over,' Susan said.

'Oh. I'm sorry to hear that. I didn't know.'

'Too unimportant to tell you.' Susan barked a bitter little laugh.

'I'm sure that's not so,' Mumtaz said.

'I'm sure it is. But anyway, thanks for letting me know. Oh, and tell Lee that Kenny Rivers has been taken into a hostel so he's not wandering the streets any more.'

'I will.'

'Thanks. Oh, and Mumtaz, look after Lee, won't you?' Susan said.

The way she said it made Mumtaz feel awkward.

'Because he really rates you,' Susan said. 'I wish he'd rated me half as much. But he was never going to.'

And then she ended the call. Mumtaz felt uncomfortable. What had Susan meant? They got on well together and she knew that Lee cared about her. But 'rating' seemed to imply something else, something she wasn't sure she was comfortable with. She distracted herself looking at Phil Rivers' photograph again and wondering when Lee would be strong enough to hear her story about him. In the meantime, she was going to go back to Gallions and see if she could spot him again. But that was after her appointment at Forest Gate police station. Vi Collins was back and she wanted to see her.

The email was as clear as glass.

'Hatem el Shamy was the father of Sara Ibrahim's foetus,' Tony Bracci told Vi Collins. 'I thought it was gonna be Dr el Masri. But the DNA results were run through the National DNA Database and up came el Shamy.'

Vi shook her head. 'The wife'll take it hard,' she said.

'Did she know that her old man had drugs in his lock-up?'

'She knew he had a lock-up and she suspected he was storing fertilizer but that was OK with her apparently,' Vi said. 'Go fucking figure? On the one hand, she's hiding her old man's John Innes number four, and on the other she's employing Lee Arnold's firm to prove his innocence.'

'Fanatics, guv.'

'Also human beings,' Vi said. 'Her husband's inside, of course she's gonna try and prove his innocence. But I've got less sympathy over what she wanted to do to her kids.'

Tony grimaced. Both el Shamy girls were temporarily in care. Their mother had wanted to take them both to Egypt, marry one off and circumcise the other.

'Why would Dr el Masri plant a bomb in el Shamy's locker?' Tony said. 'Still doesn't make sense. If el Shamy was the father of that girl's baby he could've just sacked him.'

'He could,' Vi said. 'Unless el Shamy knew something about the doctor he didn't want broadcast. Like his drug-dealing. El Masri did change Sara Ibrahim's medical records to show that he and not Hatem el Shamy had put the girl on fifteen-minute obs at the end of her life. That would seem to suggest that el Masri was trying to distance el Shamy from Sara. I wonder if el Shamy blackmailed el Masri into doing that. If el Shamy threatened to tell all about el Masri's drug dealing?'

'But el Shamy was dealing drugs too.'

'We don't know that,' Vi said. 'He had drugs in his lock-up, but maybe he was just the warehouse man. If we could get him to talk that would help, but he won't. Just like Golding.'

'That copper Lee Arnold had dealings with down in Southend said they had intel that more psych meds than ever were coming into their manor. Some of the big gangs out there are into them. That stuff's getting popular.'

'Methadone's always been top ten,' Vi said. 'But Largactil's relatively new on the scene. Cheap-ish, and it's usually safer than the so-called legal highs.'

'Unless you're a kid called Puffy.'

'And you can't get done for being in possession of prescribed meds, especially if they've got your name on on the box.'

'So we just have to prove that the doctors and their mates were shifting the stuff.'

'Yeah, but we've yet to get any evidence from the hospital,' Vi said. 'Cotton was probably over-ordering medication to supply, but we don't know that for sure yet.'

They were interrupted by Mumtaz Hakim entering their office.

Vi got them all the best tea the machine in the corridor could make (if you gave it a kicking) and asked Mumtaz what the hell she thought she'd been doing working for Salwa el Shamy. Tony wanted to hide under his desk.

'She had a compelling story about Dr el Masri sexually abusing his patients. According to Salwa, el Masri wanted Hatem to join in but he wouldn't. Hatem el Shamy was a good nurse and so el Masri had to frame him to get him out of the hospital,' Mumtaz said.

'So why didn't Hatem just grass up el Masri when he was arrested?'

'Because, according to Salwa, he was shamed by what el Masri had done and didn't want his name associated with it. Some very pious people can seem to go against logic when it comes to things like this,' she said. 'To be fair, when I started working at Ilford I did hear stories about Dr el Masri drooling over young women.'

'But not sexually abusing them?'

'Not as such but . . .'

'Hatem el Shamy was the father of Sara Ibrahim's foetus,' Vi said.

For a moment Mumtaz didn't look as if she understood.

'I've got an email,' Tony said. 'From the DNA Database. It's kosher.'

'But then why did el Masri change those observation details on Sara's records?' Mumtaz said. 'Why did he try and protect Hatem?'

'Maybe they were friends after all,' Vi said.

'But then who set the bomb?'

Vi leant back in her chair. 'Who indeed? Mumtaz, this isn't about friends or sex it's about drugs. Cotton, el Masri, Hatem el Shamy and Golding were all into making money from psychiatric drugs. We found drugs in Gallions Hotel, we found them at el Masri's flat and in Hatem el Shamy's lock-up. I don't know who set that bomb at the hospital but I do know it wasn't anything to do with terrorism. Mr Cotton's been a hard nut to crack so far and Dr Golding, well, he won't speak.'

Tony said, 'He just lays on his bed like a corpse.'

'I've a feeling he'll crack soon,' Vi said.

Tony frowned. 'Any evidence except your gut for that, guv?' he said.

'No,' Vi said. 'I just think it'll be soon.' Her phone rang. The voice at the other end sounded hysterical.

Vi said, 'All right. I'll be down. Don't leave him.'

Then she ended the call.

'What's up, guv?'

Vi stood up. 'Mr Cotton has collapsed,' she said.


Her amma's cousin, Aftab, was a nice man. Amma's family were the sort of people who respected hard work and sacrifice. Aftab Huq was the epitome of that. He ran a shop, had put two of his three daughters through university and looked after his disabled wife. He also smoked like a bonfire and sounded as if he was from a 1960s British film about chirpy Cockneys.

He drove Shazia back to the house in Forest Gate and had a look at the amount of stuff he'd have to shift at the weekend. He shook his head. 'This'll take some doing,' he said. 'What's in these boxes?'

Shazia shrugged. 'Stuff.'

'What?'

'Books, kitchen things, clothes. All sorts.'

Aftab tried to lift one box and then gave up. 'You sure you ain't got car parts or nothing in these crates?'

'No.'

Shazia hadn't been back since the night before last and she could see that there was still some packing to be done. Amma was with the police for the moment and so she was on her own with it.

'I'll have to get Uncle Baharat to give us a hand,' Aftab said. 'I've got George, me cleaner, signed up. You know George Ferguson, Shazia?'

'No.' She'd started looking out of the window, where she saw a familiar car.

'Had a trial for West Ham back in the fifties,' Aftab said. 'In goal. Got six fingers on each hand, see, which is a bit tasty when it comes to being in goal.'

'Cousin Aftab . . .'

'Yes, babe.' He walked over to her.

The familiar car had now disgorged its driver, who was also familiar.

'What you looking at?'

'That man,' Shazia said. 'I've seen him before. He sometimes sits outside the house in that car.'

Aftab wiped his glasses on his trousers and put them on. He squinted. 'I think that's Naz Sheikh,' he said.

'You know him?'

'I know of him,' Aftab said. 'Thanks be to Allah that I don't know him.'

'Why not?'

'Because the Sheikhs are gangsters,' Aftab said. 'The father's a psycho, then there's two brothers, Naz and whatever the other one's called. They'll pull your fingernails out for the price of a packet of cigs. Do you know why Naz Sheikh's been hanging about here?'

'No,' she said. She felt cold. She kind of did know. Amma had been talking to him. But what about?

'Keep away from Naz Sheikh,' Aftab said. 'Him and his lot are bad news. Especially if you're Bengali. They prey on their own, that lot. Bastards, if you'll excuse my French.'

Cotton was unconscious and Vi was beside herself.

'You know if we don't stop sending these sods up to the General, they'll stop taking them.'

She knew that Tony Bracci was ignoring her, but she carried on. 'I wonder what's wrong with him? Cotton? Out like a fucking light . . .'

Her phone rang.

'If Cotton's brief's had an aneurism in the car park, I'm handing in me cards.' Then she laughed. 'Cotton, brief, get it?' She picked up the phone. 'DI Collins.'

Ten minutes later, Tony Bracci had gone out to Ilford Hospital and Vi had Salwa el Shamy in her office. Vi told her about her husband and Sara Ibrahim.

'No, it wasn't Hatem who raped that girl!' Salwa said. 'It was el Masri!'

Vi knew it would be hard for her, but she hadn't reckoned on the screaming. Coppers outside the glass walls of her office stared.

Vi kept calm. 'Dr el Masri may have had sex with that girl, and others too, for all I know,' she said. 'But the genetic tests on Sara Ibrahim's baby show that your husband was its father.'

'But it can't be! Hatem is a good man, a pious man!'

'Mrs el Shamy, you're gonna have to accept that your husband might have lied to you,' Vi said.

'He didn't.'

There was no point contradicting her. Vi said, 'Your husband and Dr el Masri didn't get on. Your husband is a Muslim, el Masri was a Christian who supported the regime of President Mubarak, who suppressed the Muslim Brotherhood. I don't yet know if Dr el Masri did sexually abuse any of his patients. But what I do know is that your husband, el Masri and some other doctors at Ilford have been selling psychiatric drugs outside the hospital.'

Tony had been called over to Ilford because there was now some information on their drug-ordering procedures. Mr Cotton had been over-ordering and there was evidence that a whole group of fictitious patients were registered. Mumtaz Hakim had said in her statement she'd noticed some of the patients on the chronic ward didn't seem very well medicated. So Cotton and Co. had been skimming off the top of their prescriptions, too.

'No, this is a lie, those drugs were put there to incriminate my husband!'

'Like the bomb was put in his locker by someone else?'

'Yes. Why would he blow up his own locker? With his things in?'

Vi resisted the temptation to invoke the so-called 'sacrifices' of suicide bombers. Hatem hadn't set a bomb in his own locker, she'd just been making a point. 'Science doesn't lie, Mrs el Shamy. Your husband made Sara Ibrahim pregnant. I'm telling you this now out of courtesy to you. Your husband has already been made aware of this and is being questioned by us.'

'Hatem?' She began to cry. 'What did he say when you told him these lies?'

'Nothing,' Vi said. El Shamy had sat like a stone when she'd seen him.

'He didn't try to defend himself?'

'No,' Vi said. 'Why? Would you have expected him to?'

'I would expect Hatem to say when something is a lie!'

'But if it wasn't, what do you think he'd say, Mrs el Shamy?'

Mumtaz looked at her phone and then at Phil Rivers' file. Officially the case was closed. The client's legal representative had even paid Lee in full. Every communication from the client herself made Mumtaz wince. Her husband had just disappeared, taking all the proceeds from a jointly owned house with him. He'd also, it transpired, been homosexual. But his wife, Sandra, as was clear from her emails and letters, still loved him. And now Mumtaz had seen him. As far as she knew she was the only one who had. But the woman had a right to know that.

She phoned Sandra Rivers' solicitor, Derek Salmon. He was on annual leave. Then she phoned the hospital to find out if she could talk to Lee. But she was told she couldn't.

Phil Rivers' appearance at Gallions Reach could have just been a passing coincidence but for one thing. He'd been in his pyjamas. If he didn't live in the area then what had he been doing in his night attire? He'd been standing beside a man who had been coughing, who had also been in his pyjamas. Had Phil maybe been that man's one-night-stand? If he had then he'd looked curiously modest in his PJs and slippers. Not that he could have come out into the street naked. But there had been something domestic between him and the other man that encouraged Mumtaz to think that maybe they were in a relationship. Or was she just projecting her own knowledge about Phil Rivers now onto something she'd seen fleetingly two nights before?

She picked her phone up and then put it down again. The case was closed and so whatever Phil Rivers had done had been written off. Lee had been instructed to leave the whole thing alone. Then she read another one of Sandra's letters to her solicitor and Mumtaz was lost. She called Shazia just to make sure that Cousin Aftab had been to the house. She sounded a bit off and said that when Mumtaz got back they needed to talk. Then Mumtaz phoned Sandra Rivers.

## 33

They'd moved him closer to the door. Did that mean they thought he was going to die and were planning a quick exit for his corpse? Even at his least optimistic, that seemed weird. Lee was breathing on his own now and, although he was still hooked up to loads of machines, he could just about talk. They'd hoiked some other poor bastard out just before they moved him. A big tin coffin on wheels had disappeared behind the geezer's curtains and then a bloke with a face like a gibbon's bum had wheeled him away.

Now the lights were dimmed and all he could hear was the sound of other people's ventilators. He knew he was in the intensive therapy unit. He'd visited a lot of folk in places like this over the years. His dad had died in ITU, his liver liquified by the booze he'd bathed it in for over fifty years. The staff had tried to keep him comfortable but even through the diamorphine cloud they'd put him under, his dad had still felt things. Like the other people on this unit. Drugged up to their armpits, they still moaned in their sleep and sometimes they would wake up screaming.

Lee just wanted to get out. A doctor had told him that he was 'doing well', whatever that meant. He'd told Lee he'd been given some powerful psychiatric medication that had attacked his heart. He hadn't said whether his heart was going to be all right.

There was a blue tinge to everything. The white sheets, the nurses' plastic aprons, the shiny floor. It was like being under-water and oddly there was a comfort in it. Just lately some memories had surfaced about his admission to hospital. He'd been put on a trolley in a noisy place. Had that been Accident and Emergency or an operating theatre? He didn't even know whether he'd had surgery. What he could remember were bits of what had happened just before he'd come into hospital. Mumtaz had fallen asleep in that tunnel that led from Gallions Hotel to the Albert Dock. He'd been holding that doctor on the ground, while a load of coppers went off to search for some other medic. He'd thought about Derek Salmon for some reason. And then there'd been nothing.

Then the fear returned.

A hand, large but smooth, pressed itself against his mouth. Two fingers pinched his nose shut. Lee saw a pair of dark eyes in a face that, weirdly, looked terrified. The hand pressed down and Lee's heart began to hammer in his ears. Then his head filled with cotton wool.

His eyes rolled up and he couldn't see anything until, with a tiny moment of euphoria, he could breathe again. In spite of all the wires and leads that went into and came out of every part of his body, he reared up and gasped thick, hot air. It was the most incredible thing he could imagine. He saw those eyes again and for a moment he flinched away. But then he saw another pair of dark eyes too. Vi Collins smiled at him and said, 'You look like shit, Arnold.'

He saw a man being cuffed by a constable. The man was crying. Vi said to him, 'I knew you'd try and silence him. Prat.'

*

Salwa threw what she could see of the boys' clothes into a suitcase.

Asim said, 'Where are we going? I want to sleep.'

She'd just pulled them out of bed and both boys were dazed.

'Get up and get dressed,' Salwa said.

'Why?'

'Because I ask you to.'

She'd lain awake for hours before she'd made her decision, but now all Salwa wanted to do was get on with it. Again and again she'd interrogated herself about Hatem. Had he been lying to her? Salwa had used the standard anti-Western narrative to herself when she'd first left Forest Gate police station, that DI Collins must have been lying. But then when she thought about the DNA results on that girl's baby she wondered how the police could fix that if they had to take that evidence to court. Why should they? Unless they had planted the drugs in the lock-up too. They could have. But Hatem was already in custody and so why would they do that? In her heart she knew the truth.

Salwa felt more rage towards Rashida than anyone else. How could she take the police to her father's lock-up? The girl must have suspected that her father was making a bomb when she saw the bags of fertilizer in there. She had betrayed him even though she would have to have known he was only doing it for the good of Islam. That was what she'd tell everyone when she got back to Cairo. Only Salwa herself would remember those long shifts that Hatem worked when he came home not so much exhausted as satisfied.

'Come on!' she said to the boys. 'I've called a taxi and if you're not ready I'll have to leave you behind.'

'But where are we going?' Asim said.

Salwa put a heap of scarves in her suitcase. 'To Egypt.'

'So will we meet Rashida and Zizi at the airport then?' Gamal asked.

Still her favourite, she took his face between her hands and said, 'No, my soul. I am sorry but we won't.'

'We don't have tickets for tonight,' Asim yelled.

'We're going to buy other tickets at the airport,' Salwa snapped. Then she turned back to Gamal again and said, 'I'm so sorry, my little prince, your sisters are dead.'

Asim again butted in. 'No they're not, they've gone into care.'

Salwa slapped him.

'No, they didn't,' she said. 'They are dead and gone and now we must go back to Egypt and forget them!'

But she cried as she spoke and when they all finally piled into the taxi she was still crying.

Vi sat in the chair next to Cotton's bed and looked at him. His skin, which had been sallow anyway, was jaundiced, his eyes were bloodshot. Periodically he pressed a button on a small tube that hung around his neck dispensing diamorphine.

The side room Cotton had been put in was brightly lit in spite of the lateness of the hour. It helped to keep Vi awake.

'Your mate Dr Golding tried to kill PI Lee Arnold tonight,' she said. 'Silly kid thought he could do a Royal Shakespeare number called "I've Lost Me Memory" on me.'

Cotton smiled. His face was so thin it looked as if it might split in two.

'Wrong,' Vi said. 'I just told him where Mr Arnold was and then we waited and he did exactly what I knew he would. Now, of course, he's gone all silent on me again. Won't last. But what the fuck? Eh?'

'Indeed.'

'What the fuck, because I've been told by your doctor that you're dying,' she said. 'You've got cancer.'

'Yes,' Cotton said calmly. 'Early last year I had a lump cut off my leg. But too late, the tumour had metastasised and the horrid thing was in my bones. I've been under palliative care for nearly a year.'

'I'm sorry.'

He smiled again. 'No, you're not, but you want some sort of confession from me and you'll use all your charm and your sympathy to get it.'

He was a clever man, there was no point trying to pull the wool over his eyes. 'Spot on,' Vi said. 'Your ever-patient Mother Confessor, available for christenings and bar mitzvahs, that's me.'

They both sat in silence. Vi had been told that if Cotton was lucky he had a month. He could just clam up and say nothing or he could unburden himself.

'So you've a choice of beating the truth out of David Golding or hoping that I decide to tell you everything,' Cotton said.

'Mmm. The beating I don't know about,' Vi said. 'But yes, if you don't want to tell me anything, you don't have to. You'll leave Golding in a bit of a pickle but . . .' She shrugged. 'Do you like mysteries, Mr Cotton?'

'Oh, yes,' he said. 'I like them very much.'

'Then that's me well and truly fucked, isn't it?' Vi said.

He laughed and then his face fell. 'They tell me I probably won't be leaving this hospital,' he said.

'I'd've thought they'd've needed the bed.'

'You'd think so, wouldn't you?' Then he said, 'Did you instruct the consultant to tell me that to get me to talk?'

'No. Wish I'd thought of it, actually,' Vi said. 'It's a neat idea.'

'You know I like you, DI Collins,' Cotton said. 'I may even talk to you when I'm ready.'

'You're talking to me now.'

'Ah, but you, I am sure, need a cigarette and I am not ready to speak to you yet.'

'You sure?'

'Yes.'

'It's better to get things off your chest.'

'Afraid I'll die before I tell you what you want to know?'

'Yes, actually,' Vi said. She stood up.

'Well then, let me give you a taster to be going on with,' Cotton said. 'Just before I got my diagnosis I realized that I didn't have any money. Don't ask me where it went because I don't know. I'm not a boozer or a gambler and I don't take drugs. A house that was beyond my means, maybe? Two rapacious ex-wives and a child who refuses to seek gainful employment? I have all of those and I imagine their cost built up over time. Then I received my diagnosis. I looked at ways, DI Collins, whereby I might make some money in a short space of time.'

'To pay off your—'

'No,' he said, 'to have anything I wanted when I wanted it. And there was something else, too. But that's for another time.'

The interview room was silent. Tony Bracci waited. His interviewee, David Golding, shook with either cold or terror or both. But he could speak. He'd spoken to Vi when she'd arrested him. He'd played mad and now he'd been found out. He had nowhere to go. Knowing this, Tony wanted to hit him. He was a bloody doctor, for God's sake, and, at the very least, he'd hurt people. He was scum.

Golding had refused a brief and so Tony and DC Rock were on their own with him. Old muckers from training college, Tony knew that all he had to do was give Rock the nod and he'd beat the crap out of the shitbag.

'I made a bad career choice.'

Golding's sudden utterance made Tony sit up.

'What do you mean?' he said.

'Psychiatry. My dad's a psychiatrist, I thought I wanted to do it,' Golding said. 'I didn't. It was awful.'

'So change career,' Tony said. 'What do you want me to say? What's this got to do with you and Cotton and the dead bodies of Dr el Masri and his nephew?'

'Everything,' Golding said.

'Enlighten us.'

Tony leaned back in his chair.

'Mr Cotton decided to sell drugs when he found out he had cancer,' Golding said.

'Why was that?'

'He said it was because he wanted money to pay off debts he had,' Golding said. 'But if he wanted to steal drugs from the hospital he had to have an accomplice. If he ordered something like methadone, which is a heroin substitute, he'd need a counter signatory.'

'Why? He was the chief psychiatric consultant.'

'Ilford hasn't had an addiction unit for over a decade. Cotton needed to say he wanted methadone because he'd reinstated the clinic under the auspices of Dr el Masri.'

'But el Masri didn't treat addiction?'

'No. No one did. Like Cotton, el Masri wanted money. But in his case it was for what he felt was a good cause.'

'Which was?'

'He was a Coptic Christian. Those people have been discriminated against in Egypt for decades. Some of the poorer members of the community are virtually destitute. He wanted to send some money home.'

'And you?' Tony asked. 'What did you do and why?'

'I wasn't involved at first. It was just Cotton and el Masri.' He put his head down. 'I found delivery notes for methadone and I asked Mr Cotton why we were ordering heroin substitute. He fobbed me off with a story about an addicted patient on one of the acute wards. But even if such a patient had existed, the quantities were too big. Then I began to notice how many of the chronics were having their meds reduced, principally those on the antipsychotic tranquillizer Largactil. That, too, by the way, was being over-ordered. It had to be going somewhere. I guessed it was outside the institution.'

'I wanted out of the hospital and psychiatry so badly I thought that if I could get in on what Cotton and el Masri were doing I could get some cash and just go. And so, because I'm a bad man, when I confronted Cotton, I asked him to cut me in on whatever he was doing with these drugs,' Golding said. 'He didn't want to because he already had el Masri and a nurse who'd also twigged what was happening. But I followed and watched them all the time. I know what drugs can cost on the street. I know people who paid off their student loans selling drugs. I thought I'd go abroad.'

'And do what?' Rock asked.

'I don't know! Anything – anything except listen to mad people all day long and wade about on wards scented with piss.' He shuddered. 'In the end, Cotton agreed to cut me in, just like el Masri had to cut that nurse in.'

'Hatem el Shamy?'

'Yes,' Golding said. 'He and el Masri came to an arrangement.'

'What sort of arrangement?'

'A disgusting one.'

'Tell us about it.'

Golding said, 'El Shamy wouldn't sell drugs, but he would store them. He got his cut provided el Masri covered up his sexual adventures with female patients.'

Tony looked down at his notes. 'Like a girl called Sara Ibrahim?'

Golding cringed. 'She killed herself. It was because Hatem el Shamy . . .'

'He made her pregnant,' Tony said. 'But then you knew that, didn't you, Dr Golding?'

He didn't answer.

'What about Dr D'Lima?' Tony asked. 'Your other colleague. What did he know?'

For the first time, Golding smiled. 'Ferdinand? He's a dear, innocent man,' he said. 'Totally dedicated to his patients, he hardly notices that the rest of us exist.'

'Nice to know there's one decent shrink up at Ilford, guv,' Rock said.

Tony ignored him.

'So there was Cotton, el Masri, you, el Shamy . . .'

'Who started to blackmail el Masri.'

Tony frowned. 'What do you mean? El Shamy was in on it too, how could he blackmail el Masri?'

'Ragab – Dr el Masri – knew that Sara Ibrahim was pregnant by el Shamy. When the girl killed herself el Masri falsified her records to make it look as if he and not el Shamy had put her on fifteen-minute observations. El Shamy feared the girl would kill herself and he didn't want her to do that with a foetus in her belly. He feared there might be questions. But she did it anyway. El Masri had the foetus DNA-tested, which he thought he could use as insurance, if necessary, against el Shamy in the future. As Muslim and Christian they hated each other. And el Masri was proved right. El Shamy started saying he'd tell the authorities about the drugs that were being stored at his lock-up in Manor Park if el Masri told anyone about the girl. He said he was going back to Egypt, the Muslim Brotherhood had just won their general election, and that he didn't care about his colleagues and their drugs any more. That was why Dr el Masri's nephew, Butrus, came over from Egypt at that time.'

'What's he got to do with this?'

'Butrus knows – knew – how to build a bomb. He'd learnt when he was in the army,' Golding said. 'And el Masri and Mr Cotton wanted one of those.'

'To put in Hatem el Shamy's locker?'

'Yes,' he said. 'Mr Cotton is a very clever man. He knew he couldn't sack el Shamy because if he was going back to Egypt then why not tell the authorities here what Cotton and el Masri had been up to before he went? He could say they'd forced him to store the drugs for them. El Shamy had to be destroyed and the only way to do that was to implicate him in a terrorist offence.'

'So Cotton and the rest of you risked blowing up the hospital . . .'

'Not me,' Golding said. 'I wasn't involved then. And if you're wondering why el Shamy didn't just shop everyone to the police when he was arrested, then just consider that, as well as being a bomber, he also had all the drugs in his lock-up. Who would believe anything he said? If he implicated Cotton and el Masri he implicated himself. And he knew that el Masri would also make sure people back home in Egypt knew about his sexual history.

He didn't just abuse Sara Ibrahim, not according to el Masri. There were others. Radical Muslims hate that stuff.'

'I'm not keen on sexual abuse meself,' Tony said. 'So you had to leave the drugs in el Shamy's lock-up.'

'No one could touch them,' Golding said. 'And, anyway, a better place was found.'

'Gallions.'

'Yes.'

'Better in what way?'

'Nobody wants the old hotel. We rented it. El Masri lived in one of the flats overlooking it and it was he who discovered that you could get in and out of the building via an open tunnel from the Albert Dock. Two nights ago was the first time I'd been there, with Mr Cotton.'

'Did he have a key?'

'El Masri had keys made.'

'So why was el Masri killed?' Tony asked.

'Because he killed his own nephew, Butrus,' Golding said. 'It was an accident, but it threatened everything. El Masri was consumed by fear for the future, just as I was when I put my hands over Mr Arnold's mouth and nose.'

When she saw her husband for the first time in over a year, Sandra Rivers cried. Almost solidified from the cold, Sandra had sat in her car for hours, waiting for a glimpse of Phil. And now, with the sunrise, there he was. The same jaunty, fit young man she'd fallen in love with, he carried a suitcase and, after a few moments, he was joined by someone else. They kissed.

Sandra was so glad to see that Phil was alive that she hardly noticed the other person. But then they stood by the road.

Looking back towards the Gallions roundabout, they were waiting for a taxi.

Between Sandra and Phil and his companion was a large old building on a sort of an island in the middle of the blocks of flats. It looked as if it might have been an old pub or hotel at one time. Sandra didn't know the Royal Docks very well, all this was new to her. As was Phil.

He kissed the other man again, whose back was towards her, and Sandra couldn't stand it.

Weeping, she got out of her car and ran towards them. Vast in her Russian mink coat and hat, she saw the look of shock on Phil's face as she barrelled towards him.

In spite of what he'd done to her, and in spite of the man at his side, she flung her arms around her husband's neck and said, 'Oh, I thought you were dead!'

Squeezing him and kissing him, Sandra was barely aware that Phil was almost no longer breathing. Then she saw the face of the man standing beside him and Sandra suddenly disengaged from Phil.

All she said as she looked at him was, 'You.'


'Butrus el Masri stayed,' Dr Golding said. 'He liked London and his uncle promised the kid's father he'd get him a job. He didn't, but he did buy him a car and generally spoiled him. Ragab had no children of his own. He cut the boy in.'

'On the drugs.'

'Yes.'

'You lot were about the worst drug dealers going,' Tony said. 'Nobody ever tell you, you use a small core group and keep schtum when it comes to mum, dad, nephew, Uncle Tom Cobley and all.'

'Well, we're doctors . . .'

'So you shouldn't've decided you wanted to be drug dealers.'

Golding shook his head.

'Carry on,' Tony said. He looked at Rock and raised his eyebrows.

'El Masri couldn't have his nephew hanging about the hospital and so Butrus spent most of his time around the Royal Docks. He was meant to guard the drugs. But there's not much to do there for a young man and he got bored. He took to meeting up with some other young men outside some off-licence.'

'On the dole, were they?'

Golding shrugged. 'I don't know. They drank all day, I suppose so. That's what Ragab finally told Mr Cotton when the whole thing about Butrus finally blew up. Anyway, one day Butrus took these boys back to his uncle's flat where he thought he'd curry even more favour with them by letting them try out these drugs el Masri was selling.'

'The boy that took those drugs died.'

'Oh God.' He put his head in his hands. 'I knew he was sick . . .'

'He died,' Tony said. 'Largactil overdose. Just like my mate Lee Arnold. You know? The bloke you tried to smother last night when you were so "afraid". The bloke you gave an amp to, down by the Albert.'

Golding looked up. 'That wasn't me! I just hit him. Cotton injected him. You have to believe me!'

'Do I? I don't think so,' Tony said.

'I've never killed anyone! Anyone! El Masri killed his nephew because he lost his temper with him. He told Cotton that Butrus had said that he was scared and that he was going to tell the police what really happened to that boy. He knew that the bomb he'd planted at the hospital wouldn't be allowed to go off. But that boy getting sick, that was too much. From what I can gather about him, Butrus was a swaggering, spoilt young man, but not bad. He felt genuinely distraught about that boy. Butrus tried to leave the flat, but el Masri stood in his way. He knew that when the boy said he'd go to the police, he meant it. They fought and Butrus took a blow to the head that killed him. It was an accident. El Masri was distraught about it. He kept on saying he wished he'd killed himself instead.' He looked up. 'But Mr Cotton wasn't impressed.'

'What did Cotton do?'

'When we first found out, Mr Cotton went to see him in his office,' he said. 'Words were exchanged. After work the following day he went to see el Masri in his office again. He asked him what he planned to do with his nephew's body. I was walking to my office when I heard noises.'

'What noises?'

He shook his head. 'To me it sounded like strangulation. I went into el Masri's office. I saw Mr Cotton standing behind him. El Masri was sitting down. Mr Cotton was cutting his throat.'

'He had a knife with him?'

'No. It was el Masri's letter knife. It must've hurt.' He cried.

'Why'd he do that, Dr Golding? Why'd he kill him? Surely that was just making the situation worse for all of you?'

Golding struggled to get his sobbing under control. When he did, he said, 'Mr Cotton was furious about Butrus. He thought that el Masri should have just paid the boy and then sent him home after he set the bomb. Now the boy was dead and his body was a problem for all of us. El Masri kept crying and saying he wished he was dead. He didn't even try to think about how the mess he had created might be contained. Mr Cotton lost control. He said if he wanted to die, he'd fucking kill him.'

'Then what? What did you do when you saw Cotton killing el Masri?'

'Nothing.'

'Nothing? You didn't try to stop him?'

'I couldn't move.' His body began to shake. 'I watched him die. It was as if I wasn't there. And then . . . And then neither of us said a word except Cotton told me I had to help him move el Masri's body out of the way, into a cupboard.'

'Which you did?'

'Yes. We went to Mr Cotton's office after that and he gave me a drink.'

'What sort of drink?'

'Whisky.'

'Did you talk about what had just happened?'

'He did.'

'What did he say?'

Golding swallowed. 'He said that el Masri had threatened to give himself up to the police.'

'Seems to me the English branch of el Masri's family were keen to speak to us,' Tony said.

'El Masri was serious, according to Cotton. He said in the end he was cornered by el Masri and so he had no choice but to kill him.'

'What do you think, Dr Golding?'

'About Mr Cotton's choice? I think it was wrong,' he said. 'Even if it meant we all went to prison.'

'And yet, according to the advocate, Mrs Mumtaz Hakim, you helped Cotton dispose of el Masri's body. You were well aware of his plan to kill her and you were with Cotton when he, or you, spiked Mr Lee Arnold. Don't try to kid me you're a whiter shade of pale, Dr Golding. You may or may not have killed anyone but you're either weak or wicked or both.'

Golding began to weep. 'I'm not wicked. I'm not.'

'Then weak,' Tony said. 'Who was it who said that thing about evil things happening because good men do nothing?'

DC Rock shrugged.

'So when'd you find Mrs Mumtaz Hakim and how?' Tony asked.

Through sobs, Golding said, 'When we went back into el Masri's office. She had that cupboard door open. Mr Cotton hit her.'

'Mr Cotton did a lot of violent stuff for a dying man,' Tony said.

'He has cancer but he's not dying, he's in remission.'

'Not according to the doctors at Newham General,' Tony said. 'According to them he could kark it at any minute. So, Dr Golding, you'd better tell us the truth because you know, us coppers, being a bit simple-minded as we are, we do tend to believe deathbed confessions and the like. So if Mr Cotton points the finger at you on his last breath . . .'

'Then he'll be lying,' Golding said.

'I thought people didn't lie on their deathbeds?'

'Oh yes they do,' Golding said. 'Trust me, I'm a doctor, I know.'

Tony Bracci shook his head. 'Fucking hell,' he said to Rock, 'can you believe he just said that?'

## 34

Shazia was still angry with Mumtaz. She'd blatantly lied to her about Naz Sheikh and they both knew it. The night before, over dinner, Shazia had said, 'Your own cousin, Aftab, told me who he was. And I've seen you talking to him!'

'You're mistaken, Shazia,' Mumtaz had said. 'You must have seen me talking to another young man.'

'Did I say he was a young man? No,' Shazia said. 'How did you know that if you don't know this gangster boy, Amma?'

'I assumed . . .'

'And how many young men do you talk to in the street? You cover yourself—'

'Shazia!' It had been then that Mumtaz had got up from the table. 'Leave it,' she'd said. 'Just leave it.'

But Shazia hadn't been able to do that. 'Why?' she'd said. 'Is he your boyfriend or . . .'

'Don't be ridiculous, Shazia!'

'So who is he?' Shazia had screamed. 'Is he someone else my father owed money to?'

And then she'd seen her amma's face go white. So it was true. Why hadn't she told her? And now they hadn't spoken since, except when they'd had to find change for the hospital car park.

But for the moment Shazia had to forget about that. Lee was

on an ordinary hospital ward now and when she saw him she flung her arms around his neck.

'Oh blimey, this is a bit of a welcome back to the land of the living,' he said.

She kissed his cheek.

'I think I'll get a mad doctor to inject me with something deadly again.'

'Don't you dare!' she said. She sat down on the chair beside the bed and let her amma shake hands with him.

'Lee, I am so glad and so relieved,' Mumtaz said.

Lee patted the bed and said, 'Sit down, Mumtaz, you're making the place look untidy.'

She looked a little awkward. Shazia had friends who, like Amma, covered and in her opinion they all needed to get over themselves when it came to men.

But Amma sat, admittedly with her handbag primly on her knees. 'How are you?' Mumtaz asked.

'Rough. But I'll live,' he said. 'They've got to do all these heart tests to make sure the ticker's all right before I leave, and me liver's a bit damaged. But at least I don't have to give up drinking, do I?'

'No.'

'Got that covered already.'

They all laughed. Then Lee said, 'So, work . . .'

'Work I'll tell you all about when you're out of here,' Mumtaz said. 'DI Collins will be in to interview you about what happened at Gallions Reach.'

'Right.'

'I imagine that you know that the doctors are in custody.'

'I should hope the one who tried to kill me would be.'

'A doctor tried to kill you?' Shazia said. 'What? In here?'

'Not one of the hospital doctors! One of those . . .' Lee looked at Mumtaz. 'Have you told her?'

'Some of it.'

'One of the doctors at the hospital your mum was working in,' Lee said.

'Oh.'

'Everything is in hand,' her amma said.

Shazia saw Lee look into her eyes and smile.

'Mum come in first thing,' Lee told them.

'That's good.' Mumtaz smiled. 'Susan sends her regards,' she said.

Shazia had never met Susan.

'Oh, good,' he said. And then he changed the subject. 'You know, Mumtaz, for some reason I keep on thinking about that Phil Rivers case . . .'

'Ah,' her amma said. 'I might have some news about that for you . . .'

'Your mum and your brothers were picked up by the police at Heathrow,' Mrs Sidney told Rashida. 'I'm afraid the police are going to want to talk to you again.'

'What about?'

'Your father,' she said.

The father Rashida had betrayed. Separated from Zizi, Rashida was in a young people's unit full of boys and girls who'd been in care for years. Some of them were OK, but most of them scared her. Some of the girls went with men for sex when they left the building.

'Is my mum back home again?' Rashida asked.

'I don't know.'

'Do you know when I can go back to my friend MJ's house?'

She'd been there briefly but she'd liked it so much. And MJ had wanted her to stay. When she'd left they'd all cried, even MJ's mum.

'Your friend's home wasn't appropriate,' Mrs Sidney said. 'Not at the moment.'

'Why not?'

'Her mother isn't a foster carer and she's not related to you. Also they practice a different religion.'

'I don't care,' Rashida said. 'I'm a Muslim, they're Hindus, it doesn't matter. I know my religion, they won't stop me. Why would they?'

'It's not appropriate,' Mrs Sidney said.

'But I hate it here.'

'You're safe here.' She smiled.

Rashida said, 'No, I'm not. These kids frighten me. And why can't I go back to my old school?'

The unit was in Hackney, which meant Rashida couldn't commute back in to Newham to go to school. There was sense in that from the point of view of making a new life in a new place, away from her family. But it made her unhappy. It made her wonder whether what she'd done to free herself and her sister had been worth it. So she wasn't married? She was driven mad every night by the girls in the next room whispering the word 'freak' through the wall.

'I'd like to see my family,' Rashida said.

'I'm sure we can arrange for you to visit your little sister.'

'I want to see my mum and my brothers too.'

'And you can visit your brothers.'

But what about her mother? She wasn't mentioned – except in the context of having been stopped at the airport because the police wanted to speak to her.

'What's going to happen to me?'

MJ had always talked about how, when she grew up, they'd go travelling together. They'd visit Peru and see Machu Picchu, go to Cambodia and climb Angkor Wat and they'd roam the Gobi Desert on yaks and sleep in big tents called yurts. There had been nothing they wanted to do that they hadn't planned in detail.

Mrs Sidney didn't put her arm around Rashida but she could see that she wanted to. 'Look, why don't you write to MJ?' she said. 'She has been asking about you. A lot.'

'Has she?'

'Yes. If I get you some paper and stamps would you like to do that?'

'Yes!'

'Maybe if the Joshis are in agreement we can arrange for a supervised visit,' Mrs Sidney said. 'Maybe . . .'

Vi smelt death as soon as she entered the room. It was an old acquaintance. The skinny, yellowing man on the bed was leaving this world. He was also stopping her from visiting Lee Arnold.

'What do you want, Mr Cotton?' she said sharply.

The nurse checking Cotton's chart looked at her as if she'd like to stab her.

Vi didn't take any notice and sat down. The nurse left.

'It's about that deathbed confession.'

When he spoke she could hear the death rattle at the back of his throat. His lungs were flooding. It was a miracle he was even conscious.

'One of your officers kicked me,' he said. 'When I was arrested beside the Albert Dock.'

Vi flinched. 'I'm sure he had a good reason. That it?' she said.

'No. Come closer and I'll give you something you won't ignore,' he said. 'We're all corrupt in our own ways, aren't we, DI Collins? You with your thuggish officers, me, well . . . Come close. Closer.'

Vi had to make an effort not to shiver. According to Tony Bracci, Dr Golding had come across like a spoilt, thwarted child. Weak and malleable. Mr Cotton was another story.

Working against all her instincts, Vi leant across the dying man's bed and put her face close to his. His breath smelt of faeces. She felt herself gag.

'Disgusting, eh?'

She ignored him.

'You've a terrible scar on your neck, DI Collins,' he said. 'Someone try to kill you?'

'Yes, a goitre,' she said. 'Now . . .'

He laughed. It sounded like popping candy in water.

'Here is my confession,' he said. 'I don't know what Golding has told you, if anything, but let the boy go, he's a nothing.'

'He aided and abetted you.'

Cotton breathed and then he said, 'But he killed nobody. I killed Dr el Masri. That was all me.'

Vi said. 'He assisted in the abduction of Mrs Hakim.'

'She'd been poking around all day. She wanted information about Sara Ibrahim.'

'That was no reason to abduct her.'

'Maybe not. But I did it. And I injected the private eye with Largactil,' he said.

Golding hadn't confessed to that. Was Cotton telling the truth? Why would he lie?

'You confess to that act?'

But if that was the case then why had Golding tried to kill Lee Arnold on ITU?

'I do,' he said.

'I'm gonna need to get a colleague in here to back this up,' Vi said. 'If I don't I could be accused of making up stories.'

She was about to leave but then a hand that was as thin as it was strong caught her by the throat and pulled her down onto a chest that was caved in with sickness. Suddenly she was afraid.

'No. There's no time,' he said.

Given the strength in his hand she would have begged to differ but she couldn't speak.

'Hear what I say because time is very short.'

Again she tried to pull away and again he snatched her back.

He breathed. 'I know that you're wondering why I did all those terrible things just to make money to squander. But you see, I didn't do it just for that reason.'

His fingers around her throat held Vi's windpipe almost closed. It hurt where she'd been cut. She looked around to see if she could locate an emergency button. She couldn't.

'I did what I did because I knew I was dying and I wanted to know what being something I wasn't was like.' He breathed again and she heard some organ in his chest squeak. 'Wicked. I have a ward manager who is wicked, he's called Mr Pool. Many years ago I tried to stop him tormenting and manipulating his patients, but he always outwitted me. For a quiet life I stopped fighting him and then, one day, I became him. And do you know, DI Collins, for the first time in my life I felt like a man. Successful, feared and never, not for a second, afraid any more. Not even of my illness. When the worst has happened to you then what is there to lose? Bad boys always win in the end.'

He gripped her harder than ever and Vi was convinced that she was going to black out. But then, in a second, all of the strength left him and his hand flopped down onto the bed beside her. After she'd caught her breath and the weird little flashing lights she'd started to get in her eyes when her oxygen had been cut off had receded, she looked at Cotton and knew that he had been right. He had been just about to die and now he had.

But about bad boys, he was wrong. She had to think that way.

Mumtaz watched Shazia cross the road and go into college. The girl was still mad at her, but what could she do? And being angry with Cousin Aftab didn't help. He'd told Shazia who Naz Sheikh was because he'd seen him about and knew him to be a wrong 'un. She was pretty sure he didn't know about Ahmet's dealings with that family. What was worrying her was that Shazia was threatening to tell Lee about Naz when he got out of hospital. She looked up at Newham General and then began to walk back to her car.

'So, moving tomorrow?'

That voice she knew so well. She turned to face him and, as usual, Naz was smiling.

'Thought we should have a chat before the big day,' he said. 'Get our new arrangement crystal clear in our heads.'

'I thought you were going to do that after I'd moved,' Mumtaz said. 'I have to go to Forest Gate police station now.'

'Ah well, that's a coincidence then, isn't it?'

Just looking at him, all jolly and cocky, made her want to do him harm.

'Why? Are you going there?'

She took her keys out of her handbag.

'No, but I think we should have a chat about Forest Gate nick,' he said.

'What? That you should be in it?'

She walked over to her car and unlocked the driver's door.

'No, that you should be in it,' Naz said. And then he strode over to her and stood so close she could smell him. Hot breath filled with cardamom and cigarette smoke, expensive liberally applied aftershave. 'I need a pair of eyes and ears amongst the good coppers of Forest Gate and so I thought I'd use yours.'

This was the way she was going to have to pay off some of her debt.

'I need a spy,' Naz said. 'I need ears to listen for info about me and my family and eyes to see when we might be due a little visit from the plods. We like to know what they're up to but lately we seem to be finding that a bit tricky. You get me?'

She got him.

'You want me to give you warning if any of your properties are going to be raided,' she said. 'I won't be able to do that. I'm not in the police. I'm not always around them.'

'No, but your boss is.'

'No, he isn't.' She got into the car.

Naz bent down to stop her closing the door.

'He is when he's shagging DI Collins,' he said.

'What?' Many years ago, so it was said, Lee and DI Collins had had an affair but that was over. Wasn't it? Mumtaz felt odd. And angry. She fired up the engine. 'Don't be stupid.'

But she couldn't close the door because he was still in the way. 'I'm not being stupid, I'm being practical,' he said. 'On your behalf, Mumtaz. Do this and I'll give you payment holidays. Don't forget—'

'Or what? You'll burn my house down?'

As soon as she'd said it, Mumtaz regretted those words.

He let go of her car door and she saw his face harden. Then she heard him say, 'Oh no, Mrs Hakim, I won't do that. But I will hold your little daughter down and rape her.'

## 35

Three Weeks Later

Shirley decided she did want to take the plastic dinosaur pen-holder that had been given to her by a woman on the chronic ward. Not all her experiences at Ilford had been bad. In fact, apart from her own rapid exit from the Advocacy, it had all worked out for the best.

When he'd become chief consultant, Dr D'Lima had wielded a ruthless new broom. Timothy Pool was on 'gardening leave', which meant that all of the complaints against him were being investigated by the Trust. Several of his acolytes had chosen to give notice. Shirley had too.

She felt a failure. Mumtaz Huq – or Hakim, as she now knew her – had noticed that the chronics were under-medicated when she'd only been in the hospital for five minutes. She was a private detective but still Shirley felt she'd failed. After the police arrived, Mandy and Roy, traumatized by the whole experience and furious with Mumtaz for deceiving them, gave up the Advocacy. It was a shame, but Shirley didn't blame them, or Mumtaz. She'd come to Ilford to do a job and she'd done it and more. The price had been high to the reputation of the hospital but there'd been no choice. Mr Cotton, Dr el Masri and Dr Golding had been selling psychiatric drugs to gangs out in Essex and Hatem el Shamy had abused Sara Ibrahim and other women too. Poor Sara. She'd wanted to tell Shirley who had raped her that day but she couldn't quite believe it herself. Hatem el Shamy's extravagant piousness had fooled everyone. He was guilty of many crimes. Ironically, the only thing he hadn't been was a bomber.

Shirley threw the last handful of pens on the desk into her handbag. God alone knew how she'd pay the mortgage but at least she'd be free of Ilford. Dr D'Lima was going to give her a reference and she genuinely wished good luck to whoever was recruited to take her place. All the old bins were supposed to have closed years ago, but everyone knew they still had their place. People got sick and they needed somewhere to go to get better. Some needed somewhere to live. Shirley thought about the chronics. They were quiet now they were medicated. Terry no longer saw planes flying over the hospital, dropping his father's ashes at the end of his bed. The price for that was that he, and all the others on the ward, were zombies. They didn't know what time it was, what day, what year. And that wasn't right. But then, what was? Only what was wrong was entirely clear. Unfortunately it hadn't been quite crystal enough for Shirley.

As she left, Shirley saw Dylan Smith on Forensic looking out of a window. She waved to him and smiled but he just looked at her as if he'd never seen her before in his life.

It was Lee's first day back at work and Mumtaz wanted it to be easy for him. They only had one appointment in the office, which she knew he'd find fascinating; the rest of the day would be devoted to tea and catching up. On the inside she was quite

another person, one crucified by nervousness, but that couldn't
be allowed to matter for the moment.

'So how was your move?' Lee asked. His eyes were a little glassy
still, which was disconcerting.

But she smiled and put his mug of tea on his desk with a
KitKat.

'Thanks.'

'Oh, my father ran true to form, did too much and had to have
a lay down and a chocolate bar,' Mumtaz said. 'Cousin Aftab
managed to back his van into some woman's sports car and Shazia had a hissy fit over her One Direction posters. But we
survived.'

What she didn't tell him was that Naz Sheikh had watched
the whole procedure. She'd had to say yes to his request about
becoming his spy and so, she imagined, he was in some way protecting his investment. What he didn't know was that she wasn't
going to be his eyes and ears anywhere. How she wasn't going to
do it she didn't know. But she wasn't.

The office buzzer went off. Lee hadn't even had a chance to
see if they had any appointments in the diary, which was just
the way that Mumtaz had planned it. When she opened the
door, there was Sandra Rivers dressed in red.

'Sandra?'

Lee stood up.

'Cor blimey, it really has changed round here, hasn't it?' Sandra Rivers said. 'Parking's a nightmare!'

'Sandra, this is a surprise! Mumtaz told me something about
Phil and Del Salmon . . .'

'Sit down, love,' Sandra said. She smiled at Mumtaz. 'You've
not told him all of it, have you?'

'Not everything, Mrs Rivers.'

Sandra sat down and then so did Lee.

'About my Phil,' Sandra began. 'I found him. Or Mumtaz did.'

Lee looked over at her. 'Yeah, at Gallions.'

'When we were taken out of Gallions Hotel that terrible night there were some local people standing around. They'd come out to see what was up and I thought I recognized one man. I didn't know it was Mr Rivers until I got back to the office next day and I found that photograph you'd shown me.'

'So did you tell Derek Salmon?'

'He was on holiday,' she said.

'So she called me,' Sandra said.

'I couldn't call the police, that would have been against your client's wishes,' Mumtaz said to Lee.

'Mumtaz told me where she thought he might be living, Gallions Reach, and so I just went over there and waited until I saw Phil or I didn't. But I did.'

'So did you speak to him?' Lee said.

'Him and A. N. Other man were on their way out to go on their holidays to Sardinia,' Sandra said.

'I thought that Phil was afraid of . . .'

'Flying? Only with me, apparently. With his bloke he was fine! And do you know who that bloke was, Mr Arnold? Oh, I s'pose you have to know that.'

'Derek Salmon,' Lee said. 'Just before all the Gallions business I'd worked out there had to be a connection between him and Phil's bogus lawyers because their letterheads had the same fault. I didn't have him down as a . . .'

'Poofta,' Sandra said. 'Apparently they fell in love when I was ill and Del had come over to the house to get me to sign things.

Derek was in debt up to his chinstrap. Then Phil had this great idea to leave me and sell the house I'd let him stay in from under me. Del set up the fake solicitors, arranged for Phil to get a new identity – called George O'Dowd. Boy George.' She rolled her eyes. 'He's so bloody out the closet he's in the fucking bathroom.'

'So Derek could shield Phil.'

'Exactly. Until I said I wanted to know where he was but I didn't want to prosecute. Phil was no fool, he'd guessed correctly that I wouldn't come after him for money. Not then. But neither of them had thought about my just wanting him found. Put Del as the family solicitor in a bit of a spot. So he hired you, because he knew you and could pull an old pals act if he needed to. Well, that was what he thought. But when you got close, like to Barry Barber, he got some moody blokes to give you a little tap.'

'I gave him all the information he needed to track me along the way.' Lee shook his head. 'So what about the flat at Gallions?'

'Paid for, like Del Salmon's debts, with my money,' Sandra said. 'Mind you, they won't have the flat for very much longer even if I've had to kiss the rest of it goodbye.'

'You've reported them?'

'You bet I have,' she said. 'Bastards. How could they do that to me? And what about Del's wife? She'll want her cut and bloody right too.'

Lee said. 'Obviously if you need evidence from us you only have to ask.'

Then her face clouded. 'You think I'm doing the right thing, don't you, Mr Arnold?'

Mumtaz felt for her. Women, even women with money, were

always at such a disadvantage when it came to the men in their lives. Phil still had a hold over her.

'Of course you are,' Lee said.

Sandra Rivers' smiled and for a moment Mumtaz felt content. Only when Sandra had gone did she think about Shazia and her threat to tell Lee about Naz Sheikh. She'd have to stall her somehow. If she could just get her to university the kid would be safe. But that was still a long way off. Negotiating the Sheikhs and Shazia without help was daunting. But what choice did she have? She could blow a corrupt hospital apart almost single-handed. Why couldn't she take control of her own life? Then she looked up and saw that Lee was smiling at her.

He said, 'You know, I'd invite you over for dinner if I wasn't still living with Tony Bracci. To celebrate all this.'

Mumtaz's face reddened. She looked down and said nothing for a long while, then looked up at him again.

This time he was not smiling. 'Ah, sorry. Sorry,' he said. 'I've embarrassed you. Stupid.'

And although she wanted to say that what he'd said wasn't stupid she mumbled, 'That's OK.'

She went to make more tea.


The massive man with loads of keys and fists like hammers closed the cell door behind him and locked it. He looked through the hatch at him once and David made himself assume an appropriately sad expression.

When he'd gone, although he was bursting, he made himself look for a camera but he didn't find one. He looked again, just in case. Then, when he was sure he wasn't being watched, filmed or monitored, David Golding allowed himself, finally, to laugh. Good old Cotton, what a sport he'd been. How did the police think that a stick like the chief consultant had cut a large man like el Masri's throat with no assistance? David remembered it with some relish. Maybe when he did finally get out he could kill someone else.

# Acknowledgements

Acknowledging everyone and and every event that lies behind this story isn't possible for all sorts of reasons. Suffice to say, I owe the creation of this book to a lot of wonderful people who work in mental health as well as to those who suffer from mental health problems. My own many years 'in the business' have also been instructive.

If you enjoyed *Poisoned Ground*, keep reading
for an extract from

# BARBARA NADEL

## ENOUGH ROPE

A Hakim and Arnold Mystery

The brand new Hakim and Arnold Mystery
Coming in hardback and ebook August 2015

## Prologue

All the accoutrements of the last stages of alcoholism were there. Empty bottles, faeces, boots with thin soles, an anorexic ankle. There was also some gear that took DI Kevin Thorpe back to the start of his career in the nineteen-seventies. When was the last time he'd seen even the most desperate alkie heat up solid polish? Over a bonfire?

The twenty-something constable at his side said, 'What's the polish about, then?'

Such innocence, and yet the boy had probably seen more pornography than Thorpe had ever had dinners, hot or cold.

'They heat it up so they can drink it,' Thorpe said. 'Meths Boys was what we used to call them, back when this sort of thing was common. Blokes so poor and desperate they'd drink anything. Polish, methylated spirit, white spirit . . .'

'Christ.'

Thorpe had hoped he'd seen the last of the Meths Boys back in the early nineteen-eighties, but in the new shiny London of the twenty-first century, apparently some remnants of the past remained.

'So, did he set himself on fire?'

The body had been found by a runner. Shaven-headed, he'd looked like a member of the BNP, except he spoke like he'd been to Eton. Poplar was a funny place in 2014.

'No,' Thorpe said.

'How can you be so sure?' the kid asked.

The smell was a cross between scorched earth and burnt pork. The sight was worse. The body sprawled out in front of the Children's Memorial in Poplar Recreation Ground had been damaged by fire, but it was the short-handled knife in his chest that had killed the man. Thorpe pointed at it.

'Oh.'

'This is one alcoholic who didn't kill himself,' Thorpe said.

Eighteen pupils at Great North Street School in Poplar were commemorated on the Children's Memorial. They'd died in the first daylight bombing raid on London in 1917. The Memorial had been paid for by public subscription. It was a place Thorpe had always found incredibly touching. That generosity, and a love that some would call sentimentality, was something he'd always taken for granted in the East End of London. Here it was made solid in a white memorial listing eighteen names, underneath a standing angel with its wings outstretched.

Now someone had been killed in front of it, and there was even a mark in what looked like blood on the plinth. Thorpe wondered what kind of person would murder a hopeless drunk in front of a memorial to dead children.

Then, behind the memorial, he saw what looked like a bundle of rags in the middle of a flower bed. All the hairs on his neck stood up.

# 1

**Eleven Days Earlier**

'I've paid your friggin' rent!'

Yelling down over a set of rusting banisters at your landlord is not the best way to negotiate financial differences, but Lee Arnold was pissed off. Without any notice his landlord, George Papadakis, had put up the rent on his office.

'You owe me three hundred pounds!' the landlord countered.

'Yeah, so you say. But who's improved this shithole, eh? Not you, George. When I moved in here, the bog was like something out of the Ark. But you didn't give a toss, did you? I had a new one—'

'Only since Mrs Hakim came to work for you. Only then did you put that new toilet in. You didn't give a shit about it until then!' George spoke with a typical East End accent, but he waved his arms around as if he were declaiming from the steps of the Acropolis.

'I've painted the place, had the wiring done, and if you've noticed, George, my sink don't drip down into your shop any more!' Lee said. 'Three hundred quid? You owe me that, mate!'

George clicked his tongue impatiently. 'I could get twice the rent you pay from one of these rich people moving into this area. You wanna watch it, Lee, the East End is trendy now for the young people. I could make your office into a luxury flat, just like that!' He clicked his fingers.

'Then do it,' Lee said. 'If you think you can tempt some nobhead hipster kid from Shoreditch all the way out to Upton Park, then knock yourself out.'

Up in his office, Lee's phone began to ring. He threw the butt of the cigarette he'd been smoking onto the stair he'd been standing on and stepped on it.

'And stop smoking!' George said.

'When you do, I will.'

Lee ran inside his small, stuffy office and picked up the ringing phone. 'Arnold Agency.'

There was a pause. In the years since he'd left the police and started running the agency, Lee Arnold had discovered that private detection services attracted the odd and sometimes the very very timid, as well as the desperate.

'Arnold Agency. Hello?'

He didn't like answering the phone. That was one of the reasons why he'd eventually caved in and employed an assistant. But now that the woman he'd taken on to do the 'officey' things was frequently busier looking for errant daughters and dodgy husbands than he was, Lee often had to answer his own calls.

'Mr Arnold?'

It was a man. Well spoken.

'Yes.'

There was another pause and then, 'Mr Arnold, I have a problem.'

'People who ring here usually do,' Lee said. There was something familiar about the voice, but he couldn't place it. He knew a lot of people, even some posh ones. 'What can we help you with?'

'I don't know whether you can help me at all,' the man said. 'But if we could meet somewhere – I don't want to do this over the phone – then we could discuss it.'

'We could,' Lee said. 'Although I have to tell you that I won't meet anyone in a dark alley, for obvious reasons.'

'Of course not. There's a pub near your office called The Boleyn. How about that?'

If he knew Newham's most famous pub he might be local. But The Boleyn was also West Ham United's boozer – and he was a bit posh even for the most gentrified bits of the borough.

'OK, when?' Lee asked.

'Can you meet me this evening? At five?'

'Yeah.' Lee flicked the desk diary open and began to write. 'Mr . . . ?'

'Smith.'

It was almost certainly something to do with his marriage. They were always 'Smith' or 'Brown'. Lee could see him in his mind: middle-aged, white, miserable. The wife was probably having an email affair with a waiter she'd met in Morocco.

'And how will I recognise you, Mr Smith?'

There was another pause. Then, 'Oh, you'll recognise me, Mr Arnold,' and he put the phone down.

Lee Arnold went outside and lit a cigarette to steady his nerves. That 'Mr Smith' had said he'd recognise him felt ominous.

Although she didn't like to give too much credence to the fantastical theories that some of her clients had about their husbands'/ sons'/daughters' behaviour, when Mumtaz Hakim found herself following Mr Ali to Broadway Market in Hackney she had been surprised. One of the great centres of East End urban cool was not a place she would have associated with a forty-seven-year-old imam from Manor Park. Girls in ripped tights and hipsters on fixed-wheel bicycles were not obviously the kind of company Mr Ali would want to keep. Had he come to the market to taste the forbidden fruit of the excellent pork with crackling Lee Arnold had told her they sold there? She doubted it, though anything was possible. Perhaps Mr Ali had a fancy for outsized lavender cupcakes. His wife was clearly worried enough to pay good money to find out.

As a girl, if anyone had told Mumtaz that overtly religious people did anything wrong, she wouldn't have believed it. But even at the relatively tender age of thirty-three, she'd experienced enough to know that wasn't true. Her late husband had been a 'good' Muslim, but he had also been a drunk, a gambler, and had sexually abused both his own daughter and Mumtaz. Now there were other 'good' men in her life who wore their religious credentials on their sleeves while concealing the foulest sins in their corrupted hearts. Was Mr Ali one of those?

She followed him to a second-hand shop that seemed to be full of industrial artefacts – metal filing cabinets, factory lamps and furniture made from what looked like railway sleepers. It was fascinating; she could see why Mr Ali was spending so much time looking around. But then he made straight for Regent's Canal.

When she'd been a child, Regent's Canal had been a drab, smelly and forbidding waterway. Mumtaz and her two brothers had often lurked around it to throw stones at rats and jump out at unsuspecting walkers. But when a young woman was raped and thrown into the canal in 1997, Mumtaz's parents forbade the children to go. They took no notice, but their adventures hadn't been the same. In recent years, however, the canal, just like Broadway Market, had undergone a renaissance. Filled with colourful barges, some of which doubled as floating shops, it was like a holiday destination. Mr Ali, smiling as he walked towards one of the barges, obviously thought so too.

She saw him get on board, to be greeted by a middle-aged white woman who addressed him by his first name and said, 'We've got some lovely stuff for you. Really different.'

Was she some kind of madam? Mumtaz cringed. She heard a male laugh that was probably his and wondered what the 'stuff' the woman had alluded to might be. Was it new young girls brought in for his pleasure? Or some peculiar sex toy? It was only when Mumtaz saw Mr Ali and the woman emerge fully clothed onto the deck in the sunshine, carrying bulging plastic bags, that she began to get a clue that maybe she had misjudged them. Then she saw the name of the boat, *The Knitty Nora*.

She heard him say, 'I take your point about the hand-painted cashmere, Dora, but my wife wants a sweater like the one in *The Killing*, so what can I do? Twenty years we have been together. I want to give her something she will love.'

Mumtaz wondered how she was going to start the conversation she had to have with his wife.

Lee Arnold was the same build as Superintendent Paul Venus. Tall and slim, Venus was in mufti when Lee found him sitting in one of the far dark corners of The Boleyn, nursing a whisky.

'I'm assuming it's you I'm here for, Mr Smith?' Lee said. Superintendent Venus had come to Forest Gate nick after Lee had left the force, but he had made his acquaintance and still had old mates who worked for him. None of them liked him.

'Yes.' Venus looked up. In his mid-fifties, he was almost ten years older than Lee, but his skin was smooth and his hair thick, which made him look younger. On this occasion, however, he had very dark circles underneath his eyes. 'Can I get you a drink, Mr Arnold?'

Lee asked for a Diet Pepsi. Venus went to the bar.

The Boleyn, inasmuch as it advertised itself at all, promoted an image of a real East End boozer. And that was no lie. But what it meant in the twenty-first century was not what it had meant when Lee was a kid. Back in the nineteen-seventies The Boleyn had heaved with boozed-up, white, working-class blokes singing West Ham songs and having punch-ups. Now, although it still retained its early Edwardian décor, plus a faint air of chirpy cockneyism, it was a bit of a quiet billet, with the exception of home-game

Saturdays. But even though it was a shadow of its former self and he hadn't taken a drink for years, Lee Arnold loved it.

When Venus returned he said, 'I'm aware of the fact that you're friends with several of my officers, Mr Arnold. Specifically DI Collins and DS Bracci.'

Lee had worked with them both years before. He even had an ongoing, ad hoc, fuck-buddy thing happening with Violet Collins. He hoped that Venus didn't want to talk to him about that.

'But what I am going to tell you, you mustn't tell them, or anyone else. Not even your assistant,' Venus said. 'I can't stress that enough.'

Lee frowned.

'Can you give me an assurance that you will adhere to these conditions, Mr Arnold?'

Vi Collins had a theory that Venus was bent. As she perceived it, he was soft on organised crime in the borough and she speculated he was taking backhanders. Other people in the nick saw him more as a cautious operator. He was, after all, a posh type from out of the area, so fitting in was always going to be difficult.

Lee took a drink. 'Depends what it's about,' he said.

'Well, I can tell you it's not about any of my officers.'

'That's a good start.'

'And it doesn't have anything to do with any of DI Collins's theories about me either,' he said. He moved closer, leaning across the scarred pub table. 'So please put any notions you may have about my being on the make out of your mind. This is a personal matter.'

Another story that went around about Venus was that he was shagging women in the station who were half his age. He was married, to a soap star who had a great big gaff in the country that he rarely visited, but he also had a flat in Islington. Had he been taking little PCs there for some extra-curricular? Was he about to get caught?

'I need your help. I need someone who knows about being a police officer but who isn't. I need . . .'

He stopped. This *was* serious. The shadowed eyes, together with the tears Lee could see in them, made the private investigator lean in towards the policeman. 'OK,' he said, 'just between you and me.'

Venus threw what remained of his whisky down his throat. He said, 'I've got a son. Harry. He's sixteen, attends a public school in Berkshire where he's a boarder. He's bright and his mother and I love him very much.'

'That's good.'

Venus was crying, tears falling down his cheeks. What was it with Harry? Drugs? Girls? Boys?

Venus said, 'He's been kidnapped.'

Lee hadn't been expecting that.

'His mother received a phone call the day Harry disappeared and then a written demand from the kidnappers was sent to our family home in Henley-on-Thames last Friday. They, whoever they are, want a hundred thousand pounds for Harry's safe return. But if I use my police contacts, if I so much as tell the police, Harry will die. I have complied with that. My wife and I are in the process of assembling the money in the required denominations. Would you mind if I got another drink? Would you like one?'

'No, but you go for it,' Lee said.

Venus went to the bar.

His wife was an actress called Tina Wilton. Lee remembered her from vaguely saucy comedy programmes in the seventies. Blonde, curvy and a bit tarty, she'd gone on to land a role in the long-running soap *Londoners*, back in the nineteen-nineties. She played a tough matriarch, head of a crime family who, Lee always thought, were some of the worst caricatures of East End 'types' he'd ever come across. But a lot of people loved Tina Wilton and she was a regular on many panel and reality shows. Every time he saw her, Lee mourned for the way she had looked in the past, pre-Botox and plastic surgery. Had she done all that to enhance her career, or to try and please her husband?

Venus returned. 'We have to deliver the money to a PO box address on Brick Lane,' he said.

'Hold on,' Lee said. 'Do you have any proof these people have Harry?'

'Proof? What do you mean?'

'Did your wife ask to speak to Harry when they called? Have they called since? Have you spoken to them?'

'No, no.' He put his head in his hands. 'Look, I should have but I didn't. I just need to deliver the money they've asked for.'

Lee sighed. OK, it was his son, but Venus's copper's instinct should have told him to ask for proof of life. He said, 'When?'

'Monday morning at ten.' He downed his latest whisky. 'I have to do it and I'm fine with that. I just want my son back unharmed.'

'But . . .'

If that had been all he had wanted, there would have been no need to tell anyone, let alone Lee Arnold.

'I also want to know who they are,' Venus said. 'My wife picked

Harry up from school last week. Two days later he left on his bike to go and visit his friend George in Twyford, but he never arrived. Then came the phone call and the following day his mother received the demand.'

Harry was sixteen. Lee could remember being sixteen. He said, 'Look, I have to ask this – have you or your wife been having, well, issues with your son lately? Forgive me, Mr Venus, but I know you and your wife live apart. I'm just wondering how that's affected Harry. Whether it's made him—'

'Harry wouldn't put his mother and myself through something like this!' Venus said.

'I have to—'

'My wife and I haven't lived together, apart from the occasional week during school holidays, for a decade. He is accustomed to our separation. Nothing has changed for him, and in fact I would venture to guess that he has probably done very well out of having a father in London and a mother in the country.'

People often spoilt kids when their marriages failed. Lee wondered whether Harry had learned to exploit his situation. Or whether the boy, secretly unhappy, had just decided to take off with a heap of his parents' money.

'Something happened to my son between Henley and Twyford and I want you to go over there and find out what,' Venus said. 'I also want you to follow me when I drop the money on Brick Lane. I'll pay you whatever it takes. You can rip me off to your heart's content, Mr Arnold. I really don't care.'

'I won't, Mr Venus. I'm not like that.'

'I'm sorry.'

Lee could have done with a fag to help him think it over, but that meant going outside, and he didn't want to leave Venus on his own. Much as he was indifferent to him, this man was clearly very vulnerable.

'When would you want me to start?'

'Tomorrow,' Venus said, 'and I've got five hundred pounds for your immediate expenses on me now.'

'You want me in Henley-on-Thames tomorrow?'

Venus took a folder out of his briefcase and pushed it across the table. 'Yes. Here's some information about Harry, his friend George and significant locations like our family home. Plus my wife's mobile numbers and the address of the hotel I've booked you into tomorrow night.'

'You're very confident I'll say yes, aren't you?' Lee said.

Venus leaned back in his chair. 'I know you've not got a lot of work commitments, that your landlord has just put up your rent and that your assistant doesn't usually work at weekends. Your friend DI Collins has, as you know, a very penetrating voice.'

She could hear Lee's mynah bird going through his usual repertoire of West Ham United songs and lists of players as she picked up the phone. Mumtaz heard Lee yell, 'Shut up, Chronus!'

She laughed. She was in a good mood. Mr Ali had not been playing around with a long-legged blonde in Hackney, which had curtailed her job, but she'd enjoyed telling his wife about the *Killing* sweater. It was an unusual thing to do, and yet Mumtaz could see how it could happen. Some Muslim men, her own father included, had a masculine image to uphold, but inside they were really soft as butter. Mr Ali had so wanted to make something for his wife that she would treasure, that he had resorted to clandestine knitting classes. When she told Lee, she thought he'd be disappointed that the job hadn't lasted longer. But oddly, he wasn't.

'Sometimes it goes that way,' he said. 'Don't worry about it.'

'Yes, but with the office rent . . .'

'Oh, don't worry about that either,' Lee said. 'That'll get sorted. Look, the reason I phoned was to ask if you or Shazia could feed Chronus for me this weekend.'

Until recently, DS Tony Bracci had lived in Lee's spare room. His wife had thrown him out in favour of a younger man, but she'd just taken him back and so Tony was no longer available for bird-sitting.

'Yes, that'll be fine,' she said.

'Just tomorrow,' Lee said. 'I'll be back Sunday night.'

'No problem.'

'Great. Thanks.'

She didn't ask why he wouldn't be around to feed Chronus at the weekend and Lee didn't volunteer the information. It wasn't her business.

Just as the call ended, Mumtaz heard the front door open, then close, followed by the sound of her stepdaughter going to her bedroom.

'Shazia?'

The girl, a bright, tall, skinny seventeen-year-old, didn't answer. Mumtaz left the kitchen and walked the few steps to Shazia's room. After living in a five-bedroom house, the flat they shared now was cramped. It felt like living in a doll's house.

Shazia's door wasn't closed and so Mumtaz walked into her room. 'How long is this going to last?' she asked the girl.

Shazia, who was sitting on her bed emptying her bag, did not look up.

'Well?'

'I told you, as long as you insist on playing the victim, I don't want to talk to you,' the girl said. 'Go to the police or speak to Lee and I'll talk to you.'

'You know I can't do that.'

Shazia looked up. Her eyes, which were dark and huge, were also very heavily made up. She looked stunning. She said, 'I saw that Naz Sheikh today. He watched me get on the bus to college. He was smirking. Next time I see him, why don't I just punch him, eh?'

'Oh no! No!'

'Why not? He deserves it.'

Mumtaz felt her heart flutter. 'Shazia, you mustn't.'

'Mustn't?' She went back to looking at the stuff in her bag. 'Oh, just go away, Amma,' she snapped. 'Go away and leave me alone in my little rabbit hutch.'

Shazia hadn't had an easy life. Her mother had died when she was a child and her father, while fulfilling her every material whim, had sexually abused her. After his death and despite Mumtaz's best efforts, she'd also had to suffer the trauma of having to move from their lovely family home to a tiny flat so that her father's debts could be paid.

In his ignominious career as a gambler, Ahmet Hakim had

got himself in hock to a local crime family. The Sheikhs did it all. Slum-landlording, money-laundering, illegal gambling, people-trafficking and blackmail. And when the need arose to give their errant clients the occasional reminder about money owed, the Sheikh family were not backwards in coming forwards. Naz Sheikh, the youngest member of the clan, hadn't so much as flinched as he'd stabbed Ahmet Hakim to death in front of his wife on Wanstead Flats almost two years before.

'I can't believe my father still owes those people money,' Shazia said. 'They're ripping you off!'

They were. The debt Ahmet Hakim had died for had been paid in full, with interest, when Mumtaz had sold their old house. But what Shazia didn't know was that Mumtaz herself was in debt to the Sheikhs. When Naz Sheikh had killed Ahmet she'd seen him so clearly she would have easily been able to give his description to the police. But she hadn't. Instead, she'd watched her husband bleed to death into the scrubby Wanstead Flats grass. And the Sheikhs knew why. She'd hated Ahmet. He'd made her life unbearable. Naz Sheikh had been her hero, and he knew it. He played on it. But no one else knew, especially not Shazia.

'These people add interest payments onto interest payments,' Mumtaz said. 'As long as they say I owe them money, then I owe them money.'

'That's insane. You should stop paying them.'

'I can't.'

'Why not?'

'You know why not, Shazia.'

They'd talked about this.

'Because they'll hurt us? Amma, if you told the police, if you told Lee—'

'It wouldn't get any better!' Mumtaz was yelling now. She didn't like to yell. She made a conscious effort to slow her breathing. 'Just leave it to me, Shazia. Leave it to me.'

Naz Sheikh, her one-time hero, had her. The deal – pay up or Shazia gets told her precious amma had a hand in killing her own father – was unbreakable. Even though the girl had suffered so badly at her father's hands he had still been her 'abba'. Shazia would never forgive her. She would never get over it.

Mumtaz changed the subject. 'Lee wants us to feed Chronus tomorrow,' she said. 'He's away for the weekend.'

'With a girlfriend?'

'I don't know. I didn't ask.'

Mumtaz walked towards Shazia's bedroom door.

'You know you're forcing him to look elsewhere because you won't acknowledge what's happening,' Shazia said.

The girl had some notion that Lee Arnold had romantic feelings for her. It was absurd.

'Don't be silly, Shazia. I've told you about romanticising.'

'What, because he's a white man? What does that mean, Amma? My father, the one who got us into this mess in the first place, was a Bangladeshi Muslim, and look how well he turned out. Eh? God, you're so thick sometimes. Love is rare and you should never just ignore it. I know that and I'm only a kid.'

Mumtaz dismissed her with a wave of her hand. Then she went back into the kitchen and put the radio on.